"I want to know Pax. With each book he becomes more compelling, and with him, the whole saga. Some series begin with their best tale, then try to muster up sequels. The Dream Keeper Saga gets better with each book. Kathryn Butler wins our trust with her characters, engaging turns, and deeply Christian themes. I'm excited to add the Dream Keeper Saga to our family canon."

David Mathis, Senior Teacher and Executive Editor, desiringGod.org; Pastor, Cities Church, Saint Paul, Minnesota; author, *Habits of Grace*

"Two of my favorite things about the Dream Keeper Saga are the character Pax and the almost Mad-Libs-esque imaginative flow, appropriate (even necessary) to a world redeemed from humanity's collective dreams."

James D. Witmer, author, *A Year in the Big Old Garden*; *Beside the Pond*; and *The Strange New Dog*

"When was the last time you got lost in a good story? The last time you felt yourself throw off the day's troubles and sink into a tale for the ages? The wait is over. Kathryn Butler's beautiful book *Lost in the Caverns* will draw you in and hold you close. The best news is that it will point your young reader to the greatest story ever told, the redemption story. Prepare to be captivated!"

Erin Davis, author; podcaster; mother of four

"Faith, purpose, friendship, and hope. These themes and more draw young readers into a world where dreams come to life. *Lost in the Caverns* adds detail and depth as it carries the saga along with its readers."

Gloria Furman, author, *Labor with Hope* and *A Tale of Two Kings*

LOST in the CAVERNS

The DreamKeeper SAGA

LOST in the CAVERNS

Kathryn Butler

CROSSWAY®

WHEATON, ILLINOIS

Cover design: Studio Muti

Interior illustrations by Jordan Eskovitz

First printing 2023

Printed in the United States of America

Trade paperback ISBN: 978-1-4335-8778-8
ePub ISBN: 978-1-4335-8781-8
PDF ISBN: 978-1-4335-8779-5

Library of Congress Cataloging-in-Publication Data

Names: Butler, Kathryn, 1980– author. | Butler, Kathryn, 1980– Dream keeper saga ; book 3.
Title: Lost in the caverns / Kathryn Butler.
Description: Wheaton, Illinois : Crossway, [2023] | Series: The dream keeper saga ; book 3 | Audience: Ages 9–12
Identifiers: LCCN 2022017687 (print) | LCCN 2022017688 (ebook) | ISBN 9781433587788 (trade paperback) | ISBN 9781433587795 (pdf) | ISBN 9781433587818 (epub)
Subjects: LCSH: Magic—Juvenile fiction. | Dreams—Juvenile fiction. | Imaginary places—Juvenile fiction. | Quests (Expeditions)—Juvenile fiction. | Friendship—Juvenile fiction. | Adventure stories. | CYAC: Magic—Fiction. | Dreams—Fiction. | Imaginary places—Fiction. | Friendship—Fiction. | Adventure and adventurers—Fiction. | Fantasy. | LCGFT: Action and adventure fiction. | Fantasy fiction. | Novels.
Classification: LCC PZ7.1.B8935 Lo 2023 (print) | LCC PZ7.1.B8935 (ebook) | DDC 813.6 [Fic]—dc23/eng/20221003
LC record available at https://lccn.loc.gov/2022017687
LC ebook record available at https://lccn.loc.gov/2022017688

Crossway is a publishing ministry of Good News Publishers.

VP	32	31	30	29	28	27	26	25	24
15	14	13	12	11	10	9	8	7	6	5	4	3

To Jack and Christie.
When you find yourselves lost,
follow the Light.

Contents

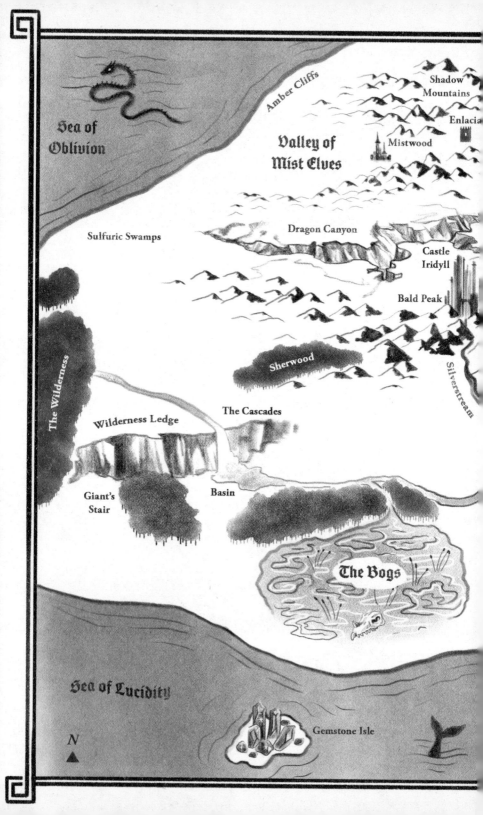

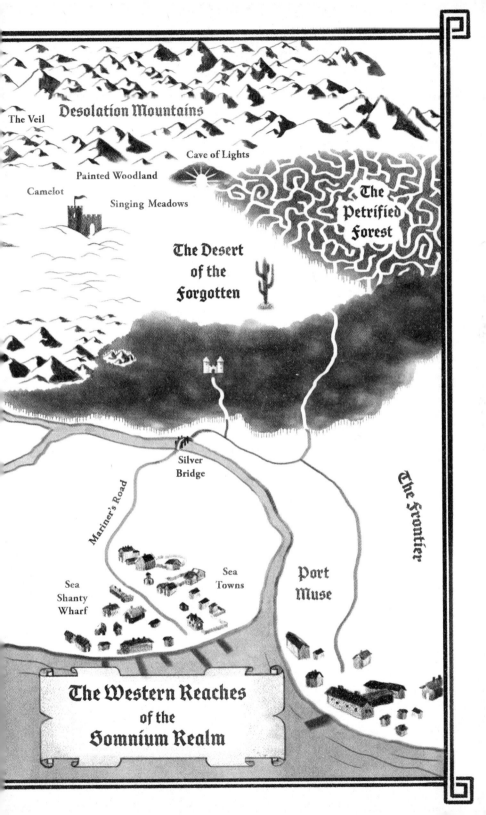

CHAPTER 1

A Light in the Darkness

Lily lingered beside Pax's tomb as the moon rose. She could still feel the hot, foul breath of the shrouds in the air around her, a reminder of how they had encircled her and mocked the fallen prince. She shivered and remembered how the gloom of the Blight had rolled back and the Realm bloomed with life again, scattering the shrouds like scraps of burnt paper. Barth was restored to human form. Scallywag was healed. Keisha and Adam had gone home, but Lily had decided that her place, for a time, was in the Realm. She was an artisan, and she would rebuild what the Blight had broken.

She placed a hand on the cool glass of the tomb. The moonlight cast a pearly sheen over the valley, lighting up the new flowers and trees as if they were fireflies. The beauty of it crashed against her pain like waves against the shore. *I know you're still with us*, Lily thought, pushing back tears. *Although I wish I could see you.*

Suddenly a great crack like thunder split the air, and the ground shook. Lily stumbled backward and shielded her eyes as the tomb glowed, its glass branches sprawling like white lightning against the night sky. A fracture split the tomb from top to bottom, and light pierced through and flooded the valley, bathing every petal and blade of grass in daylight.

The glare stung Lily's eyes, as if she'd gazed for too long at the sun, and she hid her face in the crook of her elbow. The warmth of a spring morning suddenly chased away the chill. Music drifted on the wind, and Lily strained to hear. *Are the winds singing?* As if in answer, a breeze tousled her hair, and the voices sang barely above a whisper. *They are! The winds are singing!* Though she didn't recognize their language, their song played in time with the deepest strummings of her heart.

As the light softened, Lily raised her head. The radiance had ebbed from the reaches of the valley, and night again crowded around her. A cold glitter of stars shone above. Then the source of the light snapped into form.

"Pax!"

The great unicorn reared skyward, his horn slicing the night like a new blade drawn from its sheath. As his hooves struck the ground, Lily fought to steady herself against the tremors that rattled the earth. His light stung her eyes, like the glare of daybreak reflected off a lake. With tears streaming down her face she rushed toward him, threw her arms around him, and buried her face in his neck.

"Don't cling to me, young artisan," Pax said with a laugh.

She fumbled to untangle her fingers from his mane. "I thought you'd died," she whispered. "I thought you were gone forever."

"I did die, dear one. But forever is under my authority."

"But how—"

A clatter interrupted her, and they turned to see Isla standing at the entrance to her home, her eyes wide with shock and a clay bowl of blackberries broken at her feet. At the sight of Pax she dropped to her knees. "Forgive me, lord," she said.

Pax strode toward her. "Rise, Isla."

"I am unworthy. You died because of my wickedness. The draught, the Blight, I had a hand in all of it."

"I took the Sovran Merrow's draught willingly, Isla, for you and for all the Realm. I paid the penalty." He nuzzled her. "You are forgiven, Princess Isla."

Isla stood, her eyes shimmering, and wiped the tears from her face. A smile broke through, and she gazed at the unicorn in wonder.

"Shall we dine now?" Pax said.

Isla's face fell. "Oh, of course, my lord. But we only have what my brother and I could gather from the forest, and it's not much."

"It's more than you think. Go and see."

Pax guided them through the laurel-trimmed doorway of the cottage. They entered a kitchen, where roots and dried herbs hung in clusters from a ceiling of latticed willow boughs. A row of terra-cotta bowls filled with nuts and berries awaited them on a bench, and a fire crackling in the hearth bathed the room in a golden glow. Lily's gaze flitted over these delights for a moment, before a heavy oaken table in the center of the room drew her eye. There, heaped atop silver platters, sprawled the most magnificent feast she had ever seen. Pyramids of fruit rose toward the ceiling, roasted meats and vegetables perfumed the room with rosemary and sage, and a basket overflowed with fresh bread from which tendrils of steam still coiled. In one corner a cake decorated with strawberries nestled among pastries, cookies, and the most beautiful blackberry pie, with a crust carved in the shapes of doves and stars. In another corner, Lily spotted a plate overflowing with spaghetti and meatballs and a glass dish filled exclusively with purple jelly beans. Her favorite.

Isla appeared from behind and gasped, then reprimanded her younger brother, Rowan, who had already drawn a chair up to the table and was tucking into a bowl of raspberry custard. The young lad froze when he saw Pax, a spoon with a blob of pink custard suspended in air.

"Good evening, Prince Rowan," Pax said. "May I dine with you?"

Rowan gaped at him.

"Rowan, answer!" Isla whispered.

Before he could reply, something scuffled by Rowan's feet under the table. He sprang back, his spoon clanged to the floor, and the dish followed, splattering pink custard all over the lace tablecloth.

"Get out, you grubby beast!" Rowan yelled, swiping at something with his foot.

Philippe the rabbit bounded out from beneath the table, his top hat clutched in his front paws. "*Pardon*, monsieur! I am sorry to intrude! It is just that when I saw the carrots I could not resist. They are candied in syrup, no?"

"Get out!"

"Rowan!" Isla said.

"He's stealing our food!"

"He's our guest!"

"Our *guest*? He's a filthy rodent!"

"Prince Rowan, do not deny the rabbit his place." Pax stepped into the room, his radiance drowning out even the glow of the firelight.

"I didn't invite him," Rowan said between clenched teeth.

Pax's gaze hardened. "Yet I did invite him. And whomever I call always has a place at the table." With these words a chill wind swept through the cottage as if churned up from a gale over the sea. Rowan's cheeks flushed, and without a word he rushed from the room.

"Espy, please," Isla called after him, but he ignored her and tromped out.

Lily slouched toward her jelly beans during the argument. She wanted to ask what the nickname "Espy" meant, but decided to keep mum. She felt the sting of Keisha's absence; the right words always seemed to come more quickly to her newfound friend with the notebook at her hip.

Pax nuzzled Isla's cheek. "Do not despair," he said. "Your brother is astray, but he is not lost."

"I don't know how I'm going to help him through this. Our mother was always the only one who could ever reach him," Isla said.

"Your brother awoke to find everyone and everything dear to him suddenly gone. Such wounds don't heal easily. But be at peace—they *will* heal."

Isla sank deep into thought, and a silence fell upon the room, with only the crackle of the fire and the song of crickets breaking the quiet. As Lily watched Isla, her eyes downcast in sorrow, the last shreds of anger and bitterness she'd once harbored against the princess withered away. She'd hated Isla for betraying her father, but Pax had forgiven the princess for far worse offenses. How could Lily not forgive her, too?

Philippe, a quivering puffball of fur, finally ventured from behind the table. "*Merci beaucoup, mon prince,*" he said tentatively, his paws trembling and his ears skimming the floor as he bowed before Pax. "*Enchanté—*"

"No need for formalities, Philippe," Pax said. "You are most welcome here, as are your friends."

"Friends?" Lily asked.

Pax nodded, and suddenly Glorf rolled out from under the table. Mortimer the fuzzy turtle joined him, as did Sheila the pterodactyl, who swept upward to roost on a willow bough.

Pax laughed at Lily's surprise, then invited them to give thanks and eat. They dined in the glow of the firelight as lightning bugs spun streamers outside the windows, and Pax told them old stories of things long forgotten, when the Realm first hatched from the minds of men, and even before, when the waking world had yet to spin on its axis. Lily would pause between bites of pasta to stare at Pax in awe as the images he wove unfurled like banners in her mind. In his presence, the loneliness that always stalked her like a shadow had gone, and for a delicious moment she reveled in a quiet joy. The moment reminded her of the times she'd hunched over a cup of hot cocoa after sledding outside, or when twinkling lights dazzled her on Christmas Eve. At long last, she felt *home*.

After a while, when the clink of spoons and the chatter of conversation hushed, Lily mustered the courage to ask the question burning in all their minds. "Pax, are you back for good now?"

All eyes turned to the prince. Isla leaned forward, and even Philippe, who hadn't stopped chewing since Pax invited him to the table, paused his crunching to listen.

"I will always be with you, Lily, but you'll not see me for a while. I leave tonight."

7

Lily's heart sank. How could he leave already? She opened and closed her fists beneath the table, as if somehow she could clutch the moment in her hands and stop time from tumbling forward.

"My lord, you've just arrived," Isla said, mirroring Lily's thoughts. "We've waited forty years for your return! Must you leave so soon?"

"There are others I must see, others like you who will know me for who I am. Thereafter, I must continue the work given me by our King."

"The King of the Realm?" Lily asked.

"The King of us all. I laid my life down to save the Realm, but he gave me the power to take it up again. And now I must carry on with his work, to prepare a new place and a new way. To prepare a kingdom where humans and dreams can live together again."

Lily swallowed a lump in her throat and struggled to sort the thousand questions that jostled through her head. There was so much she longed to ask him, so much she longed to know. Most of all, she desperately wanted him to stay.

"But what about the Realm?" she said, finding no other words. "The Blight destroyed so much. Doesn't it need to be rebuilt?"

Pax offered a gentle smile. "Everything has its proper time and place. The Realm will be rebuilt, but not all at once."

Lily fingered the soothstone fragment in her pocket, its contours now so familiar. She remembered her reason for returning, and the thought sparked a flicker of hope. If Pax couldn't stay, at least she had something to offer in this strange, beautiful world.

"I can rebuild it, Pax," she said. "I came back because I want to use my powers to help."

"Indeed you *will* help, although not in the way you think. I did not bring you back to rebuild, Lily."

The remark felt like a slap in the face. "I don't understand. I'm an artisan. I can use my powers to—"

"Yes, you have the gifts of an artisan, and you *will* use those gifts for good. But I called you back to the Realm after the Catacombs fell for another reason."

"*You* called me back?"

He tilted his head to one side. "Didn't you know? Think back. Why did Cedric come to find you in the school, when Glorf attacked poor Mrs. Higgins?"

"Mrs. Higgins, the lunch lady? You know about what happened in the cafeteria?"

"I know about all of it, Lily. Now, think—why did Cedric come for you?"

"So that I could try to stop the Blight. Sir Toggybiffle sent him to find me, because he thought an artisan could help."

"And how do you think the professor came upon that idea? The Blight afflicted him terribly, and he could do little more than sleep before you arrived."

"So, you're saying *you* told him to do it?"

"Not in a voice he recognized at the time, but yes, I prodded him."

"How? I mean, no one had seen you in decades."

"Lily, you've seen the powers the King has given me. Do you think time and space can thwart my work? Toggybiffle thought the idea to seek you was his own, but his inspiration came from my voice." He stepped toward her, and his gaze deepened. "I brought you back to the Realm for a different purpose than rebuilding, or even than combating the Blight. I brought you back so that you can tell others what you've seen."

"What do you mean?"

"Whomever you meet, tell them about what you have seen and heard in this valley. Tell them about what I gave for them, and won for them. This is the true reason you are here, Lily. You're here to tell others the truth—that I have overcome the darkness."

Lily's throat tightened, and her mouth felt full of sand. *I'm good at creating things, not talking!* she wanted to shout. She lowered her eyes, but could still feel Pax's gaze upon her, steady and penetrating.

"What troubles you, Lily?" Pax asked.

Lily shrugged.

"Lily."

His voice rang with tenderness and thunder all at once. Lily finally answered, although she still couldn't meet his eyes. "It's just that I thought I finally had a purpose. I thought my powers, I don't know, *mattered.*"

"They do matter, but they are not all that matters. And apart from my words, the things they build are like straw. The slightest gust of wind will blow them apart."

Lily bit her lip. "I'm not great at talking to people. I always say the wrong thing."

"Rely on my words and not your own."

"But what do I say, Pax? How do I know when to say it?

"You will know. Remember, dear one, although you will not see me for a little while, I will always be with you."

Pax bowed his head, and the tip of his horn gleamed like a tiny star. He gently touched the light to her forehead and then hovered it over her heart. A dozen tendrils of light, like stardust, coiled around her, and suddenly she felt a surge of warmth from her scalp down to the tips of her fingers. A swell of love for which she had no words accompanied it.

The next moment the light faded, and the stardust and the warmth disappeared. "Now I must depart," Pax said. He turned to Isla. "My lady, if I might have a few words with you outside, I would be grateful." Then he surveyed the room, all the occupants watching him with transfixed gazes. "I remain with you always."

Lily blinked through a sheen of tears. "I wish you didn't have to go."

Pax nuzzled her. "Always remember, Lily McKinley, that I love those in the Realm, and when its people are lost and hurting and alone, my concern for them grows all the more. Remember that I love you, no matter what storms assail you. I am with you always, and I will return and make all things new."

Pax bowed his head and strode regally out through the laurel-trimmed doorway with Isla at his side. As his light faded, a chill fell over the room, even with the fire raging. No sound of chewing or silverware broke the calm; all present held their breath.

Finally, Philippe slipped a paw into one of Lily's hands. "He was *magnifique, non?*"

Lily nodded and pulled the soothstone from her pocket. A thousand questions churned in her head.

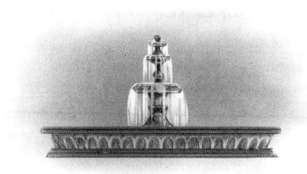

CHAPTER 2

Mistwood

Lily awoke to sunlight warming her face. For an instant she thought she was at home, and she listened for the snap of bacon sizzling in her mother's skillet, the hallmark of a Saturday morning. Then the memories from the previous night flooded back, and she bolted upright, sending a flurry of feathers from Isla's spare down bed twirling about her like snow. She remembered Pax—his words, his presence, that he'd returned after she thought him lost—and her heart thrilled. She pushed open the window above her bed with a creak and leaned out to savor the morning air . . . then rolled out and landed in a holly bush.

As the waxy leaves scratched her arms and her face flushed in embarrassment, she had a flashback to the morning when she tumbled out of her window in pursuit of Rigel, when Sheila and the other creatures escaped the Fortress. That day seemed ages ago, like a hazy dream. As she staggered to her feet and pulled twigs from her hair, Pax's words turned in her mind. Joy at his return still throbbed within her, but her uncertainty also nagged her, like a splinter worming its way down deep. *I'm an artisan, not a speaker,* she thought. *Why wouldn't Pax want me to rebuild?*

Isla strolled through the grass outside, leaning forward every so often to gather thistle and marigold blossoms and tuck them into a satchel at her hip. Lily brushed herself off and wiped a squished berry from her shoulder. She wore clothes that Isla had given her the night before—a flowy tunic shirt and a lavender cardigan, both several sizes too big and rolled up at the sleeves—and she hoped Isla wouldn't notice the berry stain on her shoulder. She felt a renewed admiration for the princess, as she had when they first met in Castle Iridyll and she struck Lily as so refined and wise. Lily urged her cheeks to stop burning and tried to act nonchalant as she strode to join the princess on the hilltop.

"Gathering a bouquet for the cottage?" Lily asked.

Isla didn't look up from her gathering. "Supplies for you and Rowan." She crouched low to examine the buds that broke through the earth toward a patch of sun. "It's hard to believe

Pax is gone again. Although truthfully, he could stay with us for a thousand years and it still wouldn't feel like enough time."

Lily nodded, then drew a breath and glanced around her. The full light of morning now blazed in the valley, draping the meadows in gold and illuminating the snowcaps of the mountains like plates of bronze. "This is such a lovely place," Lily said with a sigh. "It's so beautiful."

"Beautiful, but empty. It's not the home it was."

The splinter burrowed deeper. "Maybe I can help with that," Lily said. "I'd love to give you your old home again, Isla. That's why I came back."

Isla raised her eyes. "That's not what Pax told you last night."

"Yes, but I still I think I can help here. Just think, Isla, I can rebuild your home, and make it like it was! Wouldn't you like that?"

"That's kind, but I don't think it's the right way. Before he left, Pax told me I'd find hope for my people if I sought my old soothstone."

"Your soothstone? Really? But that's still in—"

"The Cave of Lights, yes." Isla paused from her harvesting and massaged the finger where the soothstone had burned her after she'd betrayed Lily. "The stone was like an ordinary rock when I left it, and I don't know if it will ever heed me again, but Pax knows more than I do. I have to try. I'm gathering these flowers and herbs to make some tinctures, so you and Rowan will have supplies while I'm away."

"But the Cave of Lights is so far away. And what does your old soothstone have to do with rebuilding Mistwood?"

"I don't know, but it's what Pax told me. I have to trust him."

Lily crossed her arms and chewed the inside of her cheek. She knew Isla was probably right, but her own idea wouldn't leave her alone. "Please, just let me try to do this for you and Rowan," she urged. "Just think about what it would be like to return to your old home when you get back from your trip! How wonderful would that be?"

Isla studied her for a long moment. Then, with a look of defeat, she sighed and nodded. "All right. Come along. You'll need to see our home before you can bring it back."

She led Lily to the fountain outside the cottage and waved a hand over the glassy surface of the water. Mist gathered beneath the pool, then cleared to reveal a kingdom wrought from alabaster and sapphires. The palace rose from within the city walls like a snowy mountain, and its blue banners flapped like ribbons in the wind. Fountains, like the one in front of Isla's modest cottage but much larger, bubbled with crystalline water. Vines abloom with purple flowers coiled around the balustrades, and elf children in a courtyard laughed as they tossed clumps of cloud at one another like snowballs.

Lily tingled with excitement as the pictures danced before her. "This is amazing. How did you do it?" she asked.

"It's called memory casting, a gift of my people. We deal in mist, and in many ways memories are like vapors. Drawing them out is like clearing away fog." She gazed at the images with a pained expression. "There's too much to rebuild, Lily. One artisan couldn't possibly accomplish all this."

"I still want to try. What if I start with just one part? The part that matters most to you?"

Isla closed her eyes and swept her palms over the pool. Suddenly the image of the palace magnified, and Lily felt as if she were astride an eagle soaring toward it. She could see every wall, every window, every vine snaking over the bricks. The image ducked through a window and sped down the halls. Carpeting adorned with laurels rolled down corridors, and windows cast light onto the floors in silver bars. Chandeliers hung from the vaulted ceilings, with each crystal cut into the same droplet shape of the earrings Isla wore.

The view spun into a circular room aglow with blue light, and Lily marveled at the objects lining the curved walls: a wooden horse, a tiny bow and arrow set accented with jewels, a stack of leather-bound books, a pile of white stone blocks half-assembled into a replica of the palace. At the center of the room a little girl with a cascade of lavender hair sat with a doll upon her lap.

Lily looked up in surprise. "Isla, is that you?"

Isla didn't respond but instead stood with her eyes closed, her hands dancing above the water and her brow creased in concentration. Lily returned her attention to the pool, which now displayed a grand ballroom with a crowd of elves parting like the sea before a noble couple who walked arm in arm. They both wore circlets of silver laurels upon their brows. From the flowing gray hair, Lily recognized the man as Isla's father. The woman at his arm had dark hair the color of wine, just like Rowan's.

Isla's mother . . .

The picture shifted again. She saw a courtyard with a silver tree at its center, its leaves hanging from its graceful limbs like tinsel. A young Isla galloped around the courtyard astride a white pony, one hand holding the reins and the other dancing in the air to coax lightning from the sky above her. As she performed, a crowd applauded.

The picture changed again. Lily saw a room with gauzy curtains blown inward with the breeze, the kingdom sprawling outside the large window. Isla's mother sat in a chair with a baby bundled in her lap. Isla knelt at her feet and caressed the baby's forehead with a single finger.

Another shift. A royal hall, with Isla's parents on two thrones of tangled vines gilt in silver, overseeing a banquet. Isla played a harp in the corner. Her father nodded at her, and her mother flashed a doting smile.

Yet another change. Isla as a girl, in the courtyard again, her knee skinned after a tumble from her pony. Her mother wrapped her in her arms, her robes flowing about her like billowing mist.

Then the image darkened, and Lily saw another room with drawn curtains that blocked out all sunlight. Candles flickered and cast a somber glow upon a bed hung with blood-colored drapery. Isla knelt on the side of the bed, her head in her arms as she wept. A woman whom Lily couldn't make out lay on the bed, a single pale hand stroking Isla's hair. Rowan, barely older than a toddler, hung to the back of the room, gnawing on a fingernail and clutching in his arms a ragged toy raccoon with a green ribbon around its tail.

Ripples suddenly spread across the surface of the pool and warped the image. The dark room vanished in a swirl of smoke, and Lily glanced up to see Isla crying, her tears plunking into the water. The princess shuddered, and then straightened her shoulders. "Will that be enough?" she asked, her voice slightly unsteady.

Lily wanted to tell Isla she was sorry for all she'd endured, but every time she reached for words, they fell flat. "Yes. Thanks," was all she managed to mutter. Isla nodded, then swept away toward the house, her robe fluttering behind her.

Lily stood alone in the morning light. Her heart raced from the things she'd seen, and she spent a long moment replaying every detail, examining every curtain flutter and facet of crystal in her mind. Then she closed her palm around the soothstone and marched to the crest of a hill.

The valley sprawled below, a carpet of green that stretched to the roots of the Desolation Mountains. Lily scanned the terrain for a landmark from Isla's memories to orient her. She squinted but saw only vast fields, their grasses swaying in the wind like waves upon the sea. Isla's valley had burned away in her father's fires ages ago, and every blade of grass and supple leaf was unrecognizable. Lily shook her head. *What were you thinking? You're just a kid. You can't do this by yourself.*

Not by yourself.

Lily froze. The voice had only whispered, but the words struck her distinctly. She listened again. A breeze tousled her hair and swept delicately past her face. *Not by yourself.*

Lily drew a breath. *It's the wind. The wind is speaking to me again!*

The breeze changed directions and rustled the heads of the flowers as it gusted into the valley. Lily saw the grasses bow beneath its flow and leaves spiral into the air in its wake. For a moment she lost track of it over a pile of rocks, and she jogged with a hand shielding her eyes to search for its path. Then she gasped.

A tree stood in the center of the valley and stretched its arms skyward. As the wind coiled through its branches, leaves twirled to the ground, catching the light like silver birds as they fell. Lily recognized the tree as the same one in the palace courtyard, where Isla had learned to entice lightning from the sky.

She felt the breeze through her hair again. *He's given you eyes to see,* it whispered.

Lily gazed out across the valley, and in her mind's eye she saw the palace walls rise around the tree. White cobblestones paved the courtyard, and the alabaster towers climbed toward the clouds. Then houses appeared, and roads, and the brook again wound through the valley like a strand of silver tinsel.

Lily closed her eyes. The light through her eyelids brightened, and she knew that the soothstone fragment blazed with its pale fire. From the valley below she heard the clink of stones, thousands of them knocking together and grinding into place. Then the clamor quieted except for the faint babbling of a distant brook. Something soft brushed against her hand.

"*C'est magnifique*, mademoiselle!"

Lily opened her eyes. Philippe stood beside her with his face between his paws. Below them, the kingdom of the Mist Elves gleamed like a pearl between the jaws of the mountains.

CHAPTER 3

Empty Halls

In the days that followed, Isla ventured into the valley to trace the smooth stones of the city walls and to stir ripples in the pools that dotted the courtyards. She crossed the threshold into Castle Mistwood and turned in place to gaze up at the chandeliers and tapestries in the main hall. In the playroom she caressed the yarn mane of her rocking horse and turned a set of silver marbles in her palm. She paused before portraits of her ancestors and lingered for long, quiet moments before the painting of her parents: her father regal and proud, her mother elegant, with wisdom in her eyes.

During these wanderings Isla said not a word. She drank in each detail and retreated deeper and deeper into her mind. The kitchens Lily rebuilt overflowed with fresh fruit, aged cheeses, herbs, and joints of lamb, but each night Isla climbed back up the hilltop to return to her tumbledown cottage. There, she would coax Rowan, who spent most of his time brooding in one of his fulgurites, to join her for a meager supper. Without a word she would prepare soup and bread for them all, they would eat in silence, and then Isla would clear the table and disappear into her chamber for the night.

After a week of this melancholy, Lily returned to the cottage to discover Isla in her room, folding garments and stuffing them into a leather satchel.

"Can I help you, Isla?" Lily asked, playing with a splinter in the doorframe.

Isla shook her head and continued packing.

"You're not down in the valley," Lily said. "Is everything okay? Is there something I need to change? I can fix whatever you'd like."

"You've been very kind to us, Lily. But unfortunately, not everything can be fixed."

"Did I get something wrong? If you'll just tell me what it is, I'm sure I can make it right."

"You didn't do anything wrong. The palace is wonderful. But it's also full of ghosts, Lily. This was our home not because of the stones and the carpeting, but because of our people. Our family. Without them, it feels like walking through a graveyard."

Lily swallowed. "Maybe I could still help. What if I could bring the people back? I've been able to create new dream-born before. Philippe and Mortimer and all the other creatures—they all came from my head. What if I imagined your family? Couldn't they come back, too?"

Isla's expression turned grave. "It wouldn't be *them*. They might look the same, but they would be shells of who they once were. Each dream-born is unique, just as each person in your world is unique. You can't treat people like piles of sand that you can build up or knock down at will."

As Lily struggled to think of a response, she missed her friends more than ever. Keisha would have known how to persuade Isla, and even Adam with his goofy mishaps would have offered an argument or two. On her own, however, Lily flubbed every word she spoke. Finally, she gave up. "Where will you go?" she asked, her shoulders slouching

Isla dropped a compass with a silver chain into her bag. "It's time for me to do as Pax told me. I'm going to the Cave of Lights."

"Isla, how is that going to work? The soothstone burned you when you tried to pick it up. What makes you think you can touch it now?"

"My heart was very different then. I was working with Eymah. I think that's why the stone rejected me."

"How do you know for sure?"

"I don't. But Pax told me that's where I need to go, and I trust him more than my very breath." She rolled up her cloak, then secured the tethers on her pack. "I've gathered plenty of food and supplies for you both. I need you to take care of Rowan while I'm gone. You'll do that, won't you? You'll make sure nothing happens to him?"

Lily tried to hide her disappointment. Rowan hadn't spoken two words to her since her arrival. Babysitting a sullen prince who despised her was the *last* thing she wanted to do. "I'd rather come with you," she said.

"Out of the question. I need you to look after Rowan."

"Does Rowan want that? I think he hates me."

"He doesn't hate you."

"He sure acts like he does."

"He just doesn't understand you yet. Give him time."

Lily gritted her teeth. "This isn't why I came back. I'm here to help with my soothstone, not to babysit."

She instantly regretted her words. Isla stared at her, and Lily cringed and looked away. A long silence ensued.

"You need to think carefully about why you're really here, Lily," Isla finally said. "There's a reason Pax gave you a different purpose than what you want."

Lily's face reddened, and she stared at the floor.

"And I'd advise you not to call Rowan a baby to his face. He'll throw a fit."

"No, that's not what I meant."

Isla placed a hand on Lily's shoulder. "You'll both be safe in this valley, especially now that Pax has restored it. Please be patient. And promise me you'll not let anything happen to him."

"Happen to who?" Rowan appeared in the doorway. He leaned against the doorframe, turned a piece of glass between his fingers, and studied them both through narrowed eyes.

"It's time, Espy," Isla said. "Remember what we talked about."

"I already told you, I'm not staying here."

"Yes, you are."

"This idea is ridiculous! Isla, we might have family still alive. You remember what Mother said! How can you go chasing after a rock right now?"

"Those were fairy tales, Rowan! Stories she told us as children. That's all."

"The Entwined Kingdom wasn't a fairy tale. Enlacia isn't a fairy tale either!"

"What's Enlacia?" Lily blurted. Rowan flashed her a look of scorn.

"Rowan, you are the sole surviving heir to the throne, not to mention my responsibility," Isla said. "You know the dangers I'm heading into. I want you here, where you'll be protected. And Lily, for the last time, it would mean more to me than any tower, palace, or wall that you can build, if you would please look after my brother."

Her words silenced them both. Lily looked at the ground; Rowan glared back at her and his ears turned red, but he said nothing.

"Thank you," Isla said with a nod. She leaned forward to hug Rowan, who didn't pull away but didn't return the embrace either. "I'll return as soon as I can. Look to the east." She turned to Lily. "Promise me, please."

Lily swallowed. "I promise," she said, barely able to disguise her reluctance.

For the first time in days, Isla broke into a smile. "Thank you. You've been a true friend to me." Then she shouldered her pack, hugged Rowan one more time, and began her march across the vast plain at the foot of the Desolation Mountains.

As she watched her go, Lily thought about the miles and miles of terrain she'd seen from the deck of the *Flying Emerald:* swamps and canyons, deserts, craggy peaks slick with ice. How could Isla traverse all those miles on foot?

"Hey, Isla!" she called. Her hand closed around the soothstone, and a familiar light engulfed them. When it faded, a griffin towered before them, pawed the earth, and then bowed low on its forelimbs so Isla could mount it.

Isla smiled and nodded her thanks to Lily. She climbed astride the griffin, locked eyes for one last moment with Rowan, and then took to the skies. The griffin pierced the air with its screech, and as it lifted toward the clouds, the sun glinted off its wings like firelight. The creature pirouetted twice, then sailed eastward, and Lily shielded her eyes from the glare and kept her eyes fastened on it until it appeared as nothing more than a fleck of gold on the horizon.

As Lily dropped her hands, she felt like a deflated balloon. "What am I doing here?" she asked herself. In response she heard only the sound of a lone cricket. Lily blew out a puff of air, then wrapped her arms around herself as a barrier against the loneliness that gripped her. She thought of Adam, Keisha, and Cedric, who'd journeyed alongside her through all her fears and surprises and ridiculous mistakes, and she longed for them to adventure with her again through all those dazzling lands. Instead, she stood on a hilltop over a resplendent valley, with her handiwork shimmering below, but with no real company except a kid who hated her.

Where was that kid, by the way?

She spun around. The hillside was vacant, except for the grasses bending and whispering in the wind.

"Rowan!" Lily called. The wind whipped in reply, and in the distance a wood thrush sang, but no voice answered. Lily squinted to study the hillside and the valley below.

Rowan was nowhere to be seen.

CHAPTER 4

Whoosh

"Rowan!"

Lily turned in place. The grass waved in the wind, but she saw no movement or shadow to suggest the whereabouts of Rowan. *Think, Lily, think!* She glanced down into the valley, and wondered if he'd ventured into Mistwood. *No, he's shown no interest in the kingdom at all. Why would he go there now?* Then she slapped her forehead. *His glass hideout. Of course.*

She jogged to the fulgurite where Rowan usually hid. It was the same glass tree from which Rowan would emerge for dinner every night, and which had protected him from the fires and the Blight when they first ravaged the valley. Lily crouched in front of a curtain of black canvas that hung over an arched doorway at the base of the tree, and she called Rowan's name. When he didn't respond, she rapped on the glass. Her strike echoed with a hollow tone like a bell, but Rowan didn't answer. Something scuffled inside.

"Rowan, please come out," Lily said.

No answer.

She shook her head. The last time she'd been in this position, a little girl she was babysitting had refused to come out of her closet because Lily had eaten her last green gummy bear. This moment felt just as absurd. Lily knocked on the glass again.

"Please, Rowan, I don't like this situation any more than you do, but I promised Isla I'd take care of you. Please just come out, or at least answer me."

She heard more scuffling, but still he didn't reply. Lily gritted her teeth and fought the impulse to kick the grass.

"Suit yourself, then! Stay in there as long as you want. What do I care!"

With a huff, Lily stomped down the hillside and into the valley. At least in Mistwood, she thought, she could be productive.

With her lips still pressed thin in exasperation, Lily erected a stone bridge over a stream and cajoled irises to poke through the soil along the bank. These projects elicited a few smiles from her, but not the depth of satisfaction she expected. Without someone to share in the beauty, her joy was fleeing.

She wandered into Isla and Rowan's playroom and mused about riding the rocking horse, but with Isla gone and the halls so silent, she felt too much like an intruder to displace a single wooden block.

At sunset she trudged back up the hillside to make the nightly soup. She found some leeks and mushrooms and boiled them with salt and herbs just as she'd watched Isla do, but the vegetables turned limp and soggy, and the broth tasted like stagnant water.

When she'd ladled the soup into bowls and placed a slice of stale bread beside each serving, she stood in the doorway of the cottage and called for Rowan. Again, he didn't answer.

"He has been in his glass house all day, mademoiselle." Philippe hopped up to the doorway, a parsnip jutting from his mouth.

"Has he come out at all?"

"*Non*, mademoiselle. Not that I have seen."

The sun had already sunk below the mountains, pilfering all warmth and light with it, and the sky had deepened to a somber blue-green. Lily groaned and marched out toward the fulgurite.

"Rowan, it's dinnertime!" she called, not bothering anymore to disguise her annoyance.

No answer.

"Rowan, this isn't funny. You need to eat. Come out!"

She received no reply, except for the whisper of the wind through the grass.

What a brat, Lily thought. She heaved a sigh, then threw open the canvas curtain. "Rowan, knock it off, and come out! It's the same soup that Isla—"

She stopped. Even without the sun she could see that the chamber was empty.

"Rowan! Rowan, where are you? Stop playing around!" Lily crawled through the low doorway on all fours. She fumbled about in the waning light, and scraped her knees on a rock jutting up from the earth. Then her right hand plunged into empty space, and she pitched forward and landed facedown on the dirt floor of the hideaway. Her right arm dangled in a hole in the ground beside her, and when she stretched her fingers she touched something cool, solid, and sloping at the base of the pit.

Lily spit grit from her mouth. She was about to mutter something about exasperating elf princes, when the pop of a match strike and a crackling of fire startled her. She rolled away from the hole and sat up as a spray of pink light, like a sparkler, suddenly illuminated the room. Philippe stood behind her, a light sizzling in his outstretched paw.

"Mademoiselle, it appears *le petit prince* is fond of holes," Philippe said. The sparkler in his paw was a wand, the plastic type that birthday party magicians wielded for their tricks.

"Philippe, where did you get that?"

"Surely, mademoiselle, you do not think I wear this ridiculous hat for fashion?" He removed the top hat and wrinkled his nose in disdain. "It is a magic hat, so they say. One day, some scoundrel pulled me out of it, but I had the last laugh and took it back! Then I discovered he left some of his tricks inside."

"You came from inside the hat?"

"*Oui*, mademoiselle."

"So, you live in it?"

Philippe cleared his throat in disgust, and his ears flopped about as he shook his head vigorously. "Do not be ridiculous, mademoiselle! Have you ever lived inside a hat? Impossible to clean. Lint and hairballs, they are everywhere! And the smell . . . no fresh air, mademoiselle!"

Lily shook off her confusion. "Okay. Whatever. Do you know where Rowan is?"

"*Non*, mademoiselle."

"I thought you said he was in here all day."

"*Oui*, mademoiselle."

Lily frowned at him. "So where is he, then?"

"Somewhere else, mademoiselle."

"But where?"

Philippe shrugged.

Lily rubbed her temples. "You said he never left this chamber. Are you *sure* that's true?"

"Perhaps I am mistaken, but I do not think so. I spent the afternoon harvesting roots outside the cottage. They are so good, you know, the parsnips so fragrant, they will do beautifully with a drop of olive oil and some rosemary. And yesterday, I found sage behind the old beech tree, which will be *parfait* with the turnips, although perhaps they need a bit—"

"Philippe!"

"Oh. Pardon. Ahem! The root patch is just outside this place. I saw him go in, and by sunset, he still had not come out."

"Did you hear anything?"

"I heard him moving for a while. Then I heard a sound, like eh, a *whoosh*. After that, nothing."

"A *whoosh?*"

"*Oui, ma cherie.*" He made a roller coaster motion with his free paw. "*Whoosh.*"

Lily glanced at the hole in the ground that had triggered her fall. "Can you bring that light closer?" she asked as she knelt in the dirt. The pink light of Philippe's sparkler revealed the hole as a perfect circle in the ground, its diameter barely wide enough for Lily to squeeze through. As she leaned forward, the light reflected off the floor of the hollow and cast it in a glossy sheen.

Lily frowned in concentration. Her fingers had brushed something cool and hard at the base of the pit . . . something smooth, just like . . .

"Glass."

"*Qu'est que c'est,* mademoiselle?"

"The bottom of this hole is made out of glass." She craned her neck. The opening was actually the entrance to a glass tunnel that plunged into the earth, as if someone had installed a tube slide underground. Lily studied the steep incline of the passage, and shuddered. The tunnel reminded her of a waterslide she'd been terrified to go down at an amusement park when she was six. "*Whoosh,*" she whispered to herself.

"What is that, mademoiselle?"

She stood up. "You said you heard a whooshing sound, right? This must have been it. He must have gone down there."

Philippe stepped toward the entrance and peered down the tunnel. "Are you quite sure, mademoiselle?"

"Yes, I'm sure. We need to go after him."

He sucked his teeth. "Then we will need better light than this." Before Lily could protest, Philippe extinguished his sparkler and then rummaged in his hat. "Ridiculous hat," he murmured under his breath. Then he withdrew something that sounded like plastic cups knocking together in the hands of a toddler. Philippe whistled, thumped the ground several times with his foot, and a dozen fireflies flew into the chamber, infusing the tiny space with golden light. As if upon command, the fireflies congregated into a clear, plastic half-sphere that Philippe held aloft. Once nestled inside, the rabbit closed the sphere with a second half, such that a ball filled with fireflies illuminated the night like a lantern.

Lily gawked at Philippe. "You're not an ordinary rabbit," she said.

He nonchalantly returned his hat to his head, then brushed dust off his shoulder. "Well, I believe that is, how you say? OB-vious?" He leaned over the lip of the tunnel and his firefly lantern dappled the chute with light, but Lily could make out nothing beyond a foot or two down. She crouched down to lower herself into the tunnel, but Phillipe held out a paw and waved her back. "No, no, no, mademoiselle. I suspect I know much more about such things than you. I was born in a hat, but raised in a, how you say?"

"A burrow?"

"*Burro*? You mean, 'hee haw'?"

"Ah, no—"

"I grew up in holes and tunnels under the ground."

"Yes. A burrow."

"No, there were no such creatures there. How could they dig? So clumsy, with their hooves!"

"I know, I wasn't talking about a—"

"Is it the ears?"

"What?"

"The ears. You think they are like us, because of the long ears?"

Lily's head swam. "No," she said, punctuating her words with a fist against her open palm. "I'm not talking about donkeys. You grew up in tunnels. I get it."

"Okay. Then, *allons-y*, mademoiselle."

"Who's Allan Z?"

"Ah, *sacré bleu*! *Whoosh.*"

"Oh. Yes. Let's go."

"Just follow me down the tunnel, okay? I go first. Stay close, and follow the light."

With that, Philippe leaped into the hole, and with a quick *whoosh* he disappeared. His departure plunged the chamber into darkness, and Lily strained her eyes to discern the yawning gap in the ground before her.

"This is crazy," she said aloud. "I'm alone, in the dark, following a rabbit down a hole."

Her breath clouded before her face in the chill air as she sat down on the edge of the tunnel. Three times she considered dropping down inside, but as she considered the darkness and the closeness, her courage fizzled. She'd never thought much about claustrophobia before, but the idea of shoving herself into a glass tube unnerved her. *But you have to keep your promise,* she thought. Rowan could be lost, or hurt, or worse.

Finally, with both hands braced against the ground, she closed her eyes, held her breath, and slid down into the chute.

Whoosh.

She hurtled downward into inky blackness. Her arms flew up above her head, and she fought to grind her heels against the slide to slow her descent, but her foot only ricocheted from the glass wall, twisting her ankle. The slide corkscrewed, twisted, and flipped so many times that she lost all sense of direction. As she slid down, down into the depths, a part of her worried she'd never stop sliding, and that she'd stumbled into an endless tunnel that would forever rob her of the sun. After what seemed like an eternity, the bottom of the slide suddenly dropped out from beneath her. Lily's stomach flipped as she plunged downward, and she flailed her limbs as the wind whipped through her hair. She struck something icy cold, then thrashed in panic as her nose and chest burned. She had fallen into a body of water.

Lily kicked and flapped her arms, not knowing which direction would lead her to fresh air. Finally, she glimpsed a thread of light, ghostly green, wavering above the water. Lily swam toward it and broke through the surface just as her lungs threatened to burst.

She wiped her eyes, gulped a few breaths, and glanced around her as she treaded water. She had emerged through a carpet of eerie light, a layer of green bioluminescent critters floating on the water as far as her eyes could see. Lily lifted a hand to see dozens of tiny green glowing beads slither from her arm, coalesce on the surface, and then swim away. They snaked across a wide lake and then vanished in the distance, following the course of some dark, underground stream.

As Lily squinted in the dark, she glimpsed a small yellow orb bobbing in the distance. *Philippe?* she wondered. Then, as if on cue, she saw a tiny pink flame sputter to life.

Lily swam with all her might toward the light, scattering clouds of green creatures in her wake. She reached a bank, heaved herself onto the slimy rock, and lay on her back, gasping for breath. When Philippe stooped over her, the light from his sparkler stung her eyes.

"Tsk, tsk, tsk," he said, with a tap of his foot. "I told you to follow the fireflies, mademoiselle. See what hesitation will bring you?"

Lily sat up and coughed a few times. Although the water was icy cold, on the bank the air felt stagnant and hot, like the heady steam of a jungle. "Where are we?" she asked.

"Down the tunnel."

Lily rolled her eyes. "Yes, I know *that*. I mean, what is this place?"

"That I do not know. Although I suspect we are below the mountains."

"Which mountains? Desolation?"

"I do not know."

Lily screwed up her mouth. "I thought you knew all about tunnels and burrows?"

"*Burros?*"

"Tunnels and *holes*."

"This, mademoiselle, is no rabbit hole."

Lily's shoulders sagged, and she tried not to dwell on how much she suddenly missed Cedric. He would have known where they were and what to do, and his wit would have coaxed a smile to her face even in the dark. Sighing with exasperation, she clambered to her feet, then winced as pain shot from her left ankle up her leg. She limped forward a few steps, then searched the bank for some sign of activity: tracks in the scummy earth, a tunnel, discarded bread crusts, spent coals from a fire. All she saw, however, were sludgy rock, water lapping the bank like a sea of oil, and a vast ocean of green.

"Have you seen Rowan?" she asked.

"*Non*, mademoiselle."

Lily kicked a cluster of pebbles, then instantly regretted it. She collapsed to the ground and rubbed her sore ankle. "Maybe he didn't come down here," she said with a grimace. "Maybe this was all a mistake. A massive, horrible mistake."

"He came down here."

"How do you know?"

"At least, I do believe so."

"You just said you haven't seen him."

"I have not."

"Then how do you know he's been here?"

"Some of his handiwork, I think, mademoiselle." Philippe hopped down the bank, gripping his sparkler in one paw and the firefly orb in the other. He held them both aloft, and in the strange pink and yellow light that resulted, Lily saw a large bowl of glass resting on the rocks.

"What is it?" she asked.

"A boat, I believe."

"How do you know it's his?"

"If you will see, mademoiselle, there are skid marks beside it. I believe there were two saucers." Philippe studied her. "He is a master of glass, no?"

Lily remembered how Rowan had made his fulgurites himself. "Yes, I guess so."

"It seems he has been here before. This boat was not made today."

"How can you tell?"

Philippe dropped the orb on the ground and with his nose scrunched in disgust, he pulled a shriveled, moldy potato scrap from within the boat. "This is days old. Completely inedible."

Lily followed the trajectory of the skid marks. They plunged into the water, toward the stream. "Well, I guess we have to go after him," she said. She crouched down and with a grunt tried to shove the boat into the water. The half-dome budged two inches, then ground to a stop. "Hey, can you please help me?" she asked Philippe.

No answer.

Lily turned around. Philippe reclined on the ground with one leg lazily crossed over the other as he sprinkled salt on a stump of parsnip.

"Philippe, what are you doing?"

"*Pardon, ma cherie,* but it is time for supper."

"*Supper?* Now?"

"*Bien sûr,* mademoiselle." He glanced at his furry wrist, as if examining a watch. "By the pattern of my fur, it is at least six o'clock."

"Philippe, we're wasting time! Rowan's out there somewhere, and who knows what's happened to him. He could be in trouble."

"Well," Philippe crunched a bite of his parsnip and didn't speak until he'd swallowed. "As I see it, if he is hurt, he will not go far, and we will catch up to him. And if he is not hurt, what do we have to worry about?"

"Philippe, please . . ."

The rabbit sat upright, dusted salt from his paws, and then dove into his top hat. He withdrew another parsnip and a leaf of lettuce, followed by a black pepper grinder, more salt, and what Lily barely discerned in the dim light as a small bottle of garlic aioli. "*Ma cherie,* I cannot function on an empty stomach.

C'est impossible. First, *un petit* supper. Then *un petit* sleep. Then we go."

"Philippe—"

He turned his back on her, dressed the parsnip in aioli, and proceeded to munch.

Lily flopped down on the ground and slumped forward with her head in her hands. *I can't believe this,* she thought with exasperation. *I thought I was coming back to rebuild the Realm. Instead, I'm lost in a cave, chasing after a bratty kid, waiting for a rabbit to finish dinner.* She glanced over at Philippe and felt a flicker of resentment as he tossed a mushroom into the air and caught it in his mouth. The cavern smelled of rank, decaying things, the way a dock at low tide reeks of dead fish, and she wondered how Philippe could eat his meal with such relish.

She again missed Adam and Keisha. She thought of her parents. At six o'clock on a Saturday—or was today Friday?—they would be sitting down to dim sum. Her mother would have placed a single azalea blossom in the vase on the table, plucked from their front garden. Gran would shuffle into the kitchen in her slippers and squeeze her dad's shoulder as she eased into a chair. Then the stories would come—stories of hiking and fishing and tales carried down through the years. Would they still swap stories over dumplings when she wasn't there?

Why did you bring me back here, Pax? She glanced around the dismal cavern. He'd urged her to tell others about what he'd done, but how could she do that locked away in the roots of the mountains? She heard snoring and turned to see Philippe sprawled on the ground, his hat over his eyes, fast asleep. *What am I doing here?*

"Lily."

Lily jumped at the sound of her name. The voice had been raspy, barely louder than a whisper. She glanced over at Philippe, but he still lay on the ground like a fuzzy doormat. His sparkler had gone out, and the only light in the cavern was the sea of bioluminescent mites and the ethereal glow of the fireflies in their sphere.

"Who's there?" Lily asked as she strained to see.

"It's me, Lily." Louder this time.

Lily's heart raced. The voice was so familiar, but she couldn't place it.

"Come here."

She stood up, and saw a strange profile silhouetted against the glowing water. It was short and hulking. Lily took a few steps forward but then froze in her tracks, and the hair on the back of her neck pricked up.

A pair of red eyes burned through the dark.

CHAPTER 5

Glower

Lily's heartbeat thundered in her ears. She retreated a step and with shaking hands withdrew the soothstone from her pocket. The stone glowed red, warning of a shroud nearby.

"I see you've learned much since we first met," the shroud hissed, a puff of smoke curling around him.

Lily balled both hands into fists and raised them, readying herself for an attack. "Who are you?" she asked.

The shroud's sinister laugh resounded throughout the cavern. "Don't you recognize me?"

A chill ran down Lily's spine. She searched for memories of the shrouds she'd encountered, all of them terrifying: the one who impersonated Gran, only to morph into an ogre; the one who pretended to be Adam's father, then transformed into a saber-toothed cat. The harpy, whose voice filled her veins with ice. Then, in the Catacombs . . .

"You need to think back farther," the shroud growled, as if reading her thoughts. His substance thinned as if he were a dispersing vapor.

Lily saw fangs gleaming through the murk, and the sight struck her cold. "I don't know who you are," she said, backpedaling and raising the soothstone higher.

"How disappointing. How could you forget the special times we had, all those years ago?"

He lumbered forward, and in the dim light Lily distinguished his shape for the first time.

The shroud was a black beast skulking on two knobbly, clawed legs. He had wiry hair, a reptilian tail, and two horns sprouting like scimitars from its head. He grimaced at her, his red eyes the same that threatened her from within her closet late at night when she was a little girl. Her parents had always reassured her that monsters weren't real, that the beast hunched in her closet, poised to attack, was just a figment of her imagination.

"This is impossible!" Lily stammered. "You're not real! This can't be possible!"

The shroud wavered and thinned again, and for a moment Lily saw through him to the green glowing stream snaking into the distance. Then the beast snapped back into focus.

"My name is Glower. And I am real, but only just. You can help me with that, *creator.*"

Creator? Had she really created this monstrosity before her? She looked at the soothstone in her hand, suddenly unnerved by her own powers.

"Not with that, you idiot!" he snarled, again reading her thoughts. "You seriously don't remember? After all those nights when I kept you company?"

"You're not real! There's no such thing as a monster in the closet!"

"So your elder folk told you. But I ask you, *dream keeper,* was your fear of me not real?"

Blood rushed in Lily's ears. *Pax. Cedric. Mom or Dad, somebody, please help me!*

"Fear is the food on which we shrouds thrive. It is our lifeblood. To be real we need only fear, and the fancies of an active mind. I was very real to you, wasn't I, Lily?"

"What do you want?"

"Only the same thing you want."

"What? What do you want?"

He lumbered closer, and Lily coughed as a cloud of acrid smoke swirled in her face. Her eyes stung from the vapor.

"I want a *purpose,*" Glower hissed.

"A what?"

"*A purpose.* You imagined me, but you never gave me a reason to exist. I have no story."

"Why do you need one?"

The shroud circled around her and blocked the sleeping Philippe from view. Lily retreated several steps, until her heels teetered on the edge of the bank. "For the same reason every created thing needs a purpose. You didn't finish my story, Lily McKinley."

"I was just a little kid. I was terrified of you."

"You're not so little now, and you have that magic pebble. Surely, you can use it to finish what you've started."

Lily's throat tightened, and she clenched her teeth to keep them from chattering. "Why would I ever want to help you? You terrorized me!"

He crept even closer. Lily recoiled from him, but the chilly water lapped at her heels and halted her retreat. There was nowhere to go.

"I can help you, too, Lily," he said in an oily voice that made her skin crawl. "I know what you seek."

"What did you do to Rowan?"

His cleared his throat in disgust. "That pouty little runt? I've no interest in him. I'm talking about what you *really* seek, deep, deep inside your heart."

"What are you talking about?'

"I can give you a purpose here, Lily McKinley. A role in keeping with your *true* talents."

Lily smelled his hot breath, like a mixture of car exhaust and garbage on a sweltering summer day, and she pressed her lips together against a wave of nausea. Her instincts told her to dive into the water behind her and swim as fast as she could. Yet, his words transfixed her. *What purpose could he mean?* she wondered. *I so want to create . . .* Her fingers tightened around the soothstone, the key to her powers.

"You have the power to bring him back, Lily."

She snapped out of her reverie. "To bring who back?"

"You know who I mean."

"No, I don't. Who are you talking about?"

"The great one. The lord of all fears."

Ice surged down her spine. *"Eymah?"*

The monster's teeth spread into a hideous, flashing grin.

"Why would I *ever* bring him back?" Lily cried.

"He can give you what you want, Lily. A home and a family, not in your filthy little world but here. He can give you a *purpose*, in keeping with your gifts." He motioned to the soothstone in her fist. "You know my words are true. Look at you chasing after a spoiled brat! Just think of what you could be doing instead. What you could be *creating*."

His words were like poison in her mind. She thought of Castle Mistwood, glittering in the sunlit valley, magnificent, restored . . . and abandoned. Couldn't she use her gifts for more? Didn't she have more to offer than chasing after a wayward prince in the darkness?

"That's it, dream keeper," Glower coaxed, his voice like gravel. "Complete my story. Bring me back from the shadows. Help me to bring *him* back."

Lily swallowed. Presuming victory, Glower laughed and shuffled toward her. His red eyes flashed with malice.

Remember that I love you, no matter what storms assail you, Pax had said. *I am with you, always. And I will return and make all things new.* Lily raised the soothstone higher, and Glower grinned in triumph. "That's it!" Glower cried, his shout bouncing through the cavern. "Finish my story!"

Lily's gaze hardened. "As you wish!"

The soothstone flooded the cave with its pale light. Its brilliance startled Glower, who teetered backward and tripped over his own long, scaly tail. Then a ball of fire appeared, hurtled through the air, and ignited the beast in flames.

Fire wrapped around the shroud like a cloak. He writhed and thrashed and filled the cavern with a gurgling, horrible scream that penetrated to Lily's bones. Then he shriveled and blew away in a mass of smoke. A few particles of ash on the water offered the only hint that he'd come.

Lily collapsed onto the riverbank in exhaustion, her limbs trembling and sweat soaking her hair. As she fell, she glimpsed a single, tiny flame still burning on the ground. As Lily focused on the rock beneath her cheek and fought to slow her breathing, the flame scampered toward her, climbed up her arm onto her shoulder, and tenderly swept hair away from her face.

A friend at last! she thought, as her eyes misted with tears. She propped herself up on her elbows. "Hey, Flint," she whispered, stroking the kindler's head "I can always count on you, can't I?"

Just then, she heard a snuffle. Philippe stretched his forelimbs, yawned, and bounded toward her. "Ah," he said with a sigh. "That was an exquisite nap!"

CHAPTER 6

Downriver

"I have not had my evening grooming yet. My fur, *c'est horrible*." Philippe smoothed his ears with his paws the way a young woman might brush her hair in the mirror. In response, Lily stomped toward Philippe, snatched the firefly orb from the ground beside him, and stormed away.

"Mademoiselle, what are you doing?"

Lily didn't answer. Instead, she marched to the glass saucer on the bank, tossed the orb inside, and then planted two hands on the glass rim and shoved the boat forward. She wanted to escape from that dreadful place—and from her horrific memory of Glower—as quickly as possible.

The boat skidded a few inches, then stopped as Lily's hands, still slick with perspiration, slid from the glass surface. She tried again, this time ramming her shoulder into the saucer. It budged a few more inches, then ground to a halt.

Philippe caught up his hat and loped toward her. He plunked down on the ground, crossed one foot over the other, and nibbled a carrot from out of the side of his mouth. "Forgive me for saying this, mademoiselle," he said, "but I do not think that will work."

Lily grunted through clenched teeth as she heaved again. "Rowan's out there somewhere, and we need to find him. We've already wasted too much time."

"But all the grunting and pushing, I do not think it will work. Plus, it is very bad for the digestion."

"Well, if you have any other bright ideas, I'd love to hear them." Lily's back foot slipped. She thudded to her knees, then crawled backward to nurse a scrape.

Philippe lazily swung the carrot around by its green top. "To start, perhaps you should remove the massive rock from in front of the boat, *non?*"

Lily's face flushed. She wiped sweat from her forehead with the back of her hand, then walked to the water's edge and discovered that Philippe was right: the cause of her straining and agony was a rock, wedged in front of the boat to keep it from sliding into the stream.

"Thanks," she mumbled, wanting to crawl under a rock herself. "Now can you please help me? I'll lift the boat as you yank out the rock."

"I will try, mademoiselle."

Philippe joined her and crouched down to ready himself, but then jumped back in alarm as Flint skittered down Lily's pant leg. "*Sacré bleu*! What is that?"

"That's Flint. He's a kindler."

"A what?"

"A friend."

"*Ma cherie*, where I come from, fire is not a friend!"

Lily ignored him again and stooped down. *He's even more annoying than Adam was when he first came to the Realm,* she thought. Then she recalled Adam spitting and screaming beside the riverbank on arrival, before he promptly slid down a cliff, almost dragging Lily with him. *Well, okay. Maybe not* more *annoying, but close.* She smirked at the memory and found herself wishing, for just a moment, that she was still sitting beside him in the Fortress, feeding s'mores bars to a medley of creatures again. *I wonder what he's doing right now? He'd think I was nuts, down here in this place . . .*

"Where did he come from?" Philippe asked.

"What? Who?" Lily asked, shaking away her thoughts with a tinge of embarrassment.

"Your deadly friend. The walking fire."

"I called him with the soothstone."

"*Incroyable.* Why? To help us through the tunnels? Ah, I see, so we may have light! Perhaps even a fire to roast breakfast?"

"No. To help me with something else."

"*Qu'est que c'est, ma cherie?*"

"Let's talk about it later. You missed a lot while you were napping. I mean, like, *a lot.*"

With another grunt Lily hoisted the boat from the ground. Her arms burned, but to her relief Philippe tucked his half-eaten carrot into his hat and scrounged beneath her for the rock. He snuffled, grunted, and in a moment dislodged it. Lily dropped the rim of the saucer, and with the stone no longer obstructing its path, it slid down the bank and halfway into the water. Lily scrambled aboard, and Flint scampered after her.

"You don't happen to have anything in that hat that we could use as an oar, do you?" Lily called back to Philippe.

The rabbit blinked at her, scratched behind his ear with his hind foot, then removed his hat and ducked inside. His head and forepaws disappeared, and soon his hind legs kicked awkwardly in the air. For a moment, Lily worried he'd disappear into the hat altogether, but he soon emerged, his newly smoothed fur disheveled again. He held his plastic wand in one paw and a wooden spoon in the other.

Lily groaned. "Philippe, can you *please* get your mind off food?"

"Mademoiselle, you can do great things with that rock in your pocket, but apparently it has not taught you the most important of virtues."

"What are you talking about?"

"*Patience, ma cherie.* Patience. I will not fail you." He held the spoon out in front of him, then gave a quick tap with his wand. A creaking of stressed wood sounded, and with a start Philippe dropped the spoon and hopped back three lengths. To Lily's amazement, the wooden spoon stretched to twenty times its size.

Philippe returned to his handiwork, sniffed the bowl of the spoon, and lapped up a puddle of something soupy. He preened his whiskers, then noticed Lily staring at him in disbelief. "*Un petit* bit of sauce," he said with a shrug.

Lily lugged the spoon into the boat and wondered how Philippe managed to be so exasperating and so helpful all at once. As she shook her head, the rabbit jumped into the boat after her.

"*Pardon*, mademoiselle, but where will we go now?"

"Down the river."

"But, downriver to where? Where does this tunnel go?"

"Your guess is as good as mine. Didn't you say you were an expert in tunnels?"

Philippe scanned the cold, dank walls of the cavern and the glowing slime on the surface of the water. He shivered. "I admit I was wrong. I am an expert in cozy rabbit warrens, with earth that is warm and smells of mushrooms, with perhaps even a whiff of *haricot verts* sauteed in *beurre blanc*. But this? This feels like a coffin."

The menacing eyes and sharp, grimy teeth of Glower haunted Lily, and she shuddered. "Let's hope it's not," she said, trying to ignore her queasiness.

With both Flint and Philippe safely on board, Lily used the spoon to shove off the bank, and the gentle current swept them downstream. They glided out of the vast cavern into a tunnel where the walls closed in around them, barely permitting them passage. The air grew dense and hot, and strange, oozy things clung to the rocks and slithered into the water. Lily tried to ignore the distinct impression that, true to Philippe's prediction, they were steering straight into the hollow of a coffin.

Lily perched on the edge of the boat and held the firefly lantern high to chase away the shadows that crowded around. Her eyes played tricks on her as she squinted into the gloom. Darkness would pool into the corners of her vision like a gathering mist, but when she would turn in alarm, the shadows would whisk away, leaving her searching the dim light for a sign of movement, for a cloud of smoke or a glint of fiery eyes.

They coasted through the darkness for minutes, then hours. At first Lily tried to gauge the time, but eventually she lost track. Philippe eventually dozed off to sleep again with Flint curled by his side. Every so often the rabbit's blustery snores would send the tips of Flint's flame flickering like a mop of flyaway hair.

While they slept, Lily rummaged inside Philippe's hat, half in search of food, half because she couldn't quell her curiosity about its contents. To her disappointment, she found plenty of partly-chewed turnip and carrot stubs, but none of the wands or tantalizing fireflies that Philippe had procured. As Lily's stomach rumbled, she contented herself with the carrot pieces, nibbling them as she lazily dipped the oar in the water. The green beads on the surface parted from before the saucer, then gathered in swirling rivulets behind them. Lily glanced back and watched them coil like tendrils on a vine. They seemed to intertwine, to merge and dance into shapes as she watched. Then Lily gasped. The beads coalesced and swelled out of the water. Lily darted backward and nearly dropped the oar in her panic.

"Flint! Philippe! Wake up! Look behind us!"

Her drowsy companions spluttered awake, stumbled to her side, and peered over the stern of the boat. Lily held her breath and fought to steady her trembling fingers around the oar. No one spoke. Before the travelers' eyes, the gelatinous green forms merged, rose from the water, and loomed toward them in a glowing, hulking mass.

"What is it, mademoiselle?" Philippe whispered. His voice, usually so cavalier, sounded taut with fear.

A single wing, like a bat's, poked from the thing's back, and then the creature elongated and sprouted the tail of a dolphin. It writhed and twisted above the water, picking up speed. Whatever it was, it was racing straight toward them.

Lily's knuckles whitened as she paddled furiously. "Philippe, help me!" she cried. "Paddle in the water with your feet or something! We need to outrun it!"

She rowed furiously. With her damp hair streaking across her eyes, she glanced back to see the creature gaining on them. It had swollen to double its original size.

"Faster!" Lily cried, her chest tightening with cold and fright. "Paddle faster!"

Philippe hung off the side of the boat with his forepaws and kicked at the water. "Mademoiselle, I don't think—"

"It's our only chance! Kick harder!"

"We are already going faster, *ma cherie*! Do you not see the water ahead?"

Lily swiped her hair out of her face, then cried out in dismay. The river ahead seethed with churning, green-tinted foam.

"Everyone hang on!" Lily cried. "It looks like rapids!" At her urging, Philippe huddled in the prow of the boat with one forelimb hooked over the rim, and Flint dived for shelter under Philippe's top hat. Lily jammed her paddle into the water, searching for the river bottom or a rock onto which she could ground them, but the spoon only glanced off the frothing surface. They struck a rock, soared into the air, then plunged back into the river with a crash that threatened to shatter the boat to pieces. A wave of oily green water flooded over them, and Flint squealed in terror as the wave soaked Philippe's hat. The impact threw Lily backward, and as she pitched onto her side, she lost her grip on the oar. With a whistle the oar whipped away behind her and disappeared.

Lily forced herself to her knees and crawled toward the prow of the boat, but her hands slid against the slick surface and she sprawled on her abdomen. She raised her head, but spray stung her face and blurred her vision. As her mind reeled, the riverbank seemed to fly by faster and faster.

They were speeding up.

"Mademoiselle!" Philippe shouted, his voice barely audible above the wind and the roaring rapids. "The river! I do not see it up ahead!"

Oh no. With a wave of dread Lily remembered how the river beyond the Wilderness had vanished at the precipice of the Cascades. The falls had nearly killed Adam and Cedric, and she had narrowly escaped drowning as the bracing water pounded her. Now they would endure the same trial *in the pitch dark.*

"We have to jump!" she shouted. "Philippe, look for a safe place!"

"But where? There is no place!" Philippe reached inside his hat for the wand and tapped it to ignite its sparks, but another wave immediately quenched the pink fire and tore the wand from his paw. The wand spiraled away and sent up a puff of steam as the river swallowed it up.

Lily fumbled in her pocket for the soothstone, but the endless buffeting of the boat against rocks and turbulent water knocked her onto her back. Stars flickered before her eyes, and time slowed down. She stared upward, her eyes blinking but unfocused as she gazed mindlessly into an empty blackness.

She heard a muffled cry. Who was that? Where was she?

Suddenly a large, amorphous green shape hovered over her. Lily's teeth chattered. *Get up,* she thought, her inner voice screaming. Her limbs wouldn't respond, and stars continued to blink in her vision.

It loomed closer. The blackness ceded to green, as if the beast were a greasy, phosphorescent wave cresting above her, ready to swallow her.

No. No. Leave me alone!

Another muffled cry. A splash of foul water. A jolt.

Then the green mass was around her, enveloping her, until all she could see was its unearthly glow, and all she could feel were its slimy limbs.

Another jolt. She heard Philippe shriek.

Then something lifted her. Her legs dangled above the spray, and the roar of the falls faded away. The green receded, and she again stared into blackness. She felt wet, cold stone beneath her hands, and smelled again the rank odor of the tunnel.

Lily struggled to sit up and braced herself against the grimy rock as a wave of dizziness swamped her. When the world snapped back into focus, she saw Philippe safely on the bank beside her, wringing out his sodden hat and shaking water from his ears. Flint, bedraggled and tremulous as candlelight in the wind, nuzzled into her side. Lily gave Flint's head a pat, then looked up and froze.

The creature that had coalesced from the river, with its single bat wing, dolphin's tail, and mess of unidentifiable appendages, undulated on the bank.

And beside it, with his hands folded across his chest and a scowl etched on his face, stood Rowan.

CHAPTER 7

Memories in Ruins

"Rowan, come here right now! Get away from that that monster!"

Even in the gloom of the tunnel, Lily could see Rowan raise an eyebrow. Lily backed away from the creature and searched the ground for a weapon. "I'm serious, Rowan! That thing tried to kill us!"

"Don't call him a 'thing,'" Rowan said, his voice sharp with irritation. "He wasn't attacking you; he was trying to save you from the falls." Rowan approached the creature, and Lily's heart lurched into her throat as she waited for the monster to swallow him whole. Instead, it bowed to Rowan, waved, and slid back into the river to merge with the layer of floating splotches.

"What was that thing?" Lily asked breathlessly.

Rowan shook his head in annoyance. "What are you doing here?"

"Are you kidding? What are *you* doing here? Do you realize what I had to go through to find you?"

"I didn't ask you to find me."

"You know that I promised Isla I'd look after you."

"If you really want to help, you'll leave me alone." Rowan turned his back on her and studied the rock wall of the tunnel.

Lily ground her sneaker against the slimy bank. She wanted nothing more than to turn around and do exactly as he'd suggested, to return to Mistwood and spend her hours creating. But duty bound her to the prince, even as he scorned her. "I can't do that," she said. "I promised Isla I'd protect you."

"You, protect me? Do you even know where we are?"

Lily's face reddened. "No, I don't. What is this place?"

"These are the Caverns of Unfinished Dreams. And one of those unfinished dreams just saved your life."

"That's what that thing was? An unfinished dream?"

"Stop calling him a 'thing.'"

"Sorry. *He* was an unfinished dream?"

Rowan rolled his eyes and pointed at the water. "See those green lights? Those are fragments of dreams that people—*your* people—never completed. They wait down here hoping someone will finally give them a story." He turned back to the wall, probing the rock with his fingers. "Sadly, no one ever bothers."

Give them a story? Lily's skin crawled as Glower's words haunted her. *Complete my story*, he had said.

"Rowan, do shrouds live down here too?" she asked, trying to hide her anxiety.

"What?"

"The shrouds. Are they unfinished dreams, too?"

"No! Of course not!" He pointed to the water. "Did he look like a shroud to you?"

"No, but—"

"If you were really a keeper, you'd know the difference between a shroud and an unfinished dream."

"I'm still learning, okay?"

"Why don't you just go back home? If you can't even recognize a shroud, you're a greater danger to me than anything in these caverns."

Lily clenched her fists. "I *do* know about shrouds. I've fought against them more than once. And I know that *your* family helped them to escape from the Catacombs."

Rowan scowled at her, and his mouth worried as he searched for a sharp retort. All he could manage, through gritted teeth, was, "Just go away."

"I already told you, I can't. I promised your sister I'd look after you."

"For the last time, I don't need to be looked after."

"I know you're a prince, but you're still just a kid."

"As are you."

Lily scoffed. "I'm *older* than you, Rowan."

He swiveled around, his garnet eyes flashing. "Really? Just how much older?"

Lily elongated her neck to maximize every smidgen of her height. "I'm twelve."

Rowan waved her away and returned to his examination of the tunnel wall.

"I'll be thirteen in September. I'm older than I look."

"So am I."

"How much older?"

"I've been prince of the Mist Elves for three hundred and eighty years longer than you've been alive."

His words stunned her into a momentary silence. He looked and acted like a kid. Could he really be . . . ? "You're *four hundred* years old?"

"Three hundred and ninety-two. Do they not teach mathematics in the waking world?"

"I was rounding up. Look, how—"

"Just leave me alone! Take my boat if you want, and take my oar and go back to Mistwood, or better yet, to your own home where you belong."

Lily sighed, kicked a few pebbles, and joined Rowan as he studied the wall. "What are you doing down here, anyway?"

"Looking for the same thing as my sister."

"Her soothstone? Aren't there better ways to get to the Cave of Lights than underground?"

"I'm not looking for a soothstone." Rowan wedged his fingers into a crevice in the rock, and suddenly a loud rumbling echoed throughout the cavern. Lily backed away from the wall, wary of any stalactites or dislodged rocks that might plummet down and strike them. The tunnel wall yawned open to unveil a stone staircase, and a shaft of pale, gray light poured down to illuminate the tunnel. The light revealed a layer of living, moving organisms clinging to the tunnel walls, with leafy, gelatinous appendages rippling like sea lettuce in a current. When the light touched the creatures, they sprouted spiny, articulated legs and scuttled away to darker corners.

Rowan climbed the steps as a filmy slip of gray vapor drifted down the stairway. In a heartbeat he had ascended the staircase and disappeared into the mist.

"Rowan!" Lily cried. "Don't you dare run away from me again!" She raced up the steps after him, tripped when a stair crumbled beneath her feet, and stumbled forward into the open air. A thick mist swirled around her like a scarf caught in a sea breeze. Even when filtered through the fog, however, the pale sunlight stung Lily's eyes after so many hours in darkness. Thumping and skittering footfalls told her that Philippe and Flint both joined her, but for a moment all she could see were the mist and the sun glare.

Lily called out to Rowan again and heard footsteps in the distance. She swept a hand through the mist, and for an instant it parted like a curtain to reveal the elf prince rushing into a wood, the cragged limbs of ancient trees dripping with moss around him. Pinpoints of light, like dust motes but glimmering, floated through the air. Lily's heart quickened at the sight, but in an instant the mist swirled back and concealed the enchanting image.

"I can see nothing, mademoiselle," Philippe said, swatting the fog with his hat. Lily heard a squeak and glanced down to see Flint motioning to her with a fiery limb. As he scampered ahead, his light burned through the fog like a lantern bobbing in a safe harbor. *Good old Flint*, she thought. The pang of loneliness that arose when Pax left still lingered, and she especially pined for Keisha and Adam, but at least she had Flint.

After several minutes she tracked the kindler out of the mist to a clearing, where a shower of motes floated around them like glittering snow. The turf gave way to a circle of flat stones upon the ground, the relics of an ancient, forgotten courtyard. Tiles cracked under the weight of Lily's footsteps, and weeds and grasses had long ago poked through the seams between the stones.

Lily crouched down to examine one of the tiles, and she glimpsed a hint of an old carving, its contours worn away by wind, rain, and time. What was it, she wondered? A tree? Laurels, like those that adorned so much of Isla's kingdom? She gingerly ran a finger along the relief, then glanced up and scanned the courtyard. It must have been grand once. What had happened? Was this ruin the work of the Blight, too? She stood up, and the thought cemented in her mind. *This must be from the Blight*, she thought. She slid her hand into her pocket and withdrew the soothstone. *Maybe I can help . . .*

"I wouldn't do that."

Lily jumped. Rowan appeared in the courtyard, his arms crossed behind his back.

"Sorry," Lily said, catching her breath. "I just thought maybe the Blight did all this and I could help."

"What you see has nothing to do with the Blight."

Lily cocked her head. "How can you be so sure? The Blight went everywhere."

"This is a forgotten place." He turned and followed a path of cobblestones winding out of the courtyard and into the shadows of the woods. Lily jogged to catch up with him, and Philippe and Flint trailed behind her.

"What do you mean, it's forgotten?" Lily asked.

He ignored her. He ducked into a thicket of vines that wove so low to the ground that Lily had to crawl on her hands and knees to follow him. *Where is he going now?* she wondered with exasperation. A thorn scraped across her forearm, and something wet slithered across her ankle as she grunted through the dirt. When she finally climbed out the other side, she brushed twigs from her hair and wiped a smear of unidentifiable berry juice from her face.

"Ay! *C'est terrible!*" Philippe exclaimed as he rolled out of the brush after her, his hat ragged and crumpled in his paws. Flint somersaulted through the vines like a fireball, then reeled with dizziness. When they all regained their bearings, they gasped.

71

A fortress towered among the trees. The same ancient, crumbling stones that had tiled the courtyard climbed several stories high, buttressed by gnarled tree limbs that stretched across the tower to uphold it like scaffolding. As Lily wondered at the spectacle, a flock of ravens took flight from a balcony high above and broke the mysterious quiet with their cries.

The gritty sound of moving stone drew Lily's eyes as Rowan heaved open a heavy granite door. He withdrew a large silver key from the lock in the door and gave Lily a furtive glance as he tucked the key within the folds of his cloak. Then he slipped inside.

Lily jogged after him, noting the dusty scent of ancient stone as she passed through the crumbling archway. She entered an inner court, the air cool and musty, then caught her breath. A single shaft of sunlight cascaded down through a hole in the ceiling and shined upon a medallion on the center of the floor. Vines and branches interwove across the leaning stone walls, barely hoisting them up, like weary farmers stooping to carry loads on their crooked spines. The hollow *plink* of dripping water resounded from a distant hall, and a swish of feathers announced the flight of another flock of ravens as they swooped out through the hole and cut the sunlight with their black wings.

"*Sacré bleu*, mademoiselle," Philippe whispered. "*C'est magnifique!*"

"What is this place?" Lily asked.

With his broad foot, Philippe wiped a carpet of dust from the floor to reveal the faded image of a horse. He crouched down, blew more dust away, and then with a forepaw pointed to a series of old, forgotten paintings, the pigment chipped and pale, but the delicate artistry still apparent. "Who are they, mademoiselle?" he asked.

Lily knelt. One of the paintings depicted a hunting party with noble figures on horseback. A dog leaped across a creek beside them and bayed. A young boy, a circlet around his brow, led the party with a horn raised to his lips.

Lily blinked several times, and then her brow furrowed as she studied the boy's image. She leaned closer, until her nose hovered just inches from the picture. *Am I imagining things?* Most of the paint had peeled away, but she could still make out a single lock of hair, swept back from the boy's face in the wind as he rode. Even in its faded state, Lily could tell that it was dark red, almost burgundy. It looked just like . . .

"Don't touch anything."

Lily looked up to see Rowan above her, his arms folded across his chest.

"I'm not, I just—"

Before she could finish, he had already turned and marched away. Lily shot a frustrated glance at Philippe, who only shrugged his shoulders, and Flint did the same with a subtle squeak.

Rowan walked across the court, pushed open another creaking door, and wound his way down a corridor lined with cobwebbed sconces. After several twists and bends, the hallway ended in a single, arched wooden door with a glass knob.

"Again, don't touch *anything*," Rowan repeated. "No human has ever been in here before."

"Why? What is this place?"

He withdrew the key again from his cloak, and as he turned it within the lock, a click reverberated through the fortress. Then he twisted the knob and shouldered the door open. Dust spilled down from the top of the doorway, raining into Lily's hair and face. She coughed a few times, and then blinked the dirt from her eyes and followed as Rowan stepped into the room.

They stood within a domed chamber, the ceiling so high it disappeared above them into a slip of mist. Lights lined the room from floor to ceiling, like flickering lanterns arranged in thousands of columns and rows. Each light danced from within a glass orb about the diameter of a tennis ball.

"Rowan, what is—?"

"Mnemos!" Rowan called. At the sound of his voice, the glass baubles shook, filling the room with the song of chimes. "Mnemos, are you here?"

"You're calling Minnie Mouse?" Lily asked in bewilderment.

Rowan wrinkled his face. "What?"

"Minnie Mouse. Is she here, too?"

"Not 'Minnie Mouse'! Muh-NEE-mose. It means remembrance."

A flush crept over Lily's cheeks. "Oh."

Another tinkling of glass. Rowan dropped to one knee as something small and swift bounded across the floor toward them. It was indistinct, like a shadow wavering at twilight, but as it scampered forward, Lily noted a bushy tail flying behind it.

"Is that . . . a squirrel?"

"He only looks like one. It's just the form he's chosen today."

As the squirrel approached, Lily could see straight through him to the shelves of lights on the opposite wall. His form was translucent, as if made from dandelion silk or sheer drapery. "Is it a ghost?" Lily whispered.

"You really need to stop calling the dream-born 'it.'"

"Sorry—*he*. Is he a ghost?"

"No."

"What is he, then?"

"He's the librarian."

"The *what?*"

"This is a library of memories. He's a sort of memory himself, of the one who used to tend this hall. A shadow of him is still tied to the place."

Lily scanned the shelves in wonder. "These glass balls, and the lights, what are they?"

"The most treasured memories of my people."

Lily's jaw dropped. "You can keep memories inside glass?"

"Copies of them, yes. But we only preserve the ones we care about most."

"That's amazing. But why?"

"To ensure they're never forgotten. Why else?" He reached out a hand to the squirrel, who craned his neck to sniff Rowan's fingers. As Rowan leaned forward, a wisp of dark red hair fell into his eyes, and his face softened. "And also so we can look at them and remember, when the memories in our minds start to fade."

"That painting on the floor," Lily said, studying him. "There was a boy in it who I swear was you."

"Not me. One of my ancestors."

"An ancestor? I could have sworn it was you. He looked just like you."

"Others have said that too." Rowan narrowed his eyes, as if processing a hidden pain. "His name was Esperion, the last prince of the Entwined Kingdom."

"The Entwined Kingdom?"

He pointed to another painting scrolled across the floor of the library. Lily bent to examine it and saw two thrones imprinted on the stone: one embossed with a cloud, the other with falling snow. Two groups of people flanked the thrones, those on one side adorned in blue robes and the others in white, and at the center stood two kings, their arms linked. The king in white held a glowing blue jewel in his free hand.

"Who are they?"

Rowan didn't hear her. "I wish I had something to give you, Mnemos," he said to the squirrel. "But I left in a hurry."

Lily smirked as the squirrel cleaned his face with a paw. Then he straightened, fished a pair of rectangular spectacles from his chest fur, and rubbed them clean on his tail.

"Quite all right, my prince," the squirrel said, in a voice far too deep for any rodent. He seated his spectacles on the bridge of his furry nose. "I suspect you're here for the usual?"

"Yes. And—the other one, please."

"Pardon me, sire, but my memory seems as brittle as old acorns lately. Could you please tell me which one you mean? Your first successful lightning glass? Or perhaps you're hankering after that delightful stag hunt with your father?"

Rowan's cheeks reddened ever so slightly. He leaned forward and muttered his answer under his breath. "No, Mnemos, not that one. The *other* one. The one I told you to hide away?"

Mnemos's tiny jaw dropped open, and his eyes, already magnified through his glasses, widened even further. "Surely you don't really mean *that* one, sir! You made me promise—"

"I know what I made you promise, but things have changed. I don't know when I'll be back—or if I'll be back—and I'd rather have it with me."

Lily's heart skipped a beat. *Where exactly does he think he's going?*

"Please, I'd like to have them, Mnemos. *All* of them."

Mnemos eyed him warily. "If you're quite sure, Your Majesty. If you're *quite* sure. I would just hate for something to happen to them."

"I understand. I'm sure."

Mnemos squinted at him skeptically, but finally nodded. He padded across the stone floor, murmuring to himself as he went.

He swung open a wall of shelves like a door and disappeared behind it. The tinkling of glass echoed throughout the room, along with a few exclamations in Mnemos's warbly voice. "Ah, there we are!" Mnemos said, finally reemerging.

At the sight of him, Lily retreated several steps backward and tried not to stare. The voice was the same, but instead of a squirrel, a wiry old man shuffled into view, a pair of rectangular spectacles on his crooked nose. In his knobby hands he held a handkerchief filled with baubles. "I can say with some satisfaction, Prince Rowan, that the memory that so interests you could have stayed safe here forever if you'd so chosen. I had to revert back to my old self to reach it!"

A slight smile graced Rowan's face. "I like seeing you this way."

Mnemos shuddered. "I can't fathom why. Oh, in my day I was strapping, I'll admit, but now . . . ! The arthritis is enough to drive a man mad." He held out the handkerchief in fingers that creaked like brittle twigs. "Here are your usual ones, sire," he said. "And here . . ." He drew a final bauble wrapped in a dark burgundy cloth from his robe, turned it in his palm, and hesitated. He studied Rowan from beneath bushy white eyebrows, and worry lines creased his forehead like an accordion. "Are you *quite* certain you want to take this one out of safekeeping?"

Rowan paused, as if second-guessing his decision. Finally he nodded.

"Very well," Mnemos said, holding out the parcel. "Here you are. But Your Majesty, please, *do* be careful."

Rowan accepted the bauble, still draped in cloth, as if it were a treasure liable to shatter in his fingers. Then he tucked it into his cloak, straightened his collar, and drew a breath of resolve. "Thank you, Mnemos," he said. "One day, thanks to your care, we'll bring these memories back." The resolve in his eyes deepened. "We'll bring the whole kingdom back."

"Oh, that's a good dream, sire. But I think it is still a dream."

"Not for long." He spun on his heels and marched out.

"Happy journeys, my Lord Esperion," Mnemos said, a bony hand raised in the air. His eyes shone with sadness as he watched Rowan slip from the room.

Lily followed Rowan, but dreamily, her mind too preoccupied with questions for her to focus. *Esperion?* she thought, remembering the young prince in the old paintings. *Why did Mnemos call Rowan that?* She remembered the nickname Isla had called him. *Espy . . .*

A tug at her sleeve snapped her out of her thoughts. Philippe stood at her elbow, looking up at her with pitiful eyes and thumping his foot against the ground in impatience. "Mademoiselle, it has been some time since breakfast."

Lily raised an eyebrow. "And?"

"Well, do you not think it is high time for *un petit chocolat?*" He removed his hat and began rooting. "I have a cake of radish, I believe . . ."

Lily glanced up and saw Rowan disappear through the door to the library. "Rowan, wait!" she called. She shrugged Philippe off her arm and jogged down the corridors after him, through the main hall, and out the stone door into the shady woods. Lily stumbled into the forest just in time to see Rowan stride through the trees toward a wall of mist that hovered like a vast, ghostly sea.

Flint ran ahead of her, again lighting her way, and she dodged branches and jumped over tree roots until she reached Rowan. Panting, her brow slick with sweat, she placed a hand on his shoulder. In response, the young prince whipped about, slapped away her arm, and scowled at her.

"I told you to leave me alone and go home!"

"Will you please knock it off? This game of yours—running away every time I catch up with you? It isn't funny! *At all!* I can't break my promise. Where are you going, anyway? And what did you mean when you told Minnie—when you told that librarian guy that you might not come back?"

"Isla left to look for a way forward for our people. That's what I'm doing, too."

"So you're going to find her? In the Cave of Lights?"

Rowan's eyes met hers. The intensity of his gaze uneased her. "No. I'm going in there." He pointed a finger into the swirling mist that swallowed up the forest ahead.

"What? You're joking, right?"

He didn't answer. Instead, Rowan touched the flap of his cloak that housed his memories, drew a deep breath, and then plunged into the fog.

CHAPTER 8

Lost in the Fog

Lily hesitated. She needed to follow Rowan, but the fog was unlike anything she'd ever seen—like a dense, slouching, breathing thing. She watched tendrils of mist coil like tentacles around the trees, and a shiver coursed down her spine. *Pax, why this? Why have you led me here?*

"Philippe, get out your wand," she said.

"It is lost, mademoiselle. Remember, on the river?"

Lily groaned. "Isn't there something else in your hat we can use for a light? You said it's magic, right?"

"Mademoiselle, since the prince does not want us to go, perhaps now would be a good time to sit down and roast a little—"

She waved him away, wheeled about in search of Flint, and found the kindler already standing at attention in front of her. "Can you guide us, Flint? Can you lead us through?"

Flint saluted and dove into the murk. As she approached the mist, Lily couldn't shake the impression that she was walking headlong into a massive, slumbering beast. The moment she entered, the damp chill felt like ice on her skin. She squinted and could barely see Flint up ahead, a lone candlelight in a monstrous, swirling storm. A crackle and a hiss sounded behind her, and Lily turned to see a spray of purple sparks illuminating Philippe's face. He'd procured some silk flowers and had somehow coaxed them to ignite, just like the wand he'd lost.

"Mademoiselle, I insist. I will say it again, I cannot function on an empty stomach!"

"Just come!" She grasped Philippe by a furry gray paw and dragged him deeper into the mist while he muttered complaints.

As they trudged onward, the sounds of the forest—the crickets, the chirping of birds, even the rustle of wind through the leaves—hushed into silence. Lily brushed the fog from her face, but each time the clouds regathered, smothering her like a wet scarf. Every step she took felt heavier.

Flint bobbed like a firefly struggling in a mess of cobwebs, and his light dimmed as he slogged further into the distance. "Flint, wait up!" Lily yelled. The fog yielded before her breath, then coalesced to swallow up her voice. She felt Philippe's paw slip from her hand, and she spun about to discover that he'd vanished.

"Philippe!" Lily yelled. Again her voice sounded muffled, as if she cried out with a mitten covering her mouth. She turned in place and searched the smoky gloom for the snap of a sparkler or Philippe's pert ears poking through the mist. Instead she saw only the terrible smog screening her vision.

Lily turned back on her heels, toward where she'd last seen Flint. At least, she *thought* she'd seen Flint in that direction. Or was it the other way? She turned in circles. *Left, he was to the left. No, it must have been the right . . .*

Finally, she stopped, and swallowed a lump in her throat. No matter where she looked, she could see only gray mist writhing about her, blocking out all light and color. Flint's little flame had completely vanished.

"Flint!" she shouted. "Flint, where are you? Philippe! Rowan!"

No answer.

Lily thought of asking the winds for help, but in the dense mist the only hint of a breeze was her own panting. All was still and quiet, as if all the world was a colossal, wretched animal holding its breath. Holding its breath, and waiting.

She broke into a run. The damp air pressed on her chest, and its heaviness reminded her of another time when she was cold and alone. She remembered the Petrified Forest, the thickness of the air, the chill that had turned her skin to gooseflesh. She remembered how she had taken a wrong turn in the labyrinth and then found herself alone.

Lily's heart quickened at the memory, and the mist choked her. *I have to get out of here. I have to get out!*

She sloshed through a puddle that soaked her feet to the ankles. She stretched out her arms in front of her, but her own fingers disappeared in the fog. She wished, somewhere deep down inside, that her parents would emerge from the haze and scoop her into their arms, or that Cedric would rush to her aid, with Adam and Keisha close behind. She wished this was all a nightmare and that in a moment she would awaken in her bed, see the early sunlight dancing across the books on her shelf, and sink down under the covers while the savory smells of breakfast wafted from the kitchen.

Her foot struck something. She knelt and blindly pawed the ground, then gasped as she felt something cold and clammy.

It was Rowan.

"Rowan? Rowan, are you okay?" She shook him, but he didn't respond. She could barely see his face through the mist, but she glimpsed enough to see that he was deathly pale. Lily withdrew her soothstone. *Something has to help*, she thought. *There must be something that can light the way.* She closed her eyes and tried to focus. Her heart thundered in her chest.

Her mind was blank.

Lily turned the soothstone in her palm and struggled not to let it drop as beads of condensation dotted its surface. She tried again.

Still nothing.

"Come on, work! Please work!" Lily rubbed the stone, like Aladdin polishing the magic lamp. Then her stomach flipped as the soothstone slipped from her fingers and disappeared.

Lily's heart raced wildly. She searched the ground with both hands but found only mud. Something wet slithered from between her fingers. "Oh, where is it?" she cried. "Help! Please, someone help!"

"Mademoiselle?"

The call sounded muted and distant.

"Philippe! Philippe, help me!" Lily cried.

Several thumps sounded, each closer than the last, followed by murmuring. "You need to do more than that, *mon ami*!" A squeak followed his words, then a crackle, and suddenly a blaze of fire surged up several yards away. The backdraft swept away the mist for a moment, revealing Rowan on the ground beside her, his face pale and his eyes closed. The soothstone shimmered from underneath a coating of mud.

Lily snatched up the stone, and as Flint's blaze died down, she raised it to eye level. She could barely see her own hand in the swirling fog, and she prayed through gritted teeth that she wouldn't fumble and drop the stone again. She squeezed her eyes shut and struggled to focus, her concentration so intense that her head ached. *Come on, think of something!*

Still her mind was blank. The images and colors that always danced through her head, bursting into her days to distract her at all the wrong moments, had disappeared. She felt like she was standing in an empty room, turning in circles, crying out for help and hearing only the echo of her own voice. For the first time in her life, Lily McKinley couldn't daydream.

What's wrong? Something is so wrong! Her mind spun, and she fought the urge to cry. With no images or ideas blooming in her mind, she felt stranded, abandoned, as if adrift on a raft on the open sea.

Suddenly, after all the stillness, a breeze tousled her hair. *Let the soothstone decide.*

Lily blinked away her tears and held her breath. She listened, and the voice came again: *Remember him.*

Lily pushed aside her despair and concentrated not on her predicament and not on the desolation of her own mind, but instead on Pax. His words. His goodness. How his love chased away the gloom.

The stone began to glow, and a fierce wind stirred up. When Lily opened her eyes, the fog around her swirled in a corkscrew, as if she knelt within the eye of a hurricane. A circle of blue sky glowed above her like a jewel, and threads of silver, copper, and gold wove in and out of the mist. As she peered into the churning fog in search of what the soothstone had summoned, something nipped her ear. Lily slapped her face, smearing mud against her cheek, then darted to look at what had bitten her.

"Rigel!" she cried out with joy. The star kestrel alighted on her shoulder, nuzzled her cheek, and then took flight and sailed into the vortex. Lily gazed in wonder as a hundred birds—kestrels, but also eagles and hawks, songbirds, cranes, and an albatross with a pearly sheen—revolved in a circle. Like Rigel, they glittered in an assortment of metallic colors, gold, silver, copper, and the brightest platinum, and the force of their wingbeats blew back the fog, clearing away the haze around her.

Lily brushed the sopping hair from Rowan's face. His lips were the color of an oyster. She rubbed his chest and shouted his name again, but still he didn't wake. "Flint! Philippe! Please help me!" she called.

The wind blew out Flint's blaze, and with a squeak the kindler trotted across the clearing to join Lily. Philippe soon followed, his muddy ears flopping behind him.

"We need to get him out of this place," Lily said, cradling Rowan's head in her lap.

"Mademoiselle, I do not see how. We cannot carry him, and the fog, it is too thick."

"We have to think of something!"

A group of birds suddenly broke away from the rest of the flock. They soared upward and danced around one another to weave glittering strands together, creating a hammock as Rigel had done for Lily in the Wilderness. They descended, and a golden hawk screeched for Lily to climb into the net suspended between them.

"Come on!" Lily called to Philippe and Flint. They stumbled in, and all three worked to haul Rowan in after them. Lily tangled her fingers in a mesh of silver and copper cord and held on as the birds lifted the strange crew into the air. Flint clung to Lily's wrist and shivered as they sailed upward into a sky that seemed blindingly blue against the dank and dismal fog that had surrounded them. As they cleared the mist, Lily savored the warmth of the sunlight on her face and the clean, sweet air in her lungs.

"Now, mademoiselle," Philippe panted, as he huddled shivering in a corner of the hammock, "may we *please* have something to eat?"

CHAPTER 9

Above the Clouds

They sat on a mountain peak above an ocean of clouds. The birds that saved Lily's life perched above her in the craggy limbs of a bare tree, where they preened, twittered at one another, and occasionally burst into song as the sunlight glinted off their metallic feathers. As the fog drifted to meet the sky and a flock of pearly doves cooed above her, Lily fancied that she sat on the cusp of heaven. And yet . . .

What happened down there? She turned the soothstone in her hands. She couldn't recall a single time in her life when she'd not been able to imagine something. Usually, her imagination was so vital that she could hardly cajole it to be still, and it routinely pitched her into trouble. Her daydreams drew her attention away from class, enticed her into hare-brained exploits that destroyed her mother's appliances, and triggered paper-mache pterodactyls to squawk to life at the worst possible moments. She'd never known a time when her mind was quiet, when something hadn't exploded from her thoughts to mess up her day.

Yet down in that horrible fog her mind had gone blank. She'd strained and searched for an idea, but she'd found *nothing*. Someone had swept her mind clean, removing every scrap of inspiration down to the very last speck of color. *I came back to create, and yet down there I couldn't dream up anything at all.* Lily remembered Pax's warning to her: *I did not bring you back to rebuild, Lily . . .*

A screech interrupted Lily's thoughts. She turned to see Rigel spiraling through the air with a slice of apple between his talons, and Philippe, his fur standing on end, swatting the kestrel with his hat.

"Give it back, you scoundrel!" Philippe cried. "Go eat some worms! That is not bird food!"

Lily fought a smile. "You know, Philippe, snacks are meant to be shared."

Philippe gawked at Lily with an ear flopped over one eye. "That, mademoiselle, is no snack! It is a gourmet baked apple with anise and cinnamon. If the birds, they want snacks, they can go snack on some crickets!" Then he shoved his hat back onto his head, folded his forelimbs across his chest, and stormed to the edge of the cliff, where he plopped down to brood.

Rigel floated down onto Lily's shoulder, and with a *chirrup* dropped the apple slice into her hand. Lily stifled another laugh, offered morsels to Rigel and Flint, and then took a bite herself. "You know," she whispered to Rigel, "he's got a point. This is pretty good."

A groan drew her attention as Rowan sat up and rubbed his forehead. Despite the warmth of the sun, he remained bedraggled and wet, as if he'd slogged through muddy puddles for miles or had taken a bath in a swamp. He rubbed his eyes with two fists, as a toddler would, then blinked several times.

Lily tucked some apple slices into her pocket and sidled up beside him. "Hey. Are you okay?"

Rowan scrunched his face. "Where are we?"

"You'd probably know better than me. Some mountain peak, up above all that fog. The star birds brought us here."

"The what?"

Lily pointed to the tree, where a silver owl shuffled sideways on a branch, bobbed its head, and hooted.

Rowan jumped to his feet and raced to the brink of the cliff. Lily chased after him, worried that he might do something rash, but when Rowan saw the carpet of fog sprawled out beneath him, he dropped to his knees.

"Are you okay?" Lily asked, reaching out a hand to console him.

"Don't touch me." He lowered his head in his hands, and Lily wondered if he might cry. "What happened?" he demanded, working to steady his voice.

"You passed out. I found you on the ground in the fog."

"And you took me *out* of the fog? Why would you do that?"

The sharpness of his voice took Lily aback. "I'm pretty sure you would have died if I didn't."

He frantically patted the front of his cloak, then spun in place and searched wildly inside his pockets. When he found his memory baubles, he sighed with relief, tucked them away, and slumped to the ground again.

Lily sat down across from him. She didn't understand the wounds he bore in his heart, but she thought she'd glimpsed their edges. As he slouched his shoulders, he seemed so much younger than his four hundred years. She wanted to be a friend to him. "Can you please tell me what's going on?" she said gently.

He chucked a twig off the edge of the peak and watched the fog swallow it up.

"Rowan, please. I've chased you through caves, ruins, and some weird, terrifying fog place where I seriously thought both of us would die. Please talk to me about all this."

"I never asked you to chase me."

"Well, I did. So please tell me what's so important that we needed to risk our lives down there." She cracked a twig between her fingers. "And tell me what's bothering you so much."

He threw another stick. "Are all humans so annoying?"

Lily chewed the inside of her cheek and thought for a moment. "In the case of death fog, usually."

Rowan studied the birds glittering in the trees. "You summoned them?"

Lily nodded. "The soothstone did."

"Will they heed you?"

"Hopefully."

"So, you can tell them to carry us off this mountain?"

Finally, Lily thought, *he's talking some sense.* "It might be hard for them to carry us all the way back to Mistwood, but we'll figure out something. They could definitely help for part of the way, at least."

"No, what I mean is, can they fly us *down*?"

"Down where?"

He pointed to the blanket of mist swirling below.

"Rowan, are you kidding? What could you possibly want down there? We both almost died!"

"You don't know anything about it!" His eyes flashed with anger. "What do you know? You didn't have a kingdom taken away from you or lose your entire family. You know nothing!"

Lily looked away and pressed her lips together to hold back the words she wanted to blurt. Her sympathy for him was rapidly draining away. "Actually, I do," she muttered.

"What are you talking about?"

"I know a little bit about what it's like to lose your family."

Rowan deliberated her words for a moment. Lily hoped he wouldn't ask her for specifics; after what they'd just endured, she didn't have the strength to probe old wounds. "Then you'll understand how much I want to have my family back," he finally said, his demeanor more subdued.

"Yes. But how is a bunch of fog going to help you do that?"

"It's not the fog. It's what's *in* the fog."

"I don't understand."

"I think some of my kin are living down there."

"Down *there?* In that awful place?"

Rowan nodded.

"How is that possible? How could anybody survive down there?"

"I'm not sure, but I have reason to believe it's true."

"What reason?"

Rowan shuffled his feet like a self-conscious toddler. "My mother. She told me stories."

"She told you there are Mist Elves living in that dreadful fog?"

"Not Mist Elves, but the Icelein. They were cousins of my people who lived millennia ago. You may have seen pictures of them in Enlacia."

"En-lacy-what?"

"Enlacia. The fortress with the memory library?"

Lily's heart skipped a beat. "You mean they were on the paintings in the ruins? There were two groups of people—"

"Yes. The figures in blue were the Mist Elves. Those in white were the Icelein, our kin who commanded the snow and ice."

"The king with the blue jewel in the paintings, was he one of the Icelein?"

"That was King Miran, the Icelein's last High King. The jewel is the Woven Ice, the source of the Icelein's powers. Do you see that flag out there?" He pointed to a spot far in the distance where the mist met the horizon, and Lily could barely detect a flicker of something white whipping in the wind. At first she thought it was another scrap of cloud, but as it snapped back and forth, she realized it was a flag. "That banner marks the ruins of the Icelein Towers, in the notch where the Desolation and the Shadow Mountains meet. My mother thought some of the Icelein might still live there."

"How did they build towers in *that*? You can barely see down in that fog."

"They didn't, of course. The fog fell upon the Icelein in the elder days. Tradition says that all the Icelein perished beneath it."

"But you don't think so?"

Rowan shook his head.

"Why? What did your mother tell you?"

A softness graced his face. "She said she saw one of them. She was just a girl, and my grandfather had taken her with him to Enlacia one day. She was collecting berries among the brambles, and she wandered into the fog."

"And she saw the Icelein in there?"

"One of them. Or so she thought."

"How could she be sure?"

"My mother just . . . *knew* things. Things no one else did. If she said it was one of the Icelein, that's who it was." He gazed across the expanse of mist and sky. "She said the Icelein still lived under the white banner. If I can get there, I can find them."

"Rowan, even if you do find them, what then? What are you hoping to do?"

He swallowed. "Convince them to return to Enlacia. To bring back the Entwined Kingdom again."

"Do you think they would?"

"I have to try."

"How would you convince them?"

He looked at her and drew a breath. "By telling them that I'm Prince Esperion."

Lily eyed him skeptically. "Esperion? The prince from the ruins?"

Rowan nodded. "He was the heir of the Entwined Kingdom. The Mist Elves and the Icelein were once united. Two great rulers, on two great thrones, in the same hall at Enlacia. We walked by the throne room, as a matter of fact."

"In the ruins?"

"Will you stop calling them ruins, please? It's called Enlacia. The Fortress of the Two Thrones."

"Okay, okay, Enlacia. Sorry."

"Both kings sat enthroned at Enlacia—"

"Cool name, by the way."

"What?"

"Enlacia. That's a cool name."

"What does temperature have to do with it?"

"Never mind. Sorry. Two rulers, two thrones."

"*One* joined kingdom. They ruled over the valleys between the Desolation and the Shadow Mountains for millennia. At the kingdom's pinnacle, Prince Esperion was born, and he was the hope of my people. He could wield lightning and thunder like none the Realm had ever seen. All my ancestors adored him. They thought a golden age was dawning when Esperion would rule over both dominions."

"Wait a minute . . . why would he rule over both? Wasn't there a prince or princess for the other guys, too? The Icelein?"

"At this time the king of the Icelein had no heir. It was presumed Esperion would rule alone."

"Would the Icelein like that?"

"Like what?"

"Would they be okay with a Mist Elf ruling over them?"

"Of course, they would. He was Prince Esperion, the great hope of the ages!"

Lily screwed up her lips and shrugged. "Okay. So, what happened?"

"Disaster. The Icelein lived on the slopes of mountains capped with snow. Just a few days before Esperion's three-hundredth birthday, an avalanche buried the Icelein Towers."

"*Buried* them?"

Rowan nodded. "The impact kicked up a storm of snow and fog into the sky. It's hovered over the mountains ever since." Rowan stood up, surveyed the swirling clouds below, and pointed. "It's now called the Veil."

Lily gazed down with him at the sea of fog below. *The Veil.* She remembered how the cloying vapors had confused and frightened her, and she shivered. "How awful," she said.

"Yes."

"And the Icelein were lost in the avalanche?"

"So far as legend tells us."

"So did Prince Esperion rule only over the Mist Elves, then?"

"No. Esperion and his grandfather, Eldinor, were with the Icelein when the Veil fell. They were never seen again."

Lily fell silent. She imagined the proud boy and his grandfather plunging into that cold, shadowy mist and disappearing forever. She wondered about her own fate had Flint and Philippe not rescued her.

Rowan stood up. "I need to leave. I've wasted too much time."

Lily shook herself back to attention. She stood up, dusted gravel from her pants, and studied the sky. "Yeah, you're probably right. It's getting late. We should try to get back to the valley before it gets dark."

"You should get back, you mean."

"*And* you."

Rowan shook his head. "I already told you, I'm going back down into the Veil."

"Rowan, enough of this! I get that you're lonely, and what happened to your people is terrible, but there is *no way* you're going to find the Icelein down there."

"I have a different opinion." He straightened the collar of his cloak, tightened the laces on his boots, and then pulled up his hood.

"Rowan, knock it off! You passed out the last time. What makes you think a second time will be any different?"

"I was unprepared the first time. I didn't charge up any lightning until I was already in the thick of it, and then I couldn't see. I know better this time. I'll go in ready."

"No, this is crazy! Even if you do find the Icelein—which, personally, I don't think you will, but let's say you do—how do you know they'll want to go back with you?"

"I'm going to tell them I'm Prince Esperion."

"But you're not!"

"I have evidence to suggest otherwise." Rowan's fingers wandered to the memory baubles in his robe.

"That makes zero sense."

"Call your birds down."

Lily glared at him.

"I said call your birds down!"

She folded her arms across her chest. Enough was enough. "No," she said, her gaze hard and unyielding.

"How dare you!"

"This is a crazy idea, and I won't be a part of it."

Rowan's jaw quivered. "As the heir to the throne of Mistwood, I command you to call them!"

"I'm not from Mistwood, or even from the Realm, remember? You have no authority over me."

"Fine then! I'll do it myself!" Rowan threw back his hood, craned his neck, and called to the birds roosting in the tree. "I am His Royal Highness, Rowan, the Prince of Mistwood, and I command you to escort me into the Veil!"

The owl revolved his head around a few times like a pinwheel, and a starling fluffed his feathers. Then they all blinked at Rowan. Not a single bird budged from its perch.

Rowan waved his hands and his ears reddened. "I command you! Take me down!"

The owl hooted, and an eagle screeched. Still, no one moved. Lily fought against a snicker.

"Curse you all!" Rowan shouted, kicking the ground and shaking his fist. "I'll have you all for chicken dinner one day!"

"*Coq au vin*, monsieur?" Philippe said, suddenly hopping into the conversation. A chorus of screeches and warbles erupted from the tree.

Rowan trudged back to Lily. "Will they listen to you?" he asked, his fists still clenched.

Lily tried to maintain a straight face. "I think so."

"I need to get down there. I don't expect you to understand, but I'm asking you to help me." He drew a breath. "Please."

Another pang of sympathy tugged at her. *He's annoying, but he just wants his family*, she thought. She recalled how desperately she'd longed for her father's embrace when she thought she'd lost him. In those two months, she'd yearned so ardently to hear his laugh again and to listen to another of his shining stories, that she would have done almost anything to win him back. *Even dive into a deadly fog*, she thought.

Suddenly an idea bloomed in her mind, and her heartbeat quickened. She twisted her hair around a finger, knowing somehow that her idea was wrong. Pax's words of warning about her purpose nagged her, buzzing in the back of her mind like a gnat. Yet she found the idea irresistible. "I have another suggestion," she said with a sidelong glance.

"I am *not* going back to Mistwood."

"I know. I'm not talking about Mistwood. What about that place in the forest?"

"What place?"

"En-lacy-whatever. The place with the two thrones you keep talking about."

"*Enlacia.* What about it?"

Lily's heart pounded. "What if I helped you rebuild it?"

Rowan shook his head. "I already told you. My way is down there in the Veil."

"I won't take you down there, but all your people's memories are in Enlacia, right? Maybe you can rebuild your kingdom with them somehow." She flushed with excitement. "And I can help you."

Rowan studied her. "You think you can bring it back?"

"I can try."

"What about all the people? Isla said there's no point in rebuilding if the halls are empty, like Mistwood. I think she's right."

Lily swallowed, her throat suddenly like sandpaper. "We can use the memories, and maybe—I don't know—maybe I can bring the people back too."

"Isla said that wouldn't work."

"She doesn't know for sure. She's not an artisan, right?"

He stared at her.

"Come on, Rowan, it's your kingdom! I can do this for you and Isla, and for Minnie Mouse too."

"That's not his name."

"Whatever. The librarian squirrel guy."

He studied Lily for a long moment. "Do you really think you can make it like it was?"

"I'll do my best. Here, I'll show you. Watch this." Lily stood up, withdrew the soothstone, and closed her eyes. She searched her mind for something grand and majestic to carry them to Enlacia, something sure to impress Rowan. With a surge of confidence, she drew a deep breath.

Nothing happened.

Lily's eyes fluttered open, and she glanced down at the soothstone. It remained dark. Even more troubling, its dullness reflected the state of her mind—blank. No flickers of inspiration delighted her.

Lily frowned, and an unease again turned in the pit of her stomach. She felt Rowan's gaze on her and cringed.

"So . . . did you have a favorite animal as a kid?" she asked, trying to sound nonchalant.

"A *what?*"

"In Isla's memories I saw you with a raccoon."

"Are you mad? That was a toy!"

"Okay, okay. No toys. Favorite animal—pet, or something?"

"Mist Elves don't keep *pets.*"

"Will you just tell me the name of an animal you like?"

Rowan frowned at her, but she could tell he was thinking. Finally, he held his hands behind his back, straightened, and said, "Dragonflies."

"What?"

"*Dragonflies.* I used to talk to them when—when I was hiding out in my glass caves. They'd land on the lupines that grew in the glades."

Lily beamed. "Perfect." She held the soothstone in her open palm and closed her eyes again. To her relief she saw a dragonfly in her mind, its body iridescent, its wings catching the sunlight like stained glass. *Help carry us, Pax,* she thought.

The birds in the tree behind her erupted into a fanfare of squawks, chirps, and screeches as the stone glowed in her palm. When the light faded, a dragonfly the length of a car stretched its wings on the mountaintop.

"Hi, friend," Lily said, reaching to pat the dragonfly's side. It turned its compound eyes toward her as her hand sank onto its bristled thorax. Lily clambered up onto the dragonfly's back between its cleft wings and clung to a few wiry strands to steady herself. "Come on up!" she called to Rowan.

Rowan's eyes were as large as saucers. As if in a dream, his hand shaking, he reached out for the dragonfly, which shuddered and sidled away at his touch.

"It's okay," Lily said, patting the dragonfly to soothe him. Then she deliberated on a name. She remembered how the dragonflies back home would flit about like shimmery green darts and settle on her mother's stargazers. Her mom always liked them because in humid weather when mosquitoes glutted the backyard, the dragonflies would zip around to reduce their numbers.

Lily smiled. "Sky Hunter. Your name is Sky Hunter," she said. "Don't worry, Rowan is a friend. You'll get used to him."

At these words the dragonfly calmed, and Rowan climbed aboard. Philippe and Flint scrambled up after him and nestled into Lily's back.

"What do you think?" Lily said over her shoulder. Surely, she thought, this would win Rowan over.

"I like them better when they're the right size," Rowan said uneasily.

Lily whistled for Rigel. As if reading her thoughts, the kestrel wove a harness of silver, then fluttered onto her shoulder and nuzzled her.

"Sky Hunter!" Lily cried out, wrapping the reins around her hands. "Take us to Enlacia!"

The dragonfly vaulted into the air. Philippe exclaimed something in French, and Rowan's complexion blanched, but as the wind swept Lily's hair back from her face, she could only grin. She couldn't wait to tell Adam and Keisha about this new adventure—about her ride through the sky on a dragonfly, just before she rebuilt an entire kingdom and its people.

They sailed through a sky that blushed with the setting sun. As they climbed higher, the black spines of the Desolation and Shadow Mountain ranges joined at a sharp angle. Beyond them, miles of forests and meadows unfurled into the distance. Weeks ago, the Blight had mangled these lands into gray swamps, but now the scenery billowed in velvety tones of green and auburn. On the horizon, like a faceted jewel in a golden crown, stood Castle Iridyll, its crystal spires again casting pools of color onto the valleys below.

Lily blinked away tears. *Thank you, Pax. Thank you for saving us. For saving the Realm.*

"Ow! Monsieur, please do be careful how you lean!"

Philippe's remark yanked Lily from her thoughts. Flint waved and squeaked at her from within the embroidered pocket of her shirt.

"What? What is it?"

Flint pointed behind her. Lily glanced back just in time to see Rowan, his face still a ghastly shade of green, crawling on all fours to the tip of the dragonfly's tail.

"Rowan, what are you doing?" Lily yelled.

The dragonfly veered sideways to escape a headwind. As Lily lurched and clung to the harness, she glimpsed the terrain below . . . and her heart leaped into her throat. The notch between the mountain ranges jutted through the clouds like a crooked elbow. Directly below them, flapping like a tattered dishrag, waved the white banner of the Icelein.

Sky Hunter righted himself, and Lily looked over her shoulder. "Rowan, don't you dare jump!"

She shouted to empty air. Rowan, Prince of the Mist Elves, heir to the throne of Enlacia, had plummeted into the thick fog of the Veil.

CHAPTER 10

Into the Veil

Lily steered Sky Hunter into a dive in pursuit of Rowan. The dragonfly accelerated, then reared back in disorientation as the damp clouds enveloped him. Water droplets streaked across Lily's face and soaked her hair. She waved an arm to clear the fog, but she could barely see her own hand in the murk. Flint skittered out of her pocket and flared to provide light, but the fog swallowed him up as well.

"Don't stop, Sky Hunter!" Lily urged. "We have to find him!"

"Mademoiselle!" Philippe shrieked. "I do not think this will work!"

"We have no choice!" Lily shouted back, her voice cracking. "Do you have anything in that hat that could help us see?"

"Yes, but I cannot get it."

"Why not?"

"Because my hat flew off when we hit this miserable fog!"

Lily glanced back and groaned at the sight of Philippe's bare ears whipping in the wind. Then she squinted as a flash lit the sky, and a single lightning bolt scrabbled across the clouds. Lily steered Sky Hunter toward the lightning and called out Rowan's name, but the wind drowned out her voice.

Another burst of lightning, closer this time. Lily kicked her heels into Sky Hunter's thorax to spur him on.

"Mademoiselle! What if—"

"Come on, Sky Hunter! He's just below us! You have to go faster!"

"Mademoiselle, I think the lightning, it is too close!"

Crash. Sky Hunter careened backward, as if he'd struck the bare face of a cliff. The impact threw Lily into the air, and she dashed against something cold and hard that knocked the wind out of her. Then she was tumbling, her legs dangling, the reins coiled about her right hand the only thing tethering her to the dragonfly as it plunged toward the earth.

Lily screamed for help. She reached for the soothstone, but her arms whipped to her sides in the forceful wind. She glimpsed the dragonfly free-falling through the air adjacent to her. Whatever they had struck, the impact had crippled one of his wings, and it bent at a grotesque angle. He buzzed furiously and fought to regain control.

Rigel revolved around them, shrieking as he went, and Lily saw a thread of silver flap in the wind. Lily reached for it, but over and over it slipped from her fingers and flapped away.

Sky Hunter rammed into her. She held on to him sideways and tried to scramble onto his back, but she slipped and clung for dear life to his underbelly.

We're going to crash.

Sky Hunter logrolled in midair, and Lily's knuckles whitened as she hung on. They struck a tree limb, which exploded in a spray of splinters. A shower of leaves, ice, and wood fragments blasted Lily's face, and she spit out a mouthful of debris.

Still, they plunged downward.

They struck another tree. Sky Hunter ricocheted backward and would have tossed Lily to the ground had he not wrapped a couple of spindly legs around her.

They struck the earth. A tidal wave of snow launched into the air. Sky Hunter cushioned Lily's impact, but then she rolled off and lost him. As she crawled on her hands and knees through muddy snow to find him, every joint ached and her head throbbed. Finally, her outstretched hand brushed against Sky Hunter's thorax.

Lily unwound the silver rein from her right hand and winced. The harness had cut her palm. She tore a strip of cloth from her shirt, then sucked air through her teeth as she wrapped her hand. As she cinched the filthy cloth tight, Lily could almost hear her mother's horrified warnings about infection, the same she'd issued the first time Lily slapped a bandage on a scraped knee without washing the cut first.

Mom. At the memory of her mother—her strength, her tenderness, her readiness to shoulder others' burdens—Lily's heart ached. She bit her lip to keep from crying. Would she ever see her mom again? Would she ever get out of this desolate place, this accursed fog?

We can't lose hope, Lily. Those were the words Mom had said to her the night her dad disappeared at sea. She'd held Lily for an hour and they'd cried together, then she made her a cup of hot chocolate and they cried some more. Even after their tears ran dry, Mom stroked Lily's hair and reassured her. *I don't know why this happened,* she'd said. *But we still have hope. We always have hope.* Lily didn't know then what she meant, but she memorized the words.

With her mother's words still repeating in her mind, Lily staggered to her feet and steadied herself against the still form of Sky Hunter. She whispered his name, but his only reply was a shudder.

"You're so hurt." Lily closed her hand around the soothstone and prayed she could heal the crippled dragonfly. She closed her eyes.

Nothing.

Lily opened her eyes and blinked through her tears. The moment brought her back to the night she failed to cure Scallywag from the Blight. She turned the stone over and over in her fingers and hated her helplessness. "I'm so sorry, Sky Hunter," she said, her voice cracking. "I'm so sorry I can't heal you." The dragonfly fluttered his one good wing as if to reassure her. *Why does this keep happening?* she thought with dismay. With a lump in her throat Lily turned in place as the mist swirled and gathered around her like a legion of ghosts. "Hello?" Lily cried out, her voice hoarse. "Can anybody hear me?"

Silence.

"Rowan? Philippe? Somebody, please answer me!"

She heard a rustling, and then a sucking sound, like something trudging through mud.

"Rowan? Is that you?"

More rustling, then a thump. Lily held her breath. Then, she screamed as something rough grasped her ankle and yanked her off her feet.

CHAPTER 11

Captured

Lily swung in the air like a pendulum. A vine had ensnared her ankle, and now she dangled upside down from a tree branch with her hair hanging in her face. Her efforts to wriggle free only tightened the noose around her leg.

A twig snapped somewhere on the ground. Lily froze. She could see nothing except her breath frosting before her face and mingling with the fog. Lily held her breath and wished her heart could quiet its mad thumping.

Heavy footsteps sounded, as well as the *goosh* of something lumbering through the mud. *Please, please, someone help me*, Lily thought in desperation. She remembered the Icelein from the images at Enlacia, how regal they appeared, how placid. If one of the long-lost Icelein was tromping through the mud, perhaps he or she would be equally peaceful?

Another twig snapped, and the footsteps drew closer. She heard heavy breathing, a slight wheeze at the end of each raspy breath. The rhythm of the breathing was off somehow, the breaths overlapping, as if . . .

There are two.

"Ay, Wormwood! I got one!"

"Oh, did you, now?"

"Ay! A right juicy one, me thinks!"

Lily clenched her teeth. The voices sounded gurgly, as if spoken through mouthfuls of sludge. *I don't think these are the Icelein.*

Soon Lily could hear their gravelly breathing directly beneath her. She still couldn't see anything through the fog, but she could hear them just below.

"Wot! Measley, are you daft?"

"I dunno, am I?"

"That ain't no snow rat, you donkey!"

"Are you sure? It's got four legs, don't it?"

"It's all bald-like. 'Cept for that long hair in front. And it's the wrong color!"

"Ugh. Waste of a perfectly good snare!"

"You got that right."

"Even if it's not a snow rat, d'ya think it's edible? I'm so hungry. Maybe we could just have a nibble?"

Thump.

"Ow! What ya do that for?"

"You's being daft again."

"I'm not daft! I'm just hungry, is all. Me brain is starvin'."

"Wot d'ya think Magnus would say, if he found out we'd been snacking on a new species wot's wandered into the territory?"

"Well, now, he wouldn't have to know—"

Thump.

"Aw, quit it!"

"Cut the wriggler down, Measley. You know the regulations. This one's for Magnus, it is."

"I still don't see why we can't just help ourselves to a morsel. 'Specially since we's the ones wot's caught it."

"Cut it down!"

"All right, all right. You could cut it down too, y'know. You's the taller one, after all."

Lily heard Measley grunt, and then she jostled back and forth in midair as he sawed the line holding her, presumably with a knife. The creature grunted a few more times, Wormwood scolded him from down below, and in the next minute she fell through the fog and landed in a pile of dirty snow. Lily spat, wiped debris from her swollen cheeks, and then scrambled to her feet. Before she could gain her footing to run, however, one of the creatures jerked the severed vine, whipping her tied leg out from under her. The next thing she knew, they were dragging her across a frozen wasteland, a swamp half-covered in ice and snow. She coughed, spluttered, and shielded her eyes from reeds that slapped her face as they hauled her.

"Let go of me!" Lily shouted.

"Ay, Wormwood! Didja hear that? The thing speaks!"

"Of course, I heard it, you dimwit."

"I never did hear of a snow rat that could speak, Wormwood."

"You really are a doughnut, ain't you? I already told ya, this ain't no snow rat!"

"Well, wot is it, then?"

"I don't know what it is, to tell ya the truth. But it's for Magnus, that's for sure."

"D'you think it would still talk if we took a bite?"

Thump.

"Ow! That one smarted, Wormwood! And with me brain already aching!"

Lily thrashed in the snow but couldn't break free. The vine tethering her ankle extended in a long line ahead of her and then disappeared into the mist, like the tentacle of a giant squid hidden within the Veil. She rolled onto her belly and scraped at the wet earth, but only succeeded in scooping up handfuls of snow and dirt.

"Help!" Lily screamed. "Somebody, help me!"

"Ay, it's a loud 'un, ain't it, Wormwood?"

"Just shut yer trap and keep walking, Measley. And hurry up! They'll close the threshold soon, and I am *not* keen on spendin' another night outdoors."

"Nasty last time, wasn't it, Wormwood?"

"I said quit yer yappin'!"

"How did you survive, by the way, when the marshbats attacked you?"

Thump.

"Ow, Wormwood! Knock it off, will ya?"

"I'll knock you, if you don't lock that trap and quit talking!"

"All right, all right. No need to get savage on me. Oof, this thing's gettin' heavy."

Lily's limbs ached as they lugged her through the frigid turf. Snow caked her clothing and streaked down her back, and in the chill she could no longer feel her fingers. She shut her eyes, bit her lip, and imagined the misery was all a dream. Soon, she'd awaken to sunlight pouring into her bedroom, or better yet, filtering through a stained glass window at Castle Iridyll.

After an age spent towing her through the snow and mud, Lily's captors finally halted. Lily pressed a hand to her forehead to ease the pounding, then glanced at her ankle. Her heart jolted: the line had slackened.

Lily bolted to her feet, but before she could escape, one of the creatures grabbed her by the collar and lifted her like a rag doll. Lily kicked and yelled and clawed the misty air in defense. She could feel his hot breath on the back of her neck, and the stench of onions and spoiled meat made her eyes water. With a blast of foul air, Wormwood's laughter broke the quiet.

"If you're still hungry, Measley, I reckon we'll be getting extra portions tonight for this catch. It's a live one, it is."

"I'd better get an extra portion, after Simper stole me bowl last time. She fished out all the choice bits and left me with claws and tails!"

"Stand out the way, Measley."

Suddenly, Wormword swung Lily back and forth through the air. The motion, combined with the cold, the stench, and the throbbing in her head, flipped Lily's stomach. Then Wormwood flung her. Lily sailed through the air, and the mist parted below to reveal a gaping hole in a slab of rock. Darkness enveloped her as she plunged down.

She shielded her face from whatever danger lay below, then cried out as she hit solid ground with a thud that vibrated to her bones. She winced as pain shot along her spine, and for a moment she feared she was choking. She lay on her back on a hard, rock floor, struggled to breathe, and blinked to steady the world from spinning around her. Far above she could make out the entrance to the hole into which Wormwood had flung her. A shred of fog draped into the entrance, like a cobweb yielding to a breeze.

Lily placed her palms flat on the ground, and with another wince she sat up. She had fallen into a cavern. The air felt stuffy, and somewhere in the distance she could hear the lonely drip of water against rock. The only light came from the entrance above, looming like a pale moon. Not a beam of light penetrated to the cave floor.

"Ay, Magnus!" Wormwood cried from above. "We got a live one for ya!"

Scuffling sounded from every direction. Lily glanced about the cave in wide-eyed terror as the sounds drew closer and intermixed with murmurs. Suddenly pinpricks of light burned through the pitch darkness and crowded toward her like droves of pale, green moths. At first, in a whirlwind of confusion, Lily thought she'd somehow stumbled back into the Caverns of Unfinished Dreams. Were these just incomplete dreams, yearning for her to finish their stories? Lily squinted and leaned forward to study their forms. Then she froze.

The green lights she saw weren't unfinished dreams at all. They were dozens of sinister green eyes, all of them trained on her, all of them steadily advancing.

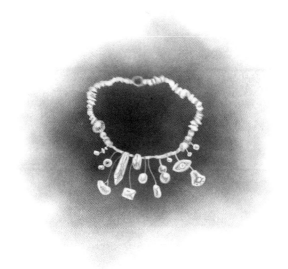

CHAPTER 12

The Dwellers

Lily searched the darkness for a corridor down which she might escape, but in every direction she saw only shadows, and scores of menacing green eyes inching toward her.

"Ay, Magnus!" a voice cackled from behind her. "Looks like we got another one of them baldy ones!"

"Two in one day! Ain't we lucky!" said another, smacking its lips.

"Should we throw this one down with the otha one, by the furnace?" a third creature rasped.

"They'd keep each otha good company behind bars!" said a fourth.

Sinister laughter rippled through the crowd. Something cold clutched Lily's ankle, then shrieked as Lily kicked it away. She scrambled to her feet and closed her hand around the soothstone . . . but again her mind was blank. Lily's heart sank with dread. *What do I do? Oh, what do I do?*

A bracing wind swept down from the entrance above, and Lily remembered the guidance the wind had offered her when she found Rowan unconscious in the Veil. *Let the stone decide,* it had whispered. Lily nodded and squared her shoulders. If she couldn't create new images, she would fill her head with old ones.

She focused on Cedric shielding her from Eymah, and her father emerging bedraggled and dazed from the Catacombs to enfold her in his arms. She remembered Pax crumpling to the ground as the shrouds gathered around him, then breaking free from his glass tomb. She heard his voice and felt his muzzle against her cheek, and her heart swelled at the remembrance of him.

Lily withdrew the stone from her pocket and opened her palm. The stone flooded the cavern with pale fire.

The cave erupted in shrieks and wails as the stone exposed every dark corner and crevice. Her assailants cowered beneath the light, their ghastly forms slinking away into tunnels still steeped in gloom. The creatures resembled humans with rags hanging from their long, lanky limbs, but their skin was deathly pale, and their eyes gleamed an unnatural, sickly green. As they squirmed beneath the light, they reminded Lily of the animals populating the darkest zone of the oceans: colorless, ghostly, drifting about in a forgotten world too deep for light to penetrate.

The soothstone faded, and then a hundred flickers of light materialized like stars or fireflies crowding the cave. As they whirled about Lily in a shining circle, she saw they were doves, their pearlescent wings blindingly bright as they beat back the ghouls. Some of Lily's attackers swatted at the birds; others swung at them with fists and clubs. Eventually, however, they all shrank back with a howl and hid themselves in lightless places. As the creatures retreated, Lily dared to breathe, and to hope for escape.

Pfft. The strike of a match sounded, and a pale green flame blazed to life and hovered in midair. At the sight of it the doves cried out, and with a panicked flapping of wings they fled from the cavern and pitched Lily into darkness again, with the flicker of that single, eerie flame the only light. Lily stood transfixed, her limbs frozen, her eyes wide as a single pair of eyes emerged from the blackness. They shone green, just as the others had, but with a coldness that coaxed gooseflesh from Lily's arms.

The green flame illuminated the creature's face. His flesh was sickly and his wet hair ragged about his gaunt face, and he towered above the others, even despite a hunch in his spine that gave him the appearance of a vulture stooping over carrion. He held a green flame in the palm of his hand, but no apparent wick or torch fueled it; it was as if the fire arose from his very skin. A dozen crystals and stone pendants clinked together from where they dangled around his neck as he stepped toward her. A brass scepter, tarnished and inlaid with a brilliant, amber-colored stone, hung in a dingy cloth sash at his waist. His eyes burned with a malice that turned Lily's blood cold.

"Few can resist my people when they hunger," the creature said in an oily voice. "That charm in your hand must have a rare power."

Lily backpedaled. "Who are you?" she stammered.

"I am the king who dwells," he sneered.

"Are you Magnus?"

"*King* Magnus to you! I am the lord of the underground, sovereign ruler of the dwellers under the mountain." He drew closer and swiped an oozing tongue across his yellowed teeth. "Why are you here?"

"I'm just looking for my friend. I won't hurt you."

He cackled, and the sound of his laughter reminded Lily of insects, rats, and other crawling vermin. "Hurt me?" he said. "What hubris! I don't negotiate with invaders, puny one. I only *crush* them, like beetles. Perhaps that's what you are. Are you a beetle, puny one?" He circled her like a wolf stalking its prey. "How much do you value your life?" he said.

A shiver rippled down Lily's spine. "What do you mean?"

"That stone you hold seems to have an old magic. I am a— *collector* of magic, you see." He toyed with the pendants around his neck and licked his lips greedily. Lily's stomach lurched as a single bead of saliva dripped from the corner of his mouth.

"I can't give it to you," Lily forced herself to answer.

"You must, if you wish to live."

Lily's fist tightened around the stone. *Please, Pax, help me.*
"I said I can't."

"Cannot, or will not?"

"Can't. It's not really mine."

"Do not try my patience!" Magnus growled. "You are stalling.
Speak to me plainly!"

"I'm just taking care of it. I'm a steward. A dream keeper." She
remembered Pax's eyes, deep as the ocean. "This stone belongs
to someone much greater than me."

Magnus slithered toward her, his gangly arms dragging near
the ground, his pale eyes disappearing beneath furrowed, hairless
brows. "*Who?*" he whispered.

"Pax. Prince Pax."

Yet another laugh, unhinged and terrible. "The unicorn from
the fairy tales? You would bet your life on a child's story?"

"It's not a story!"

"Only infants believe in Pax. Is that what you are? An infant?
Calling out to imaginary playthings in the dark?"

"Pax isn't a fairy tale!" Lily cried, her blood pulsing in her
ears. "He's real, and he saved us all from the Blight. You owe
your life to him!"

Magnus wheeled about, his eyes flashing with hate. He
loomed over Lily, and his foul breath blasted her face. "Listen,
impudent little beetle! I've reigned under this mountain since
long before the name of 'Pax' appeared in children's stories. For
centuries my people have scraped out an existence in this cursed

rock, chiseling each stinking hole with our bare hands. We've watched those we love die, and then awoken the next morning to scrounge for scraps from the swamps and to break our backs hauling stone. And in all these dark years, not *once* did any prince cross our threshold to 'save us.' We've survived *alone,* forgotten by the world, with only our blistered hands to carve our way. So, if you would, kindly keep your stories of make-believe 'saviors' to yourself, lest your insults try my patience!"

Magnus grasped her chin with a long, bony hand, and Lily's stomach flipped. "Now," he said. "For the last time. Give me that stone in your hand, and I'll let you live!"

Lily's heart thundered in her ears. *Maybe I should just give it to him. I have no role here anymore, not like I thought I would. I should just give up and go back home.* Her knees wobbled as Magnus's threatening stare bore into her, and her grip on the soothstone relaxed.

Then, in her mind's eye she saw another pair of eyes: amber, kind, with a glimmer of mischief. *Cedric.* She saw Keisha and Adam too, and Scallywag and Nyssinia. Her friends. After all they'd endured with her and for her, what would they say if they could see her now?

Lily straightened, and her fingers again closed around the stone. She drew a deep breath. "No."

Magnus growled with rage and flung his hands into the air. "Suit yourself, beetle!' he bellowed. "If you'll not give it freely, we will take it from you by force!"

The green flame flared in his palm, and by its light hordes of creatures spewed from the network of caverns. They pounced on Lily, restrained her wrists, and tore at her closed right hand. "No!" Lily screamed. "You can't take it! Leave me alone!" She kicked and thrashed, but the dwellers pried her fingers open one by one. Then, a cackling echoed in the cave, and Lily cried out in horror. Her hand was empty.

"I've got it!" the thief cried with a squeal, as he jumped back and turned circles in celebration. "Lookie 'ere, Magnus, I've got it!"

Lily pushed back tears. "Give it back! Please, give it back! You can't take it!"

"Oh yeah? Wot'll ya give me for it, eh? Looks like it's the cages for this one too, ay, Magnus?" The ghoul tossed the soothstone into the air and caught it in his other hand in mockery. His lumpy shoulders shook with laughter as he jeered at Lily with a wide, crooked grin.

Then it happened.

A yellow light flooded the cavern as the soothstone erupted in flames. The dweller screeched in pain and flung the soothstone to the ground, then grasped his burnt hand and hopped from one foot to the other in agony. With a thrill of hope Lily recalled Merlin's words when she first met him in Castle Iridyll: *If you are indeed a steward, I can't take it from you.*

As Lily's captors shielded their eyes, she wriggled free and sprang into action. She crawled on her hands and knees across the cave, dodged the tramping feet of the dwellers, and averted at least one accidental kick to her side. Amid the tangle of limbs and feet she glimpsed the stone discarded on the rock floor, still faintly glowing like a dying oakwood ember.

Lily snatched the stone from the ground. Although it still burned, it felt cool to the touch. Its light faded as soon as it nestled again in her hand, as if the stone itself were sighing with relief at having found her again.

Lily slipped the soothstone into her pocket, crouched on her hands and knees to stay low and out of sight, and then searched for a way out. The entire cavern had erupted into chaos, with the dwellers scrambling about in terror, colliding with one another and shouting. Magnus rose above them all, bellowing commands for order. "Find the puny one! *I want that stone!*" he yelled.

As Magnus shouted, his eyes wide and bulging, dwellers disgorged from every hole and corner. They poured out from channels near the ceiling and climbed up from rents in the ground. As the green light of the king's flame flickered over the damp walls, Lily squinted to discern some dark crevice in which she could hide. A hole in a far corner caught her eye. It huddled on the ground, bored into a rock face, and a faint glimmer of light like that of a campfire smoldered from within. It was the only outlet she could see from which no dwellers tumbled.

Lily held her breath, then dashed for the hole. Her right hand, where Sky Hunter's reins had cut into her palm, smarted from the pressure against the rock as she crawled, and the floor scraped her knees. She rolled out of the way as a panicked dweller nearly stomped her.

Keep going. You have to keep going.

"Find the puny one!" the king howled. "That stone is magic! I must have it!"

Screams echoed throughout the cave. Masses of dwellers, all panicked and crazed, piled atop each other and snarled in heaps.

Keep going.

Suddenly, a familiar voice boomed over the din. "I see it! It's crawling away!" Footsteps thundered behind her. Lily didn't have to look back to know that Wormwood now charged after her.

Keep going. Keep going!

"After it!" Magnus screamed. "Bring it to me! Find the stone!"

"No, you don't, you l'il grub! You'll not escape ole Wormwood!"

Lily rose to her feet to run the last few yards. As she stood up, dwellers barreled toward her from all sides. She jumped over a pile of them as they slid before her in a tackle, then darted away from another that clutched her by the shoulder. With her heart flying wildly, she wriggled away and dove to the ground. She slid toward the glowing hole. *Please, make it in time. Please, make it.* A dweller clawed at her ankle. Yet another jumped to tackle her.

She skidded across the ground, plummeting forward, and the hole swallowed her up like a fiery, gaping mouth.

Lily plunged down, down, into blistering heat. The dwellers continued their frenzied cries above her, but didn't pursue. Below, the glow of an unseen fire strengthened and stung her face.

Lily struck the ground and sprayed a cloud of dust into the air upon impact. She placed a hand to her forehead to stop the world from spinning and struggled to catch her breath as stars danced before her eyes. She sat up with a groan and glanced in the direction of the tumult overhead. She heard howls of rage, but no green eyes stared down after her.

She breathed a sigh of relief. With the back of her hand she wiped away the sweat that already beaded her brow, and then looked around her. She sat in another cave, only about the size of her bedroom, glowing orange from a fire raging in an enormous furnace at her back. *Furnace* . . . She remembered one of the dweller's words: "Should we throw this one down with the other one, by the furnace?" *Other one? Could it be* . . .

"Lily?"

The voice came from a corner of the room, where a cage made of twisted metal slouched in a corner. Inside the cage, his face filthy, his eyes forlorn, sat Rowan.

Lily's heart leapt, and she scrambled to her feet and rushed to him. "Rowan! What are you doing here? Are you all right?" She knelt before the cage and placed her hands around the bars, but withdrew them when they smarted against the hot metal.

"Lily—"

"We need to get out of here! Those things, their king wants the soothstone. We can't let him have it, Rowan!"

"Lily, I—"

"How do we get you out of this cage? Is there a key? We can't let them find us again, they'll try to take the stone!"

"Lily, look out behind you!"

She froze. For the first time, she realized they weren't alone. She turned around just as a huge, bristling shadow covered her.

CHAPTER 13

The Furnace Room

The largest rat Lily had ever seen overshadowed her, its lips curled in a sneer and soot blackening its face. It stood taller than her father, wore a leather smock, and hoisted a sledgehammer high above its head, ready to break her bones. Lily ducked out of the way just as the hammer sailed down. It missed her, smashed into Rowan's cage, and bent the bars.

Lily backed away from the cage as the rat lunged at her. She ran to the opposite wall and crashed into a shelf littered with hammers, tongs, and scraps of iron. As the tools clanged to the floor, Lily grasped a poker from among them and swiped at the creature.

"No, Lily, don't try to fight him!" Rowan cried.

"Are you crazy?"

She dodged another hammer blow, then parried forward with the poker and struck the rat in the knee. Enraged, the beast snarled and swung again with the mallet. Lily backed against the cage and was about to swing the poker again when something brushed her face. Rowan had shoved a wedge of stale bread through the bars.

"He's a rat!" Rowan whispered. "More than anything, he wants food. Give it to him, quick!"

The rat raised the hammer above his head and bared his discolored teeth. Then with a growl, he narrowed his beetle-like eyes and charged. Lily squeezed her eyes shut and held out the crust of bread as he barreled toward her. She braced herself for the end.

No strike came. The rat skidded to a stop, and his sour, hot breath blew Lily's hair from her face.

Lily dared to open one eye. The rat still hoisted the hammer high, but his forelimbs trembled, and his whiskers quivered. The anger twisting his face had vanished, and instead his eyes swam with desperate longing as he stared at the morsel of moldy bread between her fingers.

Lily's hand quivered. "Here. You can have it," she said, lifting the crust toward him.

The rat sniffed the offering and eyed her warily.

"Go on. I'm not going to hurt you."

"The king would not allow it," the rat said in a deep voice.

He speaks? Lily swallowed, and searched her mind for a response. What do you say to a giant rat determined to flatten you? "I won't tell him," she finally said.

The rat snatched the bread from Lily's hand and gnawed it ravenously. After he'd devoured the entire piece, Lily offered him the apple slices stashed in her pocket, and these, too, he gobbled up. Afterward he looked to her for more, but Lily could only open her empty hands.

In response, the rat's whiskers drooped and the light vanished from his eyes. With his shoulders stooped and his expression crestfallen, he lumbered to a corner of the room, sank to the floor, and put his head in his paws. Only then did Lily see the chain encircling his ankle, tethering him to the wall. Scars, as from the lashings of a whip, coiled down his limbs. *The poor thing,* she thought. *What's happened to him?* She recalled Magnus, the hatred gleaming in his eyes, and a spark of anger flared within her.

"Lily, how did you find me?"

Lily shook herself from her thoughts and rushed to Rowan's cage. "Are you okay? Are you hurt?"

"Not very much. How about you? How did you get down here?"

"Those monsters. They caught me in a snare, and then they tried to take the soothstone. I fell down here trying to escape from them." She looked around and shuddered. "If you could call this escape."

"They captured me too," Rowan said. "Although they used a net, not a snare. They call themselves the dwellers." He shuddered.

"I had no idea such people lived under these mountains. If my father had known, he would have routed them out."

Lily rummaged through the debris and metal equipment strewn all over the floor.

"What are you doing?" Rowan asked.

"Looking for the key. There has to be a key, or a piece of metal to pick the lock, or *something* to get you out of that cage."

"They took the key when they locked me up."

"Well, maybe there's a spare one." She fumbled with a ring dangling with metal rods. As she toyed with it, the rods suddenly sprang free from their mounts and clattered to the floor.

"Shh! You'll draw them down here!"

"I'm sorry! We need to get you out. There has to be a way we can climb back to the surface."

"I can't leave. Not just yet."

"*Excuse* me? Please don't start with this stuff again about your lost people in that stupid fog! I feel for you Rowan, I really do. It's so hard to lose your family. But enough is enough!"

"That's not what I mean." Rowan's voice cracked. "They took my memories, Lily."

Lily frowned at him, but then his meaning dawned on her. Her eyes wandered to the pockets of his cloak. "You mean—?"

Rowan nodded. "I need to get them back."

"Why? Didn't you say they were copies? Don't you still— I don't know—have the real ones in your head?"

"Yes, but you know how unreliable memories are. They change and fade over time." He gripped the bars and stared at her with wide, pleading eyes. "I can't lose them, Lily. Please."

Lily's heart softened. "Okay. But we can't find your memories if we don't break you out of those bars first." She glanced over at the rat. "Can he break it? That hammer looks like it could bust through anything." Her gaze flitted over the chain manacled to his ankle. "Come to think of it, he could probably free himself, too, couldn't he?"

"He probably could, but I don't think he will."

"Why not?"

"He's terrified of the dwellers. Especially the king."

Suddenly, a rusty hinge screeched from down a tunnel. "It's them!" Rowan whispered. "Quick, run and hide! There's a nook behind the furnace where I've seen the rat's pups crawl. Hide there."

"The rat's pups?"

"Just go! Hide!"

Lily slid behind the furnace and grimaced at the heat. She plastered herself against the back wall of the cave, as far from the furnace as she could distance herself without risking detection. Sweat soaked her hair, and she fought to quiet her breathing in the oppressive air.

The moment she crouched out of sight, three dwellers entered: Magnus, his skin bilious in the light of the fire, along with two smaller creatures who held shreds of his tattered robe in either hand. Magnus strode across the room and stopped before the rat, who dropped to his knees and lowered his shaggy face to the ground in reverence. His tail quivered.

Magnus scowled at him, then glanced at the broken shelf and the heap of tools Lily had spilled on the floor. His eyes narrowed, and without a word he delivered a swift kick to the rat's abdomen. The poor beast fell to the ground, coughing and clutching his stomach with a forepaw.

"Clean it up," Magnus said flatly. Then he strode away without a second glance and turned his attention to Rowan.

"I trust you find your accommodations here . . . comfortable?" he said. Magnus ran a finger along the bars and rubbed away a line of grease between his thumb and forefinger. "We've had another guest since your arrival. A friend of yours, I believe." He leaned his face against the bars and bared his putrid teeth. "Who is she?"

Rowan pressed his lips together and said nothing.

"Very well. If you're not keen on that subject, let's discuss a different matter." He folded his arms in front of him, and the knobby joints of his elbows protruded like tubercles. "My scholars have analyzed your trinkets, and as I suspected, they find no basis for your claim that these pretty little spheres are mere toys. Quite the contrary, in fact."

"I don't know what you're talking about."

"I find that unlikely." Magnus snapped two of his long fingers, and one of the henchmen beside him procured a memory bauble.

At the sight of it Rowan instinctively gripped the bars of the cage with both hands. "This is no ordinary glass, is it, my little caged worm?" Magnus said. "Its craftsmanship is something I've not seen in an age. And inside . . ." His voice dropped to a low whisper as he took the bauble from his henchman and examined it between his bony fingers. He traced the contour of the sphere with a single twisted fingernail. "Such *curious* fire. It moves like liquid gold, like something infused with an ancient magic I once knew, long, long ago. A magic like—well, a *memory*, that I can barely recall." He lowered the bauble and glared at Rowan.

Rowan said nothing, but sweat beaded his brow and his breathing quickened.

"Fickle things, memories," Magnus whispered. "Memories of those you love flit away with time, no matter how tightly you cling to them. And those you hate forever haunt you, no matter what you do to erase them." Magnus's spindly fingers closed around the bauble, and he leaned toward Rowan. "Where. Did. You get these?"

Rowan's hands tightened around the bars as Magnus circled the cage. Still, he said nothing. *Hang on, Rowan,* Lily thought, her heart pounding as she watched the exchange.

"I find it strange that after centuries alone in these mountains, two children wielding magical powers stumble upon my doorstep on the same day. For years, we've had no glimpse of the sun, no contact with any living creature except for the slugs that suck muck from the cave ponds, and the rats—" he kicked the poor rodent again, "—that infest our quarters. Because *no one* enters the Veil. And you expect me to believe that you and your little friend just happened to drop your toys while frolicking outside? Lose your way from Castle Iridyll, did you?" He spat at Rowan, then reached into the cage, grasped him by his collar, and flung him to the floor. The prince scuttled backward like a crab as Magnus rattled the bars with his fists. "Who are you?" he yelled, spittle flying from his mouth. His eyes bulged and his flyaway hair stood upright on his scalp. "Why are you here?"

"I—I didn't mean to come here," Rowan finally said, his voice quavering. "It was a mistake."

"Why were you in the Veil?"

"I was looking for someone."

"You're lying! No one lives in the Veil unless he writhes beneath my fist! *Why are you here?*"

"I'm looking for the Icelein!"

Magnus froze. His face lengthened in shock, and Lily's hair pricked up on the back of her neck as he leaned forward like a praying mantis about to devour its young. A long pause ensued during which Rowan cowered in the back of the cage, his eyes wide and his chest heaving. Even the rat seemed petrified with fear, with his shivering whiskers the only part of him that dared to move.

"It seems," Magnus finally said with a strange, disquieting expression on his face, "there's one method we've not yet considered, in our study of your precious toy." He turned the bauble in his fingers. "What would happen, do you conjecture, if we tested this with fire?"

Rowan's jaw tightened.

"Ah, what have we here?" Magnus said, spinning around and tearing his ragged cloak from his servants' hands. "A furnace. Fire! Just the thing we need."

Rowan stood up. "Please," he said. "Please, give it back to me. That memory isn't for you to see."

Magnus turned on him sharply. "Why? Whose is it to see, then?"

"The Icelein. I brought it to show the Icelein."

Magnus erupted into laughter. "The Icelein! We have another weaver of fairy stories in our midst, don't we?"

"It's not a fairy story!"

"Oh, indeed? Pray tell me, you squalid little leech, why the Icelein? What secrets does this pretty thing hold, what precious knowledge, to which only the esteemed, the noble, the *illustrious* Icelein have rights?" Magnus punctuated these last words by striking the memory bauble against his open palm. Then he marched toward the furnace. Upon his orders one of the minions opened the door with a bare hand, then shrieked and bounced away to nurse his burned palm. Magnus grabbed a pair of tongs, and with a sinister, eager grin, he held Rowan's captured memory over the fire.

The moment the flames touched the bauble a crescent of light projected from within it. The light shifted and wavered, the way a reflection undulates on the surface of a disturbed pond, but gradually images materialized from within.

To her surprise Lily knew the scene. The image depicted a candlelit room with burgundy bed curtains. Isla and Rowan's mother lay in the bed, her complexion sallow. This time Isla was gone, and the young Rowan stood beside the bed with his green-ribboned raccoon in hand. His mother stroked his dark hair. "Espy," she whispered. "My little Espy. Never forget who you are. You're the hope of our people, and of my heart. Prince Esperion . . . I know you'll make us whole . . . our hope . . ." She stroked his cheek, and the little boy's eyes overflowed with tears. Then, her arm fell from the curve of Rowan's face and hung limp off the edge of the bed.

The picture vanished. From across the room, Rowan's tears glistened in the firelight, and Lily's heart ached. The king, meanwhile, glowered at Rowan with a hardened, ruthless gaze. He skulked around the cage, once again adopting the stance of a predator. "*You're* Prince Esperion?" he said, his voice eerily calm.

Rowan swallowed, unsure of how to answer. With Magnus's sickly green eyes boring into him, he finally nodded.

"You're the precious prince? The hope of the age? The one who will usher in the golden era of the Two Thrones?"

A startled look flickered across Rowan's face. How did this creature living deep within caves, king over things dank and foul, know of Rowan's ancestry? Rowan nodded again, and finally found his voice. "That's why I've come. I'm looking for the Icelein, to bring them home to Enlacia and the Valley of the Mist Elves. I've come to help make our people whole again."

At these words, Magnus erupted in rage. He struck the cage with his fists again. "Is *this* what you call 'the golden age'?" He swept his arm to indicate the ruin around him. "Is this what your precious mother meant? And you come now, to bring the people you destroyed back to your valley to *grovel*? To be your slaves?"

Rowan's face paled. "What are you talking about?"

"Seize him!" At his command, his minions opened the cage, yanked Rowan from the cell, and bound him hand and foot.

"Wait, what are you doing?" Rowan shouted. "I don't understand!"

"Of course, you don't!" the king sneered. "How could you understand? How could you understand what it means to live for *centuries* without the warmth of the sun, without daylight, locked in an abyss of fog?"

"What do you want from me?"

Magnus lunged toward him and grasped his chin with a claw-like hand. His eyes were like terrible flames. "If you are who you say you are," he hissed, "I want retribution for the hundreds of years you stole from my people!"

Rowan looked horrified. "What are you—"

Magnus struck him across the face before he could finish. The pride and aloofness that had always chilled Rowan's face melted away, and Lily wanted to cry out, to hold and console him, and to hit Magnus herself. The rat, suddenly alert, shot her a look of warning to remain concealed.

"If you really are who you say you are," Magnus said, "I will take you up on your offer to return to the Valley of the Mist Elves. But on *my* terms, not yours! You would have me bow to you. Instead, I will conquer all!"

Rowan's face lengthened in horror. "There's nothing left to conquer! It's just a pile of empty halls!"

At this, the king burst into maniacal laughter. "Poetic justice! Oh, how sweet! Your words embolden my blood."

With a whip of his ragged cloak, he marched out of the furnace room. His minions trailed behind, each of them holding tightly to Rowan's limbs and dragging him as he wriggled and fought.

"Wait! Where are you taking me? You can't do this! I'm the rightful heir of the Mist Elves! I'm just looking for the Icelein, to bring our people together again!"

Magnus halted and turned about. When Lily saw his deathly pale face, with skin the color of a fish's belly, she shivered. His eyes shone with hate.

"You say you're looking for the Icelein?" he said. Then, he made a flourishing gesture with his hand, as if presenting himself at court. "Congratulations, long lost prince. You've found us!"

CHAPTER 14

Brute

Magnus and his henchmen disappeared down a tunnel with Rowan in tow. When they'd gone, Lily inched out from her hiding place and struggled to comprehend what she'd just seen. *The dwellers are the Icelein?* She tried to square Magnus's gruesomeness and cruelty with the stately, graceful people depicted in the courtyard at Enlacia, the kings' arms linked in a pledge of peace. *How could these monsters be the same people? What happened to them?*

She leaped over the pile of tools she'd upset and snatched up the poker. Whoever Magnus really was, he'd taken Rowan; all her questions would have to wait. She thought of the anguish on Rowan's face as he'd watched his memory of his mother. *All this—the whole wild-goose chase—arose from his love for her,* she thought with a twinge of pity. *The poor kid is so lost and alone.* Lily gripped the poker. *No. Not entirely alone.* With determination, she lowered her head and marched into the tunnel. *It's time to bring him back home.*

A growl stopped her.

Lily halted and warily looked over her shoulder. The rat had risen to his feet, and he stared at her with a flash of warning in his eyes, his paws clasped around the sledgehammer handle. He glanced at the poker in Lily's fist, and his scowl deepened. Lily dropped the poker and turned to face him with her empty palms raised.

"Please, I don't want any trouble," Lily said. "I just need to help my friend."

The rat's expression seemed etched in stone. "I cannot let you go," he said.

The scars on his forelimbs drew her attention. Wounds raked across his paws, muzzle, and shoulders. Someone in the bowels of the mountain had tortured him . . . and Lily believed she knew the culprit.

"Did Magnus hurt you?" she asked, mustering her courage.

The question took him aback. He shuffled from side to side, and his tail quivered like an arrow and stirred up a cloud of dust.

"Those scars," Lily tried again, pointing with one of her upraised fingers. "Did he give them to you?"

The rat shivered. "Some of them. Most."

"That's awful."

"It is my keep."

"Your *keep*?"

"I am Brute," he said, as if this would explain everything.

"Is that your name? Brute?"

He nodded, then stiffened as a jangling sounded from within the tunnel. At first, he bristled on guard, but as the sound drew nearer, the rat's eyes softened, and he let the hammer thud to the ground. Lily turned about as another rat, much smaller and dressed in rags, scurried past her. A chain, like Brute's but flimsier, dangled from her hind legs as she limped forward.

"Brute?" the rat pup squeaked.

Brute gathered her into his arms and nuzzled her. "What are you doing here?"

"I brought you this," she said. She held out a mushroom cap in her paw.

Brute hugged her again. "Thank you, little Brute," he said. He nuzzled her one last time, and then she scampered away into the tunnel, casting a nervous, sidelong glance at Lily as she passed. Before the pup disappeared, Brute called to her. "Little Brute! Be careful," he said.

She grinned at him, then vanished into the darkness. As Brute watched her go, he wrung his paws.

Lily deliberated running down the tunnel while Brute had relaxed his guard; she needed to save Rowan, after all. But something deep within told her to wait. Something she couldn't explain told her that this stooped, bruised creature chained to the wall was part of a greater story, one that she needed to unveil.

Lily lingered a moment as Brute bowed his head and retreated into his own sorrow. "Was that your daughter?" she finally asked.

Brute nodded.

"Why did you call her Brute as well?"

"We are all Brutes."

"Is that your family name or something?"

"No, not just my family. It's the name for *all* of us." He pointed to the chain manacled to his foot. "All who wear the chains are Brutes."

Lily frowned. "You mean, you don't have names? You're only known as *brutes*?"

He nodded.

She studied the chain bolted to the wall and remembered the miniature one shackled to his daughter's fragile legs. A knot twisted in her stomach. "You're a slave, aren't you?"

Brute didn't answer. Instead, he slouched to the ground and dropped his head into his paws. As he did so, Lily's fear of him melted away, and she crouched beside him and placed a hand on his shoulder. His wiry fur scratched her palm like the brush of steel wool, but she ignored the sting. Brute flinched at her touch but didn't pull away.

"Didn't you ever have a name?" Lily asked.

"We do not talk about the old times. His Majesty forbids it."

"Then you did have a name once. What happened to you?"

He hunched further into himself, and his whiskers switched back and forth as he worried his mouth.

"Please tell me. It's all right."

"The king would be displeased."

"The king isn't pleased about much, is he? I promise I'll keep your secret safe. You can trust me."

He eyed her, puffed out a sigh that blew his whiskers, and relented. "I was taken. We all were, from our homes deep in the rock."

"Magnus took you?"

He nodded. "And his soldiers."

"I'm so sorry. What was your name before they took you? You must have had one."

He opened his mouth to speak, but then stopped, as if the words lodged in his throat.

"Please tell me. I'm a friend."

His eyes glistened at the word *friend*, as if he recalled a sweet memory he'd long forgotten. He drew a deep breath. "Tobias," he finally whispered.

Lily grinned. "Tobias! That's a lovely name."

He stared at her, and she could see a flurry of questions tangling behind his eyes. "You're from up there? The surface?" He pointed upward toward the rocky ceiling.

"Yes."

"You come from outside the caves?"

"Outside the fog, actually."

Tobias's eyes widened. "You've seen the sun?"

"Many, many times."

"Is it like they say? Like a torch in the sky?"

"It's so bright it turns the sky from black to blue."

Tobias gasped. "Then, the stories are true?"

"Which stories?"

Tobias shifted uncomfortably. "Never mind. I am remembering children's tales, that's all. One of them mentions a torch in the sky that lights the warriors' path and sleeps beyond the mountains at night."

"Well, the sun is definitely real. That story's true." An idea awoke in Lily's mind. "What other stories do you know?"

"None. They are foolish."

"You have to remember *some* of them. Everyone has a favorite story."

He traced a scar on his foot and then spoke haltingly. "My father once told me of a prince. Not from the caves, but from up there." He pointed again.

"What kind of a prince?"

"A prince of light even stronger than the sun. My father said one day he would lead us out of this darkness."

"Out of the darkness of the caves?"

"Out of *our* darkness." He gestured to the chain at his ankle. "Out of this."

Lily swallowed a lump in her throat. *Oh, Pax, please give me the words. Help me to show him who you are.* "I don't think that's a fairy tale."

Tobias stared at her with wide eyes. "What do you mean? You know of such a prince?"

"His name is Pax."

"He's real?"

"He's wonderful."

Tobias stared into the fire, his breathing rapid as he processed her words. "If he is real, why has he not come?"

"His timing isn't like ours. But in a way, he's already saved you. Did you and your people recently become sick with an awful illness? It caused horrible sores and disease, and rotted everything?"

Tobias nodded. "The Deadening. His Majesty, King Magnus, saved us from it."

A flicker of anger sparked within Lily. "What?"

"King Magnus. He stopped the Deadening."

"Is that what he told you?"

Tobias drew back, unnerved by the sharpness in her voice. "He said he cured us with his magic amulets."

"He did *not* cure you! He's a lousy, no-good liar!"

"But he healed us. We owe him our lives."

"You owe him a good kick in the pants!"

"I don't understand. If he did not cure our family, who did?"

"Prince Pax did!" As Lily spoke the name, a breeze suddenly whistled through the furnace room, ruffling Tobias's fur. "Pax died for everyone," Lily said. "For you, and even those wretched dwellers, to save you all from the Blight, or the Deadening, or whatever you call it down here."

Tobias shook his head. "No prince would have died for me, or for any Brute. We are unworthy even of our names."

"This prince did. It's the truth. He saved you because . . . because . . ." She remembered Cedric's words. "Because it's who he is, and he loves you that much."

"I cannot believe it. I am only Brute. How can I believe this? How can this be true?"

Lily bit her lip. She wished she had Isla's powers of memory and could recreate images in a pool of water, or Keisha's way with words to persuade others. Even better, she wished that like Rowan she had a store of memories tucked into her pocket to share with him, to show him the things she'd seen and heard.

Pocket. She reached into her pocket and withdrew the sooth-stone. Could she somehow use it to show Tobias what she knew?

Lily clasped the stone in her hands, closed her eyes, and mined her memories for what she'd witnessed. She remembered Pax in the Catacombs, rearing upward in defiance of Eymah. She saw him rescuing Adam from the cliff's edge and healing his leg wound as if by magic. Then she saw the gloom of the Blight roll back like a scroll, and the glass tomb crack open and illuminate the valley. Colors danced through her eyelids as the stone glowed. Its light seemed stronger somehow, more piercing. Lily opened her eyes, squinted against the glare, and then felt an electric tingling travel from her chest down the extent of her arm. Suddenly, a pulse of light erupted from the soothstone and enveloped Tobias like a radiant garment.

What have I done? Lily doddered backward. Her arm prickled with electricity, and the rat stood transfixed for a moment, paralyzed; whether with fear or electrocution, Lily couldn't tell. Then, as quickly as it began, the light snuffed out, and the giant rat slumped to the ground.

Lily rushed to his side. Given the brilliance of the light, she half-expected his fur to sizzle, as Cedric's scales had when he braved Eymah's fire. As she touched him, however, he was cool and soft as before.

"Tobias!" she cried, shaking him. "Tobias, are you okay?"

He sat up with a faraway, awestruck look, and placed a paw to his forehead. "I saw what he did," he whispered. "I heard him, your Prince Pax!"

Lily gaped at him. "What did he say?"

"He said, 'Know that I love those in the Realm, and that when its people are lost and hurting and alone, my concern for them grows all the more.'"

Lily's hands trembled. She climbed to her feet and steadied herself against a wall. "That was Pax, all right," she whispered.

A change came over Tobias's face. He rose to his feet, his profile suddenly fierce and straight, more soldier than broken slave. "I will help you," he declared. "I will help you save your friend. You have shown me light again. The least I can do is help you in return."

With a mighty grunt he grasped the hammer in his paws, whirled it over his head, and then crashed it down upon his chain, breaking the links into pieces.

CHAPTER 15

Into the Mines

Tobias's severed chain clattered behind him as he led Lily into the tunnel. He gripped her hand with the self-assurance of one who had never felt the weight of shackles around his limbs. His glimpse of Pax—of the truth—had changed him. Instead of skulking and cowering he now marched with his shoulders square, as an admiral, determined to fight for the good and true, would lead his fleet into battle.

Lily wished she could draw from his well of courage. As Tobias guided her deeper into the tunnel, where the air felt dank and close and the ground oozed beneath their feet, she couldn't shake the notion that they journeyed into the burrow of an enormous, prehistoric worm. She shivered, and wondered if she'd ever glimpse the sun again.

"Here," Tobias finally said, drawing to a stop. "Climb in."

Lily squinted into the darkness. "Climb into what? I can't see anything."

"Oh, of course." Tobias released her hand, momentarily unnerving Lily as she reached for him in the darkness. In a moment, however, a torch blazed in his paw. By the light of the fire a pair of metal tracks glinted at their feet and wound into the distance. Tobias pointed to a metal cart hulking on the tracks, reminiscent of the trolleys used in coal mines decades ago in the waking world.

"Climb in," Tobias repeated. "It will lead you to your friend."

Lily's heart skipped a beat. "You mean it will lead *us*, right? Because you're coming with me?"

"The best way for me to help you is to rally my people to arms. You will not defeat King Magnus alone. Go on ahead, and I will do what I can to rouse my kinsmen to defend you."

Lily swallowed and stared down the track into the inky blackness. The tunnel gaped like the mouth of a great serpent, and she shuddered at the idea of diving into those shadows alone. "Where does it go?" she asked, trying to steady her voice.

"Deeper into the mountain. It ends in the storeroom, just before King Magnus's great hall. Climb out when you see the quicksilver stream and follow it to Magnus's court."

"Quicksilver stream?"

"Yes. Whatever you do, don't touch it. The quicksilver will poison your mind."

Perfect, Lily thought with a shudder. "Are you sure it will lead me to Rowan?"

"I think King Magnus aims to . . . *persuade* him. For this, he will want an audience. The courtroom is his preferred place to make an example of the wayward." Tobias shook his head sadly, and rubbed a scar on his forelimb.

Oh please, no, Lily thought. *Please don't let him hurt Rowan.*

"Hurry, my friend," Tobias said. "The sooner you find him, the better. I will do what I can to protect you afterward."

Lily's head swam, and she fought the impulse to cry. She knew she needed to plow ahead, especially if the scars on Tobias's limbs warned of Rowan's fate. But she couldn't bear the thought of stumbling forward into that ominous blackness alone. She hadn't even faced the Petrified Forest or Eymah alone; Cedric, Adam, and Rigel had insisted upon journeying with her, whatever the dangers.

The lump in her throat grew at the thought of her friends. What would they say, if they could see her now? Cedric had thrown himself into Eymah's fiery breath to protect her. Even Adam, who'd bullied her mercilessly before Lancelot dragged him into the Realm, had risked his life to save Scallywag when the *Flying Emerald* threatened to crash to pieces. What would they urge her to do?

The she thought of another friend. One who'd rescued her from the murky waters of the Sea of Oblivion, when she'd forgotten even her own name. One who'd given his life to save the Realm from the Blight.

What would *he* say?

Instantly, Lily knew. She drew a breath and straightened her shoulders. "Where will you go?" she asked Tobias as she hurriedly wiped her eyes. She hoped he hadn't noticed their momentary glistening.

"First, I will share your news with my family. My wife and children have known only darkness since their birth. The promise of light . . . who knows what it will do?" He placed a paw on her shoulder, and tenderness shone in his eyes. "Go now. Don't delay, and don't let anyone see you. If any of the workers glimpse you, they'll report you to the king."

Lily drew another shaky breath and nodded. He hoisted her into the cart, and she tried to muffle the echo of her footfalls on the iron base as she plunked down. The cart smelled awful, of coal dust and metal but also of old garbage. Lily wedged herself into a corner and braced her feet against the opposite wall. She pawed the sides of the cart for something to hold on to, but her hands, wet with perspiration, only slid against the bare metal.

"Stay low while you ride," Tobias added. "Good luck, seer of the sun."

Lily squeezed her eyes shut and fought to still her heart. *Please, please let me find Rowan. Please let me do the right thing.*

Tobias pulled a lever. Lily heard a clang, then a grinding of rusted gears, and the cart screeched forward. The trolley accelerated, and Lily dared to glance back toward the furnace room to glimpse her newfound friend. The light from Tobias's torch flickered and faded, then finally disappeared, pitching Lily into deepest darkness again. Deepest darkness, and aching loneliness.

The cart gained speed. Lily's hair flew back from her face, and the rattle of the iron wall at her back made her teeth vibrate and her head ache. Initially the inertia pressed her against the back wall, but as the vehicle inclined down a slope, she became airborne, the way she lifted up from the seat of a roller coaster during a family trip to an amusement park a year before. At that time she'd screamed, but a crossbar, a harness, and her father's arms had kept her safe. Now she was alone, with no restraint and only the strength of her shrimpy arms to prevent her from flying out into the abyss. Lily braced her arms against the walls and prayed for survival.

As the track leveled out, Lily toppled onto her side with a thud. She struggled to right herself but couldn't gain a foothold with the constant jostling and banging of the cart, and so instead she lay on her back and stared upward into the darkness. A light, like the gray just before dawn, soon brightened the ceiling above her, sharpening the outlines of wooden beams draped with the occasional chain. Soon torches of green flame studded the beams. As the light intensified, the trolley slowed, and soon Lily heard shouts, the clink of chains, and the gong of hammers against steel. With her heart pounding Lily grasped the edge of the cart, and slowly, carefully, she pulled herself upward to peek above the rim.

The track wove through a vast hall, with rooms and tunnels carved into six stories of rock. Giant rats, doubtless Tobias's kin, slogged in and out of the rooms and hauled heavy bags of rubble on their stooped backs. Scores of dwellers stood guard over them, hollering orders and cracking whips at the stragglers. Lily winced when a little pup rat, barely older than Tobias's daughter, stumbled under the weight of something circular and metallic, then squealed when a guard kicked him.

"Ay, stop that hutch now, vermin!"

The shout came from a guard with a single strand of greasy hair dangling over his face like a rat's tail. To Lily's horror, he pointed directly at her cart. She ducked down and pressed herself into a corner, and fought to quiet her breathing.

With a screech of rusted metal the trolley ground to a stop, and the guard's footsteps tromped closer. Lily heard him clear his throat, and although she couldn't see him, his shadow draping over her told her that he loomed just outside the cart. *Oh please. Please, don't look down.*

"All right, you filthy maggots, load 'er up!" the guard shouted.

"Grimly, got any good 'uns in that load?" another dweller hollered.

"Naw. It's all rubbish. Not even a crystal. This one's for the incinerator, it is."

"Better change the tracks then, Grimly!"

Incinerator? Lily dared to look up just as an avalanche of debris rained down atop her. She tucked her head between her knees and placed her hands over her neck as a shower of dirt, rocks, and scraps of twisted metal thundered against the floor. Chunks of rock scraped her fingers and battered the backs of her hands, and dirt covered her shoulders and piled to her chin. As it poured down and buried her head, Lily's chest tightened. She feared that if she didn't break through the rubble and take a breath soon, she'd either suffocate or explode.

Finally, the cascade of garbage dwindled, and corroded gears squealed as the cart again skidded forward. When the voices receded into the background, Lily finally broke through the heap of dirt and gasped for air. She wiped grit from her eyes, spit several times to clear dirt from her mouth, and then dwelt upon the guard's last words: *This one's for the incinerator, it is.*

Incinerator. I'm going to be burned with the garbage! Lily hauled herself up through the dirt, blinked away a few tears from residual grit, and squinted into the gathering darkness. The mines and the eerie illumination of the dwellers' torches had disappeared behind her, and she now sped toward a fork in the track. To the left, a red glow throbbed like smoldering cinders in a fireplace. To the right, she saw dim, green light, and . . . *What is that?* A silver thread glistened at the base of the tunnel.

The quicksilver stream!

Lily wiped beads of sweat from her forehead and leaned over the edge of the trolley. She peered into the darkness, then groaned at the sight of her track veering off to the left up ahead. Just as she feared, she was speeding straight toward the incinerator.

What do I do? She searched either side of the track wildly for a platform or a stairway onto which she could jump, but found nothing. Then she probed the thick iron walls for a brake handle, again to no avail. Finally, she glimpsed a loop of chain hanging from a rafter up ahead, dangling just above the fork in the track. Could she grab it?

I have to try. Lily bit her lip. If she missed, she'd hurtle on toward the incinerator without hope of escape.

Lily climbed onto the edge of the cart to reach for the chain, but she lost her footing as the rickety vehicle swayed to one side. She tried again, and once more stumbled backward into the mound of trash. With each attempt the fork in the track rushed closer, and the mounting heat in the tunnel stung her eyes. Finally, she dragged herself upward, balanced on the corner of the cart, and gripped the metal edges so tightly that her fingers throbbed. The chain dangled up ahead like a vine draping from a jungle canopy. As Lily gauged the distance, her heart raced.

I'm too short to reach it. I'll have to jump. She counted down for the leap. Ten. Nine.

The cart struck a rock on the track. It jerked to the left, sent sparks into the air, and knocked Lily off her feet again. With a grunt she scrambled back into position, her limbs burning.

Five. Four.

The heat intensified, and Lily could barely breathe. Firelight from the incinerator reflected off the links of the chain as it swung back and forth.

Three. Two.

She jumped.

Lily barely caught the chain with her right hand and cried out as the metal abraded the wound in her palm. She swung free of the cart, then toppled backward, her arms and legs flailing in the air before she thudded to the ground. The trolley careened down the track and disappeared into the inferno of the incinerator cavern.

For a moment Lily lay motionless in the darkness and fought to catch her breath. Stars spun in front of her eyes. When they finally cleared, she sat up, rubbed the back of her neck, and pulled aside her collar to glance at a welt swelling on her left shoulder. She staggered to her feet, then darted backward from something glimmering on the ground at her feet. Her sneakers had barely missed a puddle of something viscous and silver, tinted fiery orange from the glow of the incinerator. Lily shuddered as she remembered Tobias's words about the quicksilver stream: *Whatever you do, don't touch it. It will poison your mind.*

Lily backed away from the edge of the stream, then glanced down the track to ensure no more iron carts threatened to flatten her. When she saw none, she drew a deep breath and then followed the trickle of mercury into the inky blackness of the tunnel.

After several yards the air dampened and cooled. For a short while Lily could glimpse the stream weaving like a metallic streamer through the cavern, but soon the deep dark enveloped her and hid it from her eyes. She wished Philippe would appear with his sparkler wand, sizzling flowers, and lantern of fireflies.

Poor Philippe, she thought with a pang of guilt. *He never even wanted to come on this journey, and now he's lost somewhere in the Veil. Or worse . . .* As remorse pressed on her like an iron weight, Lily leaned her head against the tunnel wall and tried to ignore something slimy on the rock that squished under her arm. "Some dream keeper I've turned out to be," she groaned. "I couldn't even protect a rabbit. A *lazy* rabbit, even."

Click.

Lily craned her neck to listen. Somewhere nearby, a pebble had knocked to the ground. Lily held her breath and searched the darkness for some hint of movement, but she could discern nothing.

Then, another *clunk*, followed by scampering.

Lily withdrew the soothstone from her pocket. She turned it in her fingers and worried about whether she could coax it alive. *Whatever's been going on with my powers, right now I need light,* she thought in desperation. *Please, Pax. Please light the way again.* She imagined dozens of lanterns flaring to life down the corridor, exposing any crawling, vile things that threatened her, and prayed the flickers of her mind would materialize before her.

Suddenly the soothstone flooded the tunnel with its glow. An array of lanterns, all flickering with different shades of fire like those in the courtyard at Muzzytown, illuminated the tunnel in a kaleidoscope of colors. Lily sighed with wonder and relief. "Thank you, Pax," she whispered. Then she spotted something small and mangy shivering on the ground, and she cried out for joy.

"Philippe!" Lily rushed forward and caught the bedraggled rabbit in her arms. "Philippe, you're here! You're alive!" She spun in place, her heart bursting, his ears flapping from his head as she whirled.

"Mademoiselle, I will not be if you keep choking me!"

Lily lowered him to the ground but didn't let go. She smoothed his bedraggled fur along the top of his head. "I am so glad to see you. What are you doing here? How did you find me? How did you make it through the Veil?"

"If you wish me to answer you must let go of my neck!"

Lily released him but couldn't wipe away the ridiculous grin plastered across her face. A friend, at last! "I can't believe you're here, Philippe. I was so worried I'd never see you again."

Philippe coughed, brushed off his shoulders, then scampered to a wall of the cavern and studied the lanterns nervously. "This is not a good idea, mademoiselle," he said pointing to the lanterns with a paw. "These lights, they will draw enemies. The nasty ones will find us."

"How did you get here, Philippe?"

"How do you think? I followed you."

"Followed me?"

"Mademoiselle, it is not safe here. We must go."

"How did you follow me?"

"We must go, mademoiselle! Those pale rapscallions, they will see these lights!" Philippe planted his paws on Lily's knees and pushed her toward the entrance of the tunnel.

"No, Philippe, we have to go the other way."

"That way? No, mademoiselle! That is where the tall, horrible one is, with all the necklaces!"

"Good. That's where we need to go."

"*Sacré bleu! Ma cherie*, you have gone mad! We have just escaped that place. He is a monster!"

"I know, Philippe, but—he has Rowan."

Philippe fell silent, and one of his ears drooped. "He has the melancholy prince?"

"Yes."

He tugged on his ear, gave it a half-twist in thought, and heaved a sigh. "I heard someone cry out for help, but I did not know it was him." After a few mumbled words in French, he began to march back down the tunnel toward Magnus's court. "It is madness. Madness. But we go back to the monster's lair."

Lily trotted to catch up to him. "Thank you, Philippe. I'm so glad to see you."

Philippe groaned. "I just want a slice of carrot. Lightly salted, perhaps sautéed in a bit of *beurre blanc*. That is all."

"Still so focused on your stomach."

Philippe raised a paw in the air as if instructing her with an index finger. "Never underestimate the power of the carrot, mademoiselle."

"When all this is done, I'll see to it you have all the carrots you want and more. I promise."

Philippe grumbled something in French again.

"You still didn't answer my question. How did you find me?"

"Just now? *Par accident.* We were fleeing that terrible tall one." Philippe shuddered. "When those nasty persons took you in the fog, I followed along, but I could not find you when the mob in the cave began to riot."

"I thought I'd lost you when we fell into the Veil. I was so worried you were hurt."

"As I tell you, mademoiselle, never underestimate the powers of the carrot. It makes the rabbit invincible. Plus, our feet are designed for leaping from disaster." He puffed out his furry chest with pride.

Lily smiled, then noticed that the lantern light had dwindled behind them, and the darkness again encroached. "Soon we won't be able to see," she said. "Maybe I should try to make us another light? Something we can carry?"

"Ah, mademoiselle, you still underestimate me." He reached inside his chest fluff and withdrew something bright and flickering. Flint, rolled up like a pill bug, suddenly unfurled, hopped onto the ground, cast sparks on the cavern floor with a shake of his head, and offered Lily a low bow. Lily reached out her palm, and Flint scurried up into it. With tears in her eyes, she stroked the top of his head. "I'm so glad you're okay too, little buddy." Her thumb tingled as he planted a fiery kiss on her hand, like a tiny spark of static on a dry winter's day.

Flint hopped down and skittered down through the tunnel, and Lily followed with renewed vigor. The quicksilver stream wove through an endless network of tunnels. The deeper they marched, the more stagnant and oppressive the air felt in Lily's lungs, yet the sight of her dear friends had breathed life into her steps. Maybe together there was a chance they *could* save Rowan. Maybe they would break free from that wretched place and return to where the air was fresh and sweet, where sunlight, grass, and the silhouettes of mountains were more than a fairytale.

Philippe placed a paw on Lily's wrist as a gray circle of light appeared in the distance. "That is a dangerous place, mademoiselle. I had to hide the fiery fellow to get through. So many of the nasty ones."

"What is it?" Lily asked.

"I do not know, but it is piled high with stones. Hundreds, maybe thousands of stones and chains and all sorts of things."

The storeroom, Lily thought.

As they drew closer, Philippe urged Lily to sidle against the wall of the tunnel. He signaled for Flint, too, to hide, and the kindler scampered up Lily's arm and nestled into the pocket of her shirt, daring only occasionally to peek out and survey the scene ahead. The familiar sound of whips echoed from within the chamber, and Lily winced with each crack. She thought of Tobias and hoped that whatever he was doing he was still free, and not suffering for his bravery in helping her.

At the threshold Philippe dropped to all fours and crept forward with his nose in the air. "Follow me," he whispered.

"And stay low, mademoiselle. I see a path forward, but the way, it is narrow."

He led her down an alleyway that wound around a huge heap of rubble. As she crouched low to the ground, taking care not to step on any of the debris strewn across the cavern floor, Lily realized that they navigated not around refuse, but trinkets and jewels. Mounds of gemstones, polished rocks, pendants, and medallions piled toward the ceiling, along with talismans and rings, amulets and crystals. A dream catcher, woven from animal sinew and studded with turquoise and feathers, protruded from among the heaps.

"Philippe," Lily whispered, leaning forward. "What is all this?"

Before he could answer, a whip cracked and an angry bellow boomed through the cave. Lily's heart quickened, and she jogged forward only to ram into Philippe, who had stopped suddenly. She narrowly caught herself from tumbling over him, but before she could scold him, his slack-jawed expression silenced her. His eyes blazed with indignation.

"The rapscallions!" he whispered. Lily followed his gaze and saw the object of his fury: one of the dwellers twirled a rumpled silk top hat around his fingers.

"Ay, Lurch, give it here, eh?" another dweller growled. "That don't fit you anyways."

"It does so fit. And I likes it." Lurch jammed the hat onto his head. It was at least five sizes too small, and as he tugged, a ripping sound joined the grinding of gears and zing of whips.

A tuft of greasy, wiry hair poked through a hole that gaped open along the brim.

"Oh, now you've done it!" said Lurch's companion. "Magnus'll have your head for that one, he will!"

"Magnus don't need to know! Wot does he want with an ole 'at, anyways?"

"Same as he wants with all the rest of this rubbish, you dimwit!"

Lurch groaned, then kicked a pile of yellow crystals. "I'm tired of this, Grubbles! How many years we been collectin' this junk, eh? All of it's supposedly magic, but wot's it got us? The Veil's still thick as day-old snot!"

"He just ain't found the right magic, that's all."

"You know what I think?" He twisted the hat, and Philippe cringed as another seam split. "I'm beginning to think there ain't no magic wot can get us out of here. That's what I think."

"If Magnus says there is, then there is, you slimetoad! He saved us from the Deadening, after all."

"Well, I don't see 'ow this junk 'elped with that, neither."

They turned about, Lurch still fiddling with the torn brim of the hat, and disappeared into the shadows. Even after they'd gone, Philippe looked after them with longing in his eyes.

Lily prodded him on the back. "Philippe, we'd better—"

"That was my hat, mademoiselle. It is irreplaceable." He reached out a paw, as if to grasp the thing he'd lost, then dropped it and slumped his shoulders. "I still had radishes in there. And the most *mignon* fruit. And a carrot most *magnifique*."

Lily urged him onward. A fiery light bled through an archway at the rear of the cavern. As they approached, a voice, half-growl, half-hiss, echoed from within. *Magnus.*

Lily inched forward with her back pressed against the wall and peered out. What she saw made her heart sink.

CHAPTER 16

Magnus's Court

The archway opened onto a cliff overlooking a circular cavern, with a bonfire raging at its center and torches suspended from stalactites in the ceiling. Guards stood at attention in a ring around the fire, the points of their rusted, warped swords digging into the earth. A cragged throne hewn from the rock slouched before the fire, and upon it sat Magnus, twirling one of his necklaces around his knobby fingers. Rowan knelt before the throne with his hands bound and his hair hanging limp in front of his face.

"Let us try this once more," Magnus said. He signaled to one of his minions, who stepped into the firelight. Shattered glass littered the floor at the dweller's feet in a hundred tiny shards.

The minion grinned wickedly, a single yellowed tooth protruding over his upper lip, and he raised one of Rowan's memory baubles between two grubby fingers.

Oh, no, Lily thought with dread. She recalled the zeal with which Rowan had guarded the baubles in his cloak, and their preciousness to him. As Lily saw the despair in his eyes, and the fear, her heart broke. Those baubles had allowed him to hold and touch the people he'd loved, and had promised to preserve their memory when his own recollections faded with time. How could he bear to lose them?

"Tell me who you are," Magnus growled.

Rowan shuddered and whispered something unintelligible.

"I. Can't. Hear you! Answer me, you pitiful worm!"

"I'm Prince Esperion."

"So you say. If that is really who you are, then you have something of value to me. Something that does not belong to you." Magnus rose from his throne and circled Rowan like a ravenous wolf.

"I told you, I don't know what you're talking about," Rowan said.

"Do not mock me, you sniveling little larva!" Magnus sprang forward and grasped Rowan by the collar. "You stole it from me! If you are who you say you are, then you either have it or you know where it is!"

Rowan, always so stoic and aloof, shook like a leaf in a gust of wind. His bottom lip quavered. "I don't have anything of yours, I swear!" he said, his voice cracking.

Magnus struck Rowan across the face and sent him sprawling across the floor. In her shock Lily involuntarily cried out, and Philippe leaped up to cover her mouth with his paw. "No, mademoiselle! You must wait, or he will capture us all!" he whispered.

Magnus yanked Rowan's collar again and drew their faces together until their noses nearly touched. "*Where is the Woven Ice?*" he shouted, spittle flying from his lips.

"I don't know!"

"Wrong answer!" Magnus snapped his fingers. "Mudge! Another one!" On cue, the dweller hurled a memory bauble to the ground. There was a crash, a clinking of glass, and the ball shattered into a hundred pieces. The golden flame at its center escaped into the air, pirouetted a turn or two, and then vanished like a coil of smoke.

Rowan's tears streamed down his cheeks. "Please. Please don't break any more. I'm just looking for family, or people like me."

"Your words make my ears bleed. You want family and you have the audacity to come *here*? To us? When *you* condemned us to misery?"

"What are you talking about?"

"If you are who you say you are, *you* are responsible for the Veil!"

Rowan gaped in horror. "That's not true. You're lying! I don't have anything to do with the Veil!"

"Oh, don't you? We've dabbled in your memories, long lost prince. Now feast your eyes upon some of my own! Behold *your* legacy, noble Prince Esperion!"

Magnus withdrew a handful of dust from a satchel at his side and flung it into the bonfire. The flames turned green, flared upward, and then coalesced into ghostly images that danced and wavered. A palace of ice, like that in the Diurnal Mountains but with sharp spires and intricate carvings, emerged from the fire. White flags whipped in the breeze. On the grounds below, elves clad in white robes, like those in the paintings at Enlacia, tended ice sculptures. A child barely younger than Lily knelt and held out her hand to an arctic fox, who warily padded closer to nibble at something in her palm.

A rumbling sounded and the image shook. The elves in the picture turned to face the mountain beyond the palace, then lifted the hems of their robes and ran screaming as a wave of snow barreled down upon them, engulfing their kingdom in a white tide.

A tall elf wearing a silver circlet ran out to meet the avalanche. A blue crystal glowed at his breast, and as he held his hands aloft against the oncoming surge of ice and snow, Lily faintly recognized the strength of his jaw and the nobility of his profile. *It's the king from the painting*, she thought. *The king on the throne of the Icelein.*

The light from the crystal intensified, and the surge slowed to a crawl. The king shouted words in a language unfamiliar to Lily, and the avalanche halted as if restrained by an invisible wall. For a moment Lily thought it might reverse on itself and fold backward at the king's command.

Then the jewel dimmed. With a groan the avalanche regained momentum, pummeled the king off his feet, and swept him away in a flood of snow, ice, and debris. Soon the palace, the people, and even the king himself disappeared. The entire image swirled into a white mass, as if a blizzard had overwhelmed the world.

Gradually the haze cleared. A few elves, shaken and bruised, dragged themselves from the drifts, then wailed aloud at the sight of those they loved and the home they cherished buried in the catastrophe.

The image shifted toward the shade of a coniferous forest, where a single arm protruded from the snow and a brilliant blue jewel lay atop the crust several feet away. The hand suddenly sprang into motion, snow flung into the air, and the king broke through and gasped for breath. Although he struggled, he couldn't free himself from the vice grip of the snow and ice around his chest that locked him into place. With his fingers splayed wide he stretched out his hand to grasp the blue gemstone just beyond his reach.

A shadow darkened the image. The king glanced up, and his face softened with relief as he recognized his visitors. He reached out his hand, anticipating they would free him from his trap.

Instead, they regarded him with disgust, as if he were a worm writhing on the pavement after a rainstorm. One, a wizened old man with gray hair that draped down his back, tilted his head to one side and faintly smirked. The other, just a boy with garnet-colored hair that flowed around his shoulders, stared blankly, as if the great monarch trapped in snow were nothing more than an insect flipped on its back. The king glanced from one face to the other, and his own expression fell. The hope in his eyes dwindled away, and his brow wrinkled. He stretched out his arm in desperation and pleaded with them to help.

Instead, the old man strode toward the blue stone, scooped it up, and brushed snow from its facets. The smirk that had only vaguely turned his lips now widened into a leering grin. He tossed the crystal into the air, caught it, and with a laugh tucked it into the folds of his robes. Then with a last, cold glance at the king, the iciness of which chilled Lily to the bone, the gray-haired elf placed a hand on the young boy's shoulder, and they turned their backs on the buried kingdom.

The king flailed and screamed, but his betrayers never looked back. The magic jewel glimmered in the elder's hand as they slowly marched away, abandoning the king and his subjects to their icy prison. Just before they vanished into the distance, the younger, red-haired elf raised his arms and circled them above his head. Suddenly the clouds, gray and heavy in the sky above, gathered above him in a thick cloak. With a flourish of his hands the boy cast the clouds back over the palace, and soon the entire kingdom up to the root of the mountains disappeared beneath an impenetrable blanket of mist.

The Veil.

The images flickered out. Rowan stood speechless, the color completely drained from his face.

"What do you have to say for yourself, Esperion?" Magnus hissed as he resumed his predatory circling.

Rowan shook his head in disbelief. "It can't be. This can't be true!"

"You destroyed my kingdom! You tried to wipe us from the Realm like smears of grease!"

"No. Esperion was supposed to unite the two kingdoms! He was the hope of our kind. He wouldn't have done something like this!"

Magnus growled with rage and snatched another memory bauble from the bundle in Mudge's arms. Before Rowan could protest, he hurled it to the ground, where it split into shards and the memory housed within disappeared in a whisper of gold. "The Woven Ice was the hope of our kind!" Magnus shouted. "It gave us the might of the snow, the ferocity of the ice, and the power to harness all we chose for our glory! *That* was our hope! *That* was our heritage! And you stole it from me and left us all to die, while I bayed and wriggled like a dog!"

Stole it from him? Lily stared at the ghostly, haggard, contorted figure of Magnus. She could see no trace of the delicate nose, the strong jaw, and wise eyes of the king in the images. What was he talking about?

Rowan echoed her thoughts. "Stole it from *you?*" he said, recoiling from the king. "You mean from King Miran, right?"

Magnus again loomed over him. "I mean what I said. You stole it *from me.*"

"You're—you're King Miran?"

Magnus recoiled at the name and growled with rage. "That name lost its power long ago! Yes, Prince Worm, Miran I was. But Magnus now reigns! I am the Great One, the one who dwells in the deep!" Magnus slithered toward him. "After you drenched us in that accursed fog, we dove into the mountains. Without the sun or the sky, we had no future above ground, but the depths of the earth offered . . . prizes." He lifted his collection of amulets, which clinked against each other like wind chimes. "We've found secrets of our own in the heart of the mountains. Magic lurks in the deep places, Prince Worm."

"But you're nothing like Miran, or like any of our people. You're—you're—"

"Rotten? Putrid? Oh, poor, ignorant, petulant prince, I daresay even your ivory complexion would suffer when cut off from the sunlight for a millennium!"

Rowan shook his head. "I don't believe it. You can't be him. Our people would never have caused the Veil. None of this is true!"

"What you believe doesn't matter! I have no interest in what you choose to believe or deny. I want two things from you: the Woven Ice, and my revenge!"

"I already told you, I don't have the Woven Ice! I didn't take it!"

"You try my patience, weakling! Mudge!" The minion shuffled over with his mouth still curled in a ridiculous smirk. Magnus rifled through Rowan's memories, and he withdrew one with a sneer and a malicious flash of his green eyes. "Perhaps we can prod your memory along."

Rowan looked desperate and stricken. "Please," he said, his voice barely above a whisper. "Please, don't break it. Not that one."

Magnus turned the bauble in his fingers. "This one is worth something to you, isn't it?"

"Just don't break it. I'll do whatever you want. I'll help you find the Woven Ice. Just please don't break it."

Magnus placed a hand on Rowan's shoulder. "I grew up without a mother too, you know. She died fighting against the shrouds in the ancient wars. A fool's errand it was, madness. To grow up without a mother leaves such a hole. There's an emptiness no magic can fill." He tossed the sphere into the air and caught it again. "Don't you think so, Prince Esperion? Don't you just cleave to every memory of her, every hint and flicker, as if they were your life's breath?"

"Don't. Please."

Magnus's grip on Rowan's shoulder tightened. "Who. Are. You?"

"Please, I didn't mean any harm."

"Who. Are. You?"

Rowan's words burst from his mouth as if under pressure. "I'm a prince of the Mist Elves, but I'm not Esperion. I'm Rowan. I just look like Esperion. My people all died during the Blight and I'm—I'm just looking for family. To rebuild our kingdom."

Magnus's pale lips stretched into a thin grin. "There now, was that so hard? Tell me, Prince Not-Esperion of the Mist Elves, how did you find us? How did you travel through the Veil without going insane?"

"A—a friend. A friend flew me in."

"*Flew* you in?"

Rowan nodded, and stared at the ground in exhaustion and defeat. "She created a huge dragonfly that carried us into the Veil."

"Created it? I don't recall the Mist Elves possessing such talents, as to *create* flying creatures."

"She's—she's a dream keeper."

A corrupt fire flared in Magnus's eyes. He licked his lips. "Do you think she could fly you *out* of the Veil as well as into it?"

"I hope so."

"Fascinating." Magnus paused and suddenly scanned the upper reaches of the cavern. "And this 'friend,' is she a brave girl? Is she, say, loyal?"

At these words, the hair on the back of Lily's neck prickled. She crouched lower to the ground.

Rowan looked up. He met Magnus's eyes, and a storm of conflicting thoughts danced across his face. "Yes, she's loyal," he finally answered. "She's very loyal."

Magnus's eyes narrowed to slits. "Perhaps we should test that loyalty." Then he leapt upon his throne and raised the bauble over his head. "You must have been an ungrateful child as well as a foolish one, Prince Worm. Why else would you dare to place such a cherished memory in so fragile a plaything as a crystal ball?"

Tears streamed down Rowan's face. "I told you the truth. Please, give it back!"

"Sorry, Prince Rowan!" Magnus bellowed. "You should learn to be more careful with your memories!" Magnus reared back a skeletal arm. Howls and cheers erupted from the guards, who rapped their weapons against the ground.

"Don't! Please, don't!" Rowan screamed.

Lily saw the memory in Magnus's hand reflecting the firelight like a small flame. She imagined it smashing to the ground. Rowan's most treasured memory of his mother, his one record beyond the imperfect, fickle images in his own mind, would vanish forever in the putrid smoke of the bonfire.

Lily couldn't hold back. She sprinted to the edge of the cliff.

"No, mademoiselle!" Philippe shouted as he reached to restrain her, but she shrugged him off and rushed ahead. She skidded to the edge and waved her hands to keep from pitching over the cliff. Then, she shouted.

"Stop!"

The chaos within the cave fell silent. Lily broke into a sweat as dozens of beady eyes, some bewildered, some gleaming with hunger, trained on her.

"Please," she said, her voice shaking. "Don't destroy it."

Magnus locked eyes with her, and then his face lengthened into a sinister grin. "So, our young friend proves her loyalty at last," he said. "Seize her!"

CHAPTER 17

Battle in the Deep

Magnus's soldiers lashed their twisted blades to their backs, gnashed their teeth, and surged toward the cliff like a swarm of locusts. "Magnus'll have your head on a platter, girl!" a guard at the foot of the cliff bellowed. Then he clenched his dagger between his teeth and scuttled up the rock face on all fours, like a cockroach scaling the wall.

"Mademoiselle! We must go!" Philippe yanked Lily's shirt-sleeve, and Flint tugged her pant leg and pleaded with her to run as dwellers thronged up the cliff like rock crabs.

Lily backpedaled several steps. She heard Philippe yell for her again, pleading for her to retreat, but her gaze fixed on Rowan, still kneeling on the ground before Magnus's throne. "We can't leave him!" she cried.

"But we must, mademoiselle! This is madness!"

Her fingers closed around the soothstone. *Please, Pax. Please, let the stone work. Please let me save him.*

As if in answer, in her mind she heard Pax's voice: *Know that I will return and make all things new.*

Lily straightened her shoulders and hardened her gaze. "Get back, both of you! Take cover!" she commanded Philippe and Flint. She imagined a great net appearing in midair at the top of the cliff, and raised the stone to eye level. Suddenly its light pierced between her fingers like the rays that had burst through the cracks of Pax's tomb. As Lily opened her palm, a halo radiated outward from the stone like ripples on a lake, and the dwellers crawling up the cliff face shielded their eyes from the glare. Some lost their grip and toppled downward with a squeal to disappear in the stomping, grinding, snarling mob below. Others froze on the cliff face like frightened rats. Then the light faded, and an enormous silver net cascaded down from the ledge on which Lily stood. The net gathered the dwellers in its weave like a jellyfish engulfing a school of fish, and it dragged them screaming to the bottom of the cavern.

Oh, thank you, Pax! Lily whispered as she watched the dwellers fall. Her powers had truly returned! For a brief, delicious moment she felt invigorated, even invincible. *I'm still an artisan!* she thought with relief and delight.

While she still rejoiced, another wave of dwellers plowed up the cliff. Lily stretched out her hand, and with a flash a flock of star birds appeared and swooped down to peck at contorted faces and pry greasy hands away from the rock.

Crash.

A blast struck the rock wall against which Lily leaned, barely missing her head and spraying debris into the air. Lily rolled to the ground and shrank away just in time to evade another projectile that pulverized the outcropping on which she stood. She peered over the edge of the cliff and glimpsed the source of the threat: two dwellers stretched a wide band between them, while a third loaded it with rocks and pulled it taut like a giant slingshot.

Crash.

Another boulder struck the archway above them. Lily grabbed hold of Philippe and dragged him out of the way as the entryway caved in, driving them back into the storeroom and blocking their access to the cliff with a wall of shattered rock. As the dust settled, Lily coughed, wiped dirt from her eyes, and rushed to dismantle the barrier. She heaved stones from the mound and tossed rocks over her shoulder in her panic to clear the way.

"Help me, Philippe! We have to get back through!"

"Mademoiselle, I cannot!"

"Stop whining and *help!* I don't care how hungry you are! We can't leave him!"

"I cannot, mademoiselle!"

"Philippe, I've had enough of your—"

She whirled around to scold him, then froze. She'd expected to see Philippe wringing his ears between his paws or clutching his abdomen in another bellyache. Instead, he dangled in the air. Grubbles the dweller, his mouth curled into a sneer, clutched Philippe's ears in his knobby fist. Lurch stood beside him, his grimy hair protruding from the tear in Philippe's hat like weeds from a garden bed.

"Ay, Lurch, what we got here, eh?" Grubbles said.

"Looks like a couple of tasty morsels, I say." Lurch slapped his palm with a coiled-up whip.

Lily gritted her teeth. "Let him go," she said.

"Well, that's rich, ay, Lurch? This li'l girl acts like she owns the place, don't she?"

"Aye. Better watch them words, lassy."

"I said let him go!" Lily shouted.

"Wot'll ya give us for him?"

Philippe whimpered as Grubbles squeezed his ears. Lily glanced at the whip in Lurch's hand, and an idea awoke in her mind. She raised the soothstone. "I'm not negotiating," she said. "Let him go, or I promise there'll be trouble."

The dwellers both guffawed. Lurch's Adam's apple bobbed like a cork, and Grubbles threw his head back and slapped his gelatinous belly. "Oh, there'll be trouble, lassy," Lurch said between laughs. "I guarantee it!" In a quick motion he unfurled the whip and snapped at Lily's feet. Then he wound his arm back.

As Lily watched, the moment seemed to unfold in slow motion: the whip flying back behind him; spittle spraying from his gaping mouth; his front foot lifting off the floor of the cavern as he wound up. In the next instant, the whip would shoot out to ensnare her.

The soothstone's light blazed forth. In a quick flash the whip flew out of Lurch's hand and landed on the ground behind him. The light snuffed out and Lurch blinked dumbly, then studied his empty hands in confusion. A throaty growl sounded behind him.

Instead of a whip, a massive alligator hunched on the ground, ready to strike.

Grubbles and Lurch both screamed. Grubbles tossed Philippe aside and sprang away just as the beast lunged forward with a hiss and a snap of its jaws. The alligator twisted about and then attacked Lurch, who likewise fled deeper into the cavern with his arms raised in terror. The gator gave chase, writhing over rocks and treasure piles with a swish of its tail. Before it disappeared into the darkness of the cavern, it turned, caught Lily's eye, and winked.

Lily nodded her thanks, then rushed to Philippe's side and gingerly touched his bruised ears. "Are you okay?"

"It is humiliating, to be hung by the ears," Philippe said, massaging one of them. "But it seems I am victorious, no?" He reached behind him and withdrew the top hat that had flown from Lurch's head as he ran. It looked more like a soiled dishrag than a hat, and the ripped seam gave it an awkward tilt, but it was his once again. Philippe situated it back onto his head with a grin of pride.

Another crash shook the cavern and jostled them both to the ground. Lily propped herself on her elbows and squinted into a crescent of firelight. The concussion had rent a hole in the rock pile.

Lily sprang to her feet. "Come on, Philippe! We can get through!"

She scrambled over the loose rocks but lost her footing. In an instant her feet skidded out from under her, and she gasped for breath as she landed on her chest against the rocks. For a moment Lily's vision blurred. She gulped air into her lungs and waited for the world to snap back into focus.

When it did, a dweller, his green eyes narrowed with malice, peered back at her through the opening in the wall.

Before Lily could react, the dweller grabbed her by the collar and dragged her through the hole. "And just where do you think you're goin', you slippery li'l worm? You belongs to Magnus, you does!" He tossed her to the ground, pinned her leg beneath his tattered boot, and raised a club high above his head. Lily cried out for help as veins bulged from his arms and his face spread into a triumphant grin.

Suddenly, her attacker's tattered shirtsleeve burst into flames. He released Lily and flung away his club, then ran frantically in a circle and batted his burning arm to extinguish the fire. As

Lily backed away, she glimpsed a tiny light skittering away into the rocks.

Flint!

Shouts sounded as more dwellers scaled the cliff. Three of them hauled themselves up from the edge, shook the dust from their limbs, and growled at her with weapons raised.

Lily lifted the soothstone and imagined a wind sweeping across the cliff face. With a flash a tempest whipped up, wrenched the dwellers from the cliff, and carried them hollering to the cavern below.

More dwellers replaced them, grunting as they clawed the rock and heaved themselves onto the ledge. Lily then envisioned miniature marshmallows in place of the granite wall to which they clung, and with another flare of the soothstone the ledge gave way and her pursuers tumbled downward in a shower of sugary puffs.

An iron grip seized Lily from behind, spun her around, and twisted her arm behind her back. Lily stared into the face of yet another dweller, a filthy patch covering one of his eyes, his hot breath smelling of rotten eggs. Lily fought to free herself, and stomped on the monster's foot, but the dweller only growled in annoyance. "You think you's fancy with yer pretty li'l marble, don't you? Well, let's have you see Magnus, and then we'll see who's fancy!"

"*Charge!*"

At the cry Lily searched the cliff edge, expecting another dweller with a battle axe or a mace to barrel toward her. Instead, a blur of gray and orange light, like an electrified dust bunny, sailed through the air and struck her captor square in the face. The dweller released Lily, lumbered backward, and howled just as the sizzling projectile returned to career into his throat.

"Wot's the big idea?" the dweller shouted, his voice raspy from the blow. He reached for a dagger, but scarcely had he withdrawn it from its sheath when the mysterious assailant kicked it out of his hand. The knife whipped over the edge, and moments later the clink of metal against stone echoed throughout the cavern.

The gray blur rushed in again, and this time the orange light connected with the dweller's foot and sprayed a plume of fiery sparks. The dweller howled, cradled his burned foot, and hopped about, whining in agony and blowing on his smoking toes to cool them. As if on cue, Flint then burst into view and puffed himself into a blazing fireball. The dweller took one look at Flint, and then fled screaming down the cliff.

Lily gaped as the electric dust ball stopped its whirling and came to a halt. As her enigmatic hero emerged, his chest puffed out, an orange sword gleaming in his paws like a neon light, Lily burst into laughter.

"Philippe? Where did you get a *lightsaber*?"

He raised his weapon: it was a long, straight sword with a green hilt, and with a blade that pulsed with electrifying orange light. He tapped the crumpled brim of his hat. "I told you, mademoiselle! The hat, it is irreplaceable! And never underestimate the power of the carrot!"

A screech interrupted them. Lily glanced up, then shouted for Philippe to take cover as a bat as large as a horse swooped toward them. Despite his huge size, the bat was decrepit, a pale, shriveled bundle of crooked wings and scraggly hide stretched over bones. A scar raked across his right eye, and his twisted wings barely held him aloft. A female dweller rode on its back, her grimy hair flying behind her and reins wrapped around her palms as she lashed the poor beast with a whip.

"Go on, you filthy bag of bones!" she shrieked. "After her! Don't let her get away!"

Philippe bounded back into the storeroom, dropping his flaming carrot as he fled. Lily thought of dashing after him and cowering behind the rocks, but another screech stopped her. She turned, and her heart leapt into her throat. The bat barreled through the air toward her.

Lily snatched Philippe's light saber from the ground, and with her limbs shaking and perspiration slicking her palms, she gripped the hilt and raised the sword.

Crack.

A flick of the whip cut her face. Lily staggered backward, stunned, and winced as she touched the wound.

Snap.

Another cut. Lily backed against the rock pile and scanned the ledge for some means of escape. The hulking figures of more dwellers crawled over the ledge. Above her, the crippled bat stirred up dust clouds with each wobbly stroke of his wings.

"Time's up, deary!" the dweller astride the beast shrieked. "There ain't nowhere to go but down!" She cackled, then cracked the whip against the bat's flank. The beast spiraled downward toward Lily in a turbulent nosedive.

Lily's heart raced. The beating of the bat's lopsided wings swept her hair away from her face as she tightened her grip around the sword hilt. Cedric wouldn't have backed down; neither would she.

Suddenly, the bat veered away. The dweller screeched in protest and lashed the beast several times with the whip, but instead of attacking Lily it turned lopsided circles in the air above her.

Lily watched in astonishment, and for a terrible moment the bat locked eyes with her. Far from the menacing glint she'd seen in the eyes of the dwellers, in the bat's face Lily saw only remorse. *He doesn't want to hurt me.*

The dweller delivered another cruel cut with the whip, and the bat screeched and teetered in the air.

Another crack. Another shriek.

Then, with a gurgling sigh and a glance of apology at Lily, the bat plunged into another nosedive.

As he plummeted toward her, Lily had no choice but to strike. She swung the light saber, sparks sizzled in the air, and the smell of burnt fur stung Lily's nose. Then the bat flipped over backward, slammed onto the ledge, and slid across the ground until he skidded to a halt against the rock pile.

In a flood of emotion Lily threw down the saber and knelt beside the creature. His chest heaved as he struggled to breath. A wound, Lily's own handiwork, raked across his torso.

"I'm so sorry," Lily whispered, stroking his fur with shaky hands as tears welled in her eyes. The bat croaked in response and opened his eyes. Lily expected anger in his gaze, or accusation, but she saw only sorrow.

What have I done?

"Got you now, slime!"

The dweller snagged her fingers in Lily's hair and yanked her backward. Lily cried out, kicked, and thrashed, but the dweller grabbed hold of her collar and dragged Lily across the ledge. "No!" Lily cried. "Let go!"

Philippe bounded out from his hiding place and sailed through the air to kick Lily's assailant, but she shoved him off. Flint also appeared, and scurried up the dweller's sleeve, but she swatted him away like a mosquito. She hauled Lily to the very edge of the cliff. Below, a horde of minions waited with hunger in their eyes.

"Supper's on, boys!"

A shout echoed through the cavern as dozens of slavering jaws awaited their prize. Lily flailed and struggled, but to no avail. With a last shriek of laughter, the dweller flung Lily over the cliff.

CHAPTER 18

The Broken Memory

For an instant Lily hovered above a scene reminiscent of *Gulliver's Travels* or *Alice in Wonderland*. Everything below appeared tiny, almost quaint. The figures of Magnus and Rowan looked like dolls discarded on a child's floor. The central bonfire reminded her of a candle flame, and the guards swarmed below like an army of ants. For a wild moment Lily thought she was dreaming, and that she'd concocted the entire crazy story of fallen kings and dwellers in her mind. In a moment, she thought, she'd awaken. Perhaps she'd hear her mother softly humming as she prepared breakfast. Perhaps she'd rub her eyes to see sunlight streaming in a golden veil through a window in Isla's cottage, or even glimpse the valley below Castle Iridyll soaking in the morning warmth.

But then, gravity seized her in its iron grip. Lily clawed the air, and her heart sank with dread. She screamed as she plummeted toward the courtyard below.

A grimy pair of hands caught her leg and arrested her fall. At first Lily felt relieved, but when she smelled the sour stench of the one who held her, her brief reassurance turned to panic. She hung upside down, her cardigan dangling around her face, while a pair of beady eyes, blank and pitiless as those of a spider, glared at her.

"Look wot I've got, lads!" her captor cried out. He clutched Lily's leg with both hands and clung to the side of the cliff with his feet, as if minuscule barbs on his soles anchored him to the rock. With a chortle he walked down the cliff and shouldered the other guards out of his path. "Out the way!" he shouted. "I've got her, she's mine! Make way, will ye?" When he reached the bottom, dwellers congregated around him, ogling and poking at Lily as if she were a prized turkey towed home from the hunt.

The dweller stomped through the courtyard and paused before Magnus's throne. He bowed clumsily, then chucked Lily to the ground at Magnus's feet, as a cat might present a dead mouse to its owner. Magnus laughed through his nostrils and slunk from his throne. "You are brave, little louse," he said to Lily. "Stupid, of course. Exceedingly stupid. But braver than I expected."

Pax, please help. Lily gaped at Magnus in horror and ground her teeth to keep them from chattering. His muddy eyes reminded her of the pools of muck in the Wilderness that housed vile, crawling things. *How can I get out of this? Maybe I should do what he wants. Maybe, if I don't fight, he'll let me go.*

From the corner of her eye, she glimpsed Rowan still crumpled on the ground beside her. She thought of the abused bat bleeding on the ledge, and of Tobias stripped even of his name. Magnus had orchestrated all this cruelty. And he'd lied about the Blight.

In that moment images of Pax flashed through her mind. She saw his graceful form shudder and be still as shrouds encircled him. She saw him step triumphantly from the tomb, wreathed in pale fire.

Lily's anger broke through her fear. On wobbly limbs she tottered to a stand and clenched her hands into fists. "You can't win," she said, staring at Magnus the way she'd glared at Adam when he'd bullied the boy in the schoolyard. "Let us go, and we won't harm you."

Magnus's eyes widened, contorting his face into something wild and malignant. "You've crossed the line from bravery to imbecility. Harm *me*? I assure you, impudent louse, there's no risk of that!" He nodded to the guard who'd captured her, and Lily collapsed beneath a blow from the dweller's fist. The world blackened momentarily, and when it finally brightened, darts of color danced and swam before her eyes.

"The real question, my pretty little beetle," Magnus continued, "is whether or not I'll let you keep your life. And that depends entirely on you. You have something of value to me, something of a magic I've not seen in a thousand years. Something that rivals even the Woven Ice in its power."

Lily fought to stand but the world spun. Magnus squatted beside her and leaned forward to whisper in her ear. "I know what you have in your pocket, little girl. And if you wish to live, you'll give to me."

"You can't take it from me," Lily said in a raspy voice. "The stone won't let you."

Magnus growled. "You've been talking to that flimflam Merlin, haven't you? Well, if I can't take it from you, perhaps a little *persuasion* might move you to give it freely." He held Rowan's most treasured memory bauble between two of his fingers. "Give me that stone in your pocket, or your pathetic little prince loses his mother forever."

Lily glanced at Rowan, who now sat upright, his breathing rapid as he pleaded with her through his eyes. At the sight of their exchange Magnus flashed a sinister grin. He drew within inches of Lily's face, until she could see the green slime clinging to his teeth. "I will give you to the count of three, louse," he said. "One."

With a groan Lily hauled herself to her feet. *Pax, please, be with me.*

"Two."

She slipped her hand into her pocket and wrapped her fingers around the soothstone.

"Three!"

Lily withdrew the soothstone. For a moment Magnus's satisfied grin widened, but as Lily stared back at him in defiance his smile contorted into a grimace.

"Drop it," Lily said. "Give it back to him."

A low growl rumbled in Magnus's throat. "Suit yourself," he hissed. "Prince, say farewell to your precious mother!"

Rowan shouted in protest, but it was too late. The sphere twirled through the air, its glittery innards flashing like gold at the bottom of a creek bed. Then it struck the ground and shattered into hundreds of pieces. Rowan cried out in anguish with his arms outstretched as the shimmery ribbon of his memory unfurled into the air.

Flash.

Rowan and Magnus both jumped back, and the guards grunted in alarm as a familiar blue-white light enveloped the room. Lily stepped toward the shards of the ruined memory bauble. She closed her eyes and fixed her mind on Pax, his light splitting the tomb, his love healing the Realm. Through the sheen of that memory, she imagined the bauble reassembling, all the jagged pieces and splinters of glass coalescing and melding back together to house the images Rowan couldn't bear to lose.

When Lily opened her eyes, the bauble hovered in the air before her fully intact, the memory again safely pirouetting within its glass chamber. At the sight Rowan sprang forward and caught the memory bauble in his hand. Tears misted his eyes, and he flashed Lily a grateful smile.

Magnus howled with rage. Guards stumbled forward to apprehend Rowan, but the crazed king shoved them out of the way, lashing out with his lanky arms at anything that crossed his path. He pounced upon the young prince like a hyena upon a carcass, withdrew a rusted dagger, and held it to Rowan's throat. As he pivoted around to face Lily, his eyes burned with hatred.

"Let me persuade you with less subtlety!" he shouted. "Your curio can mend a glass ball. But let me ask you, how does it perform in the face of death? Can you put a life back together, once it's drained away? Can you close up a wound with that pretty little gem of yours?" He pressed the point of the blade against Rowan's throat, and Rowan sucked air through his teeth at the sting.

Color drained from Lily's face. She remembered Jaggers Scallywag, and the deathly pallor that washed over his face when she failed to save him from the Blight. Only Pax had the power to heal him. In the face of death, Lily's soothstone was nothing more than a party favor. Suddenly Lily felt small and helpless again, less like a dream keeper than like the shrimpy kid who always said the wrong thing in class.

"Please," Lily said, her voice shaking. "Please, let him go."

Magnus stood with one hand holding the blade, and the other wrapped around Rowan's shoulders. He opened the palm of his restraining hand while still anchoring Rowan with his forearm. "Give it to me, and perhaps I will."

"Only if you let him go first."

"Do not toy with me, louse! Give me the stone, or the boy dies!"

Lily struggled not to cry.

"Let's try this again!" Magnus said. "His life, for your stone. I'll count to three. One."

What do I do? What do I do? She opened her palm and stared at the soothstone, but no images bubbled to the surface, and she couldn't piece her fragmented thoughts into something whole. The stone remained as dark and dormant as her hopes.

"Two!"

Help. Oh Pax, please, please, help.

"Three!"

The groan of a horn echoed throughout the cavern. Magnus started in alarm, and his eyes boggled as he searched the walls of the court.

Dozens of lights suddenly flared in the tunnels and halls surrounding the cave. The horn blew again, and Lily followed its sound, then gasped.

Tobias stood atop the cliff with a red cloak draped over his back. He held a torch in one hand and a ramshackle horn of twisted metal in the other. Dozens of his compatriots appeared from within the shadows, their torches held high and their chains broken.

CHAPTER 19

The Uprising

Tobias blasted his horn again, and the torch lights in the cavern tripled as an entire army of rats of all ages and sizes congregated on the cliffs. Their shiny black eyes glinted wildly in the firelight as they raised shovels, pickaxes, and blacksmith mallets above their heads.

"My brothers and sisters!" Tobias bellowed like a general on the battlefield. "For too long, we have slaved away in soot and fire. For too long, we have shoveled filth for those who would call us brutes. We have forgotten who we are. We have surrendered our claim even to our own names!"

An outraged cry rippled through the crowd.

"My brethren, no longer will we bow to the sting of the whip! Tonight, we reclaim what we have lost! Tonight, we cast off our bonds and remember who we are: a people loved by the one prince, the *true* prince, the ruler of the Realm who saved us all!"

More shouts. Some rapped their weapons against the ground.

"I, Tobias the Valiant, Commander of the Army in the Rock and servant of Prince Pax, beseech you: remember your names!"

"I am Lionel the Strong!" a voice rang out.

"Penelope the Fair!" called another.

"Myra the Gentle!"

"Cyril the Clever!"

A chorus of names unspoken for decades reverberated through the cavern. As the volume rose, Magnus shoved Rowan aside, cowered behind his throne, and frantically rifled through the trinkets around his neck. "No! You are brutes!" he screamed, the veins along his temples bulging as he fumbled with the crystals and medallions in search of something to save himself. "You are all brutes!"

The echoes of reclaimed names drowned out Magnus's voice. "Brethren! Sisters! Daughters and sons!" Tobias cried. "Out of love for your family, in honor of your ancestors, and in reverence of Pax: take back your home! Remember who it was that stole your names! Remember the Prince of Light, who won them back for you! Now is the hour! Fight with me!" Tobias pointed his torch at Magnus, and his whiskers quivered with anticipation. He drew a deep breath. Then, with a thousand emotions storming across his face, he shouted the order: "Charge!"

Tobias's soldiers swept over the cliffs, determination gleaming in their eyes as they shouted the names of those who lost their lives to Magnus's cruelty long ago. Their voices joined together into a single battle cry, a cry for freedom, a cry of hope after so many long years toiling in mire.

The onslaught pitched the dwellers into chaos. Some fled into the tunnels to escape. Others brandished clubs and swords, but in their panic they tangled together and smacked heads with each other.

Magnus rummaged through his jewelry in a frenzy. He muttered words over a green gem, then dropped it when it turned some of his nearby troops into frogs. He kissed a silver medallion, but in response it blew a hole in the ceiling above him. Magnus vaulted from behind his throne just as a shower of rocks crashed down and split the royal seat in two.

When Magnus stood up, a ring of rats encircled him. A single shaft of gray light—the first inkling of daylight to penetrate that subterranean world in centuries—pierced through the rent in the ceiling and illuminated the resolve in their eyes. Magnus backed away with his fists in the air, his own eyes glassy and bulging. "I command you to stand down!" he shouted. "Have you forgotten all I've done for you? If it were not for me, none of you would be alive! I saved you from the Deadening!"

The ring of soldiers surrounding Magnus parted, and a hush fell over the crowd. Tobias marched forward, his eyes piercing, his head held high. As he approached, two rat sentries bound Magnus's arms.

"Let go of me! I am your king!" Magnus hissed through clenched teeth.

Tobias stopped and scowled at Magnus. His whiskers twitched. "You are a king of lies!" he said. "We bow to you no longer."

"I gave you a home!"

"You stole our home, and our names, and everything that is good!"

"I saved you! I saved you and all your putrid little filth from the Deadening! You owe your lives to me!"

Tobias's expression darkened. He passed his torch to a nearby soldier and wrapped his paw around the bouquet of trinkets hanging from Magnus's neck. "You did *not* save us from the Deadening. The one who did is far greater than you and is more noble than you'll ever be. *He* is our king!" Tobias yanked, and the tinkling of metal and glass against stone echoed throughout the cavern as Magnus's chains wrenched apart. Tobias tossed the lot to the ground, then crunched stray bits of glass under his feet. Stones, metal, and crystal fragments scattered throughout the courtyard, rolled into crevices in the rock, and disappeared.

Afterward, Tobias turned his back to Magnus and signaled to his troops with a wave of his forelimb. The soldiers dragged Magnus across the courtyard and hauled him, bound, up one of the cliffs. At the sight of their monarch in binds, a few straggling dwellers looked to each other in befuddlement, then dashed for their lives into the caves.

"Don't run, you nitwits! Fight!" Magnus shrieked at his fleeing minions. "If you value your lives, do something! These vermin are going to kill me!"

Tobias halted, then strode back toward Magnus with his snout wrinkled into a frown. "We are not like you, false king!" he said. "We will not kill you. We will only return you to the place from which you came."

Magnus's eyes boggled with horror. "Not the Veil! I can't survive in the Veil, no one can! It will drive me insane!"

Tobias didn't flinch. "You have not only survived but ravaged and conquered in dark places for centuries. Survival is in your blood. You'll find a way." He nodded to his soldiers, who carried Magnus kicking and screaming from the courtyard. Then Tobias approached Lily. He offered her a gentle smile and softly placed a paw on her shoulder. "Thank you, my friend," he said. "In sharing the truth, you set us free." His expression turned grave. "You must flee now," he said. "This court is steeped in anguished memories and has no place in our restored home. We mean to destroy it."

Lily's eyes widened. "Destroy it?"

"You will be our honored guest once we've rebuilt our halls and again adorned them with the crafts of our kind. But for now, flee. Follow the westward tunnels, and don't stop until you reach the surface." He pointed to an entrance on the far wall gaping like an open mouth. Then he touched Lily's face. "Go, my friend. Go and see the sun again!" Then he turned, and his cloak whipped behind him as he rushed away. He ascended a cliff, and the army and their prisoners followed behind him.

Lily watched Tobias go, and her mind turned in wonder until Rowan placed a hand on her shoulder. "We have to get out of here, Lily. Now."

Lily nodded, and raced with him toward the tunnel to which Tobias had pointed them. Just as they reached the entrance, however, Lily skidded to a stop. *Philippe. Flint!* She turned and glimpsed her friends stranded high on a cliff, jumping up and down and waving at her frantically. "Wait! We have to get the others!"

"Lily, there's no time!"

Suddenly a pair of angry green eyes appeared behind Rowan. Lily screamed for Rowan to duck as a dweller lurking in the darkness of the tunnel swung a mace at Rowan's head. Rowan rolled out of the way, and the dweller roared in dismay as the mace struck the rock wall. The blow cracked the stone archway, and a pile of rubble thundered down and sealed off their escape route.

Rowan emerged coughing and covered in dust just as the cry of Tobias's horn again pealed through the cavern. A group of rats had gathered on a cliff, crouched around something stout and black . . . a cauldron. A red gleam burned at its center.

"We need to find another way out!" cried Rowan.

"What is that up there?"

"Iron. It's melted iron."

The blood drained from Lily's face. "What? What are they doing with—"

"He already told you, they're destroying this place. We have to go! Now!"

"But we can't leave Philippe and Flint!"

"I said there's no time, Lily! Do you want to die down here? Come on!"

Just then, a group of rats huddled around the cauldron. They crouched low to the ground, then grunted as they heaved the rim of the massive pot.

"No! Not yet!" Lily shouted, waving her arms. "Tobias, stop! We're not out yet! Stop!"

But it was too late. With a final groan the rats tipped the cauldron over. A stream of blazing hot metal gushed out and ran down the cliff like a fiery waterfall, and as it struck the cave floor, steam sizzled up from the rocks and clouded the air. Then the horn blew again, and in unison three more cauldrons emptied their contents down adjacent cliff faces. The few lingering dwellers in the courtyard howled and ran, their grungy hair whipping behind them and their weapons discarded on the ground as they fled.

"Lily, use your stone!" Rowan shouted. "We have to get out of here!"

Lily didn't answer. She couldn't answer. She couldn't even hear Rowan or see him out of the corner of her eye.

"Lily! What's wrong with you?"

Lily's heart raced in her chest. *This is impossible!* she thought, aghast. Rowan continued to shout her name and wave for her to follow him, but she didn't notice him. All she saw, with his hair bristling and his green teeth bared, was Glower as he materialized in front of her.

"You never did finish my story, dream keeper," Glower growled. "Shall we end it here? You know you can't escape. You know you're not *really* who they say you are."

"No," Lily muttered, barely audibly. "You're not real. You can't be real! I destroyed you! I watched you burn up!"

"And yet, here I am. What does that say about your powers, dream keeper? You may have fooled your fancy elf friends, but you don't fool *me*. You know what I say is true. You're a fraud!"

Lily shook her head, and her throat tightened. "No. It's not true. You're lying!"

"Oh, am I? Prove it! Go ahead, try making something with that stone in your pocket. See how easy it is now."

A flash of light enveloped the cave. At first Lily thought it was the soothstone, but then thunder rumbled, followed by the groan of shifting rock and an electric, burnt smell. In the next instant, an enormous fulgurite stretched toward the ceiling like a twisted tree.

Rowan yanked at Lily's arm. "What's wrong with you? We need to climb! Now!"

She pointed to the monster glaring at her. "Don't you see—"

"*Now*, Lily!"

The rats cheered from their stations on the cliffs as a wave of iron consumed the remains of Magnus's throne. Steam billowed up and stung Lily's eyes, hiding Glower from view. When the vapor cleared, the monster had vanished, and in his place a flood of liquid metal rushed toward her.

Rowan climbed up the fulgurite as if it were the trunk of a massive, ancient oak. He called for Lily to follow, but she slipped and slid to the foot of the structure. As the torrent of gleaming hot iron rippled toward her, each breath felt like scorching fire in her throat and tasted of metal. She cried out for help, but in the oppressive heat her voice thinned to a rasp.

A hand clutched her wrist. Clumsily Lily gained a foothold and stumbled up the trunk of the fulgurite as Rowan, his brow furrowed in concentration and his hair matted, led her steadily up the slope. When the fulgurite branched, Rowan carefully guided her onto a limb, and Lily braced herself against the trunk of the glass tree and dared to glance down. The entire floor of the courtyard seethed with steaming, molten metal. They perched in a tree with roots that seemed to tunnel to the world's fiery core.

"Please," Rowan said, his voice barely above a whisper. "Please get us out of here!" He motioned to the hole in the ceiling, where mist from the Veil curled into the room in smoky tendrils.

With shaking hands Lily withdrew the soothstone from her pocket, closed her eyes, and prayed she could find a way out. She prayed Glower's words were only a lie, and that in a moment her mind would sparkle with pictures and ideas as it had when she combated the dwellers on the cliff. Her grip tightened around the stone as she strained to concentrate.

Her mind was a complete blank.

"Lily, please! Hurry up!"

She choked back tears. She searched for that flicker of delight that a new creation always sparked in her, but the images in her head were amorphous, drifting like shapeless jellyfish in a vast, empty sea. Glower's words echoed in her mind like a curse: *Try making something with that stone in your pocket. You're not really who they say you are.*

She slumped against the glass and met Rowan's eyes. "I can't do it. I'm so sorry, Rowan, I can't do it."

The tree lurched. Rowan nearly lost his footing, and Lily wrapped both arms around the branch to guard herself against a fall.

"You *have* to do it, Lily! The heat is softening the glass, and it's all going to come crashing down. You have to get us out of here!"

Another lurch, and the tree groaned into a lean. Lily's heart pounded.

"Just call something! Anything!" Rowan shouted. "Look, I was wrong. You *are* an artisan! You *do* belong here! I saw what you did up on that cliff, and I know you can do it again! You can save us, Lily!"

"I can't! My mind is blank!"

"Then call something! You have to—"

Screech.

The fulgurite listed forward. Rowan slipped, and Lily screamed as he slid down the limb. A sharp tine of glass caught his cloak, and he dangled in the air like a rag on a hook.

Lily cried out his name and inched down the limb after him, but a ripping sound told her she was too late. His cloak tore. In the next instant, Prince Rowan, heir of the Mist Elves, plummeted through the air toward a sea of molten metal.

No. This can't be happening! This can't be happening! Glower's words reverberated in Lily's mind, and each syllable pulverized her hopes like the pounding of a mallet. *There's no use. I can't save anyone. There's no hope.*

There is always hope.

The words came to her like a match strike through the darkness. Her mom had reassured her with them. Then Cedric had spoken them when they first glimpsed Castle Iridyll shimmering over a dying landscape. The tenth spire had shone like a jewel, a beacon of hope above the Blight-sickened valleys and streams . . . a light in the darkness, pointing to another light, a greater light . . .

"Pax!" Lily cried, her voice suddenly finding strength. "Prince Pax of the Realm! Help us!'

Suddenly the soothstone blazed. Aurora, one of the swans who had saved Lily and her friends when the Flying Emerald fell from the sky, appeared and parted the steam with each beat of her wings. At the sight of her, tears gathered in the corners of Lily's eyes.

The swan trumpeted, then circled about. A quick turn, a flash of prismatic feathers, and the swan dove and glided just a foot from the scorching floor of the courtyard. Rowan landed on her back and clung to her feathers, and the swan's wings churned up steam as she banked upward.

A crack and the sound of splintering glass split the air. Like a mighty sequoia surrendering to an axe blow the fulgurite groaned, leaned, and pitched into a harrowing plunge toward the ground. Rowan shouted Lily's name. In the distance, Lily could hear Tobias cry out in alarm, and even Philippe's high-pitched protest from the cliff rose above the din of crackling glass.

It's over, Lily thought. The wind hissed in her ears.

Rowan cried out again.

Please. Please help me, Pax.

"Save her!" Philippe called.

The molten metal covering the floor of the cavern still sizzled, and as she fell, its heat stung her face. She shut her eyes. Memories broke through the blankness of her mind like fresh shoots through soil, and Lily saw her parents, hiking through the woods and then curled on a couch reading her stories. She saw Adam and Keisha. Cedric. And she saw Pax, his eyes windows to infinity, his light renewing the fields and valleys. *This is the end,* Lily thought.

Suddenly something jerked Lily's collar and broke her grip on the glass limb. Whatever had snatched Lily lifted her into the air, and the fulgurite fell away below her. It crashed to the ground and fragments of glass flew into the air, catching the light from the glowing metal and appearing like thousands of tiny embers. Lily glanced up. She hung from Aurora's beak like a kitten dangling from its mother's jaws.

Lily squinted into the shaft of daylight that cut through the gloom as Aurora veered toward the rent in the ceiling. Hope stirred within her, until she remembered the high, urgent voice that had called out to her as the fulgurite collapsed.

"Wait!" Lily called to Aurora. "We can't leave yet!"

"Are you mad?" Rowan yelled from astride the swan.

Lily ignored him. She pointed to the cliff. "We have to pick up Philippe and Flint first. We can't leave them here!"

Aurora changed course. As they circled the courtyard, Lily could see Philippe bouncing at the cliff's edge, waving his flaming carrot in the air and begging Lily not to abandon him. Flint revolved around and around Philippe's feet like a whirling dervish. They both retreated from the edge of the cliff as Aurora approached, and a few stray marshmallows blew away beneath the strident beats of the swan's majestic wings.

Aurora landed on the ledge, released Lily from her beak, and bowed her graceful neck in invitation for all to climb aboard. Philippe and Flint needed no urging to scamper up. Lily ran to follow them, but the movement of something hulking and gray just askance of her vision stopped her. She turned, and her heart sank at the sight of the old, decrepit, and abused bat whom she'd wounded. He lay on the ground in a heap, his right wing twisted and broken, his dark eyes glazed and staring at her imploringly. He tried to call to her, but the only sound he managed was a gurgling squeak in his throat.

Lily ran to his side, dropped to one knee, and placed a hand on his back. The poor wretch shuddered at her touch.

"Lily, what are you doing?" Rowan shouted. "Come on! Now is our chance!"

Lily glanced over her shoulder, and locked eyes with Aurora. "We need to take him too," she said.

Rowan's jaw dropped. "You really are mad, aren't you?"

Lily crouched and wrapped her arms around the bat's neck to lift him, but he was too heavy. She grunted, laid him back down, and tried to ignore how the creature winced with each movement. "Please, help me lift him!" Lily cried. "We need to bring him too!"

"You can't be serious," Rowan said.

"Mademoiselle, he tried to kill us!" Philippe added, equally incredulous.

Lily scowled at them both. "He didn't try to kill us! The dweller who was *whipping* him did. He didn't deserve his wounds any more than you did, Rowan!"

Rowan gritted his teeth but said nothing. Lily motioned for Aurora's help, and dutifully the swan leaned forward to grasp the bat by the scruff of the neck. As gently as she would have with her own cygnets, Aurora nestled the bat into the plumage between her wings, then arched her neck for Lily to follow.

Once all sat astride Aurora, they soared into the air. The pool of iron had started to cool below them, its edges darkening to the color of pewter. As they sailed toward the opening in the ceiling, Tobias raised a single paw in gratitude. Lily waved in reply, drew a deep breath, and said a prayer of thanks.

As they escaped the shadowy caverns, the outraged cry of Magnus, the fallen, twisted king of the Icelein, chased them into the cloying murk of the Veil.

CHAPTER 20

The Painted Woodland

They broke through the Veil to find the sun hanging low on the horizon like a bronze coin, the sky over the Shadow and Desolation Mountains washed in the coral hues of sunset. Lily drew fresh air into her lungs, sweet and cool after so many hours—or was it days?—within the grime of the caverns and the suffocating fog of the Veil. The breath felt like a blossom opening in her chest. She savored the breeze against her face, and her heart thrilled as forests and meadows rolled beneath them in colors even richer and more vibrant than she'd remembered.

Every so often she thought she could glimpse the crystal spires of Castle Iridyll, but then the moment would pass, the light would flicker away, and she would again scan the horizon with yearning. As time passed and the sun ducked below the mountains, uneasy thoughts troubled her. She wondered how Magnus had survived all those years underground, and what had so corrupted him. She struggled with disbelief that Glower had returned to haunt her after she'd so soundly defeated him in the Caverns of Unfinished Dreams. Most of all, she worried about the sudden blandness of her imagination. Why had her powers failed her again? Why did this keep happening? She shivered as she remembered Glower's words: *Try making something with that stone in your pocket. You're not really who they say you are.*

But I am an artisan. I am. She wrung her hands, as if she could mold the word *artisan* between her fingers and make it her own. Before Cedric had whisked her into the Realm, her life limped forward in a jumble of missteps. Every day she'd miss the bus, daydream through class, flush with embarrassment as kids laughed at her, and then stumble into the house with her book clasped to her chest like a life preserver. In her own world, she was a bumbler. She was a dreamer who could never manage to make life work.

But here? In the Realm, she was an *artisan*. She had a purpose. She mattered. How could she let that gift slip away?

I won't let it, she thought with determination, closing her hands into fists. *I've just been scared and distracted, that's all. I need to get back to someplace safe and beautiful. Someplace where my mind can wander and I can feel inspired. Someplace like . . .*

Philippe's snoring interrupted her thoughts. He and Flint huddled together beside her, snuggled into the down of Aurora's back and snoozing as they sailed through the sky. The bat also slept, but he moaned and shuddered as if a nightmare troubled him. Lily stroked the wiry fur on his forehead, and he seemed to quiet at her touch. Then her fingers wandered to a chain around his neck, and she traced the links to a pendant of rough, yellow stone. *I wonder what this is for?*

"I still don't know why you brought him."

Lily glanced up at Rowan. For an hour he'd sat half-buried in a tuft of Aurora's feathers, brooding and turning his memory bauble in his fingers. He'd not spoken since their escape. Lily wanted to sidle up beside him and place a reassuring hand on his shoulder, but Philippe leaned against her like a sack of potatoes and drooled into the crook of her elbow. She grimaced, then studied Rowan warily. "Are you okay?" she finally asked.

He glanced up, and his eyes brewed a storm of emotions. "I'm sorry for everything I dragged you into."

"It's all right," Lily said with a shrug.

"No, it's not. I've been an idiot."

"I wouldn't say an *idiot*."

"A fool then."

"Maybe. But if I had to pick one thing, I'd say you've been a big snob."

"A what?"

"A snob."

He screwed up his face. "The gunk inside your nose?"

"No, not snot! *Snob.* You've acted like you're better than everyone else."

"Oh." He screwed up his mouth, then shrugged. "Fair enough."

"Look, don't worry about it. I could tell you about loads of things I've messed up. See this scar?" She lifted her hand and pointed to a pale knot of flesh. "I got that trying to make flying shoes."

He raised an eyebrow. "Did it work?"

"Not even close."

A hint of a smile graced his face, but just as quickly it flew away. "Thank you for helping me. And for saving this." He raised the memory bauble. "I'm sorry about everything. I wanted so much to bring our kingdom back, but I was stupid and selfish to drag you into it."

"It's all right. I'm just glad you're okay."

He didn't answer.

"*Are* you okay?"

"Not really. I don't know what's real anymore. All my life I've believed my mother's stories about Esperion, that he was the hope of our people. Because I look like him, I thought maybe I could be great, too. But now I see all that was a lie."

"Rowan, you don't know that!"

"If what Magnus claims is true, Esperion and Eldinor abandoned all those people to die in the Veil. He wasn't the hope of our people at all, Lily. He was a traitor!"

"Again, you don't know that. I've never met your mom, but based on what I've seen, I trust her more than Magnus. How can you be sure he told you the truth about all this?"

Rowan scanned the mountains as if searching for help. "I don't know what to think anymore. All I know is that my hope for a kingdom of our own is gone." He tucked his memory bauble back into his cloak, a motion that reminded Lily of Adam when he would wrap his arms around his knees. Rowan's proud exterior had melted away. When Lily looked at him, her heart aching, she no longer saw an arrogant prince, but rather a lost little kid searching for home.

Lily searched for the right words to say. What would Cedric have whispered into her ear? What would Keisha do? Suddenly, a delicious idea resurfaced. The longer she pondered, the more irresistible it grew. "Maybe there's still a way," she said.

"A way to what?"

"To bring your kingdom back."

Rowan furrowed his brow. "If there is, I can't see it."

"What about Enlacia?"

"What *about* Enlacia?"

"I can try to rebuild it for you, Rowan. Maybe . . . maybe I can bring it all back."

Rowan stared at her. "What exactly are you thinking?"

"You've got a library full of memories, right? Show them to me, and I'll try to rebuild everything."

"Didn't you have trouble using the stone back in Magnus's court? How can you be sure it will work?"

Lily's face reddened. "I think if I'm in the right place, someplace beautiful and full of mystery, I'll be able to get it working again."

He eyed her warily. "And you'll try to bring everything back?"

"Yes."

"Even our people?"

Lily remembered Isla's caution: any people Lily re-created would be shells of themselves. She remembered her even sterner warning that, according to Pax, the future of the Mist Elves lay in the Cave of Lights, not in rebuilding broken kingdoms.

Still, the idea wouldn't leave Lily alone. *What harm could there be in trying?* she wondered. "Even your people," she declared with a nod.

Rowan frowned. "Isla said that wouldn't work. She said you can fix the buildings, but you can't bring back the people. It would be like Mistwood, just a bunch of empty halls."

"Isla doesn't know that for certain."

"Doesn't she? She's used a soothstone for ages."

The comment irritated Lily. "But she's not an artisan. She doesn't know *everything*. Please, Rowan, just let me try. I really, really want to do this for you. Let me help you."

Rowan breathed a sigh. "One empty castle is as good as the next, I suppose. Tell your swan to take us to Enlacia."

"Oh, thank you, Rowan, thank you! You won't regret it."

Her outburst jostled Philippe awake. As he stretched his forepaws and yawned, Lily shook away the pins and needles

In her arm and tried not to laugh at Philippe's goofy face. He blinked groggily with droopy lids and smacked his lips a few times.

"Good evening, Philippe," Lily said with a smirk.

"Good evening? Mademoiselle, why did you not wake me? I narrowly missed dinner!" He tugged off his hat, still torn along the outer rim, and frantically rummaged inside.

"Speaking of which," Lily said, "I'm starving. Who knows how long we were stuck down in those caves? It feels like days. I'm so hungry."

"A turnip, mademoiselle?" Philippe pulled a limp purple root from his hat and dangled it by its greens.

"No thanks."

"*Non?* Suit yourself." The rabbit crunched into the turnip, strewing wet nibblets into the air.

"Rowan, how far are we from Enlacia?" Lily asked. "Maybe we can stop somewhere for food."

He scanned the landscape. "We can get there by morning if we fly all night. We need to head northwest, though. Right now, we're going the wrong way."

"We need to fly *all* night?"

"If we want to get there by tomorrow."

Lily tried to hide her disappointment, but her stomach betrayed her with a growl.

Rowan rolled his eyes. "All right. Let's camp down below and look for some food."

Lily signaled to Aurora to descend. Behind them, the Shadow and Desolation mountain ranges retreated like black snakes writhing into brush, and to the south Lily thought she recognized Bald Peak. The dense forest below them, however, sprawled in patterns unrecognizable to her. The foliage quivered and shifted, like bands of sunlight reflected within a pool of water. Colors, not only green but gold, red, and the faintest blue, swirled and flickered like fish darting beneath the surface of a pond.

"What's that place down there?" Lily asked.

"We're over the Painted Woodland. We should find some food there."

Aurora glided beneath the stray stars that had just blinked into view and down through a canopy of wispy clouds. As they descended below the treetops, the fiery light of sunset disappeared and shadows crowded around them. Lily buried her hands into Aurora's feathers and held on as tree branches snapped against the swan's wings. Leaves and the torn tendrils of vines flew into Lily's face. She spat out a few pine needles, then hid her face as Aurora crashed through the trees, banked upward, then finally settled on the ground.

Lily had expected to see the shadows and haunting shapes of a darkened wood. Instead, the Woodland teemed with color, light, and movement. Aurora had landed not within a dense forest steeped in night, but on a sunlit path winding through trees unlike any Lily had ever seen. Noonday sunlight dappled the path, even though Lily had so intently watched the sun sink into the distance and spill its fading colors across the horizon.

Aurora lowered a wing, and Lily slid to the ground and turned in place with her eyes wide and her mouth agape. At first she thought the trees lining the path were birches sheathed in white, papery bark, but on closer inspection they seemed to shimmer. Streaks of blue and mauve dashed across the trunks, and leaves of gold, crimson, and deepest green shivered on the branches. What was this strange place? And how could daylight shine within a forest while the rest of the Realm slept?

Lily glanced upward to orient herself. Instead of a blue, sunlit sky, or even a firmament of twinkling stars, she saw a swirling palette of brush strokes. Blue and yellow strands curved across the sky like a horse's tail, and halos radiated from the stars like ripples on a lake. To the west a crescent moon stood vigil over the churning color, but it, too, seemed to lurk underwater, and to cast out wavelets of light across the sky. The sight was strange and breathtaking, and somehow . . . vaguely familiar. Lily studied the sky and searched her memories. *I know I've seen this somewhere. Somewhere in a book . . .*

"*The Starry Night!*" Lily covered her mouth in disbelief and pointed to the sky. "I know this! This is a painting!"

Rowan slid from Aurora's back and joined her with his hands folded across his chest. "Of course, it's a painting."

"No, I'm serious, I *know* this one! It was in a book my mom gave me about famous paintings. The guy's name was Van—Van something."

"Van something? I thought Vincent painted it. You can still see his signature above the treetops."

Lily could barely catch her breath. "How is this possible? How can *The Starry Night* actually be in the sky?"

Rowan smirked. "What did you expect in the Painted Woodland?"

"The Painted—." She glanced around, and thought she might faint. "You mean the Woodland is made from *actual paintings*? As in, the stuff people paint is *real* here?"

"Surely you've seen more impressive things in the Realm than this."

"I've seen dreams come to life, sure, but these are *real* paintings!"

"Why are you so surprised? A painting can be like a dream if it's a *true* painting."

Lily's eyes welled with tears. "It's so beautiful," she said, awestruck.

"It's also a good place to find food if you know where to look," he said, turning toward the path. "Come on."

At the mention of food, Philippe predictably rolled off Aurora's back and scampered after him, and Flint followed as well, grabbing twigs from the ground as he walked. As they strode down the path, trees waved on either side of the companions like fronds of seaweed drifting in a quiet ocean. Lily, still awash in wonder, followed in a dreamlike state until Aurora's trumpeting stopped her. She turned around, and the swan motioned to something dark and limp that still flopped on her back.

"Oh, of course," Lily said. "The bat." She returned to Aurora and found the creature crumpled in a heap among her feathers. Lily wrapped her arms around his torso to lift him, but at her touch the bat groaned, and his dark, glassy eyes shot open in alarm. Lily whispered an apology, then crouched down in another attempt to lift him. When the bat screeched in pain, however, Lily stood up in defeat, her arms limp at her side and perspiration dotting her hairline.

"I need help!" Lily called to Rowan. "Can you please help me get him down?"

Rowan didn't answer. He stared at her with his arms folded across his chest and with a familiar look of disinterest lengthening his face. *Oh no, not this version of Rowan again,* she thought. She looked to Philippe and Flint, but neither of them moved. Philippe nonchalantly munched the fringe of a lettuce leaf.

"Come on, you guys! We can't just leave him."

"Why did you even bring him?" Rowan asked. "He tried to kill you."

Aurora clacked her beak, grasped the bat by the scruff of the neck, and gingerly lifted him onto the ground. Lily thanked Aurora, then slid down, knelt beside the bat, and stroked his fur to soothe him.

Rowan shook his head. "Personally, I've wasted enough time on creatures intent upon killing me. I'm going to get us some food." He turned away, leaving Lily red-faced and scowling.

"I thought you had more respect for creatures of the Realm than that!" she shouted, remembering how staunchly he'd defended the unfinished dream who'd frightened her. Rowan ignored her and continued down the path.

"Deep wounds."

Lily's eyes widened. The bat still lay flaccid and panting on the ground, but he'd turned his glazed eyes toward her.

"Did you say something?" Lily asked.

"Wounds," the bat choked out. "Deep."

The words twisted Lily's heart. "I know. I'm so sorry. I didn't want to hurt you."

The bat coughed several times. "Not mine. His."

"Whose?"

His gaze shifted toward the path down which Rowan had disappeared. Lily stared at the bat in disbelief. *He means Rowan's wounds.*

"Water," the bat whispered. "Please."

"Yes. Yes, of course you need water." Lily stood up and turned in a circle. The stones along the path were dry, as was the turf around her. She searched the tree trunks and branches for a drape of damp moss, and in response the trees seemed to incline toward her in curiosity, like a row of spindly women leaning to pinch the cheeks of a little girl. Lily tried not to dwell on their strangeness, and instead strained her ears to listen. Ever so faintly, she heard the croak of a frog followed by a tiny splash.

Bingo. "I'll be right back," she said, gently touching the bat's neck. The creature closed his eyes and nodded.

Lily wove between the trees. After a short walk, the elegant birches parted to form a gateway to a garden swaying with blossoms of lavender, roses, and poppies. Lily jogged through the flowers and followed a stone walkway trimmed with daffodils and yellow lilies. The path led her to a mirror-like pond studded with water lilies, with weeping willows draped along the banks. A teal-colored wooden footbridge that arched over the pond struck Lily as familiar. She mined her memory for the image, trying to recall the pages in the book from her mother, but the splash of a turtle sliding from its sunning perch on a log snapped her back to the present. She'd found water; now she needed to carry it back.

Lily glanced around for something in which to collect it, but found nothing. She withdrew the soothstone, closed her eyes, and tried to focus her mind on some receptacle to help, but as in Magnus's caverns she drew a blank. *What's wrong with me?* she worried. She closed her eyes, focused, and tried again: nothing. *It's because I'm so exhausted. That must be it. It will be better at Enlacia. It has to be.* Lily searched the banks for a garden ornament, or a discarded cup, or *something* to help. She reached into the pond and tugged up a lily pad to use as a makeshift bowl, but when she scooped up water it dribbled back out. With a groan of frustration Lily pulled off her cardigan, doused it in water, and placed it sopping on the lily pad. She hated the idea of giving the bat water that had soaked into her filthy sweater, grimed from the dirt and soot of the caverns, but she didn't know what else to do.

Lily jogged back through the garden and the birch grove. When she arrived on the path, she found Aurora dozing with her head tucked under one wing. Lily rushed to where she'd left the bat crumpled on the ground.

He was nowhere to be found.

CHAPTER 21

Alister

Lily scanned the woods for the bat but saw no trace of him. She dropped the lily pad she'd so painstakingly carried from the garden, and tousled Aurora's tail feathers to wake her. "Aurora, what happened?" Lily asked, as the swan blinked and shook her head. "The bat's gone! Where did he go?"

Aurora cocked her head to one side as if the question confused her, then pointed with her beak down the path. Lily followed the gesture, and gasped.

The bat stood beside a birch tree. His stance was upright, and his eyes were clear and bright. Beside him, with the dappled sunlight dancing off his horn, stood Pax.

Lily burst into tears and raced toward them. Pax laughed, and as Lily threw her arms around the unicorn's neck, she felt herself carried away again to a place where she belonged, to a place where fear was a figment of her imagination.

"You're back!" Lily exclaimed. "Pax, you've come back!"

"I told you, young artisan. I'm always with you."

Lily pulled away to wipe the tears from her eyes. Her face hurt from smiling, and the words flew from her mouth. "I'm so glad to see you! Rowan got us into a heap of trouble, and we almost died!"

"I know."

"It was awful. There are these caverns under the Veil—that's this place where there's fog that doesn't go away—and these awful people captured us. They're related to Rowan's ancestors, but they've turned horrible. Their king wanted the soothstone, and he made all these rats his slaves, and we barely escaped. He tried to destroy Rowan's memory copies, even the one of his mother."

"I know."

Lily caught herself. "Of course, you know," she said, flushing slightly. Then she threw her arms around him again and held on for dear life.

"Thank you for helping me, my lady."

Lily let go of Pax and glanced backward. The bat had spoken in a baritone that Lily would never have expected when she first encountered him screeching and flapping in the caverns, or even when he choked out a few raspy words on the ground. Although scars still raked through his fur, his wounds had healed and his stooping posture had straightened, like a withering stem suddenly uncurling toward the sun. He stood with his wings folded over his breast as if he wore the coat of a military general, and the amber stone around his neck shone like a medal of honor. A clean burgundy cloak now draped over his back.

"I'm so sorry I hurt you," Lily said, suddenly humbled by his stately appearance.

"Do not apologize, young lady. I'm sorry I could not resist my captors and help you. I was a coward."

"You weren't a coward. They were torturing you."

"No longer, thanks to your bravery. And thanks to the prince. He gave me water and now, somehow, I find myself well." The bat gazed reverently at Pax. "My name is Alister, and I am at your service in your quest."

"Oh, thank you, but there's no need. We're going to—" She stopped, and her face reddened. She could feel Pax's eyes boring into her.

"Where are you going, Lily?" Pax asked. The tenor of his voice sent a shiver down her spine. He already knew the answer.

"Mistwood," Lily said, avoiding his eyes. "The Valley of the Mist Elves."

His gaze hardened. "Speak the truth, Lily McKinley."

Lily swallowed. She wanted to crawl underground and hide. "Enlacia."

"Why are you going there?"

"To rebuild it. I'm doing it for Rowan, to help rebuild a kingdom for him."

"The fate of Rowan's kingdom lies in the Cave of Lights, where I sent his sister."

"Yes, yes, I know, but it would be so wonderful to rebuild that fortress in the meantime. I mean, it couldn't hurt, could it? After all, I *am* an artisan, and it's my job to rebuild what's broken in the Realm."

A wind suddenly swept across the path. Lily shivered as the gust buffeted her back, and then died down.

"That is not why I brought you back," Pax said.

Guilt flooded over Lily, and her knees weakened.

"Your powers are a gift, Lily McKinley, but be careful of the space they occupy in your heart. Do not let them lead you into temptation."

"I'm sorry. I just—"

"Wanted to be important?"

Lily nodded.

Pax's demeanor softened, and he nuzzled her cheek. "You already are important, Lily, but not because of a rock in your pocket. You will forever be important because you arose from the mind of our King, and so bear his mark. And you are special because my love also marks you."

Lily couldn't raise her eyes. "I wanted what I did to matter."

"It does matter, my dear. *You* matter. You've already been faithful in the purpose for which I called you."

Lily looked up. "What do you mean?"

"Remember Tobias. What inspired him to lead his people to freedom, after so many long years in slavery?"

"I told him about you, about what you did."

Pax nodded. "As I instructed you to do. Your gifts *are* special, Lily. But my words can accomplish more than the imagination of humankind. Even if that imagination is as vibrant as yours."

Lily wiped away her tears. "I'm sorry, Pax."

"You are forgiven, dear one," he said, nuzzling her again. "Enlacia will rise again, and you *will* help Rowan reclaim his kingdom. But not yet. Everything has its proper time, and right now your path, and his, is toward the Cave of Lights."

"We need to follow Isla?"

Pax nodded. "Whomever you find, tell them about what you've seen and heard. Tell them my words. And take heart, dear one. You will rebuild Enlacia at the right time."

"How will I know when it's the right time?"

"You'll not be tempted to hide the truth from me."

As Lily processed his words, Pax turned to Aurora. "Thank you, madam, for carrying these little ones to safety. I believe Alister can usher them hence; he still has a part to play in this story. Return to your young."

Aurora bowed, shook out her wings, and then soared into *The Starry Night*. Her pearly form mingled with the quivering, round stars before she disappeared into the distance.

"Now I must leave you," Pax said. "But remember my words."

Lily reached out a hand to stop him. "Pax, please wait. Before you go—I think there's something wrong with the soothstone. I can still call things, but it's really hard for me to make new stuff."

"How, dear one?"

"I don't know. It will work for a while, and then all of a sudden . . . my mind just goes blank."

"The answer to that mystery also awaits you in the Cave of Lights."

Lily bit her lip. "Can't you—can't you just fix it now?"

Pax stared at her, and Lily shrank in embarrassment. "Okay, I know. Everything in its proper time."

He turned.

"One more thing! There's—there's this *thing* that's been following me. He's like a shroud, but he keeps coming back. I thought I got rid of him once, but he appeared again as we were fighting Magnus."

"Glower?"

The hair on the back of Lily's neck pricked up. "Yes. Yes, that's him."

"You can't get rid of him, Lily. He arises from your own fears."

Lily's heart sank. *I can't get rid of him? What do I do?*

Pax turned to face her, his eyes somber but kind. "You can keep him at bay though. Remember that I'm still with you, and my words will chase away even the darkest of fears."

At these words Pax nodded to Alister, who in response bowed low to the ground. Then Pax cast Lily a last, knowing glance and walked down the path. After a few paces, his image wavered like a mirage in the desert, and he disappeared.

The moment he vanished, Rowan, Philippe, and Flint sauntered back into view. Rowan carried a catch of fish over his shoulder, while Philippe bounded behind him with his forepaws overloaded with apples. At the sight of Alister, healed and standing upright, Rowan stopped in his tracks. Philippe collided with him, spilling the heap of fruit all over the path.

"What are you doing? All the *petits fruits*, they will be ruined!" Then Philippe froze. "*Sacré bleu!* What has happened, mademoiselle? The bat, he is—"

"We had a visitor." Lily offered a weary smile.

Rowan stared at Lily, then at Alister, and back again. "Was it—?"

Lily nodded. "Looks like you got quite a haul."

Rowan gestured toward Philippe. "He pillaged a Cézanne."

Philippe scrambled to salvage the fallen fruit, and Flint tried to help but only succeeded in roasting an apple he picked up.

"We need all the food we can get," Lily said. "We have a bit of a journey ahead of us tomorrow."

"To Enlacia?"

"No. Not to Enlacia."

"Why? What did the unicorn say?"

Lily drew a breath. "We're going to the Cave of Lights."

CHAPTER 22

The Stolen Dream

After their dinner of fish and apples, the unlikely party wandered through the Painted Woodland in search of a spot where it was night—someplace where the sky and the light at ground level coincided. Despite searching for hours, they found no such place. They meandered over meadows of poppies and fields of haystacks, into shaded woods and beneath more starlit skies, but no matter how brightly the moon and stars burned above them, the turf at their feet was always warm and sunlit, the pools they passed reflecting deep blue skies swathed in clouds like fleece.

They finally settled on a field of sunflowers, their brilliant heads turned away from a panel of blue-green mountains like flames swept in a breeze. Lily nestled down among the flowers, and struggled against the images that stirred her mind to wakefulness, images of dark caverns and green fire, swirling skies and Glower's muddy teeth bared in a grimace. Finally, at long last, she drifted into a fitful sleep.

She awoke to Rowan standing nearby, assembling his belongings into a pack.

"Are you sure about this?" he asked her when she sat up.

Lily picked a few stray leaves from the knit of her grimy cardigan, and hoped—as she'd wrecked it—that Isla didn't want the sweater back. "You mean going to the Cave of Lights? Yes, I'm sure. Pax told me."

"That's not what I mean. I mean are you sure about *him*?" Rowan pointed to Alister, who dabbed his mouth with a leaf after finishing a breakfast of mosquitoes. His eyes teared in the early morning sun, and after a final swallow he ducked beneath the heads of a few sunflowers to escape the glare.

"Yes," Lily whispered. "Pax said he had a part to play."

"How do you know it's not a bad part?"

"Come on, Rowan. It was *Pax*."

"But that bat tried to kill you."

"For the last time Rowan, he didn't! I almost killed him."

"Even more cause for concern. What if he wants revenge?"

"He *doesn't* want revenge. He's grateful we got him out of Magnus's cave."

Rowan raised an eyebrow. "You're sure? You're absolutely sure?"

"The only thing I'm sure of is that Pax told me, and so that's what I need to do. I've messed up enough lately to know that ignoring him is a bad idea."

"All right. But you're riding in front."

Lily rolled her eyes. She shook the leaves and grass blades off her damp sweater, then followed a trail of chewed yellow petals to Philippe. He'd gorged himself on sunflowers until his belly swelled taut like a watermelon, and she found him stuffing blossoms into his top hat until they spewed through the rip in the seam. Still, he crammed in more, pausing only to jam another petal into his already puffy cheeks.

"Ahem!" Lily said with a single eyebrow raised.

Philippe froze, his cheeks still protruding. "Ma-moo-sew," he said, his mouth still filled to the brim. "Mmph ee—"

"Is all this really necessary, Philippe? Alister thinks we should be at the Cave of Lights by nightfall. I don't think you need to hoard food."

Philippe finally swallowed and scowled at her. "*Pardon*, but do they have *un bistro* at this Cave of Lights?"

Lily tried not to snicker. "No."

"Do they have gardens, then? Or an orchard? Perhaps *un café*?"

"Nope."

Philippe folded his forepaws over his chest. "Then mademoiselle, you confirm that these flowers are indeed *very* necessary. Twice now you have led me into nasty caves with not a smidgen, not a *hint* of *la grande cuisine*. Now, you bring me to paradise for one night, only to drag me away to cave number three. Experience tells me that for my stomach these flowers are *absolutement* necessary, mademoiselle!"

"Okay, okay, calm down! It's your hat. You can carry all the flowers you want. Although I think you're losing the battle, Philippe." She pointed to the tear in the brim, through which blossoms protruded as quickly as Philippe stuffed them.

"Do we depart soon, my lady?" Alister emerged from a row of sunflowers, squinting and shielding his face with a single wing.

"Does the light hurt your eyes? I thought that was a myth," Lily said.

"A myth, madam?"

"My friend Adam told me bats aren't really blind."

"What is myth in your world is not always so here. But I am not blind, no, just unaccustomed to the light. I've not seen sunlight in decades. Alas, as in all of life, in one way or another I must adjust."

Lily smiled. Even with his scars and his grizzled fur, Alister reminded her of someone refined, like a host she'd seen wearing a tweed jacket and gripping a pipe as he introduced classic movies on British television.

"Thank you for helping us, Alister. Especially after everything we put you through."

"My lady, it is my honor." He bowed low. "You freed me from captivity. I've not felt the wind against my face for an age, and for that gift alone I thank you."

"What happened to you?"

"The same that happened to Tobias and his people. King Magnus came from above ground and brought terror with him. We were a peaceful people, no match for his brutality." He shuddered. "Most of my people fell long ago, and only a few of us remain."

"I'm so sorry. Who are your people?"

Alister straightened. "I am of the race of Nightwatchers. We are guardians of the Amber Beacons." He motioned with his wing to the yellow stone at his neck.

"I noticed that stone before; it's beautiful. What does it do?"

"The Beacons are a gift to my people, for us to protect. They call light to themselves in dark places, to illuminate a path for the wandering and lost. When Magnus stumbled into our caves, he tried to take them from us, but we are bound to them. He could torture us, but he could never wrench them from us. When we lose our lives, they, too, vanish; when they are torn from us, they disappear, and we with them. Our lives are tied to these stones. When he could not steal them from us, he enslaved us so that we would waste and fade away even as we bore them."

Lily fought tears. "I'm so sorry. What an awful thing to happen to you, to watch your whole family die . . ."

Alister shook his head. "Not my family. My people. I have no family."

"You mean you're orphaned?"

"I mean I don't know. I do not remember ever having a family."

"No one? Not a mother or a father?"

"No."

"Not any sisters or brothers?"

Alister shook his head. "My earliest memory is awakening in the council chamber with the Amber Beacon around my neck. Before then, there is nothing."

"Were you born into slavery?"

Alister cringed. "You have seen Magnus's scepter? The one with a yellow jewel, like mine?"

"Yes, I remember it."

"Its power governs ours. While it glows, he is sovereign over us."

Lily shook her head, and a darkness turned within her. "I hate him. What an awful creature."

"Feel pity, not hate, my lady. Magnus's heart is twisted. His lust for magic consumes him." Alister lifted his chin in the air, and he reminded Lily of one of the queen's guards outside Buckingham Palace. "But it has not consumed us. Some of us remain, and while we do, the Beacons are safe."

Lily smiled. The story seemed familiar somehow, like one of the tales her dad had woven before kissing her forehead and turning out her light some night when she was young.

"Shall we make ready?" Alister asked. "I struggle to read the sky here, but I imagine the day grows long."

Lily called for the others, and they climbed astride Alister. At first Lily sat up front, as Rowan had insisted, but when the proud prince realized he'd have to hold on to someone else's waist, he changed his mind. They nestled between Alister's leathery wings, Rowan tightly grasped the chain around his neck, and they took off into the sky, sending the heads of the sunflowers swaying and bowing in farewell.

They crested the blue-green mountains hemming in the sunflower field, and suddenly the scene changed. The swirling colors, alive with the movement and energy of a painter's brush, fell away like a curtain. In their wake the sky stretched in an expanse of flawless blue, and a sun piercingly bright blazed down. As she breathed in the fresh, crisp air, Lily felt like she'd just awoken from a dream.

Her wonder was short-lived. Alister suddenly shrieked, then bucked and wobbled in midair. Philippe hollered, and Rowan wrapped the chain around his palm to keep from plunging off the bat's back.

"Alister, what's going on?" Lily yelled.

"It's too bright, my lady!"

"Can your eyes adjust?"

Alister ventured to open an eyelid, then shrieked, squeezed it shut, and bucked again. "I don't think so, it burns. I've been too long underground!"

Lily knotted her fingers in Alister's hair to keep from sliding off, and Philippe swore as his stash of sunflowers blew away.

"Lily, use the stone!" Rowan shouted.

Lily's mind raced. She searched again for some image to help, but no pictures or flicker of inspiration surfaced from her churning, frightened thoughts.

"I can't! My mind's blank!"

"Just ask the stone for help! Let it choose!"

Lily's arms burned as she held on for dear life. How could she reach for the stone in her pocket when she was barely hanging on?

"Monsieur Rowan, hold my ears!" Philippe cried. A shower of sunflower blossoms suddenly littered the air and smacked Lily in the face. Lily spit out a few petals and opened her eyes to see Philippe, his ears in Rowan's fist, blindly rummaging in the hat with a single paw. He grumbled and gritted his teeth, then pulled out what looked like a green rubber ball. "Monsieur Rowan!" he shouted. "For the bat's eyes!"

Rowan anchored his arm in the chain and took the ball from Philippe, who huddled back into place and clung to the bat's fur. Lily saw Rowan reach toward Alister's head with his free hand just as the bat started to nosedive.

They all screamed. The wind whipped them as they dived faster and faster, like a meteor plowing toward earth.

Suddenly, Alister leveled out his flight and ascended toward the sun. The wind lulled to a gentle breeze as he silently cruised past the clouds.

Lily's hands stung as she relaxed her grip upon Alister's wiry hair. Flint had scrambled into her pocket before he swooned and fainted, and Rowan wiped sweat from his brow and stared about as if dazed. Only Philippe, still huddled in place, grumbled to himself as if their close encounter with death was more annoyance than threat.

"This is mortifying."

Alister's lament broke the quiet. Lily shook herself into the present and tried to piece together what had happened. What was that ball? Why had Alister suddenly regained control? Then Alister glanced back, and Lily stifled a laugh. A pair of green and yellow striped sunglasses encircled his eyes. As Lily studied them, she realized they weren't sunglasses at all but rather two worms with cartoonish eyes and goofy smiles that had wound themselves together. A shadow passed between them, creating the "lenses" of the glasses.

"Mortifying, but necessary," Philippe said flatly. "Monsieur bat, you nearly killed us all!"

"Forgive me, I was foolish to fly without preparation. But is this really the only answer?"

"You need shade for your eyes. What better way than with shadeworms?"

"Philippe," Rowan said, "I have to say, I'm *very* grateful for that hat of yours."

———

They kept pace with the sun's swift march across the sky. Philippe chewed on the few stray sunflower petals that he'd salvaged, while Flint dozed in Lily's pocket. Alister continued to mumble to himself in humiliation. Eventually a melody rose from the winds below them, and Lily glanced down and saw that they flew over a vast meadow, with grasses waving like swells on a wide, golden sea. Flowers sprinkled the terrain with splashes of purple, red, and yellow. From among those waves, a song arose even more beautiful than what Nyssinia had sung, or what Lily heard when the winds spoke to her. Lily couldn't make out the words, but the harmony struck a familiar chord. It reminded her of the music of the sea against the shore, or of birdsong, or of the leaves of a maple tree rustling in the wind.

"What is it?" Lily asked breathlessly, to anyone who would answer.

"The Singing Meadows," Alister said. "My people used to venture here long ago, before the Veil descended."

Lily closed her eyes and focused on the music. As colors waltzed through her eyelids, she found herself riding the waves of stories that thrilled and delighted her—stories her father had told her, stories her mother had read to her, stories she'd scrawled in her math notebook when she was supposed to be paying attention in class.

She opened her eyes as the song faded. As the meadows receded into the distance, a great cliff rose from the landscape and blotted out the sky. Lily recognized the vast Desert of the Forgotten atop the cliff, sprawling into the distance like the surface of a barren, lifeless moon. She shuddered at her memories of the desert: the ghostly figures that had emerged from behind the rocks to capture Adam, and the sinkhole that belched hot wind as it yawned open beneath her in the sand. *What an awful place,* Lily thought. As she mulled over the haunting images, she spotted a dark blotch midway up the cliff face. It was the Cave of Lights, tucked into the side of the rock wall.

They landed as the sun began its descent over the horizon. As Lily slid off Alister's back and onto the ledge before the entrance, an eerie sensation overtook her. The last time she'd entered this cave, excitement about finding her father had crackled within her like electricity, only to snuff out when she found the cave empty. Now, she felt a foreboding that their long journey would end in similar calamity.

She looked at Rowan to gauge his thoughts. He wouldn't make eye contact, but his shoulders slouched just a little, as if the prospect of recounting his misadventures to Isla humbled him. He walked into the cave without a glance at any of his companions, his hands clenched into fists. Lily, Philippe, and Flint followed, while Alister stood guard on the ledge. He'd cast off his sunglasses at the first possible moment, and the shadeworms squeaked at each other and inched about on the bare rock.

The ethereal sound of harbor bells greeted them as they stepped into the cool, damp cave. Lily recognized the turquoise light throbbing from within, and she quickened her pace as the corridor opened into the central cavern. She felt a sudden thrill at the promise of glimpsing the fledgling dreams again as they drifted over the turquoise pool like an array of floating Christmas lights.

When she reached the central cavern, however, she froze. Instead of the spectacle of lights she expected, only a handful of fledgling dreams hovered above the water, drifting aimlessly like fireflies that had lost their way.

"What's happened? Why are there so few dreams?" she asked Rowan.

Rowan didn't answer at first, but instead turned in place with a scowl etched across his face. "She's not here," he finally said in disbelief.

"What?"

"Isla. She's not here."

The hair on the back of Lily's neck pricked up. "Isla!" she called with sudden urgency. "Isla, are you here?"

"She's gone." Rowan knelt to study the ground for some trace of his sister's footsteps. Flint joined him, flitting from one streak in the dust to another, and even Philippe paused his chewing to study the cave walls.

"Maybe she didn't come here after all?" Lily ventured.

"No. She came."

"How do you know?"

"Her soothstone isn't here."

Lily glanced around and realized that he was right. No magenta stone glinted within the cave. "Maybe she went back to the Valley, then? We may have traveled all this way when she's already back at Castle Mistwood."

"She didn't return to Mistwood."

"How do you know?"

"She's my sister. I know." Rowan stood up and pointed to a swipe in the dirt. "This was her." He followed the trail a few steps. "She didn't go home. She was running."

Lily scrunched her face. To her, the mark only looked like an ordinary, nondescript scuffle in the dust. "Why would she be running? You don't think she was trying to escape something, do you?"

"To escape . . . or to follow something."

"Like what?"

Rowan traced the trail outside the cave. At his appearance Alister scrambled to position the shadeworms back onto his face, but no one paid any attention. Rowan stopped at the edge of the cliff and pointed to a clawed print at the verge of the rock. "She called a bird of prey. Looks like an eagle."

"Maybe she flew home?"

"She didn't fly home. If she'd succeeded in her quest and was returning home, she would have walked, not run. It's the way of our people."

"Oh, that's right. You guys are super proud."

Rowan glared at her, and Lily bit her lip. *Oops.* "What would she be chasing, Rowan?"

Before he could answer, a wavering blue light flashed alive behind them. Alister jumped back from the glare, and Lily and Rowan turned around and gasped.

A fledgling dream trembled in midair at the entrance to the cave. It quivered and jolted as if fighting against an unseen force, and thrust out spines of blue light in its effort to break free. Then its glow faded and dimmed. Rowan and Lily watched aghast as something sinister, like the hand of a malevolent, invisible giant, dragged the fledgling up the cliff. With a last glimmer of blue like a cry for help, it disappeared into the Desert of the Forgotten.

CHAPTER 23

The Desert of the Forgotten

Alister stumbled forward as Rowan clambered atop his back without invitation. "Good sir!" Alister cried. "Kindly wait a moment!"

Lily stared at them in bewilderment. "Rowan, what are you doing?"

"Something is very wrong here. Fledglings never leave the Cave of Lights like that one just did. They disappear when they're ready to bloom into mature dreams, but never before that, and never through the cave entrance."

"What do you think is going on?"

"I don't know, but I don't like it. Did you see how that fledgling fought not to leave? It's like something was dragging it. We have to follow it."

Lily's stomach lurched. "But it went into the Desert of the Forgotten."

"So?"

She fumbled with the grimy cuffs of her sweater and bit her lip. "That place is so dangerous, Rowan. Isla and I almost died there."

"Lily, you said yourself that the fledgling dreams were missing. Isla ran out of that cave in a hurry and took off. Where else do you think she would go, except to chase after them?"

Lily remembered the determination in Isla's eyes as she rode a griffin to attack a sky full of harpies. "I guess you're right. But can't there be another way? I hate to go back there."

He met Lily's eyes. "The fact that you're scared is exactly why we need to find her. She's in danger, Lily. And—and she's all I have. I can't fail her."

Rowan suddenly seemed much older than when Lily first met him, and his resolve encouraged her. Yet as she remembered the rusted, rickety robot seizing Adam's leg, and the Forgotten swarming around her and dragging her into the abyss, her hands shook. She crossed her arms to hide her trembling.

Philippe appeared at the entrance to the cave. "Mademoiselle, one of the lights, it—"

"Yes, we know, Philippe," Rowan said. "Please, come with us. We need to go after it."

"After it? Where? Where do we go now?"

"The Desert of the Forgotten."

"Oh. It is above ground, yes? No more dark and nasty caves?"

Lily remembered the sinkhole and raised an eyebrow. She let Rowan answer.

"Not for a while, at least," he said.

They climbed astride Alister, who insisted that his eyes had, indeed, adjusted to the sunlight and the shadeworms could return to Philippe's hat. Philippe stuffed them inside, and Lily cast a last, wary glance at the cave entrance as they took off. She knotted her fingers in Alister's coat and tried to quiet the thundering of her heart.

As they cleared the cliff, an expanse of desert stretched out for miles beneath the setting sun, the light of which bled orange and red over the sparse terrain. The cracked earth unscrolled beneath them like an endless, crumbling parchment, dotted only rarely with a desiccated shrub or a creaking tree. Lily spotted a desert willow stooping like an old man, and remembered the trunk she'd leaned against when they paused for rest before the Forgotten attacked. At the memory she twisted her fists in Alister's fur.

"Ow!" Alister cried. "Please, my lady! I am not a swaddling blanket!"

Lily mumbled an apology. She relaxed her fingers but gritted her teeth until her jaw hurt.

The sun sank toward the earth, and soon the impending night chilled the air. As the sky turned from crimson to navy, Lily wondered if nightfall would still find them chasing after a stolen dream. "Rowan, can you still see it?" she asked, after searching the horizon.

"There." Rowan pointed to what Lily had presumed was an early star, but as she squinted, she realized that it was blue. "It's slowing down," Rowan said. "We'll gain on it soon."

Just then another light soared past them like a red comet. *Another fledgling. Rowan's right, it's like something is stealing them.* As Lily watched it dart and sway ahead of them, an uneasy question pricked her mind: *What happens when there are no dreams left?*

The sun disappeared. Constellations paraded across the sky, and as Lily glanced up she was delighted to recognize a few from her stargazing back home. She searched for the nebula within Orion's sword, then gasped as the hunter pulled the blade from his belt and whacked the Great Bear on the nose broadside. Cassiopeia, reclining lazily upon her divan, yawned and waved them away.

The red fledgling halted in midair, then circled around the blue one as if they were binary stars. For a moment Lily watched them with wonder, but then the earth beneath them blackened and a familiar roar rumbled over the desert. A sinkhole, like the one that had nearly claimed Lily's life, gaped open. The two fledgling dreams quivered, then sank into the chasm as if drawn by a net. With a tremendous groan the earth sealed closed again, and a cascade of sand obscured any evidence that the dreams had ever existed.

Alister hovered in midair, unsure of what to do. Philippe blinked into the gathering darkness, his shock so profound that he'd dropped a carrot from his forepaw and failed to notice. At Rowan's urging, Alister silently glided down onto the sand, still hot from hours of baking in the scorching daylight. All the while, Lily's heart knocked in her chest.

Rowan slid off Alister's back and walked around the terrain where the lights had disappeared. "We need to follow them down there," he said. "But how?"

No one answered.

Rowan sifted a pile of sand with his foot and turned in a circle. "So strange. There's no seam or crack in the ground. It's as if that hole we just saw never existed."

Lily's mouth felt full of sand, and she had to force herself to speak. "I can help," she said.

Rowan approached her. "How, Lily?"

She didn't answer. Her knuckles whitened as she clung to Alister.

"Please, Lily. What do you know?"

Lily released her grip and Alister sighed with relief. "I think I can call one of the Forgotten."

Rowan raised his eyebrows. "You know the Forgotten?"

Moments from her childhood, spent on the carpet with a pile of toys and crouched in the treehouse drawing sketches, resurfaced to Lily's mind. She'd had companions during those moments, imaginary ones that she'd forgotten long ago. "I know some of them, I think," she said, struggling to steady her voice. "One especially."

"And they'll show us the way down?"

Lily swallowed. "Based on what I saw the last time I was here, I think they'll *force* us down."

Rowan studied her and weighed her words. "All right," he finally said. "If you think they can get us down, let's do it."

Lily slid from Alister's back and stepped across the desert sands. A wind rushed by and tousled her hair, and for a moment she thought she heard it speak, but she couldn't make out the words. She glanced up at the constellations; they had ceased their movements, as if waiting in suspense to see what would happen.

Lily drew a breath. "Aristotle Otter!" she shouted. Her voice echoed across the cold, barren desert.

Philippe murmured in puzzlement. "Ahem. Aristotle what?"

Lily felt her cheeks flush. "I made up the name when I was little, okay? I was only five."

"Five?" Philippe asked.

"Okay, maybe eight."

"I do not judge, mademoiselle."

Lily held her breath, waited, and counted the seconds.

You will not find what you seek, dream keeper.

Lily's heart raced. It was Glower's voice. "Did you hear that?" she asked, her voice shaking as she searched the dark for the glow of the monster's menacing eyes.

"Hear what, mademoiselle?" Philippe, Rowan, and Alister all gawked at her in befuddlement. Even Flint peeked his head from within her pocket and squeaked in confusion.

It was my imagination, she told herself. *Just my imagination.* Then the voice came again. *This is a fool's errand, little girl. You can't escape. He* is *watching.*

Leave me alone! Lily clasped the soothstone and called out Aristotle Otter's name once more. Again, only silence met her cry.

Rowan stepped toward her hesitantly. "Maybe we have other options. There are bound to be more fledglings that pass this way. Maybe if we camp here, we can follow—"

A scuffling noise sounded across the sand. Flint puffed himself into a blaze to illuminate the patch of desert on which they stood. As his firelight danced against the dry earth, something small scampered out from behind a rock. It was long and covered with brown fur, but bare in spots, as if someone had pulled out patches from its coat. One ear was misshapen. It was also translucent, like a phantom, and seemed to flicker in and out of existence, one minute there, the next vanished.

Lily's heart twinged with pity at the sight of her old friend so mangy and browbeaten. Years ago, Lily imagined the little otter climbing up into the Fortress with her and listening while she created stories about knights, dragons, and birds that became stars. Back then his coat was shiny and his eyes bright, but now . . . *What's happened to you?* she wondered with dismay.

Aristotle stood on his hind feet, tilted his head to one side, and then squeaked as if asking Lily her name.

"Yes, Aristotle. It's me. Come here, buddy."

He dropped to all fours and bounded toward her. Then he paused, stood upright like a meerkat, and with a mix of joy and astonishment he squeaked again.

Lily nodded with tears in her eyes. "It's me, Aristotle. I'm here."

Aristotle flopped onto her, wrapped his stubby arms around her waist in a hug, and buried his face in her sweater. Lily returned his embrace and tried not to cry as she felt him shake with a sob. "It's okay," she said as she gently stroked the scruffy, tangled fur on the back of his neck. "I'm here now. Everything's going to be okay."

A familiar roar sounded from deep within the earth. Lily clenched her teeth and drew Aristotle closer as the sand before her sank into a gaping black hole. She glanced up at her friends, who rushed to her side and crowded around her. A hot, putrid wind belched out from the depths below and stung her eyes.

Lily felt the ground beneath her give way. As she plummeted into the abyss, with her long-lost friend clutched to her chest, the eyes of Glower burned through the darkness at the edge of the pit. His green teeth spread into a malicious grin as he watched her fall.

CHAPTER 24

Down the Rabbit Hole

As the stars disappeared from view, Lily had the impression she'd fallen down the rabbit hole from *Alice in Wonderland*. Their descent dragged on for so long that she wouldn't have been surprised to see cupboards lining the walls of the cavern, perhaps stocked with a jar or two of orange marmalade or a tin of Earl Grey. As they plunged deeper, however, the air grew hot and stifling, ripe with the stench of spoiled meat. Lily recognized the smell from her first encounter with this cursed desert, and she steeled herself against a wave of nausea.

After plummeting for an age, Lily and Aristotle finally landed in something large and soft. A cloud of dust poofed up into their faces, and as Lily fanned it away, a flurry of moths rose and circled around her. She wiped the dirt from her eyes and glanced about. She'd landed on an enormous, tattered mattress coated in dust. Torches lined the walls around her, casting haunting orange light across the floor of yet another cave.

Rowan, Philippe, and Flint soon thudded onto the mattress beside her and sent up their own plumes of dirt, while Alister flapped to rest on the ground. They stared at each other in confusion for a moment as they struggled to orient themselves. The heat felt oppressive, and Lily gagged at the smell. "Where are we?" she asked. "And what is that stink?"

"Aaaah! Mademoiselle!"

Philippe bounded backward in panic and pointed to something behind her. Lily turned.

An enormous dragon dozed at the end of the mattress.

Like the Forgotten, the dragon was translucent and the color of dirty dishwater. Patches of scales had rubbed off from its flanks. Cobwebs slung between its horns, and as it snored, its wide, armored chest expanded like a bellows and gusts of foul breath sent the cobwebs swaying and fluttering.

"Lily," Rowan whispered, "you need to back up. Slowly and carefully." He slid silently off the mattress, guiding Philippe and Flint with him, and retreated to the entrance of a tunnel leading deeper underground.

Lily gaped at the beast with her eyes as wide as saucers. She knew she had to move, but when smoke billowed from the monster's nostrils, she couldn't will her joints to budge.

"Come on, Lily! Back away!"

She inched backward. The dragon groaned, and Lily watched in horror as it scratched its neck with one of its hind claws. The beast had only two legs, rather than four. *It's a wyvern*, she realized. She struggled to remember details she'd read from *King Arthur* and other legends. *It doesn't breathe fire . . . but there's something about its tail . . .*

"Lily, come on!" Rowan urged her.

With her heart thundering, Lily crab-walked backward toward the edge of the mattress. Aristotle still clung to her midsection with his face buried in her sweater, and this made the task awkward. She felt behind her for the edge of the mattress, pawing the air while her eyes remained fixed on the threat snoring before her.

Clomp.

She fell backward and bumped to the ground. Although she suffered only a minor bruise on the spine, she accidentally squashed Aristotle's tail in the fall. Before she could react, the otter yelped.

Lily scooped Aristotle up, clasped a hand over his mouth, and held her breath. *Maybe it's a deep sleeper*, she hoped. Too terrified to glance away, she stared at the wyvern and prayed he would continue to snooze.

Instead, a single, yellow eye opened, trained on her, and narrowed with suspicion.

"Run!" Rowan shouted.

The monster roared and leaped into the air, kicking the mattress out from under it and spreading its sharp-tipped wings wide. Lily scrambled to her feet, but the blast of the wyvern's acrid breath knocked her to the ground. The fumes cleared from Lily's eyes just as the wyvern loomed over her with its dagger-like teeth bared and its eyes flashing with rage. She fumbled for her soothstone, but once again her mind was as empty as a drained pool.

The wyvern growled as it crouched low to the ground and lifted its barbed tail into the air. A drop of black venom oozed from the tail, and for a horrible moment Lily remembered the details from medieval legend: *wyverns couldn't breathe fire, but had venomous tails.* As the terrible reality sunk in, Lily remembered the scorpion in Ash Canyon. At that time, Cedric had saved her. Now, her only hope for rescue was a stone in her pocket that refused to comply.

Suddenly a screech split the air, and a gray form swept down and struck the wyvern's head. The enraged dragon snapped its slavering jaws at its assailant, but with a quick flapping of wings Lily's rescuer dashed away, the yellow jewel at its neck gleaming like a drop of sunlight.

Alister! Lily thought with a rush of gratitude. The monster gave chase, its neck undulating back and forth like a cobra swaying to a charmer's pipe, but it could not keep pace. Alister darted to strike the wyvern's eyes, then withdrew again,

Rowan rushed to Lily's side and helped her to her feet. "There's a door back there at the end of the tunnel!" he shouted. "We have to get through!" Aristotle squealed in protest as Philippe and Flint pried him away from Lily, grasped his shabby paws, and raced down the tunnel.

Another roar shook the cave like an earthquake. Rocks rained down and pelted them as they ran. Aristotle whimpered ceaselessly, then finally knocked Philippe to the ground and rushed back toward Lily. Lily saw the rabbit fall, skidded to a stop, and scooped up both animals into her arms.

"Don't stop!" Rowan cried. "We have to get out of here! Now!"

With both Philippe and Aristotle bundled in her arms, Lily barely dodged a boulder that crashed down in front of her. The light around them dimmed as they darted beneath an outcropping of rock, and Flint skittered ahead and flared into a blaze to light their way.

Another roar. *Crash.* A shriek rang out behind them, and Lily glanced over her shoulder in time to see the wyvern fling Alister against a wall of the cave. The bat ricocheted off the rock, flipped several times in midair, then landed on the ground with a sickening thud.

Lily cried out Alister's name. She ran a few paces back before Rowan seized her arm. "Stop! You'll be killed!" he cried, his garnet eyes wild with fear.

"We can't leave him! He's done so much for us!"

"He's already lost, Lily. Leave him! There's nothing you can do!"

"I *won't* abandon him!" She flashed Rowan a hard look, then shoved Philippe and Aristotle into his arms. Rowan called her name one more time as she ran back through the tunnel, plunged into the shadow of the wyvern, and slid to a stop beside Alister. The bat's eyes were closed, and when Lily touched him, he only grunted.

"Alister! You need to get up! Now!" she said, shaking him.

His eyelids fluttered open. "My lady—"

"Up, up! Get up!" She crouched low and tucked her hands beneath him to lift him from the ground. Another roar. Lily glanced up, and her heart sank into her stomach as the wyvern wheeled around and fixed her in its penetrating, unearthly stare. "Alister, you need to fly! Now!" she cried.

"I can't, my lady! I think my wing is broken."

"Then crawl! Flap! *Something!*"

Alister squeezed his eyes shut, and with a grimace he dug a single winged claw into the ground, then shimmied himself forward. He did it again, crawling at a painstakingly slow pace and cringing with every inch gained.

The wyvern thundered toward them. It hunched low to the ground, and a black droplet of venom dripped from its tail and sizzled upon impact with the earth. Lily glanced from the beast, to Alister barely limping forward in the dirt, and back. Rowan, Philippe, and Flint dashed to her side and tugged at Alister to prod him on, but he collapsed to the ground in pain and exhaustion. "Leave me, friends," he whispered. "Run, and save yourselves!"

Lily's heart raced. She shoved a hand into her pocket and withdrew the soothstone.

The wyvern's footfalls fractured the earth and cracks spider-webbed in every direction. It raised its tail high.

Her mind was blank and the stone equally dull. *Help us*, Lily pleaded. *Please, just help!*

A bright flash illuminated the cave. Lily breathed with relief, then glanced down at the stone, expecting it to blaze white.

It remained dark and lifeless.

Lily shielded her eyes from the blinding glare. The scents of smoke and scorched earth filled the air, and the terrible howl of a wounded animal reverberated from the rock walls. When the light faded, spots danced before Lily's eyes. She blinked them away, and when the world slowly snapped back into focus, she gasped.

Isla stood before them, the remnants of a lightning bolt still crackling within a storm cloud between her palms.

CHAPTER 25

The Princess and the Wyvern

"All of you, get back!" Isla shouted.

"Isla!" cried Rowan. "Are you—"

"I said *get back!*"

The group fled into the tunnel, dragging Alister along as Isla confronted the thrashing wyvern. A scorch mark blackened the wyvern's thigh, and the monster foamed at the mouth as it seethed with rage. It whipped its tail, slicing its poison dagger through rock and earth and swiping just inches away from Isla's torso. Isla darted back, raised her palms, and narrowed her eyes as another shaft of brilliant white lightning pulsed from a cloud that broiled between her hands.

The wyvern charged at her. It lashed its tail again, and this time it struck Isla in the side and swept her against a wall of the cave. The lightning between Isla's hands sputtered and fizzled as the worm pinned her against the rock.

Rowan shouted Isla's name and ran into the fray with a storm cloud gathering between his own outstretched hands. Without hesitation, the wyvern cast the prince aside with a swift kick, and Rowan tumbled to the ground, slammed against a boulder, and held his head in pain.

Isla clawed at the wyvern's tail, but it pressed her against the wall like a vice. The pressure squeezed the breath from her body, and the deadly tip of its tail hovered just inches from her face.

Flint flared himself into a blaze and rolled toward the wyvern like a flaming tumbleweed, but the monster stomped him beneath a fearsome clawed foot. The blow divided Flint into six miniature flames, all of which darted and flitted chaotically before converging again and running for cover. Even Philippe rushed in, shouting something unintelligible in French and raising his carrot saber over his shoulder as he bounded toward the beast. Another kick sent the rabbit careening backward into the shadows.

A laugh rumbled from the wyvern's throat, and its mouth drew back in an evil sneer of triumph. It licked the air with a slender, forked tongue, then lowered its terrible face toward Isla.

Isla lifted a single trembling hand into the air, balled into a fist. At first Lily thought she was gesturing in a final stand of defiance, but then Lily saw it: a tiny magenta light gleaming on Isla's finger. Isla was wearing her soothstone.

With a flash the stone flooded the cave with rose light, and in its halo the beast withdrew and shielded its eyes. Suddenly a second giant beast appeared, stretched its wings wide, and shook the rocks with its roar. It was a winged lion, its mighty paws as wide as boulders, its eagle's wings fanned in victory.

The wyvern released Isla to deal with this new threat, and Isla ran, coughing and panting, to help her brother from where he still lay on the ground. Lily rushed to join her, and together they revived Rowan and led him to the shelter of the tunnel. . Philippe, Aristotle, and Flint followed afterward, and Alister, who had barely reached the tunnel entrance, crawled in painstaking, cumbersome jerks. Lily fell back to help him as the others ran deeper into the tunnel.

A terrible pounding rattled the cave as the two beasts clashed in midair, the wyvern whipping its tail and snapping at the lion with teeth like razors, the lion slashing at the wyvern's throat with its claws. The wyvern had loosened rocks and debris from the cavern walls, and now the cataclysmic battle that raged threatened to crack the foundation of the cave in two. Rifts split the cave walls as the beasts pummeled each other, and Lily planted a hand against the tunnel wall to steady herself.

They raced to the door, a circular, wooden gateway with a brass ring for a handle. The earth shook again and a crevice snaked down the tunnel after them. "Come on!" Rowan cried.

He dashed ahead, grasped the handle with both hands, and yanked.

It wouldn't budge.

"Monsieur, stand aside, I will slice it open!" Philippe declared.

"No, stop!" Isla cried. "It won't—"

She was too late. Philippe hoisted the blade above his head and brought it swiftly down upon the door handle and lock. A burst of orange sparks exploded from the impact, singeing Philippe's ears and Isla's hair. Afterward, Philippe dropped his weapon and stood with his ears drooping and his chest heaving. A black, scorched line now marred the door, but the entrance remained sealed tight.

"You can't force it! I've been trying for days," Isla said in exasperation. "The door only opens if—"

An earsplitting roar stopped the words in her mouth. Even the beasts, grappling in midair, suddenly fell silent as a deafening noise drowned out all other sound. It sounded as if the entire world was ripping apart at the seams.

From her position at the tunnel entrance Lily watched a waterfall of sand cascade into the cavern through a hole gaping far above. Rocks, stalactites, and gallons of sand rained down as the entryway widened to reveal a dim panel of stars. The winged lion escaped through the opening to avoid the falling debris, but to Lily's surprise the wyvern suddenly seemed serene. It shuffled toward the rear of the cavern and cocked its head to one side in amusement as the gap in the earth widened. Eventually the roaring ceased, the cascade of sand slowed to a trickle, and all fell quiet and still. Lily held her breath.

A soft, purple light illuminated the cavern. The wyvern straightened as if standing at attention as a violet orb, like a shining sea urchin, descended into the cave. It jostled and quivered as if towed by an unseen force. *A fledgling*, Lily thought.

The infant dream hovered in the center of the cave for a moment, then slid into the tunnel. Flint and Philippe scrambled to the sides of the tunnel and pressed themselves against the black rock to let the dream pass, and Lily stared in wonder as it paused just inches from her face. She expected it to emanate heat, like a flame, but instead it cooled the air around her and smelled faintly of eucalyptus. Although it radiated purple light, its heart swirled with a thousand colors.

Lily reached out a hand to touch it, and her heart soared. As she dipped her fingers into the fledgling's light, her mind, so agonizingly empty, suddenly crackled with images and ideas, as if a dozen movie reels played in her head at once. Lily relished the moment, savoring each flicker and nuance, until the dream slipped from her fingers and sped through the door. The clack of a latch sounded, the wooden door creaked open, and the fledgling sped through the doorway and disappeared. As it vanished, Lily's imagination again quieted.

"Amazing. Did you guys just feel—"

"There's no time!" Isla said. "This is our chance. Quick, into the tunnel!"

Rowan, Philippe, Flint, and even Aristotle promptly obeyed, but Lily hesitated. Alister still lay listless and exhausted on the ground just inside the tunnel entrance. Without another glance at the rest of her friends, Lily rushed to him.

"Lily, what are you doing?" Isla called.

Lily ignored her. She stooped down and placed a hand on Alister's back. His breathing rattled beneath her palm. "Go on, my lady," he wheezed.

Lily shook her head. "No. I'm not leaving you." Her eyes flitted over the broken wing, protruding from his body at a sickly angle. She reached into her pocket for the soothstone. *Please, please work*, she prayed. *Please, just this one time.*

She closed her eyes and struggled to imagine the wing as it once was, intact and smooth, lifting them into the clear skies above the Painted Woodland. She tried to cling to the ideas that moments before had flourished in the fledgling's presence. As she remembered, hope fluttered in her chest like a dove in flight.

Then her heart sank. When Lily opened her eyes, the soothstone was dark. The shimmering newborn dream had taken all her inspiration with it.

A puff of foul breath struck the back of her neck. Lily turned around to see the wyvern glaring at her with sickly yellow eyes.

CHAPTER 26

Wendell

The wyvern puffed smoke through its nostrils, glared at her . . . and then withdrew. As his head slunk away from the tunnel entrance, Lily dared to hope. *Has he really gone? Is he going to leave us alone?* she wondered. Her heart knocked in her chest and every muscle tensed as she waited.

Then, it came. The wyvern's roar shook the cave, and a shower of rancid spittle sprayed into the tunnel. Lily backed away just as the wyvern rammed its head into the stone archway, splitting the rock and widening the entrance to admit its grisly scarred head. Isla screamed, and Rowan and Philippe howled Lily's name as the entrance crumbled and the wyvern plowed into the tunnel.

The monster growled at her, then glimpsed Alister, who dragged himself painstakingly across the ground with a single claw. A low growl rumbled in the wyvern's throat, and threads of saliva strung between its fangs as it opened its ravenous jaws wide.

"Alister!" Lily cried in horror. She rushed forward with her hands upraised to protect her friend, but the wyvern whipped to face her and knocked her down with one blow. Lily kicked at the beast, but with a snap of its jaws it snagged the cuff of her pants. Lily screamed and dug her fingernails into the dirt as the wyvern dragged her like a dead rat out of the tunnel. She flailed and thrashed, but her cuff remained caught in a single crooked fang.

The wyvern flung her across the cave, and she skidded through the dirt, then rolled over in time to see the wyvern towering over her. Its barbed tail glistened with black poison, and its mottled lips curled into a wicked sneer as it poised to strike. Lily squeezed her eyes shut. A medley of faces paraded through her mind. Her parents. Cedric. Adam and Keisha. Pax. *I'm so sorry*, she thought, her chest tightening with panic and dismay. She lingered over the memory of Pax, over the miracles he worked. Then she drew a breath and braced herself.

Sniff. Sniff.

SNIFFFFF.

What on earth . . . ? Lily opened one eye. She expected to see the wyvern looming above her, its evil face contorted into a crazed grin. Instead, it crouched low, its eyes narrowed with concentration, and pressed its mucousy nostrils against her ankles.

Sniff. Sniff sniff sniffff.

The wyvern straightened its neck, leaving a gob of greenish goo on Lily's ankle. She fought the urge to throw up—even ogre slobber hadn't been this gross. Then, Lily watched in amazement as the bloodthirsty wyvern rolled onto its side, curled up its hind limbs like a kitten, and gazed at her with googly eyes.

Is this really happening? With shaking limbs Lily propped herself on her elbows, half-afraid the wyvern would lunge forward and swallow her in one gulp. Instead, the dragon met her eyes and cooed.

"You're—you're not going to eat me?" Lily stammered, hardly believing the words had left her mouth.

In response the wyvern cooed again, and gazed at her with the earnestness of a doting puppy. For the first time Lily noticed a collar around its neck, tattered and frayed, with a single tarnished tag dangling from a rusted link: *WENDELL.*

"Unbelievable." Lily glanced over her shoulder to see Isla, with the others hiding behind her. At the sight of the others congregated around Lily, the wyvern narrowed its eyes and growled.

"Whoa! Wendell? Is that your name?" Lily said. "It's okay, Wendell. These people are my friends."

He stared at her with another anxious puppy expression, then, when convinced she spoke the truth, he lazily rolled onto his side to show her his belly to scratch.

"I don't understand," Lily said, her voice still quavering as she tentatively reached out an arm to pet the wyvern. "He was ready to kill me."

"He was ready to kill us all, mademoiselle!" Philippe said.

"I can't believe I didn't realize it before," Isla said. "It's because you're *human*, Lily. He's a Forgotten wyvern, and he wants to be loved. Preferably by the one who created him, but I suppose the love of any human is better than nothing."

Lily scratched Wendell's neck. In response he thumped his tail, sending droplets of black venom flying through the air like splattered paint.

"Unbelievable," Isla said again.

"This is all *très intéressant*, but shall we, say, *go*?" said Philippe.

"The door's closed," Isla said. "We missed our chance to get through."

"Why do we not go the way of the lion?" Philippe said, pointing his paw to the sinkhole high above them. "Back out where the sun still shines?"

The moment he spoke these words, sand and debris floated back into place above them, and the broken fragments of earth locked together like pieces of a jigsaw puzzle. The hole in the ceiling sealed up, locking them once more underground.

Philippe used his ears as a handkerchief and hid his face. "Caves! I hate these caves!"

"Didn't you say you grew up in tunnels, Philippe?" Lily said.

Philippe shot her a look of indignation. "Do not compare these filthy holes to my home, mademoiselle! My warren has down beds and lavender. There is a hearth with a clock that has been in my family for generations, and the most *magnifique* stores of vegetables. These—these—*caves* have slime and dark things and monsters who steal hats!" He stomped his foot to emphasize this last point, then stormed off down the tunnel, fuming as he went.

"Maybe he's right about going out through the ceiling," Rowan said. "When another fledgling comes, perhaps we can escape out the opening?"

"We? Forget *we*." Isla frowned at Rowan with her arms folded in front of her. "When another fledgling comes, I'm following it through that door, and *you* are going home. Do you understand?"

Rowan's face reddened. "Isla, I don't think—"

"What are you even doing here, Rowan?"

"We didn't find you in the Cave of Lights, and when I saw—"

"What were you doing in the Cave of Lights in the first place?"

Rowan's eyes swam as he searched for the right words. Finally, he just shrugged. "It's a long story."

"No story could excuse this! My instructions were for you to stay at home! Don't you realize what could have happened?"

Rowan looked stricken, and as Lily watched the argument, she again saw the little boy with the tattered raccoon. "I didn't mean to cause problems," Rowan said, his voice shaky. "It's just that—"

"I'm so disappointed in you, Rowan. I can't believe you could be so irresponsible. If something had happened to you, everything our family has worked for would be lost. Lost! Don't you see that? You're the heir to our kingdom! How can you be so reckless?"

Finally Rowan gritted his teeth, and a flash of anger burned in his eyes. "Heir to *what* kingdom?" he retorted. "There's nothing left! Isla, I went to—"

"Enough! I don't want to hear anymore. The next time a fledgling comes through that hole, I'm calling you a steed and you're going *home*. Do you understand?"

"But Isla, I—"

"I said enough! You're going home, and you're staying there until I get back!"

Rowan opened and closed his fists and worried his mouth, as he debated whether to say the words itching to burst out. Finally, he shuffled away down the tunnel, his shoulders slouching, his face dark with dejection. As Lily watched him slink away, she wrangled with the impulse to run after him and wrap an arm around his shoulder. She'd never had a little brother, but the more time she spent with this sullen prince, the stronger grew her stirrings to protect him.

She felt Isla's eyes on her. Lily drew a breath and spoke tentatively. "Isla," she ventured. "I know he shouldn't have left, but he was determined to find a way for your people. And then when you were gone from the Cave of Lights, nothing could have stopped him from finding you. He was reckless, sure, but it's because he cares. He's been through a lot. If you only knew half of what—"

"Quiet, Lily. You're just as guilty. The only thing I asked you to do was keep him safe, and you've failed miserably."

Lily felt as if Isla had slapped her. She drew a breath to compose herself. "He wouldn't listen to me," she insisted. "He was dead set on finding—"

"On finding me, when I explicitly told him not to."

"No, that's not it. I mean, eventually yes, but at first he was looking for your lost people."

"What are you talking about?"

"In the Veil. He went into the Veil to look for the Icelein."

Isla's jaw dropped. *"What?"*

"He remembered a story your mom used to tell, about seeing one of the Icelein in the Veil, and he tried to find them and bring them back to Mistwood."

The color drained from Isla's face. "How could he do that? The Veil is so deadly. Lily, how could you let him?"

"I didn't have much choice. He ran away, and I chased after him."

"You followed him?"

"Yes."

"You followed him *into* the Veil?"

Lily nodded.

Isla studied her. "You risked your life, Lily."

Lily lowered her eyes and played with her sweater buttons. She shrugged.

"What happened in there? What did you find?"

Lily searched for the words to capture what they'd endured, but nothing seemed to do the experience justice. "Let's just say we barely made it back out," she finally said.

Isla's eyes misted as she gazed after her brother. Rowan sat slouched against a wall of the tunnel, turning his memory bauble between his fingers. With a rush of emotion Isla swept to his side, joined him on the ground, and slipped an arm around him. Lily heard her say, "Espy," then felt like she was eavesdropping and wandered back down the tunnel. At least, she thought, she'd been able to diffuse some of the tension between them.

As she walked through the shadows, she found Alister lying against the wooden door, his broken wing jutting upward like a flag. He grimaced as she crouched down beside him and accidentally brushed against the wing.

"I'm so sorry. That was so stupid of me," Lily said.

"It's not the wing," Alister said, still wincing. "It's that I've failed you, my lady, and Pax as well. He said I had some role to play in all this. I certainly don't see how I can fulfill it."

"Don't say that. How do you know you haven't fulfilled it already? You brought us all this way safely."

"And it seems I can bring you no farther."

Lily felt a pang of regret, and suddenly the soothstone felt heavy in her pocket. *If only I could mend his wing . . .*

Footsteps sounded behind them, and Isla and Rowan appeared. "Thank you for looking after my brother," Isla said. "I wish you'd both stayed home, but I understand why you came, and I'm grateful."

"It's okay," Lily said. "What do we do now?"

"I need to get through that door somehow. Something is stealing the fledgling dreams, and I have to figure out what it is and notify Merlin."

"What do you think could be happening?"

"I don't know, but I suspect ill intent. The fledglings are bound to the Cave of Lights until they bloom into full dreams. It's unheard of that they would leave before then. Whoever is doing this, I doubt he or she is a friend of the Realm."

The hair on the back of Lily's neck pricked up. "Any ideas how to get in?"

"Other than wait for a fledgling to arrive and steal in after it? No. The door is firmly locked. I've been waiting for days for the chance to follow after a fledgling, but each time one would arrive your scaly friend was too close for me to sneak by." She glanced at Wendell, who scratched his neck with his leg like a dog, then gnawed at his flank as if to eradicate a flea.

"Actually, maybe he can help us," Lily offered. She climbed over the rubble scattered across the entrance to the tunnel to speak to Wendell. He had abandoned his itch and now occupied himself by crunching the bones of some ill-fated animal between his teeth.

Lily cleared her throat. "Ahem! Wendell?"

He glanced up, a femur bone protruding from his mouth like a toothpick, and crouched down in front of her. Even though he adored her, the stench that wafted toward her with his every breath made Lily nauseous, and his black claws unnerved her as they gouged ruts in the earth.

"Um, hey there, Wendell. Any chance you know how to get through that door?"

Wendell glanced down the tunnel, narrowed his eyes, and with a look of determination snaked his head and neck down the corridor. Flint and Aristotle darted to the side, and Philippe rolled Alister out of the way just as the monster rammed his snout against the wooden door with a deafening *BOOM*.

Wendell withdrew from the tunnel, shook his head, and blinked as he waited for a wave of dizziness to pass. Then he plowed in again, and another *BOOM* resounded as he smashed into the door a second time.

When he withdrew, doddering and unsteady, Lily glanced hopefully down the tunnel. Dust clouded the corridor in a gray haze, and as she watched the particles settle, a flicker of hope flared within her.

Then her heart sank as she realized the door remained untouched.

A squeak sounded from down the tunnel, and Flint bobbed into view. He pointed to himself, then to the door, and waited for Lily to give her permission to charge forward. The little kindler had proven himself time and again, and so Lily nodded.

Flint burst into a conflagration at the base of the door, filling the entire tunnel with firelight and heat. Burning debris snapped and crackled, and Philippe and Alister coughed as smoke billowed into the cavern. Finally, the flames petered out, and Flint returned to his usual diminutive size. He scampered about the tunnel fanning away the smoke. Even before he'd cleared it, Lily could see that the door remained intact.

"Let me try again, mademoiselle!" Philippe cried out. He plunged headfirst into his hat and rummaged around before he reemerged with a crowbar between his paws.

"Philippe, are you daft?" said Rowan. "That won't work!"

Philippe screwed up his face in offense. "Do you have a better idea, monsieur prince?"

"Yes, I do. Isla, you've got your soothstone back. Why don't you use it?"

"And do what?" Isla said. "Call a key?"

"Perhaps *le petit prince* has in mind a battering ram."

"Don't be sarcastic."

"Monsieur, after chasing after you underground for days and narrowly escaping death about sixty thousand times, I believe I have a right to sarcasm!"

"Both of you, stop arguing!" Isla said.

Flint skittered back and forth between parties and squeaked unintelligibly, pointing a glowing finger at one person, then another. Soon, what began as a minor disagreement escalated into a quarrel. Shouts echoed through the tunnel. As her anxiety mounted, something jerked Lily's sleeve.

"Not now, Aristotle," she said, waving away the otter as he tugged on her shirt.

"Rowan, why are you even arguing about this in the first place? You're not coming," Isla said.

"Of course, I'm coming!"

"No, you're not! You're staying right here. Lily will mend that bat's broken wing with her soothstone, and you'll fly out of here when the next fledgling comes."

"That's ridiculous. I came all the way across the desert to find you, and I'm staying with you!"

"Out of the question. I appreciate why you came, but there's too much at stake for you to continue with me. I'll go on, and you'll fly home."

"We couldn't go home on the bat if we wanted to! Lily can't fix the bat's wing. She's already tried!"

Isla looked at Lily with an eyebrow raised.

"He's right. I did try," Lily said, averting her eyes.

"I don't understand. You recreated our entire kingdom in the valley. Why can't you mend a bat's broken wing?"

Aristotle tugged Lily's sleeve more urgently. Lily pulled away and crossed her arms. "Something's wrong with the soothstone. Or me. I don't know which."

"It's not working at all?"

"No, not exactly. I can still call things, but I'm having a hard time make anything *new*. It's like my mind is blank. The stone just stays dark whenever I try."

"Your mind is *blank*?"

"It's so strange. There's this awful emptiness in my head. It feels, I don't know, like I'm on a desert island by myself."

Isla stiffened. "That's our proof. I *need* to get through that door. Now."

The urgency in her voice unsettled Lily. "Why? Isla, what do you know?"

Aristotle squeaked at Lily yet again to get her attention, but she batted him away.

"The fledglings! Without fledglings, there's no inspiration for dreams. No ideas. Nothing *new*."

Lily's eyes widened. "You mean, I'm struggling to create things with the stone because—"

"Because the fledgling dreams are disappearing from the Cave of Lights. If they leave the cave, they can't bloom. And if they can't bloom . . . dreams are just a memory."

Lily fell into stunned silence. *A world without dreams? No more inspiration, no more ability to imagine and create?* The terrible idea settled in, and she felt sick to her stomach. *How could we go on?*

The otter squeaked again, shriller this time.

"Aristotle, please!" Lily barked. "Not now!" She turned to flash him an angry look, but in the next instant her irritation melted away.

The otter stood in front of the doorway and nonchalantly shoved it open with a single paw. The door swung agape to reveal a tunnel emanating an eerie blue light.

CHAPTER 27

The Lairs of the Forgotten

Aristotle grinned so widely that his eyes disappeared. Then he giggled and released the door. Everyone cried out in protest as it clanged shut.

"*Sacre bleu,* why did you let it close?" Philippe yelled as he jumped up and down and wrenched his ears. Aristotle shrugged, then pressed a tiny metal button above the door handle. It looked like a bolt, the same as a dozen others that studded the heavy oak beams, but when the otter touched it, a click sounded. Aristotle pushed, and the door creaked open again.

"Great job, Aristotle!" Lily said, beaming.

"Why could the furry fellow not do that to begin with?" Philippe muttered. "It would have saved me from dulling my blade."

Aristotle shrugged. "You didn't ask."

They all gawked at him. His voice reminded Lily of cartoon chipmunks she had watched as a kid.

"You can talk? Why did you say nothing before?" Philippe asked.

Aristotle shrugged again. "You didn't ask me anything."

Lily suppressed a snicker, then put a hand on Isla's shoulder to stop her from running through the doorway. "We need to help Alister," Lily said. "He's saved our lives too many times. We can't just leave him here."

"He'll slow us down with that broken wing," Isla said. "Are you sure you can't mend it?"

"I've tried, but there's nothing in my head."

Isla tilted her head and narrowed her eyes. "That's not true. Even if the dreams are dwindling, you have something in your head."

"Maybe, but nothing that could help us in this situation." She chuckled. "Before he became my friend, Adam once asked if I had anything between my ears. Now I can truthfully say no."

Isla shook her head, then placed her palm on Lily's forehead and closed her eyes.

"Isla, what are you—"

"Hush. Let me focus."

Suddenly, in her mind's eye Lily saw herself flying through vast, winding corridors steeped in darkness. The hallways led to rooms that housed her memories, each chamber brilliant and teeming with the images, sounds, and even smells from her past. She returned to a campfire casting fingers of light across her dad's tent, and heard Gran's laughter after she won at gin rummy with a gathering of friends from a book club. She winced at the memory of Amanda Weatherby flicking a wad of gum into her hair, then saw Cedric emerge from the gnarled vines of the Wilderness with a plaid-colored melon in his claws. The flurry of visions dizzied her, and she braced herself with a hand against the rock wall.

Suddenly the motion stopped, and in her mind, clear as daylight, Lily saw Pax in the Painted Woodland. Beside him stood Alister, proud, newly healed, with his sharp, leathery wings folded at his side.

"I see him," Lily whispered. "Isla, I see him!"

"Good," Isla said, lowering her hand. "Work quickly. Even if you can't envision something new, you have your memories as a template. Use them."

Lily placed one hand on Alister's twisted wing, and she closed the other around the soothstone. She shut her eyes, and with all her might she focused on her memory of Alister: his regal posture, the amber jewel at his neck, his humility before Pax.

A familiar white light flooded the tunnel, and when it faded, the angle of Alister's wing was set right. Alister turned in place and spread his wings with a grin. "Oh, thank you, my lady!" he said with a bow. "You are indeed a heroine! A genius, even."

Lily's heart skipped a beat at his words, and she relished their sound in her ears. *Heroine. Genius.* As she turned the stone in her fingers, however, she remembered Pax's words: *Your powers are a gift, Lily McKinley . . . but be careful of the space they occupy in your heart.*

"Thank you, Alister, but not really. Pax is the real hero. He's just given me a wonderful gift, that's all."

Alister tilted his head and regarded her with admiration. "True, my lady. Still, I am indebted to you. Allow me to lead the way. I am made for dark places, and if I go ahead, I may guard you against danger."

Lily nodded, and Alister bowed again and then took flight down the tunnel. Before the door closed behind them, Lily cast a final glance at Wendell, who gazed after her with his neck drooping and his eyes downcast. "I'm sorry," Lily said with a twinge of sympathy. "We'll be back, I promise." The moment she said these words, she wondered if she could really keep her promise. Just before the door creaked shut, Wendell slumped onto the floor of the cave and whimpered, his eyes glassy with worry.

The tunnel shimmered with light that seemed infused into the very rock. It shifted colors as they walked, transitioning from blue to gold to deepest green. "It's an echo of the fledglings," Isla whispered when she noticed Lily frozen in awe. "It's proof that they've passed this way."

"It's beautiful," Lily said breathlessly.

Isla nodded. "A reflection of their maker."

They continued onward, and the tunnel meandered through so many twists and turns that Lily soon became disoriented. The trail of color in the rock was the only hint of light to guide their way, and as they traveled deeper below the desert, the air became close and stale. Philippe mumbled nervously under his breath, and Aristotle shivered and clung to Lily's hand with two velvety paws. Oddly, Lily's anxiety ebbed the farther they plunged. As they neared the hiding place of the fledgling dreams, the sparks of her imagination flickered back to life, and gradually she began to feel like herself again.

Isla raised a hand for them to pause. The tunnel opened into a large room lit with pools of pale, yellow light, more reminiscent of the glow of incandescent lamps than of the glittering starlight of the fledgling trails. "Stay low," Isla mouthed, and she stepped into the cavern.

The room rose stories high, and dilapidated toys piled along its walls from top to bottom. Rocking horses with chipped paint and broken rockers lay heaped in one corner. In another, rusted cars and trains formed a junk pile. Cobwebs draped over roller skates, tricycles, and board games, and moths fluttered up from a mountain of moldy teddy bears. The Forgotten wandered among the dusty relics, drifting aimlessly and tripping over piles of blocks that had spilled into their way.

Isla directed them against a wall, then pointed above to where Alister swooped in circles beneath a glint of blue. He was following a fledgling trail that clung to the very top of the cavern in a glittery ribbon. Isla waved them onward, and Lily looked over her shoulder to ensure Rowan had seen Isla's signal. She stopped.

Rowan had vanished.

Oh, no! With a wave of déjà vu, Lily pressed herself against the wall and looked from one side of the cavern to the other, scanning for some sign of the elf prince. Although Aristotle still toddled beside her, the rest of the group took no notice and disappeared amid the piles of discarded toys.

"Rowan!" Lily whispered. She sidled along the wall and froze as a Forgotten airplane with a missing wheel and a cracked windshield wobbled past. Then, she glimpsed Rowan lingering near a heap of stuffed animals. He had a single hand outstretched toward something among the pile.

"Rowan, what are you doing?" Lily whispered as she crept up. He turned toward her, but didn't raise his eyes. Instead, he stared in disbelief at something clutched in his hands: a faded, mangy stuffed raccoon with black beady eyes and a green ribbon around its tail.

"I don't understand it," he whispered to her, his brow furrowed in confusion. "What is he doing here?"

"Rowan, we need to go. Someone might see you!"

"You don't understand. This is—"

"I know it's your raccoon. Just leave it! We need to go; we'll lose the others!" She slipped her free hand into his, and gently led him back into the shadows. He didn't resist, but as she guided him back against the wall, he repeatedly glanced over his shoulder at the raccoon that stared sappily back at him from the pile of animals.

Lily squinted through the darkness in search of the fledgling trail. She could barely see it, and without the guidance of Isla and Alister she struggled to discern its trajectory. "Rowan, can you see where we're supposed to go?" she asked.

Just then, a walking fish missing half its scales flopped by them. It held a cane and balanced on its tail fins as if they were feet. Lily dragged Rowan and Aristotle against the wall and froze until the creature passed.

"I just don't understand it. What is he doing *here?*" Rowan said once they were safe again.

"That fish? You know him?"

Rowan blinked, as if he'd not even noticed the dapper codfish who'd nearly blown their cover. "I'm talking about my raccoon," he said.

"Are you kidding? Rowan, let it go!"

"You don't understand, Lily. It shouldn't be here! I'm dream-born!"

"Can't we talk about this later?"

"The Forgotten only care about humans. They filch *human* toys to remind them of the children who made them. Why would they care about my raccoon?"

"They filch toys? From whom?"

"From the humans who dreamed them up. Didn't you ever lose a toy as a child?"

"Of course, I did."

"Where do you think it went? Who do you think took it?"

Lily's eyes widened, and then she shot Aristotle an appalled look. The otter avoided eye contact and busied himself with cleaning his paws.

"Aristotle?"

He fluffed his fur and pretended not to hear.

"Aristotle! Did *you* take Poky Penguin?"

The otter glanced up, shrugged, and squeaked.

"How could you? What else did you take?" She gasped. "Don't tell me Diggy the Dragon! Aristotle, say you didn't!"

"He took them all, Lily, just accept it," Rowan said. "The point is, although the Forgotten steal human toys, I've never heard of them taking things from the dream-born before."

"Are you sure it's the same raccoon?"

"You saw my memory, didn't you?"

A brilliant green fledgling suddenly flickered above and floated along the ceiling of the cavern, bathing all the decrepit toys in a mysterious glow. It zigzagged among stalactites, then floated toward an entryway opposite where Lily, Rowan, and Aristotle stood.

"Here's our chance!" Lily whispered. "We can follow it to the others."

Rowan nodded, crouched low, and then grasped Lily's hand and took the lead. He nimbly sidestepped a hill of marbles and wove between mounds of soccer balls to keep pace with the fledgling above them. Every time a green ray of light from the fledgling touched Lily, her imagination came afire, with ideas and pictures sparking so quickly and abundantly that she could hardly sort them. As she reveled in the joy of it, she tipped her head backward to gaze in appreciation at the fledgling, and then stepped on Aristotle's tail.

The otter uttered a shrill squeak. Rowan wheeled around to hush her, and Lily flushed with mortification. "Sorry, I tripped," she whispered.

Rowan didn't answer. Instead, his eyes widened, and he pointed to a familiar glow shining through her pocket. The soothstone had come afire like breaking daylight. As the soothstone faded, dozens of sprites, each small enough to fit within Lily's palm, floated about the cavern like the willowy heads of dandelion seeds.

Lily stifled a laugh. *It's back!* she thought with delight. *My power to create is back!* While she beamed, the sprites gossiped with one another in voices like wind chimes. They swirled about in a celebratory dance, and their spinning quickened, faster and faster, until they eventually formed a funnel cloud that whooshed about the cavern. The sprites swept up the dirt, cobwebs, and dust from everything they touched, polishing the surfaces of plastic balls and toy trains long forgotten.

Oh, how lovely! Lily thought. She looked to Rowan, eager to share her joy with him, but the moment she spotted him her exhilaration fizzled.

"Lily, what have you done?"

Lily snapped out of her reverie as Rowan backed toward her, his hands upheld in self-defense. The sprites' clean-up job had drawn attention. A crowd of the Forgotten gathered around them in a circle, staring intently at Lily with wild desperation. As Lily looked into their haggard, worn faces, she recognized the same distress and hunger that had glinted in the eyes of the Forgotten who attacked her in the desert.

"Uh oh," Aristotle squeaked.

A slimy frog grabbed hold of Lily's ankle with two webbed forelimbs. Lily kicked it off and backed away from the crowd. "Please, just let us pass," Lily said, her voice cracking. She thought of Wendell at the entrance to the lairs, and remembered Isla's remark: *He's a forgotten wyvern, and he wants to be loved.* "I'll try to care for you," Lily added. "But I can't all at once. There's— there's only one of me. Please."

More and more of the Forgotten emerged, creaking and drooling as they crept from the shadows. A miniature pirate, his peg leg splintered and his eye patch faded to gray, brandished a rusty cutlass. "Fancy seein' the likes of you here, lass," he said with a toothless grin. Behind him, an amphibious creature raised a net tangled with seaweed as if to cast it over her.

"Please! I can't help all of you at once! I'm not trying to run away, please just let me pass!"

Aristotle clung to Lily's hand so tightly that pins and needles shot through her fingers. "Not good," he squeaked. "Must go!"

A spider scuttled up Aristotle's shoulder, and a dog with a chewed ear latched onto Lily's leg.

"Run!" Rowan cried. He whipped his arms in the air, and a blinding flash of lightning sizzled into the ground. The Forgotten cowered from the blaze and shrank back, shielding their eyes and squealing in terror. A screen of smoke billowed up from the scorched earth and kindled Lily's hope that Rowan had stopped their advance, but in the next instant the Forgotten stumbled through the smoke as if it were a ragged curtain. They paraded forward, slack-jawed and moaning with their limbs outstretched.

Rowan's cry and the cold slap of a jellyfish against Lily's neck prodded her to dash ahead. She swerved to avoid a miniature superhero with a tattered cape, then leaped over a plush snake that coiled on the ground ready to strike. A litter of kittens with mangy faces and a robot with a spring protruding from its head gained on her as she raced after Rowan, the both of them running deeper and deeper into the hollows beneath the desert.

Suddenly, Rowan skidded to a stop. Lily saw him too late, ran past him, and slammed into a sheer rock face. She spun around, and panicked when she realized she'd struck a dead end. "Aristotle!" she cried, pawing the wall in search of an escape route. "Do you know about any more buttons?"

Aristotle clung to her leg in terror with his eyes squeezed shut. He didn't answer.

A growl broke through the din, and Lily whirled around to discover a wolf with a twisted leg crouched on its haunches. The wolf snarled, and its black lips curled back to reveal yellowed teeth.

"Easy there, buddy," Lily said, raising her arms. "I'm not going to hurt you. I'm just looking for my other friends, okay?"

The wolf cocked its head, and for a moment Lily thought it might flop to the ground and roll over, as Wendell had done. Instead, it bared its teeth, growled, and then leapt. Lily screamed and huddled against the wall with her arms over her head as the wolf sailed toward her in a mass of mangy fur.

"I've got you, Lily!"

Light filtered through Lily's closed eyelids. She peeked through her arms just in time to see Rowan rush to her side and unleash a shower of lightning bolts. A familiar groaning filled the air as the lightning penetrated the ground like a gnarled network of roots, and then an enormous wall of glass ascended through the cavern, knocked stalactites from their bases, and stopped flush with the ceiling. A thud and a whimper sounded outside the glass wall as the wolf struck the dome and recoiled backward.

Lily's relief at Rowan's appearance melted away as she studied the glass wall into which he'd locked them. She placed a hand on the smooth glass, and knocked on it as if testing its integrity. "You just trapped us in," she said, her voice faraway and disbelieving.

"I saved your life."

"But you've locked us in!"

"To save you! If it hadn't been for me, you'd be smothered in the Forgotten right now."

"Great, thanks. But do you see where you've trapped us?" She turned in place and swept her arms to indicate the rock and glass walls that imprisoned them. "This is pretty close to being smothered!"

"We'll be fine, trust me."

"We're in a tomb!"

BANG. The mob of Forgotten had reached them and pounded against the glass wall. Aristotle squealed and pointed toward the ceiling.

"Great. Just great," Lily said.

"Stop complaining and let me think."

BANG. The Forgotten hoisted a withered tree trunk with eyes and spectacles and rammed the glass.

"Which way would Isla have gone?" Rowan said.

"Whichever way the fledgling went."

"And which way is that?"

"How should I know?"

Another *BANG.* Aristotle's squeaks turned frantic, and Lily finally followed the direction of his paw. This last sound hadn't come from the Forgotten at all, but rather from the green fledgling as it repeatedly smacked into the wall like a bumblebee against a windshield.

Lily and Rowan backed against the rock as a starburst of cracks splayed along the glass. The fledgling reared back, barreled forward in one final impact, and broke through. As it slid through the hole, the Forgotten immediately seized their opportunity. A woodpecker—made out of wood—tottered through the rent in the glass with rickety flaps of its wings, and a tiny, winged pony soon followed.

Lily's heart raced as the fledgling hovered above her and flitted back and forth across the wall in search of an exit. It stopped in front of a mural scrawled across the rock face in charcoal. The sketch depicted something serpentine, with a long tail and a neck arched like an eel. It had a long, beak-like snout, and its eyes were . . .

Lily's blood turned cold. The drawing portrayed a vicious black dragon. "Rowan, do you see this?" she asked.

Before he could answer, the stone between the charcoal dragon's jaws opened. Light poured from the resulting gap in the rock, as if the beast were calling out a mystical song. In an instant, the fledgling shot into the dragon's mouth like a comet through the dark, and disappeared.

"That's our way out!" Rowan shouted. He unleashed another lightning bolt, and a fulgurite twisted up from the earth and leaned against the mural. Rowan nimbly ascended the glass tree and dove into the tunnel as the narrow entryway through the dragon's mouth started to spiral closed.

The splintering of glass pierced the air, and Lily hid her face as dozens of shards pattered down. The Forgotten had smashed through the glass wall and now streamed in like water.

Lily scrambled up the fulgurite, but something held her. She glanced down. Aristotle still clung to her, whimpering and trembling, too frightened to climb up himself.

"Come on, Aristotle! We have to go!"

He said nothing, but instead tightened his grip around her ankle and shuddered.

"Lily, it's closing!" Rowan screamed from within the wall. "Come on!"

Lily kicked her leg in desperation, but Aristotle only clamped tighter. His weight dragged her down the sloping glass, while a mob of the Forgotten crowded around the base of the fulgurite and clawed at her shoes.

"Aristotle, please!" she begged.

The otter looked up at her, his helpless eyes shining like black beads. As Lily locked eyes with him, a memory suddenly flashed into her mind. She recalled Aristotle gazing up at her in the Fortress back home as they pretended to battle a mob of ogres. Minions with gnashing green teeth had surrounded them on all sides, and Aristotle, fearing all hope had faded, pleaded with her to surrender. Lily had puffed up her chest and raised the tree branch she'd commandeered as a sword, and declared, "Fear not . . ."

"Good will overcome." Lily spoke the words blankly at first, but at the sound of them, Aristotle's frightened eyes glistened. "Fear not, good will overcome! I'll save you!" she cried.

The terror on the otter's face melted away. With a gush of love, he rallied his courage, cried out, and scurried up the fulgurite, calling for Lily to follow. Lily scrambled up after him and stretched out her hand to clasp Rowan's.

As their fingers interlocked, something rough and sharp grasped Lily's ankle and wrenched her back down the glass. A crocodile with broken teeth had latched onto her right leg, and a mangled teddy bear soon wrapped his tattered paws around the left. As she slid downward, Lily grasped for a foothold, but her hands slipped against the glass.

Another flash. Another billow of smoke, and the Forgotten released their grip on her. Rowan reached through the storm cloud he'd procured and called out Lily's name, but he still couldn't reach her.

Aristotle dashed out. "Tail!" he cried to Rowan.

Rowan fumbled at first, then perceived Aristotle's meaning and clutched his tail. The otter raced down the slope and grabbed onto Lily's outstretched arm with both front paws. Rowan grunted, Aristotle yelped, and with a heave they dragged Lily up the fulgurite and into the shrinking expanse of the dragon's mouth. The Forgotten cried out in anguish as Lily pitched forward into the tunnel, and then the dragon's mouth sealed shut with a crash.

Lily lay on her back on a stone floor, and for a moment she rested with her eyes closed and tried to still her heartbeat.

"Save you," Aristotle cooed, nuzzling her.

Lily smiled and opened her eyes. She stroked Aristotle's head, and he lapped at her cheek with a tiny pink tongue. "Thank you, little friend," she said. "Without you, I would have—"

The spectacle around her stunned her into silence. They had landed in a cylindrical chamber, like an ancient well with stones eternally dripping from the runoff from some forgotten, subterranean river. From floor to ceiling, thousands of fledglings floated together, brilliant and glittering.

The throng of newborn dreams coaxed a hundred colors, images, and hopes from Lily's mind like sparklers. She suddenly felt the impulses to play, draw, paint, sculpt, and write all at once.

The spectacle didn't faze Rowan. "Isla!" he called out. "Isla, are you here?"

"Rowan."

They squinted through the mass of lights. The voice was Isla's, but it was thin and trembling, exuding none of the princess's steely confidence.

"Isla, where are you?"

"I'm here, Rowan. It's all right. Everything is all right."

Rowan walked around the perimeter of the chamber with Lily and Aristotle in tow. They found Isla, Alister, Philippe, and Flint standing alongside a figure with its back to them. The figure was short, about Lily's height, and wore a gray cloak. Isla had a strange, faraway expression on her face, as if she'd just seen a ghost, or witnessed the mountains uproot themselves and wander off.

"What is it?" Rowan asked, trying to read her face. "What's happened?"

"Pax was right, Rowan. He was right."

"What are you talking about? Right about what?"

"He said the fate of our people was tied to the soothstone."

"And?"

She gazed with wonder at the figure beside her. "My quest for the soothstone brought me to the Cave of Lights, and then here. To *her*."

"Isla, to whom? What are you talking about?"

The figure turned around, and a pair of small, slender hands pulled back the hood of the cloak. A young girl—a *human* girl—smiled back at them. Her eyes were dark, and she'd tied her hair back in a low ponytail, just like the girl in a photograph Lily had recently seen.

Just like the girl in the photograph in Barth's journal.

CHAPTER 28

The Lost Girl

Even with the myriad colors from the newborn dreams dappling her face, the girl's dark eyes, and the intelligence in them, were unmistakable. She wore her hair at the nape of her neck, just like Barth's daughter Mattie in the pictures he'd shown Lily while they sailed in the *Flying Emerald*.

But how could she still just be a girl? Lily wondered. *Barth left our world years ago, and said she'd be a grown woman by now.* As Lily pondered, Cedric's words surfaced from her memories: *Time in the Realm is much more fluid . . .*

"Mattie?" Lily whispered, but the girl was too busy grinning at Rowan to notice.

"It's amazing that you're here!" Mattie cried. "I was excited to see Isla, but you've *both* come!" She clapped her hands together, as a little girl might upon discovering a truckload of presents under the Christmas tree.

Rowan looked startled. "Who are you? How do you know my name?"

"Don't you know me?"

His brow furrowed. "I know your voice. But why? Who are you?"

"Rowan, I *made* you. You're a character in my drawings."

The ruts in Rowan's forehead deepened. He looked to Isla for answers, but she just smiled back at him. "I don't understand," Rowan said.

"You said you knew her voice," Isla said. "So do I. Rowan, this must be what Pax meant by the hope for our people! It's her! She's the human who dreamed us up. Maybe she can find a way forward for us!"

Rowan's eyes narrowed with suspicion. "This is really strange. This little girl is our hope?"

"Her name's Mattie," Lily said.

Mattie glanced at Lily in surprise. "You know my name?"

Lily nodded. "I'm Lily."

Mattie studied her. "You're not from here. You're like me, aren't you? How did you find me?"

"That's a really, really long story. What about you? What are you doing down here?"

"I came here by accident, ages ago. I was following my father—"

"Barth?"

Mattie's eyes widened. "How do you know that?"

"I know him. He was kind of a teacher to me, and a friend. I know who you are because he showed me your picture."

Mattie opened her mouth to speak, but the grinding of rock interrupted her. A stone door slid open to reveal a passageway in the ceiling above them.

"It's him," Mattie said with sudden unease. "Come on, let's go somewhere else. I can't think straight with all these lights here anyway."

"Too many ideas in your head?" Lily asked.

Mattie smiled. "Of things to draw, yes."

Mattie felt along the seams between the stones in the wall and pressed her fingers into an indentation. With a clamor the bricks folded back to reveal a tunnel, and she led them into a room bathed in the soft glow of candlelight. A canopy bed with lilac curtains nestled in one corner of the room, piled high with pillows in mismatched shams—lace and plaid and floral patterns all mixed up. Drawings scrawled in charcoal, painted in tempera, and shaded with chalk wallpapered the room from floor to ceiling.

As Lily's eyes flitted from one sketch to the next, her heartbeat quickened. She recognized the willow trees beside the rushing river near the Wilderness, and Isla's home with the fountain out front. The regal towers of Castle Mistwood glimmered in the

Valley of the Mist Elves like a silver crown. A familiar laurel-leaf pattern, the same that adorned both Lily's cottage and Mattie's journal pages, curled and wove through the sketches.

Isla spied Mistwood among the drawings, and she tenderly traced its lines with a single finger. Rowan, meanwhile, stood transfixed before the images of a stone fortress peeking up from the tree line, and beyond it, a gleaming white tower with flags waving in an icy wind.

"It all came from you?" Isla said breathlessly.

"I drew all this, if that's what you mean," Mattie said. When she spoke, her voice was pressured, as if her words burst from a firehose. "I can't believe you're here! I mean, I guess I *should* believe it. My owl, Sonia, is here too, and I figured out pretty quickly that this is a magical place. But I never thought I'd meet both of you! I have pictures of you and Rowan somewhere around here if I can find them." The rusted hinges of a dilapidated chest squeaked as she opened it and rifled through a stack of papers. She pulled out a sketch: Isla, just her head and shoulders, her hair sweeping across her face and her eyes hardened as if readying herself for battle.

"Rowan, look at this!" Isla said, taking the paper as if it might crumble to dust in her fingers. "It's amazing!"

"My raccoon," Rowan mumbled to himself.

"What?" Isla asked.

"I found my old raccoon among all those toys back there." He pointed to Mattie. "I think I know how it got here."

"Oh, sorry." Mattie shrugged her shoulders and grinned sheepishly. "I didn't mean to take it from you. I drew a picture of it and was longing for a friend, and then *poof!* One of the Seekers—an old dog with a chewed ear, I think—brought the racoon to me in his jaws. He wanted to cheer me up. Anyway, what are you all doing here? How did you find me?"

"We followed the fledgling dreams here," Isla said.

"The what?"

"The lights, gathered in that chamber?"

"Oh, you mean the cures."

"Pardon me?"

"The cures. That's what the Dream Catcher calls them. They cured a terrible disease that was running through these caves. I didn't get sick, but all the Seekers were dying."

"The *what* were dying?" Lily asked.

"The Seekers. You know, all the shabby creatures that live down here?"

"Oh, you mean the Forgotten."

Mattie wrinkled her nose. "The Forgotten?"

"Yeah. That's what they're called."

"That's not what they call themselves."

"They're imaginary friends, caught between our world and this one."

Mattie's eyes sparkled. "I knew it. This place really is another world, isn't it?"

"It's called the Somnium Realm. It's like a dream world."

Mattie stared in wonder. "All these years, I didn't even know its name. The Seekers could never explain it to me, and the Dream Catcher doesn't tell me much."

"How long have you been down here, exactly?"

Mattie's face fell. "I'm not sure. I kept track for a while, but eventually there didn't seem to be any point." She gestured to a wall cluttered with dozens and dozens of tally marks.

Lily's heart ached as she imagined the long years Mattie had spent in solitude, all while Barth pined for her. "How is it that you came here?" she asked.

Mattie sat down on the canopy bed, one leg tucked under her, and swept her ponytail over her shoulder to anxiously pull at the strands. "My dad was going on a business trip, and as he left, I realized he'd taken my journal with him. He was like that. He'd forget things when he was talking or really focused on something else. I ran out the door after him, but instead of getting into his car he started walking into the park, toward our tree. The tree wasn't *really* ours, obviously, but he called it that. It was this huge maple with three trunks, and I used to climb in it when we'd go out for walks. He stopped under it, flipping through my notebook. I ran and called his name, and then—" She faltered.

"What, Mattie? Then what?"

"Something happened. Something awful. There was a flash of light, and suddenly everything around us disappeared."

Lily exchanged a knowing glance with Isla. *Barth's soothstone.*

"I felt dizzy, like the world was spinning around me. I tried to call out for my dad, but he didn't hear me, and then all of a sudden I saw Sonia." She glanced up at Lily. "You said something about imaginary friends?"

Lily nodded.

"Sonia was one of mine. She's this clockwork owl I made up, after I saw a fantastic clock in one of my mom's catalogs. My mom's into stuff from Germany. Anyway, I saw her and reached out for her, and then all the spinning stopped. Except my dad had vanished, and I wasn't home anymore. I was in this horrible desert. Sonia was with me, but she was different, old and broken, and her gears were all bent. Then there was this terrible roaring—"

"And a hole opened up in the ground," Lily finished.

Mattie nodded. Her chin quivered, as if she were holding back tears. "I've been here ever since."

"Ever since?" Lily asked. "Didn't you try to escape?"

"Of course I did, at first, but the Seekers wouldn't let me. They're so lonely, and every time I'd try to find a way out, they'd stop me. Then, of course, the Dream Catcher came and told me the truth. After that I didn't try anymore."

"Truth? What truth?"

"That it's not safe up above ground, and I'll die if I leave. And that my dad abandoned me here because he doesn't care about me."

Lily's face reddened with anger. "That's not true, Mattie! Not true at all!"

Mattie twisted her hair and suddenly appeared like a little girl who'd lost her parents in a crowd. "How could it not be true? No one ever came back to find me."

"Who is this Dream Catcher, exactly?" Isla said.

"He takes care of me. He has the Seekers bring me food, but he protects me from them, too. They mean well, but they're so desperate for company that they can be scary sometimes. The Dream Catcher doesn't let them come in here. Except for Sonia, of course."

At the mention of her name Mattie's clockwork owl, a rickety fistful of rusted gears, hobbled into the room. Two clock faces set at contrasting times, with their hands bent and crooked, formed the bird's eyes, and a spring protruded from her head like an antenna. Sonia glanced warily from Mattie to her visitors, and back again.

"But who *is* the Dream Catcher?" Isla repeated. "I used to be on the Council, and I've never heard of him."

"You were on the what?" Mattie said.

"Never mind. Please, tell us, who is he?"

"I don't know, really. I've never actually *seen* him. He wears a cloak, like mine—he gave this one to me, actually—but he always lingers back in the shadows." Mattie shuddered. "To tell you the truth, I don't think he has a body. He's kind of like a phantom and, if I'm honest, he scares me. But he's helped me, and he saved everyone down here from the sickness, so I have to trust him."

"*He* saved everyone?" Lily said with indignation. She thought of Magnus's similar claim, and her blood boiled.

"With the cures. When he filled that chamber with the lights, everyone was healed."

"That's a lie," Rowan said, suddenly joining the group. "Those aren't cures, and they don't belong to this Dream Catcher character, whoever he is."

"How does the Dream Catcher capture the cures?" Isla asked. "How does he bring them here?"

A faint flush of pride tinted Mattie's cheeks. "He used my idea, actually." She pointed to her sketches of the towers of the Icelein, stretching up like fingers from the snow-covered peaks of the mountains. A figure in a white robe stood upon the highest tower with his arms raised, a blue jewel in his hand as he cast a silvery net into the sky. Pinpoints of color dotted the net. *King Miran?* Lily wondered.

"I'd made up a magic gemstone that casts invisible nets into the air," Mattie said. "I originally imagined it could control ice and snow, but over time I thought it could catch other things, stars and moonbeams and such. It turns out the Dream Catcher had the stone but didn't know how to use it. Once I taught him, he harnessed the cures and healed the Seekers."

"What is it called?" Rowan suddenly snapped. He stood with every muscle tensed, and had clenched his hands into fists.

His outburst took Mattie aback. "I'm sorry?"

"The gemstone. What is it called?"

"The Woven Ice. I named it the Woven Ice."

Rowan's breathing quickened. "The Woven Ice is here? You have it?"

"I don't have it; it's in the chamber. The Dream Catcher controls it."

"How did he get it?"

"He told me King Miran gave it to him, ages ago."

Rowan's face reddened. "Where is this Dream Catcher now?"

"Probably back in the chamber that we just left. I don't think he'd like—"

"I need to talk to him. Take me to him, right now!"

"Rowan, why are you so agitated?" Isla asked.

"I don't know who this Dream Catcher person is, but he's lying."

"I agree with you, but what more do you know? What haven't you told me?"

Rowan opened and closed his fists and wavered in place, as if deciding whether to reveal all he'd seen.

"Please, Rowan," Isla urged.

Rowan drew a breath. "I met King Miran."

Isla gaped at him. "Rowan, what are you talking about?"

"He's alive, Isla. All the Icelein are, except they're nothing like what mother and father told us. They call themselves *dwellers* now. They retreated under the mountains when the Veil fell and have lived there for centuries."

"I had no idea." She thought for a moment, and then her face brightened. "Rowan, this means Mother was right all along! She always said the Icelein were still alive, and you were the only one who believed her. But she was right! This is wonderful news!"

"She was right, but it's not wonderful news. They've become horrible, Isla. Miran calls himself Magnus now, and he's so obsessed with finding magic stones like the Woven Ice that he enslaves everyone who gets in his way. He tortures people and forces them to mine the caves for stones."

"How could that be? Legend says King Miran was so regal and wise. To think he'd fall so low . . ."

For a moment Rowan suddenly looked older, more noble. He straightened his shoulders, and the intensity of his eyes reminded Lily more of a prince than a little brother. "Our father fell too, Isla. Why wouldn't Miran?"

Isla fell silent, and the sorrow in her eyes hinted that she reflected upon her own betrayals. "Why not any of us?" she said softly. "Still, it's hard to wrap my mind around it all. You said Magnus is obsessed with finding the Woven Ice, but why would that be, when he gave it to the Dream Catcher, like Mattie just told us?"

"He didn't give it to him."

"How do you know?"

Rowan looked grief-stricken. "Because Eldinor and Esperion took it from him. They betrayed him, Isla."

Isla's face grew ashen. "Rowan, no. No, that's not possible. You must be mistaken."

"There's no mistake. Magnus showed me everything. There was an avalanche, just like we thought, but instead of helping, Eldinor and Esperion *stole* the Woven Ice from Miran, and then they called down the Veil. Esperion was supposed to be the hope of our people, but the truth is he left all our kin to die."

Isla's eyes misted with tears. "This can't be. It just can't."

"It's true, Isla, as awful as it is. I saw it myself."

"I don't understand something," Lily interjected. "If Esperion and Eldinor took the Woven Ice, how did this Dream Catcher guy get it?"

"The Dream Catcher told me Miran gave the Ice to him as a token of devotion," Mattie said.

"That's a lie, too," said Rowan.

"Well obviously *someone's* lying," Isla said. She thought for a moment, then became suddenly animated. "Rowan, how vivid is your memory of what Miran showed you?"

"It was horrific. It's burned into my mind."

"Can you show me?"

"I don't have a memory bauble of it."

"No, but can you *show* me?"

"Oh, Isla!" He kicked the ground. "I hate when you do this."

"Please. If I sift your memories, I might be able to find it."

"I hate this. It makes me feel like a child."

"Why? It's not exactly a childish skill."

"I know, but you always sifted my memories to tattle on me for sneaking lemon biscuits."

"Obviously, this is different."

He wrung his hands. "Is it even worth it, though? You'll be sifting a memory of a memory. It might not be accurate."

"I'll be the judge of that." When Rowan didn't answer, Isla raised an eyebrow and crossed her arms in impatience.

"All right, all right," Rowan groaned. "But don't blame me if you see things you don't like."

Isla smirked, then placed her palm against Rowan's forehead, just as she had done with Lily back in the tunnel. She closed her eyes, then opened them again and wrinkled her face.

"I told you, you'll not like all of it!" Rowan said.

Isla smirked and closed her eyes again. As the seconds passed, her face darkened, and Rowan soon closed his eyes and folded his arms in front of his chest, barricading himself from the pain. Finally, Isla gasped, withdrew her hand, and for a moment stood stunned as Rowan rubbed his forehead and stared at the ground.

"I told you it was awful," Rowan muttered.

"Yes, it was, but there's something more, something that bothers me. That memory was off."

"I told you, it's a memory of a memory. It's bound to be fuzzy."

"No, it's more than that. There was this *blip* in the images, like something had been cut out."

Rowan looked up in alarm. "What?"

"The Icelein were memory workers too, Rowan. They could have interfered with it."

"What are you talking about?" Lily asked.

"Someone has tampered with the memory," Isla said. "Part of it was erased."

They fell silent, each one staring at the next.

"There's something else too, something I can't quite grasp. Something about Esperion that wasn't quite right."

"We know he wasn't quite right. He betrayed our brethren."

"Rowan, I'm serious. I mean something about *him* was wrong."

"Like what?"

"I don't know. If I could just try one more time—"

Rowan batted away her outstretched hands. "Out of the question! Be grateful that I let you try once!"

"*Pardon*," Philippe said, sauntering forward while swinging a turnip by the greens. "But how does all this fascinating conversation help us in our efforts to, say, get out?"

"You have a point, Philippe," Isla said. "We still need to free the fledglings. Mattie, how exactly does the Dream Catcher use the Woven Ice?"

"He commands the stone to cast out a net. It's invisible, and made from crystal fibers, like ice. He snares the cures, and draws them into the chamber. It's almost like fishing . . . except from *really* far away, of course. He just pictures what he's catching in his mind, and it works."

"Where does he cast the net?"

"Into a cave, beyond the desert. That's all he's told me. To be honest, I didn't even know it could reach that far."

"Is there a way to disable the net?"

Mattie frowned. "Why would we want to do that? He's helped so many of the Seekers with it."

"The only thing he's done is ensure no more Forgotten— or Seekers, as you call them—ever appear again. Those lights aren't cures, they're newborn dreams. The Dream Catcher is stealing humankind's ability to dream and create."

Mattie looked from one person to the next in bewilderment. "But that doesn't make sense. The Seekers all became well again when he brought in those lights!"

"Someone else cured them," Lily said. "Trust us, we know who it was."

"We need to free those fledglings," Isla said gravely. "Otherwise, the entire Realm is in jeopardy. As is your own world."

"Why? How?"

"We're created when your people dream. If that stops, our Realm will cease to exist. And as for your world, you're made to create, as reflections of the one who created you. Imagine what would happen if your people lost that gift? Imagine the desolation and the despair."

Mattie looked stricken. She dropped her head into her hands and rubbed her forehead with both palms. "I'm so confused. The Dream Catcher scares me, but he watches over and protects me. Why would he do this?"

"I don't think he is who he claims to be," Isla said.

"He's the only one who's ever cared for me."

"That's not true," Lily said. "Your dad cares for you."

"How can you say that, when he abandoned me here?"

"He didn't know you were here. He's been missing you for years and finally just returned home to find you again."

Mattie raised her head and examined Lily with reddened eyes. "I want to believe what you're saying, but I don't know who to trust. I haven't seen another person in years and years, and just met you. How can I be sure you're telling me the truth? How do I know you're even who you say you are?"

"Because I know your dad."

"How can I be sure of that?"

Lily's thoughts flew. "The journal," she blurted. "Your dad showed me your journal. There were drawings of willows and Mistwood and Isla's house."

"You could guess that just from sitting in this room. These walls are covered in those drawings."

Lily bit her lip and concentrated. "Frisbee," she finally said. "He told me about the walks you'd take together. You lived near Golden Gate Park, and you'd play Frisbee with the dog. He'd get you soft serve ice cream, and you'd feed it to the dog when you thought he wasn't looking."

Both joy and grief washed over Mattie's face. "Bruiser. The dog's name was Bruiser."

"He didn't tell me that much, sorry."

Mattie laughed, and pushed a lock of hair out of her face. "He drove my mom nuts. He was cute but smelly." She laughed again, then wrung her hands and fought against tears that welled in her eyes. "I've missed him so much. I've missed all my family so much."

Mattie broke down, and Lily wrapped her arms around her shoulders. Aristotle gave a squeak of pity and nuzzled against Mattie's knee. Even Flint and Philippe drew closer.

"Your dad loves you," Lily said. "He's gone back to look for you."

"Why didn't he look sooner?"

"He didn't know you were here, and he was too ashamed to go back home."

"Ashamed? Why? Why would he leave my mom and me?"

"He made some mistakes," Isla said. "Like we all do. He loved you too much to disgrace you."

They sat in silence and let Mattie's tears pour out. Lily weighed different words to say, but a glance from Isla warned her to wait and to give Mattie space to grieve. Finally, Mattie sat up, wiped her eyes, and smoothed the stray hair back into her ponytail. "Can you help me find him?" she asked, looking at Lily imploringly.

"What do you mean?"

"My dad. You said he's gone back home to look for me. Can you take me to him?"

Lily hesitated. She hadn't planned to return to the waking world anytime soon. She missed Keisha, Adam, and her family, but how could she leave when she hadn't yet explored so much of the Realm? How could she walk away from so many mysteries and tantalizing wonders, especially when her own world chafed her like an ill-fitting glove? She couldn't. It was out of the question.

And yet. Mattie leaned forward in earnest, twisting the hem of her shirt between her hands as if her very life depended on Lily's answer. Lily recognized the desperation in Mattie's eyes, and the hope. She'd felt the same swirling emotions when Nyssinia revealed that her father hadn't died at sea.

"Yes," Lily finally said. "Yes, I will." She tried to hide her disappointment, but she slouched a little, as if she were a slowly deflating balloon.

"Oh, thank you! Thank you!" Mattie said. She hugged Lily in a rush of gratitude. The embrace took Lily aback, but she smiled as she patted Mattie's shoulder. Somehow, she knew Mattie would be a fast friend.

Isla watched the two girls with an uneasy expression. "Mattie?" she said hesitantly. "Wouldn't you want to come back to Mistwood? To live with us?"

Mattie thought for a long while. "I need the same thing you do, Isla." She met Isla's eyes. "I need my family. I want to find my dad."

Isla clenched her jaw, and her gaze flitted over the sketches on the walls as if she were searching them for answers. Isla had thought Mattie would restore her kingdom, that *she* was her people's destiny. How could that be, if she left the Realm to return home?

"So what do we do now?" Rowan asked. "We still have to deal with this Dream Catcher character."

"Yes. Yes, of course." Isla shook off her thoughts and straightened. "First, we have to find a way to free the fledgling dreams. Then we need to capture the Woven Ice, to ensure the Dream Catcher doesn't abuse its powers again."

"I don't know if we can," Mattie said. "I'm worried about what he'll do."

"Excuse me, madam." Alister had stood at attention during their banter and silently observed the scene. "I believe I may be of service. The amber jewel at my neck draws light to itself. I believe I can use it to draw the fledgling dreams out of these caves."

Lily's heart skipped a beat. "Alister, that's genius! You can fly out and use the jewel to lure them after you!"

"And lead them back to the Cave of Lights," Isla added with growing excitement. "I can go with him; a soothstone will help as we cross the Desert of the Forgotten. Now we just need a plan to take the Woven Ice. Mattie, where does he keep it?"

"It's mounted in the ceiling of the chamber."

"I can do it," Rowan said.

"How are you going to climb up to the ceiling?" Isla asked.

"Lily can call something to fly me up. Right, Lily?"

Lily thought for a moment. *Could she?* She remembered how her thoughts danced in the presence of the fledglings. "Yes. Yes, I can. Even better, I'll call Rigel and he can retrieve it for us."

"Great," Rowan said. "How soon can we start?"

"The Dream Catcher comes every night to count the cures," Mattie said. "A few days ago, the Woven Ice fell from its mount and some of the lights escaped him. It made him pretty angry, so lately he's been coming every night to ensure the numbers are correct."

A few days ago? Lily remembered how her powers transiently returned during their fight against Magnus, only to vanish again. Perhaps that sudden return of inspiration coincided with the fledglings escaping the Dream Catcher's grasp.

"He's probably in there now, but he usually leaves after sunrise," Mattie said. "We can sneak into the chamber then."

"How do you know it's sunrise when you're underground?" Lily asked.

Mattie motioned to Sonia, who approached her for a head scratch. Mattie pointed to the owl's belly, where a brass moon anchored to a clock hand leaned to the right, signaling the end of night. "When Sonia's sun rises, it's usually safe."

Isla nodded. "It's settled then. When Sonia's sun rises, we act."

They spent a few fretful hours waiting for the brass sun within Sonia's creaky innards to rear its head. Flint and Aristotle played a game with little marbles of flame, while Philippe chewed distractedly on some parsnips dipped in *mole* sauce. Isla and Rowan paced the room, first studying the drawings, then staring off into the wells of their own memories.

Lily decided to call Rigel before they ventured into the chamber, and when light flowed from the soothstone, Mattie bolted upright and stared as if she'd seen a ghost. When her shock wore off, she collected the belongings she wanted to take with her, stuffing stacks and stacks of drawings into a tatty pillow sham. Eventually, however, the load became too heavy, and she dumped the sketches into a pile on the floor, never to gather them again. Then she curled up on the bed, hugged a pillow to her chest, and played with the brass feathers splayed out from Sonia's tail.

A grinding sound finally broke the quiet, followed by the dysphonic clank of broken chimes. They all glanced at Sonia, who hooted miserably as a tarnished sunburst creaked into her chest.

"Sunrise," Isla said.

Mattie clutched Sonia beneath her arm and led them through the tunnel into the chamber. The circular door in the ceiling remained shut, like a sewer drain closed with a manhole cover. Lily whispered in Rigel's ear, and the star kestrel took flight. He pirouetted several times, then disappeared among the swirling lights of the chamber to search for the Woven Ice.

Isla climbed onto Alister's back, and with a great flapping of his wings and a sweep of his cloak the bat lifted into the air. The amber jewel at his neck radiated a brilliant gold light, like the rays of the sun when it first peeks over the horizon at daybreak. As its beams pierced through the gloom of the chamber, all the fledgling dreams halted their frenetic vibrations, as if all at once they paused and held their breath.

Alister flew toward the ceiling, and Isla probed the cracks between the stones for the mechanism to draw back the door. With a quick intake of air, she found it, then depressed it. The grinding of stone echoed throughout the chamber as the door retracted to reveal a tunnel snaking into the blackness. Alister twirled once in the air, and the jewel at his throat pulsed a vibrant flash of light. Then he swooped up the tunnel.

A tidal wave of light followed, as if all the stars in the sky converged at once and heaved on the swell of a great sea. Unborn dreams rushed in a brilliant stream of color up the passageway, surging in unison like a synchronized flock of birds. When the last few stragglers spun their way up the tunnel, Lily's heart ached. The chamber darkened as they disappeared.

Rigel trilled, and Lily turned to see him hovering beside her with an oblong jewel, turquoise in color but translucent like ice, glowing from within his beak. "Thanks, Rigel," Lily said with a smile. She reached out a hand to take it from him.

"I'll take that."

Rowan placed one hand on Lily's shoulder and showed her the open palm of the other. The pressure on her shoulder was heavy, and the insistence in his voice made her uneasy. Rowan wasn't asking her; he was commanding.

Rigel didn't respond, but instead turned a circle in the air and awaited Lily's signal. Warily, Lily nodded. Rigel dropped the Woven Ice into Rowan's hand, and the prince immediately closed his fingers around it and clutched it to his breast. A darkness in his eyes unsettled her.

"Mademoiselle, we must leave," Philippe said, tugging at Lily's sleeve. "If that tunnel closes, who knows when we can get out again?"

"Indeed, miserable rodent. And what will you do then, trapped here in the dark?"

Oh, no.

The voice turned Lily's blood to ice. She suddenly felt sick, as if all the hope within her had drained away. She turned in a circle to locate the voice, but it seemed to echo from all around and envelope them in the dark, empty chamber.

"It's the Dream Catcher!" Mattie whispered, gripping Lily's arm. "We have to get out of here, now!"

"You disappoint me, Matilda. After all I've done for you. After I've treated you like my own daughter."

Lily's heart pounded. *I know that voice! It can't be!* She glanced down. The red glow of the soothstone shone through her pocket.

A figure draped in a gray cloak, like Matilda's but flowing as if whipped by an invisible wind, stepped into the center of the chamber. The hood enshrouded no face, but instead a mass of swirling smoke. He had neither form nor features, but Lily knew his identity without doubt.

"Welcome back, dream steward. How fitting that we should meet again underground!"

Eymah's eyes burned through the dark like flaming coals.

CHAPTER 29

The Dream Catcher

"Mattie, get away from him!" Lily cried.

Eymah cackled, his laugh sounding like the click of some heinous insect. "I see you've retained your spirit, Lily McKinley. What a pity that you would not join me. Imagine what we could have accomplished together, you and I! How pathetic to see you now, a bedraggled imp of a girl squandering your talents when you could have been so much more." He circled her, as if examining her for weaknesses. "It's not too late for you though, Lily. You can still rise to greatness. You can still prove the full scope of your powers. Imagine what people would say if you brought back the lord of the Realm! Imagine what such a feat would prove about your talents, Lily, about your *importance!*"

Waves of bracing cold seized Lily, as if Eymah sucked all warmth from her with each ghastly word. She tightened her hands into fists. "Pax is already Lord of the Realm!" she shouted. She tried to sound self-assured, but her voice cracked.

The phantom growled. "The unicorn? Tell me, esteemed dream keeper, where is your precious prince now? The Sovran Merrow tells me he's a bit . . . under the weather."

Under the weather? Lily's heartbeat quickened with a flicker of hope. *He doesn't know. He doesn't know Pax is alive!*

Eymah drew within inches of Lily's face. His vapors swirled around her, sucking all joy from her heart, and his eyes pierced through her. "*I* am lord! Restore me to power, Lily. Use that pebble in your pocket to give me a new form, something awesome, something great and terrible. Then all the glory of the Realm will be yours. Then all will know the name of the greatest artisan in the history of the Realm! You've raised castles and walls, Lily McKinley. Now raise me!"

Lily steeled herself against his words. She slid her hand into her pocket, closed her fingers around the soothstone, and focused on Pax, his light, his majesty. "You can't win!" Lily said through chattering teeth.

Eymah cleared his throat in disgust. "Can't I, dream steward?" He flung his cloak as if snapping a whip and laughed as the stone door to the passageway ground shut, trapping them within the chamber.

Philippe withdrew his carrot saber, bellowed a war cry, and charged at Eymah. He swung the blade and scattered sparks into the air, but with a *whoosh* the saber passed through the villain without impact, as if he were nothing but vapor. Rigel dove in next, striking at Eymah with his beak and talons, but with a flap of his cloak Eymah whisked him away like a mosquito. Finally, Flint rushed in, rolling forward and bursting into a conflagration that swallowed Eymah in flames. Yet even before the fire died, Eymah's detestable laugh echoed throughout the chamber. Flint spun backward panting and spent, while Eymah's eyes flared red with malice.

"You cannot destroy me, vermin," Eymah hissed. "True, your prince deprived me of form when he pitched me into the Catacombs. It is an existence I have *loathed*, scrabbling about in the filthy places of the Realm. And yet, it is not without its advantages."

"Open the door."

Eymah blinked in surprise as Rowan stepped toward him with the Woven Ice held aloft. The stone pulsed blue in his hand.

"And what have we here?"

"I said open the door! Now!"

Eymah's eyes flashed. "You're the Mist Elf's boy, aren't you?" he said.

Rowan's jaw tightened. "I am Rowan, Prince of the Mist Elves. And I command you to open that door above us!"

A wind whipped through the room, and Eymah swept within inches of Rowan's face. "My, my, you *are* like your father, aren't you? You have the same nose. I wonder, is that all you share?"

Rowan's face changed, as if he'd been struck. "I'm warning you!" he shouted. "Open. That. Door!"

"Ah, there it is. The outrage of the Mist Elves. Tell me, fair prince, do you also brood when you don't get your way? Do you covet power as much as your father did?"

Rowan's breathing quickened, and Lily recognized the change that came over him. Eymah was casting the same dismal spell over Rowan that he'd used against her in the Catacombs, when he'd poisoned her mind with lies. "Don't listen to him, Rowan!" she shouted. "He's trying to trick you! You can't believe what he says!"

Eymah dropped his voice to a whisper. "You can have all you desire, young prince. A kingdom all your own, where everyone will adore you, just as you've always wanted. That *is* what you've always wanted, isn't it, young prince? Young *Esperion*?"

Rowan's face appeared wan in the pale blue light of the Woven Ice. "How do you know what I want?" he said, his voice thin and tremulous.

"Oh, foolish, brash, proud prince! You are the weakling child of a spineless king. Do you really think the workings of your heart are so secret? They cry out to me like screams in the dark." He whirled around Rowan. "But I can set you free. I can give you more power than you've ever imagined."

"Don't listen to him! He's lying to you!"

Eymah snarled. "I've had just about enough of you, dream steward! Rowan, silence her!"

Rowan's eyes widened. "What?"

Suddenly the Woven Ice emitted a burst of light, and a web shot from the stone and trapped Lily in a cage of ice. Lily stumbled backward as the spokes imprisoned her, and the soothstone slipped from her hands and tumbled just beyond her reach. Mattie cried out and ran forward to help.

"Take one more step, Matilda, and I'll rip you to shreds!" Eymah growled.

Mattie froze. "You can't hurt me," she stammered. "You have no body!"

"No, but I have loyal servants for arms." Eymah swept his cloak again, and suddenly a pair of familiar, hungry eyes materialized from within the shadows.

"I told her I'd find her for you, master," a gravelly voice said.

At the sound, Lily's heart threatened to fly from her chest. *It can't be . . . Please, oh please, not this . . .*

"You've done well, Glower," Eymah said. "Although sadly, as the girl will not cooperate, I have no further use of her. Dispose of her!"

"With pleasure." Glower growled, baring his green teeth in an evil grin. "I've been looking forward to this, *creator.* You wouldn't finish my story. Now, I'll finish yours!"

In panic, Lily dropped on all fours and reached for the soothstone through the bars of the cage. Her fingers barely skimmed its tangled surface. She jammed her shoulder against the cold metal and tried again, but to no avail.

Glower loomed closer. "You can't win, creator. You know you can't. You always flounder. You always do the wrong thing."

Lily gritted her teeth and tried to ignore Glower's words. He was like an echo of Eymah, his speech just as twisted and vile as his master's.

"Leave her alone!" Rowan cried. Although he meant to defend her, he himself looked like a toddler grappling with a runaway dog. The Woven Ice jostled in his hand, casting flashes of color like a strobe light across the chamber walls, and he could barely hold on to it.

As Glower grimaced and raised his claws high, Flint sprang into action. He slammed against the cage and melted a hole at its base through which Lily could escape. Then he wheeled about to face Glower, but before he could charge, the shroud swatted him away with one swipe of his claws.

Lily scrambled through the rent in the cage and searched for the soothstone, but in her desperation she inadvertently knocked it farther beyond her reach. *Please, Pax*, Lily pleaded. *Please. I know you are with me. Help me now.*

"Goodbye, creator," Glower said. "It seems not all stories end happily." He barreled toward her, his red eyes burning through the gloom, his claws uplifted like a pair of tridents.

Lily shut her eyes. She could smell Glower's fowl breath, stinking of rotten eggs and moldering garbage.

Please. Please, Pax.

Glower's claws clacked against the rock floor.

Please, Pax. I know you've already won.

Suddenly, Glower cried out in rage. Lily opened her eyes to discover Philippe swinging his saber at the beast, then batting him across the head with both broad feet. On the ground just beyond lay the soothstone.

Lily rushed forward and snatched the soothstone from the ground. As she raised the stone to eye level, she remembered Pax, his eyes deep as the sea, carrying her to safety across turbulent waters. She remembered his words: *Remember that I love you, no matter what storms assail you. I am with you always, and I will return and make all things new.*

The stone burst aglow. Philippe sprang back and cried out in alarm as a tornado of white flame appeared and swirled through the chamber. Glower shrank back and screamed. The flames chased away the darkness and exposed him not as a deadly threat, but rather as a mangy, stooped mess of wiry hair and jutting limbs, a wretched thing powerless without the shadows of a closet. For a moment Lily locked eyes with him, as she had from beneath her bedcovers as a little girl. On those frightening nights, she'd shivered, clutched her pillow, and prayed for rescue. Now, with the blinding light revealing him in all his meagerness, she could only shake her head with a twinge of pity.

Philippe held his saber aloft and tightened his paws around the hilt, readying himself for an attack. It never came. In an instant the tornado swallowed Glower up, engulfing him from head to tail. The monster moaned, writhed, and cried out for help from his master still hovering at a distance. When no help came, Glower vanished in a puff of smoke.

"Lily! Are you—"

A gust of wind blasted through the chamber and knocked Mattie off her feet.

Lily rushed to her side; a small gash streaked across Mattie's scalp. Lily glanced up. Eymah loomed above her, his cloak whipping in the wind he'd stirred up with one swipe of his arm.

"This is not over, dream keeper!" Eymah screamed. "You don't yet know the meaning of fear! No one can help you here! Your precious unicorn is dead!"

"Call for help, Lily!" Rowan yelled as he wrestled the Woven Ice.

I will return and make all things new. Lily lifted the soothstone. For an instant, a gleam of horror flickered in Eymah's eyes. Then he shrank back and screamed as the glare of the stone bleached him white.

A roar sounded, followed by the crash of splintering rock. The soothstone's light dimmed, and in its wake Wendell the wyvern crouched in the cavern, his tail glistening with poison. The dragon bared his teeth, narrowed his yellow eyes, and growled as he scanned the room.

"Wendell!" Lily cried. "Get us out of here!"

Wendell turned toward the sound of Lily's voice, and at the sight of her he stooped his head low. Lily called for her companions to follow her as she climbed atop Wendell. Just as she crested the curve of his back, however, something seized her by the ankles and whipped her feet out from under her. Lily slid backward and barely clung to one of the spikes along Wendell's spine. She kicked her feet to free herself from the icy grip tethering her, and looked over her shoulder in bewilderment. She could see no obvious rope binding her leg, yet something cold and biting dragged her toward the ground.

Rowan stood with his feet firmly planted on the ground, the Woven Ice casting a ghastly hue on his face as he held it high. A wave of panic gripped Lily as she realized that the frozen snare around her leg arose from the ancient gemstone.

"Rowan, what are you doing?" Lily cried.

"I'm not doing it! It's like it has a mind of its own!"

"Then drop it! Get rid of it!"

"I can't do that."

"You have to!"

"I can't! Don't you see that I can't? Everything depends on this stone!"

Eymah's wicked laugh echoed from the chamber walls. "You see, dream keeper? Even when I am without form, you are no match for me!"

The invisible lashings tightened around Lily's ankles, and her hands, wet with perspiration, began to slip. "Please, Rowan!

Please, drop the stone!" she cried. She glanced back, and saw tears, silver blue in the light of the stone, threading down Rowan's face. He looked back at her helplessly.

Finally, her grasp gave way. With a cry she tumbled to the ground, and the snare from the Woven Ice dragged her across the stone floor. As she fought, kicked, and clawed at the stones beneath her, the phantasmal, cloaked figure of Eymah awaited her with smoky arms outstretched.

"Where is your precious Pax now, dream keeper?" Eymah sneered.

"Rowan!" Lily screamed. "Please!"

Wendell reared upward, and Philippe and Mattie screamed as the dragon rammed his head against the ceiling of the chamber. Upon impact the stone cracked, and soon fissures ran down the walls along either side of the room like spreading fingers of frost. Then Wendell roared, and acrid smoke spewed from his nostrils as he crouched low and raised his venomous tail.

"A lizard?" Eymah hissed with disdain. "This is what you call to save you?"

Wendell shook the chamber with another roar. His yellow eyes flashed with rage, and his claws scratched grooves into the stone floor. Then, he spread his wings wide and charged at Eymah.

The tethers around Lily's ankles loosened. She clambered to her feet and raced toward Wendell, but then skidded to a stop and gaped in horror as the wyvern suddenly whimpered. Something had arrested Wendell's leap, and he hung suspended in midair as if an invisible wire had caught him about the throat. He thrashed and whined, his tail lashing about like a writhing snake and his eyes pleading with Lily for help. Then he crashed to the ground, kicking up a tidal wave of rocks as the floor buckled beneath his massive weight.

"Rowan, drop the Woven Ice!" Lily screamed. "Eymah's still controlling it! Let it go!"

Rowan stared at her in wide-eyed dismay, but he couldn't push himself to surrender the stone. As Wendell gasped for breath and writhed on the ground, the lashings caught Lily's ankles again and dragged her. Lily raked her fingers against the stones, but nothing could stall her as the snares from the Woven Ice towed her toward Eymah.

"Now we finish this, dream keeper!" Eymah shouted. "You are mine! No unicorn can save you now!"

The stones scraped her knees. *Please, Pax. I know you're alive.*

A thump sounded, and Lily scudded to a halt. The straps binding her again melted away, and she scrambled to her feet. Mattie had slid off Wendell's back and wrapped both of her arms around Rowan's shoulders from behind. Rowan appeared dazed and frantic as she wrestled him to the ground.

"No, you can't! You can't take it from me! It's mine!" he yelled in desperation. He planted a foot against Mattie's chest and threw her off, but she dove upon him again.

"I'm sorry, Rowan. I never meant for this to happen."

"You can't have it! It's mine!"

"It was never meant to be yours."

Mattie wrenched the Woven Ice from Rowan's grasp. She backpedaled and held it overhead, and for a moment it bathed all the faces in the cavern in a cold, unearthly blue light.

"Give it back!" Rowan cried, scrambling to his feet and charging at Mattie in rage. "That's not yours!"

Mattie didn't back away from him, but instead, with cool determination in her eyes, she stood her ground. "This isn't part of your story, Rowan."

"I'll kill you! I'll kill you if you don't give it to me!"

Mattie looked at him with pity and compassion, then raised her eyes to Eymah. Her gaze hardened. "No more lies!" she cried, her voice drawing from a strength that seemed years beyond her age. "The story ends here!"

Eymah's eyes suddenly widened in alarm. "Matilda, don't be foolish—"

"I made the Woven Ice. I'm the one who needs to destroy it."

"Matilda!"

Mattie lifted the crystal over her head, and Rowan howled in agony as she hurled it to the ground. The jewel emanated a burst of light like a flash of lightning, then shattered into pieces.

Eymah screamed, and in desperation he swept upon Lily, enveloping her in a cloud of smoke thicker than the most wretched corners of the Veil. As he descended upon her, every shred of hope, every ounce of joy drained away, leaving Lily hollow and wretched.

"You are mine!" Eymah rasped. "You cannot escape me!"

Darkness pooled over Lily's eyes, and her teeth chattered from the pulse of ice in her veins. "Pax," she barely whispered.

"No! That name cannot save you!"

Eymah's darkness enshrouded her thoughts, and his stench choked her. Her movements seemed to slow, the seconds lengthening until she perceived each breath and sound in amplification.

And yet, in that mire, she clung to Pax's name.

My words chase away the darkest of fears. As his words reverberated in her mind, something deep within Lily turned over, like a breaker rolling onto the shore. She stared straight into the burning fires of Eymah's eyes. "I will not be afraid of you," she whispered. "Pax has stripped you of your power."

"Pax. Is. Dead!"

Lily drew a breath. "No, he has risen!"

The soothstone erupted into light. A pulse of electricity traveled from Lily's heart and down her arm, just as it had when the stone had revealed her memories to Tobias. White flame shot from the stone and enveloped Eymah, and his blood-curdling scream shook the cavern.

Lily struggled to her feet. A windstorm churned through the chamber, sweeping her hair from her face. She stretched out her arm, and with Pax's words emboldening her, she marched forward with fire blazing from her hand. "Pax has risen!" she cried again. "You have no power here!"

Eymah arched his back, then writhed and contorted like a serpent. The stones of the chamber cracked and shifted, as if a great, slumbering animal had awoken and rolled over beneath their feet. Then a gust of wind blasted the room, and with a last, ghostly wail, the lord of terrors disappeared in rivulets of smoke.

Lily stood dazed, her chest heaving. She stared at the sooth-stone in her hand and stretched her fingers. They tingled, as if still coursing with the power that had saved her . . . a power beyond herself.

"Come on, Lily, we have to go!" Mattie tugged at Lily's elbow and urged her to run. Lily climbed atop Wendell's back as the walls of the room came apart at the seams, and the domed ceiling above them caved in to permit a single beam of sunlight and a swathe of blue. As the cavern collapsed, Rowan stooped on his hands and knees, his head bent as he harriedly searched for the fragments of the Woven Ice.

"Rowan! Come on!" Lily shouted.

Mattie dropped beside him and lifted his chin until his garnet eyes met her own. A moment of silence passed between them, and then suddenly Rowan stood up, leaning on Mattie in his exhaustion and anguish.

The tumult of the cave-in mounted to a deafening roar, and the earth rumbled and lurched around them, as if the Realm itself was turning inside out. Although muffled, the fearful cries of the Forgotten penetrated the chamber walls.

"We have to go!" Lily shouted to Mattie and Rowan. "Run! Now!"

They climbed atop Wendell, the sky above them broke through, and the wyvern soared upward into the blue. They burst through the ground like a shoot through the earth, trailing sand behind them as Wendell arced into the sky. The sunlight stung Lily's eyes after the gloom and shadow of the caverns, and for a moment she feared she couldn't stand it, so brilliant and delicious and painful was it through her eyelids and against her skin. She cast her eyes downward and blinked at the disaster below as the entire kingdom of the Forgotten crumbled.

The rent through which they had escaped yawned open into a cragged ravine. Thousands of the Forgotten emerged from the crevasse, blinking and groaning as they wobbled into the sunlight.

"Wendell, can we land there?" Lily asked, pointing to a dune adjacent to the ravine. Wendell spiraled down to land gently on the hill of sand. As they dismounted, Aristotle and Sonia clung close to Lily and Mattie, and they shuddered as they surveyed the wreckage of their home.

"What will we do now?" someone cried from the foot of the dune. A rabble of the Forgotten were already ascending the hill, with a flea-bitten dog leading them on his hind legs. "Where will we go?" the dog said. "We have no home!" He slumped to the ground and buried his head in his paws. Soon, scores of the Forgotten followed suit. Some of them wept, others bawled, still more drifted about in a trance through the windswept sand.

"How awful for them," Lily said, turning to Mattie and Rowan. Mattie nodded and wiped tears from her eyes. Her bedraggled hair had pulled from her ponytail, and she looked like a dried leaf in the wind, a fragile thing about to crumble and break. Rowan, also shocked, retreated to stare off into the remote corners of the desert in silence.

As Lily watched the Forgotten straggle up the dune, her mind reeled. *The Dream Catcher was Eymah, all along? But how did he get the Woven Ice?* She strained to piece together the events, then wondered, as the dog slipped and rolled back down the hill, how the Forgotten would find a way forward. What home did they have? What hope? She glanced at Rowan. And what home did he have now? What would become of Rowan's kingdom?

Rowan suddenly rose to his feet. "There's something out there."

Lily squinted at the line between sand and sky that blurred and wavered in the heat. "I don't see anything."

"There's something there."

"What? What is it?"

He shook his head, but his piercing eyes remained fixed in the distance. "It's coming this way." Rowan scrabbled atop Wendell. The wyvern snorted in protest, but Rowan ignored him, and climbed until he perched between the horns on Wendell's head. He shielded his eyes from the sun and scanned the terrain.

"Oh no," he finally said after a long pause.

His words struck Lily like lead weights. She recognized the dismay in his voice, the same as when he'd knelt before Magnus's throne and bargained for his memories. "What? What is it?" she asked, her anxiety mounting.

"An army. It's an army."

"*What?* What army? Who are they?"

"They can't be the Seekers. Or, I mean, the Forgotten," said Mattie, stepping to the edge of the dune and peering at the horizon herself. "All the Forgotten are here."

"It's not the Forgotten."

"Then *who*, Rowan? Tell us, who are they?"

"I can't believe it. It's *him*."

Lily's heart sank. "Eymah? How is that possible, when we just watched him burn up?"

Rowan didn't answer, but he didn't need to. At that moment Lily saw it: a thin, dark shadow cresting the parched earth, advancing toward them like a murky tide. Above the army a creature hovered in the air, its iridescent wings glittering in the sunlight.

It was Sky Hunter. And astride him, with his amber-studded scepter raised like a banner of war, sat Magnus.

CHAPTER 30

Battle in the Sand

The Forgotten, many still scaling the rocky slopes of the trench that had claimed their kingdom, turned, dumbfounded, and gawked at the oncoming horde. The army of dwellers brooded on the horizon like a gathering storm and stirred up a cloud of sand that blotted out the sun. As the tide of soldiers swept toward them, the Forgotten wailed in panic and then scattered, littering the dry earth behind them with scraps of their belongings. Magnus raised his scepter high and bellowed a command to attack, and soon the dwellers' crazed shouts and the clang of their rusted steel weapons echoed across the desert like the wails of banshees.

"We need to get out of here!" Rowan shouted.

"*Oui!* Mademoiselle, it is the nasty person! We must go!" Philippe leapt atop Wendell, and Flint and Sonia followed. Lily placed her hands against Wendell's scaly flank to climb aboard, but before she could hoist herself up, a furry paw grasped her arm. Aristotle clutched her wrist, whimpered, and pleaded with her to stay.

"Aristotle, come with us!" she said. In response, Aristotle pointed to the scene unfolding below them. At the foot of the dune, a Forgotten weasel, thin, grungy, and neglected, ran screaming from beneath the stomping feet of a dweller who hurled a metal rod at him. A rabbit with a torn ear loped along the edge of the crevasse, urging a flock of chicks onward until a dweller grasped him by the ears and dragged him crying through the dust. Just beyond, the dwellers bound a crowd of the Forgotten in cords and towed them away through the hot sand. In desperation for their freedom, some of the Forgotten fled over the dunes until their substance wavered like mirages and they disappeared. Others turned to fight, only to suffer beneath the blows of decrepit blades and hammers that pitched them into the sand.

As Lily watched the terror unfold, her hand tightened around Aristotle's paw. "Save you," he'd said to her back in the Lairs of the Forgotten. Didn't she owe him the same dedication? Didn't his people deserve rescue from the twisted and depraved clutches of the dwellers? But as the screams of the terrified Forgotten filled her ears, her heart sank. How could she save them from all this? How could any of them overcome such evil?

Suddenly, she remembered the words—the words she knew to her bones, the words in time with her heart. *His* words: *I have overcome the darkness.*

Lily blinked away tears. *Of course.*

She met Aristotle's shiny black eyes and saw the same plaintive, earnest pleading. Lily nodded, and squeezed his hand again. "Fear not, buddy," she said. "Good will overcome."

Aristotle's face curled into a puffy smile, his whiskers poking out askew from his face, as Lily backed away from Wendell's side.

"Lily, what are you doing?" Rowan said from astride Wendell. "Climb up, now! We have to fly!"

"No. We have to help them."

"Are you insane? We need to get out of here! Now!"

"This isn't the Forgotten's fault, Rowan! We brought all this on them. Magnus is after *us*, not them. We can't just abandon them!" She patted Wendell to draw his attention. "We have to go down there," Lily said. In response, the wyvern stretched his wings and belted a roar that rolled through the desert for miles.

"This is crazy, Lily!" Rowan protested.

"Just hold on." Lily climbed back atop Wendell, and Rigel appeared with a screech and wove a harness in a few rapid loops. Wendell grunted when Lily slipped it over his snout, but he settled after a few soothing words. Then Lily tapped Wendell's side, and the wyvern shot upward, racing above sand

and through sky until wisps of cloud dampened Lily's face. She pointed to a group of the Forgotten cowering beneath a dweller's whip, and with a shriek Wendell dived down toward the trembling huddle. The dwellers fled from beneath Wendell's shadow and lunged headfirst into the sand as he skimmed the ground. Wendell snatched the captives by the ropes holding them, and lifted them as if they were a parcel of letters.

Lily directed Wendell to another group, and then another. They saved a pack of ragged puppies, a family of tattered dolls, and a gecko in a dusty trench coat. They rescued a shabby lion quailing beneath a dweller's blade, and a fish in a moth-eaten sailor's hat who flopped away from the onslaught. With another roar and a flourish, Wendell flew to a flat-topped hill, like the mesas from the deserts of Arizona and New Mexico. There he gently settled the Forgotten among some sage plants, and took to the skies again while they huddled together, shivering with fright but safe. Rigel stayed behind to bind their wounds with his silver bandages.

Screams drew Lily to the crevasse, where a mass of jeering dwellers brandished their whips and blades and pressed a group of the Forgotten toward the cliff edge. Wendell struck the dwellers with a midair kick, scattering them like scraps of paper and liberating the Forgotten to run free. Then he tackled one horde preying upon a group of woodchucks and another racing across the desert with the Forgotten slung over their backs like burlap sacks. A swipe of his tail reduced an entire infantry of dwellers to its knees, and the beat of his wings stirred up a whirlwind that sent others into panic. The dwellers cast their weapons to the ground and fled west toward the dismal murk of the Veil from which they'd come. For a delicious moment, Lily dared to hope she and her friends might triumph, and that the Forgotten, poor, downtrodden, and lonely, might be free.

Then a familiar, gravelly laugh sent a shiver down Lily's spine. She glanced over her shoulder, and her momentary excitement gave way to dread as she saw Magnus, his hair blown back to reveal his deathly face contorted in a grimace as he flew toward them astride Sky Hunter. One of the dragonfly's wings bent at a sickly angle, and Magnus struck him with his scepter whenever he teetered in flight.

Wendell wheeled about to face Magnus, and sand pelted their faces as he barreled toward him in attack. Philippe brandished his saber, and Flint worked himself into a blaze. Lily reached for the soothstone, gritted her teeth, and prayed for courage.

The wyvern and the dragonfly collided in the sky. Sky Hunter, already battered and bruised, faltered and wobbled in the air, and Wendell reared back in triumph. He shook the dunes with another roar, then charged forward for a second attack. Lily's heart raced. She squeezed her eyes shut and braced herself for another impact.

Instead, calamity struck. As Wendell rushed close, Magnus howled with rage and scattered a shower of green dust into the wyvern's face. Wendall coughed, bucked, and shook his head to clear the toxic smoke from his eyes, but the cloud adhered to him as if woven into his scales. With an anguished roar Wendell lost control and fell from the sky, all the while violently shaking his head and swiping his tail at the noxious fumes. His convulsions threw Lily and her party to the ground, sending up a cloud of dust as they hit the mesa below. Lily struggled to her feet and watched with dismay as Wendell careened against the slope of the mesa and rolled down, whimpering until he struck the bottom.

"Thought you could get away, did you?"

The back of Lily's neck prickled as the voice growled behind her. She turned around, and groaned in dejection as Magnus landed the dragonfly atop the mesa. His triumphant sneer revealed his green teeth, slimy like pebbles at the bottom of a muck pond.

"I should have warned you never to steal from the Icelein, you pathetic larva!" Magnus said. He raised his scepter, and its amber jewel glowed like a burning coal. The sight of it triggered Lily's memory. What had Alister said about Magnus's scepter? Something about it controlling him . . . something about it being tied to the Amber Beacons . . .

"Yes, beetle," Magnus said, as if he'd read her mind. "Once you escaped with my slave, the stone in my scepter gleamed like fire. It led me straight out of the Veil, and its pulse has betrayed your every movement, your every step across forest, mountain, and field. When it dimmed, I feared I'd lost you. Then it brightened again, and when it guided me northward I rallied my troops to arms . . . only to discover you and your little party had ravaged the desert itself. How could I not join in the frivolity?" He laughed, and spittle flew from his gray lips. "After all those long years in the dark, to be freed by a child's foolish mistake! Your compassion for that pathetic bat was your undoing. Tell me, beetle, was the bat really worth it? You should have listened to the sniveling little elf prince and left the miserable wretch to die!"

Suddenly, he stopped laughing. His face lengthened in shock as he stared at something behind Lily. Lily turned around.

Rowan stood with his face stern and his legs like two tree trunks rooted in the ground. He held something small and blue in his palm, barely larger than a pea.

It was a fragment of the Woven Ice.

Magnus's clawlike hands tightened around his scepter as the shard of the Woven Ice bathed his face in a ghastly glow.

"Rowan, what are you doing?" Mattie said in alarm. Rowan shot her a reassuring glance and cupped the fragment in both palms.

"*You* have it," Magnus whispered, the muscles in his face twitching. "You've had it all along!"

"I'll give it to you," Rowan said, "only if you leave here and never come back. Go back to the Veil and take the Woven Ice with you. Use it to clear away the Icelein Towers and reclaim your home. Just let us go. Let *everyone* go."

Magnus's frown deepened into a scowl. "You've had it all along, you impudent liar!"

"I didn't have it. But I'm offering it to you now. Go home, and live in peace."

"You filthy, lying vermin! It was never yours! You stole it from me!" Magnus's green eyes flashed as he raised his scepter, its jewel blazing like fire. Lily cried out Rowan's name.

A blow to the head stopped Magnus midattack. With a cry Philippe flipped in the air and kicked him, then rebounded and slashed with his flaming carrot. He hollered a battle cry, but with a single clip of his staff Magnus silenced him and sent him tumbling into the dust.

Lily raised the soothstone. A quick flash burst forth and a centaur wielding a bow and arrow appeared. Magnus ducked as the centaur loosed an arrow that whistled past his head. Lily raised the soothstone again and narrowed her eyes, and with another flash an eagle as massive as a boulder appeared, its wings tipped in flame. It soared toward Magnus with a piercing screech, and unseated the king from atop Sky Hunter's back with one slash of its talons. Magnus toppled into the sand, and Sky Hunter, finally free, whizzed away in panic.

Philippe lifted his saber above his head and bounded toward Magnus with his ears flung back. Just before Philippe brought the flaming carrot down, the king rose from the sand and met Philippe's attack with a block of his scepter. Philippe struck again, then again, but Magnus parried each blow. Finally, Magnus hurled the rabbit off the mesa with one sweep of his staff.

The centaur and the eagle both attacked next, each striking from an opposite flank. Magnus cast another handful of green dust into the eyes of the eagle, who arched backward with a shriek and tumbled out of sight. The centaur unsheathed a dagger and galloped to overtake Magnus, but the king whipped around and struck him. Another green cloud billowed into the air, and the centaur, his hand over his tearing eyes, slid down into the dunes.

Lily raised the soothstone again, but Magnus pounced upon her and knocked her to the ground. "I've had enough of your magic!" he snarled. The veins of his arms bulged and the whites of his eyes reddened as he raised his scepter above his head with both hands. Lily stared into his crazed face, gripped the sand, and stammered a cry for help, but fear and the scorching wind of the desert had stolen her voice. She fixed her mind on Pax, on his goodness, on his light. *Please, help us!*

"Miran!"

Magnus froze. He still upheld his weapon, but with a befuddled expression he unfastened his eyes from Lily and followed the voice.

Mattie stepped closer. "Miran, son of Tiran, king of the Icelein!" she said. "Do you know my voice?"

His green eyes narrowed. "What is this devilry?"

Mattie's eyes flitted to a large, gray shadow over Magnus's shoulder in the distance. Something yellow, like the jewel in Magnus's scepter, glinted in the sunlight. *Alister*, Lily thought. *Alister and Isla.* She made eye contact with Mattie and nodded to encourage her to keep stalling.

"You know my voice, don't you?" Mattie said, straightening with authority as she spoke.

Magnus lowered the scepter. "I said, what is this devilry? Who are you?" he said.

Alister's profile grew larger by the second.

"I've known you since the beginning."

The stone in the scepter pulsed brighter. An unruly, angry light flared in Magnus's eyes as he pointed the staff at Mattie's forehead. "I'm warning you!" he growled. "Explain yourself now, or I'll silence your vile mouth forever! Who *are* you?"

Mattie's chin trembled. "You know me, don't you?"

"Answer me!" Magnus screamed. "Answer me now, or I'll kill you both!"

Mattie's eyes widened. Lily drew a breath.

With a shriek, Alister barreled Magnus over.

The king fell backward and gasped for breath, then struggled to his feet and rasped a scream. Alister whirled about as Isla, astride him, charged a lightning bolt between her fingers. She locked eyes with the fallen king, and for a moment she hesitated. A deep, ancient sorrow passed over her face, as if long-buried memories had churned to the surface of her mind. She lowered her hands slightly.

In response, Magnus growled with rage. He rushed forward and released another plume of toxic vapor into the air. Alister lurched backward, and with a flourish of her arms Isla unleased the lightning bolt. It sizzled at Magnus's feet, charring the earth and driving him to the edge of the mesa. Magnus's eyes boggled, and he flailed his arms wildly. Then, with a gut-wrenching scream, he lost his balance and plummeted down the slope.

Alister landed and Isla slid off his back. "My ladies, are you okay?" he asked. Lily nodded, although her limbs trembled and her chest heaved. Mattie offered a weak smile.

"Are the fledglings safe?" Rowan asked.

"Yes," Isla said. "We didn't even need to cross the desert. Once freed from the chamber, they all sped home to the Cave of Lights without our bidding. Only a magic as powerful as the Woven Ice could have restrained them." She glanced around at the wreckage and at the fighting still raging below. "What happened here? We've come back to find you at war!"

"It was Eymah," Lily said. "He was the Dream Catcher all along. We barely escaped him, and when we did, Magnus and his dwellers attacked."

"*Eymah?*" Isla looked like she might be sick. "He's back?"

"I don't think he ever really left. He's just weaker."

"And that one was Magnus," Isla glanced over the hill. It was a declaration, not a question, and the sadness returned to her eyes. "That creature used to be King Miran."

"Yes. And all these were the Icelein." Lily motioned to the hordes of dwellers below.

Isla shook her head. "It's crushing, how far we can fall. And Eymah had the Woven Ice all this time." She narrowed her eyes as she sorted through her thoughts, then raised a hand to her mouth. "Oh my!"

"What is it?"

"The eyes." She looked at Rowan in astonishment. "I just realized what was wrong with that memory, the one Magnus shared. Something was erased, but do you remember there was also something I couldn't identify that seemed wrong? It was the *eyes*, Rowan! Esperion's eyes, and Eldinor's! They were the wrong color!"

"What color were they?"

"Red."

"Like Rowan's?" Lily asked.

"No, not like Rowan's. Rowan's are the color of wine held up to the light. These were *red*. Blood red. Red like . . ."

"Like the eyes of a shroud," Rowan said.

Lily's jaw dropped. "Those people in Magnus's memory were really shrouds?"

"Yes, I think they were."

"So, it wasn't Esperion and Eldinor who took the Woven Ice. They were actually shrouds! Esperion didn't betray Magnus after all!"

A snarl interrupted them. With a start they turned.

Magnus, covered in sand, scowled at them from the edge of the mesa with his scepter held aloft.

"No, clever little lice," he said with a sneer. "I betrayed *him*!"

CHAPTER 31

The Lost Prince

At the mention of Magnus's betrayal, a change came over Alister. He cried out, his usually subdued voice suddenly bellowing with the power of the sea against a cliff. He called out Pax's name and then charged at Magnus, the Amber Beacon at his neck piercingly bright.

He was no match for the twisted king. With a wave of his scepter Magnus arrested Alister in midair, then slung him onto the ground. Alister shrieked, then rolled over and arched his back in agony. The jewel at the center of Magnus's scepter glowed and faded like a breathing thing, and with each pulse Alister cried out in pain. Finally, he slumped on the ground like a worn dishrag.

Rowan, Mattie, and Lily stood frozen in terror. *What do we do?* Lily asked herself over and over, her heart breaking as she watched Alister twitch on the ground. Then, with a sweep of her cloak and her head held high, Isla stepped forward. "Leave him alone," she said with a hardened gaze.

Magnus's face curled into a hideous grin. "Another Mist Elf. And a royal one, I see." He gestured to her silver circlet with a bony finger. "How quaint. Does the imminence of your death embolden you?"

"I said let him go!" Isla raised her palms above her head. In an instant a storm cloud whirled between her fingers.

Magnus growled at her, but complied. As he lowered the scepter, its jewel snuffed out and Alister drew a deep draught of air into his lungs.

"What did you do to Esperion?" Isla said, the cloud still broiling between her fingers.

Magnus wrinkled his brow and sneered.

"What did you do to Prince Esperion? Tell me the truth, or I'll bury you in the ground with your jewels!" A thunderclap cracked through the air, and the storm intensified.

Magnus's guttural laugh echoed over the desert. "Oh, how ironic! You threaten to bury me in the desert. Meanwhile, I buried your ancestors in the snow so many centuries ago!"

The cloud between her fingers blackened. "What are you talking about?"

"Your hope for the ages has spent an age sleeping in the snow, fair princess. He's nothing but a pile of frozen bones!"

"Esperion? You're talking about Esperion?"

"Naturally."

"So he *was* killed in the avalanche, just like we thought."

"Indeed."

Her eyes turned cold as metal. "How was an avalanche your doing?"

He didn't answer, but the menace in his eyes intensified.

Isla's face darkened in horror. "You *caused* it, didn't you? You caused the avalanche that buried the Icelein Towers. You brought an avalanche down on your own people!"

"Another power caused it, but I lured the fair prince into it. I rejoiced as the snow swallowed him up."

"You watched him die?"

"With relish."

Understanding flickered across Isla's face. "That's it. That's the distortion in the memory, the part that was deleted. You didn't try to stop the avalanche; you *planned* it! You orchestrated it to kill Esperion!"

Magnus's vulgar mouth upturned in a smirk.

"How could you?" Isla said her voice cracking. "All these years we've grieved for you, but we should have condemned you! You're a murderer!"

With a snarl Magnus whipped his scepter through the air, and Alister again writhed in pain. "I am a king who guards what is rightfully his!" he hollered. "Can you imagine my mortification, when your family insisted I grovel to Esperion? To a *child*? Can you believe their insolence, to suggest I give up my throne to a pouty-faced boy? I wielded the Woven Ice! I was the most powerful in the northwest reaches! All Mistwood should have bowed before me! "

Angry tears misted Isla's eyes. "Our family trusted you."

"Your family was a thorn in my side" he growled, lumbering toward her. "And with Eymah's help, I plucked that thorn out."

"So you *did* work with Eymah. What bargain did you make with him? How much of your soul did you sell to him, if he would only help you murder an innocent child?"

Magnus's eyes narrowed. "I promised him Esperion's throne. If Eymah got rid of the child, he would rule beside me at Enlacia. There would be two worthy rulers, on Two Thrones, as was always intended."

"And you *believed* he would share power with you? You actually trusted Eymah, the lord of terrors, to keep his word?"

"I trusted in his power! Which is more than I can say for your miserable race!"

"Your pact condemned all your own people to ruin. The Veil happened because of you!"

"You don't know that! Who's to say those shrouds were acting under Eymah's authority? I did what was necessary to protect my crown. The Veil was a small price to pay to protect what was mine!"

Isla shook her head in disgust. "You're a fool."

Magnus glared at her. "What did you call me?"

"You're a fool. Your plan failed because you're a fool!"

"My plan was perfect! The shrouds took the form of Eldinor and Esperion when they loosened boulders from the mountain. If anything went awry, we could blame the avalanche on Mistwood."

"But something went very awry, didn't it? The shrouds betrayed you and stole the Woven Ice right out of your hand."

Magnus growled, saliva dripping from his green teeth.

Isla suddenly raised her voice. "For how many centuries have you lied to your people?" As her words echoed across the desert, a few dwellers paused in their pursuit of the Forgotten and turned their eyes toward Magnus.

Magnus glanced nervously down at the multitudes below. "I am the ruler of my people!" he shouted. "I am the only reason my people are still alive! I am the bearer of the Ice!"

"You mean this one?" Rowan stood at the edge of the dune, the fragment of the Woven Ice glowing between two fingers.

"Give it to me, worm!" Magnus growled. "Before I smash all of you into a pulp!"

Rowan shot Mattie a long, knowing look. Then he turned to Magnus and drew a deep breath. "The time of the Woven Ice is over," he said. He raised his arm, and the Woven Ice glinted like a blue star as he threw it over the edge of the mesa.

Magnus howled like a wounded animal as the stone hurtled over the cliff. He lunged at Rowan, and in his passion he dropped his scepter. As it struck the earth, the light of its jewel flickered out.

The moment the jewel dimmed, Alister straightened and spread his wings, coming to life like a flower bud unfurling its petals. He drew a breath, set his shrewd eyes on Magnus, and sprang at the king in a blur of gray. As he plowed Magnus to the ground, Isla and Rowan each rushed forward with lightning crackling between their fingers.

Magnus screamed, then tossed green dust into the air that ignited into a shield of green flame. As Alister, Rowan, and Lily shrank back from the fire, Lily called a flock of star birds, who soon glutted the sky with shimmering light. As they pelted and dive-bombed the king, Philippe, Rigel, and Flint also surged in, and soon flames and the glitter of metallic birds swarmed around Magnus like hornets around a nest.

Magnus flailed and shrieked. His assailants drove him to the edge of the mesa, and Lily's heart pounded as her hope rose. *We can do this*, she thought. *Good will overcome . . .*

Magnus cried out words Lily didn't understand. Suddenly, a strange hush swept over the desert. In answer to his call the dwellers below paused midbattle, their fists suspended in the air and their swords midswipe, and they craned their necks toward the cliff.

Magnus repeated his cry. Then, suddenly, the dwellers erupted in a roar. A boom of battle cries shook the ground, and with their weapons upheld the soldiers charged up the mesa.

As the tide stormed forward with teeth gnashing, Magnus released another toxic cloud into the air, and the star birds scattered in confusion. Philippe backed away with his paws to his eyes, then retreated down the opposite slope as a dweller swung a meaty fist at him. Lily cried out for Wendell, but he still rolled at the bottom of the cliff, his eyes red and watering.

A dweller with a scar across his eye crested the mesa and knocked Lily to the ground. He loomed above her, his face contorted in a hideous grin, and pressed a jagged dagger to her throat. "Where you think you're goin', lassy?" he sneered.

Lily planted a kick to his chest. She struggled to her feet and raised the soothstone. A giant octopus appeared and latched onto the dweller's face. The dweller clawed and scratched at the tentacles, but to no avail. The octopus nodded his gelatinous head at Lily in solidarity before the dweller fell over backward down the mesa.

A thunderclap boomed, and lightning from Isla's hands sent a mob of dwellers wailing back down the mesa, their discarded weapons clanging against the rocks. Lily ducked as another dweller threw a metal ball at her head; a flourish of the soothstone turned the ball into a porcupine. A dozen dwellers fled as the porcupine ejected its quills in a circle of barbs.

With another thunderclap Isla barricaded a group within a ring of fire, then called out to Lily over the din of battle. "Lily, where's Rowan?" she cried. "Keep Rowan safe!" Another burst of lightning erupted from her palms and stopped a dweller in his tracks.

Lily scanned the mesa, her eyes darting wildly between gangs of dwellers that stormed the hill. She saw no trace of Rowan.

She ran to the cliff edge to search the landscape and saw the Forgotten huddled together in a single translucent mass, like lost children unsure of what to do. Halfway down the slope, Lily finally spotted Rowan. He chased Magnus, sliding through the sand as the king hunted for the Woven Ice fragment on the ground.

"Rowan!" Lily cried. She started for the edge, but Alister stopped her.

"Do not go, my lady. Please, let me go."

Lily studied him. Bruises and scratches lined Alister's face, and dirt caked his fur, but the depths of his eyes still seemed so vast for a bat. "Be careful," she said with a nod.

Alister bowed, then glided down and knocked Magnus off his feet. A cloud of sand obscured them, and suddenly Alister appeared with the Woven Ice clutched in his claws. He flew down the hill, and Magnus slid after him and leapt atop his back. Rowan chased after them, then circled them with lightning sizzling between his fingers. He searched for a window to strike Magnus but risked injuring Alister with the same bolt.

Alister flapped his wings in desperation. He flopped around in the dust, while Magnus wrestled him for the Ice. As Magnus's rage boiled over, a flurry of flying limbs and sand obscured Lily's vision. Suddenly, Alister slumped onto the ground and lay still, and the Woven Ice fell from his claws.

Magnus snatched up the Ice, and then, with a savage growl that Lily could hear even from her height, Magnus coiled Alister's chain around his fingers. He seethed words Lily couldn't discern through clenched teeth. Then, with a violent yank, Magnus tore the amber pendant from around Alister's neck. As the chain broke and an orange flash swallowed them up, Lily remembered Alister's words: *Our lives are tied to these stones.*

"No!" Lily screamed. Her stomach twisted into a knot and her throat tightened. She stared at Alister, willing him to wake up, to roll over and again draw himself to a stand like a knight rising to protect his queen. Instead, he remained still, the rustling of the hot wind through his fur the only movement.

While she still wrangled with her grief, a sharp sting cut into Lily's shoulder. She spun around to see a dweller with a whip in one hand and a dagger in the other. He raised the knife high, but with a flash of the soothstone Lily unleashed a tidal wave that swept over the top of the mesa and knocked her assailant and scores like him to their knees. When the water and foam dwindled, the dwellers shook themselves like soaked dogs, then sent up a howl of war that sent chills down Lily's back. Their cry died out, and another mob of dwellers scaled the cliff.

Another attacker struck Lily's shoulder, and she fell to the ground in a cloud of dust. Lily raised the soothstone, and the sand billowing around her came alive and battered her opponent away. As she stood up, Lily saw the numbers swell around her. She heard weapons clang, Isla cry out, and Philippe call for help. The entire mesa swarmed with dwellers . . . and still, they came.

And now Alister was dead.

Lily slumped to the ground. The scene blurred around her like a spinning carousel, the colors and lines blending together. A hot wind blasted her face with sand. She felt numb, hollowed out, as if she perched at the end of the world.

Lily stared down at the soothstone in her hands, and suddenly it seemed just like an ordinary pebble. It was over. It was all over. Magnus would win, and he would enslave everyone in his path. She'd never see her parents again. Or her friends. There was no hope, only fear and dread.

Another blast of wind, and something on the breeze penetrated Lily's thoughts. It was just a whisper at first, but as another gust swept her hair away from her face, it grew louder and more insistent. Lily blinked away her tears as she recognized a voice on the wind.

The voice spoke, and suddenly a warmth and vigor welled up within her. The voice was powerful, unmistakable, familiar as the sea: *My words are more powerful than any rock, Lily McKinley. And my presence chases away even the darkest of fears.*

Lily's heart quickened, and a sudden rush of confidence surged through her. She stood up.

Tell them my words, the voice said.

She raced to Isla's side. "Isla, I need you to cover me," Lily blurted.

"What?" Isla glanced over her shoulder, then whipped back around to fend off three dwellers with a fan of lighting.

"I said cover me!"

A dweller astraddle an enormous, dingy crow swooped down and hit Isla on the shoulder with a metal pipe. Isla raised her hands, and another flash of lightning zapped the dweller and chased him into the distance. "How can I cover you when I'm fighting for my life?" Isla panted.

"Isla." The hardness of Lily's voice made her pause, and their eyes met. "Only one person can win this."

Isla's hands fell to her sides, although sparks still flickered between her fingers. The light in her eyes changed. "Do you think Pax will come?" she asked.

Lily swallowed. She remembered the tingling in her hand, and how the soothstone burst into fire on its own accord when she'd faced Eymah. "In a way," she said, "I think he's already here."

Isla looked at the soothstone on her finger and deliberated for a moment. Then she nodded. "Go. I'll do what I can." She raised both her hands; a web of blue sparks gathered in her left, and on her right the soothstone glowed magenta. The stone flashed, and a fleet of white tigers appeared and ran amok among the crowd, slashing with their claws and roaring. Then, with her left hand she unleashed a lightning bolt to char the ground at the feet of a group of marauders. Another mob raced toward her from behind, and Isla whirled around in time to call a flock of eagles with the soothstone. The eagles attacked the dwellers from all directions, then churned up a storm that tore weapons from the dweller's hands and drove them back down the hill.

Lily scanned the hilltop and spotted an outcropping of rocks heaped up in a peak atop the mesa, with a vantage above the entire desert. She scrambled up, kicking stones into the face of a slobbering dweller who lumbered after her. When she reached the top, she sent a flock of bronze falcons fluttering and shrieking after her pursuer. Then she clutched the soothstone in her fist and gazed out at the valley below her.

The dwellers swallowed up the sand like ants upon an apple core. At the sight of them Lily felt dizzy. Her hands shook.

Yet Pax's words thundered in her mind, and held her: *Know that I love you, no matter what storms assail you. Know that I am with you, always. And know that I will return and make all things new.*

Tell them my words.

Lily's eyes snapped open. Light surged from the soothstone— not the pale, cool, blue-white light that so often ushered her dreams to life, but something far stronger, like the burst of a supernova against the void of space. A familiar electricity traveled from Lily's chest down the extent of her arm, and a ray of light shot out from the soothstone and pierced across the valley. It was the same beam that had enveloped Tobias, but now it split into a thousand different threads, like a prism splintering light into its colors. Each beam wrapped around a dweller, or a member of the Forgotten, like a brilliant cloak.

The entire desert held its breath. Every figure froze in place with wide, unbelieving eyes. Lily's arm trembled with exhaustion, and she fought to hold the soothstone aloft, even as she felt her knees buckle. She bowed her head and fought not to faint. *Know that I love you, no matter what storms assail you*, she remembered. Her arm steadied as her memories of Pax replayed in her own mind. She prayed those down below could see these images, too. She prayed they could see the truth.

The light faded, and Lily stretched out on the ground and felt the warm earth against her face. With one palm she pressed into the dust. With the other, she still clutched the soothstone in trembling fingers.

"He lied to us."

At the words Lily clambered to her feet and stretched out her arms against a wave of dizziness. The voice came from far below, where the dwellers and the Forgotten alike stared up the mesa with mouths agape. One of the dwellers looked directly at her and scratched his head with a meaty arm.

"The unicorn, he's the one wot saved us." He turned to Magnus, an angry glint flickering in his eyes. "You lied to us!"

A murmuring swelled in the crowd, as others echoed the truth.

"He didn't save us from the Deadening at all!"

"'Twas the unicorn wot done it!"

"He's a liar! He lied to us!"

Lily stood frozen in amazement, but Isla scrambled up onto the rocks beside her and seized the opportunity to guide the throng. "Yes, he lied to you," she said in a voice that reflected her noble heritage, "but not just about the Blight!" With a wave of her arms Isla projected a memory. It was the exchange from just moments before, when in his pride Magnus had confessed that he, himself, had condemned all his people to darkness. At the words "the Veil was a small price to pay to protect what was mine," the entire nation of the dwellers went into an uproar.

Magnus's eyes widened as all the hatred, anger, and bitterness he'd cultivated in his people suddenly boiled over onto him. The masses of dwellers rushed at him with their rusted weapons raised. Magnus backed away and searched the desert for escape. "No!" Magnus cried. "I am your kin! I am the one who saved you from the Deadening! The unicorn is just a fairy tale!" He upheld the Woven Ice fragment in his fist, but its facets had dimmed, like a lightbulb switching off.

The crowd advanced like a slick of oil seeping across the desert. Magnus sifted through the few stray pendants still dangling about his neck. He grasped one, then the other. All remained dark, silent, and lifeless.

"Finish him!" a dweller screeched.

"He betrayed us!" bellowed another.

Magnus turned and fled. As he jumped over rocks and kicked up sand behind him, his tattered cloak, its fringes stained with blood, fell off his shoulders and flapped behind him like a winged creature hurtling to the ground. He howled for help, but the only response was the echo of his own voice and the outraged cries of his people behind him.

"Murderer!"

"Traitor!"

"Liar!"

The shouts came in waves, and the Woven Ice fell from Magnus's fingers and skittered across the ground. As it struck the sand, it came to life again, burning brilliant blue against the dull, scorched earth of the desert. Then it tumbled over the ravine of the Forgotten and disappeared into its depths.

His eyes wild with panic, Magnus followed it. He skidded across the sand and stopped just short of the precipice, swinging his arms to keep from falling over the edge, and then he turned to the onslaught. He glanced over his shoulder, into the darkness down which the Ice had fallen. Then he looked back to his attackers with eyes bulging in terror. A cloud of dust blocked out the horizon behind them as they charged.

"You will not have me!" Magnus cried. Then, with a final growl, he fell back into the abyss.

The earth itself groaned as it accepted the twisted king, and the desert heaved, like a giant rolling over in its sleep. Lily clung to the rocks around her to keep from falling down the slope as the land itself buckled and swayed. The dunes flattened out, spilling their contents into the black ravine, and then the walls of the ravine lifted themselves and drew together, like a seam closing. With a mighty boom the ravine sealed, trapping Magnus of the dwellers, fallen king of the Icelein, in its boundless depths.

For a moment all were silent. Lily, who had hidden her face from the flying sand, looked up, wiped dust from her eyes, and spit it from her mouth. Then she glanced beside her, to where a shivering Aristotle clung to her arm. She lovingly wiped sand from his forehead, then gasped.

"Aristotle? What happened to you?"

The little creature glanced up and sneezed, blowing a circle of dust into the air. He shook the sand from his fur, and Lily's eyes widened. Where mange and bare patches had once spotted Aristotle's coat, there was now silky brown fur, perfect and sleek, as if he'd just shimmied out from a riverbank to frolic. His eyes were glassy and clear.

"Aristotle, you're like new!" Lily said in wonder.

He blinked at her, and a meek smile brightened his face. "The prince," he said softly. "The prince did not forget me."

"Mademoiselle!" Philippe beckoned to Lily with his forepaws. "Mademoiselle, look at them all!"

Lily skidded down the hill, rushed to the edge of the mesa, and gasped. Across the desert the Forgotten stared in awe at their limbs and at each other, and rejoiced. Rusted robots now gleamed. Animals' coats shone. Pax's light had repaired every crack and mended every torn seam. And the Forgotten were no longer translucent but solid, as real in substance as Lily herself.

"Isla!" Lily cried with joy. "Do you see this? Do you see what Pax has done?"

Isla didn't answer. Lily glanced around her, then remembered Isla had dashed down the slope to protect Rowan. With her heart still pounding Lily ran to join them.

"Isla, do you see—"

The puzzlement on Isla's face halted Lily mid-sentence. Isla crouched on the ground, her arm still around Rowan, staring at a form in the dust before them. Lily followed her gaze.

A figure lay heaped in the dirt. Lily recognized Alister's cape and remembered the flash of light when Magnus had ripped away the Amber Beacon. She rushed forward, dropped to the ground beside him, and placed a hand on his shoulder, praying her brave friend had survived. Then she pulled away and placed her hand to her mouth.

A figure she didn't expect lay in Alister's place, with his eyes closed and his head resting on the crook of his elbow. He was an elf like Isla, but with a paler complexion, and he had long, wine-colored hair streaked with gray. It was a color Lily knew—the same color as Rowan's hair. Alister's cape clung about the elf's neck, and the Amber Beacon, freed from its chain, lay in the dirt beside him.

"I don't understand," Lily said. "What happened to Alister? Where's Alister?"

"His name was never Alister."

Mattie appeared beside Lily. She dropped beside the fallen elf and carefully touched the Amber Beacon. It was dull and scorched, as if dipped in smoke.

"What happened to him?" Lily asked. "Where's Alister?"

"His name was never really Alister," Mattie repeated.

"What do you mean? Who is he?"

Mattie drew a breath. "His name is Esperion."

CHAPTER 32

Beginnings and Endings

At the sound of his name Prince Esperion drew a breath and stirred. Lily and Isla stood at attention, knowing instinctively they were in the presence of a legend. Rowan, his eyes red and swimming, clasped his memory bauble to his heart.

Esperion stood up, and his hair draped about his face as he rubbed his temples. He raised his eyes and squinted against the light as if seeing the sun for the first time. A smile graced his face as he recognized Lily, and he nodded somberly at Isla and Rowan. Then he saw Mattie, and he dropped to one knee before her.

"My lady, are you injured?"

Mattie smiled through her tears. "No, of course not. Stand up."

Esperion complied, but reluctantly. "I owe you my very being, dear lady. I sensed it before, but—"

"You didn't remember the great prince you were."

Esperion tilted his head to one side thoughtfully. "I did not remember who I was, no. But please don't call me a great prince. There is a prince much greater than I. I had this dream. There was a unicorn"

"It wasn't a dream," Lily said. "You saw the truth."

A flicker of wonder danced in his eyes.

"Alister—I mean, Esperion—what happened to you?" Lily asked.

"Miran," he said with a shudder. He stretched out his hand, tentatively, as if marveling that his fingers still worked. Then a projection of his memories appeared over the hot earth like a mirage. In the images the avalanche barreled down the mountainside. Esperion cried out for Eldinor and stretched out a hand to grasp his, but the wall of snow and rubble swept them both away. The scene turned white and blurred as Esperion flipped head over heels down the mountain, smothered in a curtain of snow. Then the whirling stopped, and all was white and silent.

In the memory a spark suddenly shone, and a blue bolt burst from Esperion's fingertips to melt a tunnel through the snow. The lightning struck the mountain, and a rock face opened with a crack. Soaked and coughing, the young prince crawled down the pathway and peered into the cave that yawned open before him. A wind, like a breath, blew his hair back from his face, and suddenly dozens of amber lights flickered within the cave and converged toward him.

The memory wavered and disappeared. "They protected me," Esperion said with a faraway look as he lingered over his recollections. "The Nightwatchers kept me safe and taught me their ways. Then Miran mined into the mountains, and as he dug deeper in his lust for magic, he stumbled into their halls. He killed most of them immediately and spared the rest only because the power of the Beacons intrigued him." Esperion gritted his teeth. "The Nightwatchers knew that if he found me, Miran would kill me. And so they adopted me as one of their own. One of them, named Alister, passed his Beacon on to me, and eventually all memories of my life before the caves faded away. The Beacon molded me into the image of its original bearer."

They all stood in silence, awestruck by his words. Isla wrapped Rowan in an embrace and leaned her head against his as she wept.

"Your Majesty."

A dweller had crept near to the party. At the sight of him Philippe brandished his carrot saber and Isla lifted her sooth-stone, but Esperion raised a hand to still them. He stepped toward the dweller, his regal figure in sharp contrast to the pale, grisly creature before him. Lily held her breath, expecting the dweller to attack.

Instead, to Lily's astonishment the dweller dropped to his knees and bowed his head. "Your Majesty, forgive us," he said.

"Magnus lied to us. We thought you'd betrayed us and destroyed our kingdom. We see now it was all a lie."

A low rumble sounded over the desert as scores of dwellers murmured their agreement. The clink of metal filled the blistering air as they dropped their weapons into the dirt, churning up clouds of dust that hovered like a fog. Behind them, the Forgotten gathered in an outer circle, rimming them with color like the corona of an eclipse.

Rowan approached Esperion with tears streaming down his face. His tough veneer of pride had cracked and crumbled away, and as Lily watched him she felt the urge to wrap him in a hug. "They called me Espy," Rowan said, his voice cracking. "But that's not my name." With a tumult of emotion in his eyes, he dropped to his knees, reached into the folds of his robes, and withdrew the silver key of Enlacia. "This belongs to you, my lord," he said, lowering his eyes and presenting Esperion with the key.

Esperion placed a hand on Rowan's shoulder and stooped to regard him at eye level. "You and I are family, young prince," he said. Then he rose, and in a stately voice he addressed the dwellers still stooped on the ground. "As are all of you, my friends. Magnus called you dwellers, but you are the Icelein. You are my kin." He turned in a circle, gazing upon his fallen and broken people. Then he focused on the throngs of the Forgotten huddled just beyond, and his eyes softened with sympathy. "My dear, lost friends. I know what it means to live in darkness. I know the agony that afflicts the heart when those you love forget you. I know the emptiness that lingers, when you forget who you are and where you belong." He raised a hand in salute. "The time of the dwellers and the Forgotten has passed. The era of the Two Thrones dawns again. My brethren, dwell in darkness no longer! This day, join me and rebuild a kingdom of our own! I beseech you, *all* of you, to accompany me to Enlacia. Icelein! Forgotten! My family, both lost and found, join me, and together we will rebuild our rightful home! Together, we will found a kingdom not upon magic stones or upon futile hopes to reclaim the past, but upon the *truth*: that the great Prince of the Realm has overcome! That his love for us burns on! And that his sovereign power will make all things new!"

Waves of applause rippled through the crowds, and soon the desert thundered with cries of jubilation. The Icelein and the Forgotten embraced one another between shouts of joy. Rowan locked eyes with Lily and smiled through tears before Isla wrapped her arms around him.

———

Wendell led them through the sky and out of the desert. The Forgotten and the Icelein followed on a medley of winged steeds, griffins and eagles, and enormous flying hedgehogs. They crossed over the Singing Meadows and the dancing colors of the Painted Woodland, and then Wendell's shadow cut across the

Veil, which broiled below them like a brewing storm. At Esperion's signal the wyvern descended just beyond the fog, east of the Valley of the Mist Elves, into the cool of a familiar forest. Lily slid from Wendell's back and breathed the air as a shower of motes floated down from the trees and a shaft of sunlight bathed Enlacia in gold.

Esperion dismounted and gazed upon the crumbling ruins of the once grand fortress. For a long moment no one spoke.

"Ruined," Esperion finally whispered, his face drawn with grief. "Was there a battle here?"

Isla sighed. "Only the battle waged by time. Over centuries the wind and the rain have pummeled the stones."

"And what of Mistwood? Does the castle still stand?"

Isla nodded, but averted her eyes. "It stands, but its halls are empty."

A rush of cloaks and the flapping of wings sounded from behind them as a fleet of sandhawks and griffins landed in the glade. The Icelein slid to the ground and gasped. They whispered to each other, the memories swirling in their minds like fog thicker than the Veil.

"It's fallen apart," one said.

"Nothin' like wot it was," another said with a groan.

As Lily watched the sadness wash over them, a thrill rose in her chest. *When the time is right, you will know,* Pax had said.

"I can rebuild it," she suddenly blurted. All turned toward her, and Lily's cheeks burned. "I mean, I think I can do it."

"I've never seen Enlacia intact, Lily," Isla said. "I only have memories of ruins. Perhaps we could find a memory from the library to help? Or Esperion, can you—"

"I can help her." Mattie appeared, her face still smudged with soot. She pulled a dingy piece of paper from her pocket, creased and flimsy from years of wear. On it, Mattie had scrawled archways and towers buttressed by vines and branches. She handed it to Lily.

Lily studied the drawing, then closed her eyes. The glow of the soothstone shone through her eyelids. She heard a rush of wind through the leaves, the creak of tree limbs stretching. Stones clinked together as they reassembled. Gasps rushed through the crowd, followed by cheers, and Lily opened her eyes. She laughed aloud at the sight of the Fortress of Enlacia made new, its archways resplendent, its tinted glass windows casting crescent moons of color on the courtyard stones. Mnemos stood grinning at the restored gate, his hands clasped in gratitude, his squirrel attire exchanged for that of a wizened professor with a flowing white beard.

"Well done, my dear, well done!" Mnemos said, adjusting his rectangular spectacles. "And Prince Esperion, I knew you would return! We'll again have a king on the throne!"

"Two, my old friend," Esperion said. He extended a hand to Rowan.

Rowan looked about him, as if Esperion had spoken to someone else.

"Come, my son," Esperion said.

The color drained from Rowan's face, and he pointed to himself. "You don't mean me?"

Esperion smiled

"But I don't understand. I'm not—"

"You are rightful heir of the Mist Elves, Prince Rowan. From this day forth, you will rule beside me as my beloved son. Two rulers, on the Two Thrones at last."

Rowan gaped in shock, then fought against the tears of joy that welled in his eyes. He could hardly breathe. He joined Esperion and turned to welcome his new people to Enlacia: the Icelein, and also the Forgotten, whose flying hedgehogs and other wobbly creatures carried them, at last, to a home of their own. The great oaken doors of Enlacia creaked open to welcome all to a coronation feast.

"*Pardon*, mademoiselle?" Philippe tugged at Lily's sleeve. "A feast, I believe it is, how you say—"

"Go ahead, Philippe. Eat all you like. You've earned it."

Philippe turned a somersault, shouted for joy, and then raced into the Fortress. Aristotle, less clingy since his transformation, smiled at Lily and then loped through the entrance to join his brethren. Lily meant to follow them, but a glimmer of something shining deep in the brush caught her eye. *What was—?*

"Won't you join us?" Lily turned back toward the fortress to see Isla striding toward her. Her eyes shimmered with a peace that Lily had never seen in the princess before.

"Yes, I will in a minute," Lily said, trying to hide her distraction. "Thanks."

"No, thank *you*, Lily. For this . . . ," her gaze drifted over the resplendent archways of the fortress, "but for the rest of it, too. For everything."

She tilted her head and studied Lily thoughtfully for a moment. "How did you do it? That moment in the desert, when those rays of light swallowed up the armies . . . I've never seen anything like it. The few times I saw the dream guardians at work they, too, wielded light, but they could only manage a few shrouds at a time. What you did, it was—well, it was astonishing."

Lily remembered Pax's words in the Painted Woodland, and how memories of him had changed the hearts of those warring on the battlefield. "I'm not sure how it happened, but it wasn't really me, you know."

A smile graced her face. "Yes, I suppose it wasn't. But thank you for walking the path Pax gave you. You've given us our home back."

Lily nodded. "Thank you, too. If you hadn't covered me back there in the desert, I don't think any of us would be here right now."

Isla smiled. "I think we have Pax to thank for that, too." She held up her hand to display the soothstone. "He said if I went back for the soothstone, I'd find hope for my people. When I think about the number of ways that's come true, I'm awestruck." She placed a hand on Lily's shoulder. "I once mocked you and your father. The notion that I could learn anything from a human insulted me. I was such a fool. You've taught me more than I've learned myself in a hundred years."

Lily's ears reddened, and she glanced away uncomfortably. "It's nothing," she said with a shrug, and immediately felt idiotic. Why couldn't she ever find more intelligent words?

Thankfully, Isla didn't mind. She cracked a smile.

"It's wonderful, about Rowan," Lily said. "This whole time he's wanted to bring your family back, and your kingdom. Now he has everything he wanted."

Isla raised an eyebrow and nodded. "Yes. Although, he had family even before Esperion returned to us."

"You, of course. You're so protective of him."

"Not just me." She looked intently at Lily. "He considers you a little sister now, Lily."

Lily flushed again, stammered a few words, then faltered. She cocked her head. "*Little* sister?" she finally eked out.

Isla laughed. "Whether younger or elder, he considers you family. As do I, my sister." Isla squeezed Lily's shoulder, then walked back toward the Fortress.

Lily's heart fluttered for a moment as she lingered over Isla's words. Just days ago, Rowan had shown her such scorn and bitterness. During her first journey to the Realm, Isla had tried to kill her. Yet now, they considered her a sister. Family. *Thank you, Pax,* Lily thought, craning her neck skyward to marvel as the fire of sunset softened into twilight.

Pax . . .

Lily suddenly remembered the glimmer she'd spotted in the woods. She crouched low and ducked through the trees, parting the branches that crisscrossed her path. The deeper she advanced into the forest, the brighter the light grew, like moonlight against the snow on a clear night. She tripped on a tree root and spat grit from her mouth as a pine branch slapped her in the face. Then, she stepped into a clearing and her heart leapt.

"Pax!"

Lily ran forward with her heart bursting. She leaned against his neck and relished the feel of his mane against her cheek. *He's here. He's here at last!*

"Well done, young artisan," Pax said.

She pulled away and gazed at him adoringly. "I'm so glad you're here! You were right, Pax. You were right about everything."

Pax didn't answer, but only nuzzled her.

"Are you here to stay? Are you going to oversee Enlacia being rebuilt? And what about Mistwood?"

"I'm here to see you and Mattie off."

Lily's face fell. "You want me to leave? But Enlacia's just been rebuilt."

"Don't forget your promise, Lily." He looked back toward Enlacia, and rustling sounded, followed by the snap of a twig as Mattie entered the clearing.

At the sight of Pax Mattie gasped with delight. "It's him!" she cried. "Oh, it's him, isn't it, Lily? I mean, I'm sorry, you're right there—it's *you!*"

Pax laughed. "You were very brave, Mattie. Few could have withstood the Dream Catcher's dangers as you did. Thanks to your courage, both the Icelein and the Forgotten have a home. Now, it's time for you to return to yours."

Mattie flushed. "Can I truly go home?"

"Indeed, I think you must. Your parents will be eager to see you again. Your father is searching for you as we speak."

"He's looking for me? Really and truly?"

"Most fervently, my dear."

Mattie's eyes sparkled with excitement. "I can't believe I get to see my dad again! What do I say to him, after all these years!"

"The right words will come. But make haste. Lily knows the way and can take you."

Lily's throat tightened. *I have to go back? Now? After everything that's just happened?* How could she bear it? How could she bear to be away, when there was so much of the Realm she'd yet to explore, so many shining corners to see and adventures to embrace? How could she leave, when she felt more at home in the Realm—among its wonders and her friends, among the beauty and majesty that Pax oversaw—than she did on any of the streets of her own hometown?

Then she looked at Mattie, her dark eyes shining with joy. She remembered Barth's grief over having lost her, and Mattie's own heartache for so many long years locked away beneath the desert. As Lily considered these thoughts, her heart softened, Lily's she felt a twinge of shame at her initial reaction. "Yes. Yes, of course," she said. "Of course I'll take you home safely."

"Oh, thank you! Thank you, Lily!" Mattie hugged her, and Lily's disappointment melted a touch. How could she not help such a friend? How could she not help Mattie return home, when she'd saved Lily's life more than once?

But Pax was *there*. Pax was in the Realm, with her at that moment. How could she leave? How could she stand a world that didn't know his wisdom or understand his love?

"Take heart, both of you," Pax said, intuiting Lily's concerns. "We *will* meet again. In the meantime, cling to my words." He nuzzled Lily's cheek. "You have done well, dream keeper. Take courage, and know that I am with you. Always." Then he turned, and a chill gripped the air as Pax disappeared.

Lily watched the spot where Pax had vanished, and for a long while she said nothing. She clenched and unclenched her fists and struggled with the reality that once again she was leaving.

"Should we go now?"

Lily met Mattie's eyes. She cleaved to Pax's words. "Yes. Yes, let's go."

They held hands. Lily closed her eyes, then opened them again when the clearing glittered with light. In a brief burst of hope she thought Pax may have returned, but instead she saw Rigel swooping around her head. Flint followed, skittering up her pant leg and into her shirt pocket with a squeak. Lily smiled, patted the pocket, and then closed her eyes again.

The light flared, and the cool of the forest yielded to something new. The scent of dried leaves filled the air, and the laughter of a stream floated toward them. Lily opened her eyes to see another fortress, less impressive but equally beloved as Enlacia, nestled within the trunk of her favorite tree.

Home.

Mattie shivered with excitement and Lily grinned in spite of herself. She warned Rigel to stay low and out of sight, and then she led Mattie out through the dusky forest, their footfalls crunching in the leaves as they walked. Mattie was too excited, and Lily too pensive, for either of them to notice the shadow that trailed behind them.

Continue Reading the
Dream Keeper Saga

The story continues in *The Quest for the Guardians*,
book 4 of the Dream Keeper Saga!
Read on for a sneak peek at a sample chapter.

To learn more about this series, visit
crossway.org/TheDreamKeeperSaga.

CHAPTER 1

Home

The light of the soothstone faded, and Lily wrapped her sweater around herself to fend off the chill of twilight. She stood among trees she knew by heart, their every branch and knot markers of the stories she'd spun in the woods when she was little, long before she knew anything about soothstones and dwarf dragons, shrouds and caves teeming with lights. As leaves rustled beneath her feet and crickets graced the evening with song, Lily wondered if all she had just endured, and all the beauty she had just left, were only a dream. Had the caverns, the Veil, and the Painted Woodland sprung from her own thoughts? Were Enlacia's gleaming walls only the product of her imagination?

Then she scratched her arm. Lily glanced down at her hands and rubbed grains of sand from the Desert of the Forgotten between her fingers. She stood in the cool of the woods, *her* woods, far removed from any hint of dreams run amok, and yet the Somnium Realm still clung to her. To eliminate all doubt, Lily's favorite star kestrel landed on her shoulder and nipped her ear.

"Better stay out of sight, Rigel," Lily whispered. Rigel scattered silver dust onto the forest floor as he flew into a nearby tree, and Lily patted her pocket, where Flint snuggled down into hiding.

"Where do we go?" Mattie sidled up beside her. Her dark eyes shone bright and earnest in the dwindling light. "Do you know this place?"

Lily brushed the sand from her fingers. "Definitely. This is home for me. My dad built that tree house over there."

When Lily pointed at the Fortress, Mattie sighed with admiration. "I always dreamed about a tree house. My dad said he wanted to build me one, but we only had the maple tree in the park. We pretended it was ours, but, you know, it wasn't *really*."

"I'll bet he'll build one with you now."

"Do you really think so?"

"I'm sure he'd like nothing better."

Mattie's eyes sparkled, and Lily couldn't help but smile at her eagerness. She'd known Mattie for such a brief time, but in that short span Mattie had already saved Lily's life more than once. For her bravery, and her sincerity, Lily considered her a true friend . . . something Lily happened upon readily in the Realm but somehow struggled to find in the waking world.

As they wove through the trees, Lily wondered with a twinge of anxiety about the scene awaiting her at home. Cedric had called her back to the Realm to tackle the Blight just weeks before the end of the school year, with summer only flirting with the land and sky. Now, the cicadas, the smell of a charcoal grill, and the rattle of a nearby lawn sprinkler told Lily that summer had tightened its grip. How long had she been gone? She remembered the note she'd hurriedly scribbled to her parents, promising that she'd return, and wondered if Barth had delivered it. How much did they know? How much would she have to explain . . . and would they understand?

A boy in the front yard of a neighbor's house threw a tennis ball at a mutt dog, then froze and stared at Lily and Mattie with his mouth agape. Lily suddenly realized that she still wore Isla's tunic and sweater, their lavender fibers now smeared with grime from her explorations of the caverns. Lily offered the boy a timid wave; in response, he dashed into the house and screamed for his mother.

"You don't have the friendliest of neighbors," Mattie remarked.

Lily groaned. "No, not really. Although, I guess I can't blame him. We do look like a mess."

"It's not our fault. I'd like to see him try to stay clean while fighting against Magnus and his dwellers!"

They turned the corner, and Lily glimpsed her mailbox. The lid hung open and the surrounding grass was unkempt, a sure sign that something had distracted her parents from the usual business of keeping the house. Lily bit her lip as she walked up the steps. She tripped on the stoop, then winced as the rusty hinges on the screen door squeaked. She entered the house, grimaced at her grimy face in the mirror, and then loitered in the doorway.

"Dan? Is that you?"

Mom. Lily's heart thrilled. She opened her mouth to respond, but words failed her. *What can I even say? "Mom, I'm home!" sounds ridiculous . . .*

"Dan, are you okay? Dinner will be ready in—"

Lily's mother stepped into the corridor. She held a wooden spoon—the same one Lily had grabbed to defend herself against Cedric when he ransacked her kitchen—and wore an apron dotted with tomato sauce over her scrubs. In one moment, she stared at Lily in wide-eyed disbelief. In the next, the spoon clattered to the floor and she swept Lily into her arms.

"Lily! My sweet girl, you're okay! You've come back! I didn't know—we were so worried—"

Lily squeezed her eyes shut as her mother shook with sobbing. "I'm okay, Mom," she whispered. "Everything's all right."

Her mother pulled away and gripped both of Lily's shoulders, squeezing them to convince herself that her daughter was real. Then she cupped Lily's face in both of her palms, stroked her cheeks, and finally gathered her into another hug and whispered a prayer of thanks. She stroked Lily's hair, as she'd done so many nights while reading her stories before bed, ever since Lily could remember.

Lily's dad appeared, and he, too, cried out and then joined in the embrace. They held each other for a long moment, most of their words only fragments. In the warmth of their arms and the familiarity of home, Lily's worries washed away.

"Lily, are you all right? You're *sure* you're all right?" her dad finally said, pulling away and studying her.

"I'm fine, Dad. I'm fine."

"What happened to you? What did you go through?"

"It's a long story. A *really* long story."

"We've been so worried."

"I know, Dad, but I'm fine, I promise you."

He gathered her in a hug again, but then over her shoulder he noticed Mattie still standing in the doorway. "Hi," Mattie said with a bashful smile as she met his eyes. "I'm Mattie."

At the mention of the name, Dad's eyes widened and his arms loosened from around Lily. "Barth's daughter? Mattie, as in Barth's daughter?"

Mattie beamed. "Yes! How did you know? Have you seen him?"

"I know Barth. He was here a couple of weeks ago."

"That's great! Oh, Lily, It's just like Pax said! This is wonderful!"

An expression Lily couldn't pinpoint flickered over her father's face as he looked from Lily, to Mattie, and back again. "Where did you come from?" he asked Mattie.

Mattie bobbed up and down on her heels in her excitement. "Lily and I met in the Realm, and she brought me back. Do you know where I can find my dad?"

Dad studied her for a moment, and opened his mouth to speak, but then decided against it. As Lily wondered what thoughts troubled him, he clapped his hands and adopted a lighter demeanor. "You know what? We have a lot to catch up on. Why don't you girls go get cleaned up, and we can talk about everything over dinner?"

"Good idea," Lily's mom added. "Mattie, please make yourself at home. Lily, why don't you give her some fresh clothes? I need to get back to the sauce before it bubbles over." She planted a kiss on Lily's cheek, then hustled back to the kitchen. Her dad lingered for a moment before wrapping Lily in one more hug. "I'm so glad you're home, Scout," he said. A glint of pain shone in his eyes, but it quickly vanished as he followed Mom into the kitchen.

Lily ran her hands along the walls in the main hallway and pressed her fingers into a familiar crescent-shaped divot in the plaster, the product of a collision when she once tried to roller skate on the carpet. She glimpsed Gran in her favorite chair in the living room, asleep with a photo album on her lap, and she motioned for Mattie to go on ahead while she slipped into the room. She padded silently toward Gran, placed a hand on the back of her chair, and smiled at the pictures of her grandparents, decades younger, waving at the camera during one of their many cross-country expeditions. In each photo Lily's grandfather wrapped a sturdy arm around Gran, who leaned into him as if he were a mighty sycamore shielding her from a storm. A lock of hair —her signature—dangled in front of Gran's eyes in each picture. Her mother now tacked that lock back with a bobby pin, and Lily had the sudden urge to loosen the pin, fan out the strands, and recapture a glimpse of the woman in the photographs.

Gran's eyelids fluttered open. She blinked at Lily for a moment, and then her eyes moistened and a huge smile brightened her face. She reached out a single finger to stroke Lily's cheek. "Lily!" she said.

"Hi Gran. I'm home." Lily clasped her hand. When her dad first disappeared, Gran's understanding and language seemed to vanish with him. The memory lapses they'd noticed for so long worsened precipitously, and she could never remember Lily's name. The change was so unsettling that Lily's heart had leapt when she first heard Gran talking like herself in the Wilderness, only to discover, with horror, that it was really a shroud impersonating her grandmother. The sound of her own name on Gran's lips now sounded like music. She felt like she was recapturing something she'd lost.

Gran's eyes wandered again to the pictures. When she glimpsed Mount Rainier towering above a field of wildflowers she gasped. "Look at that," she said, tracing the silhouette of the mountain. Gran couldn't remember her trip to Rainier, or the fact that she'd taken the picture herself, but her capacity to wonder still burned. As Lily kissed her cheek and turned away, she heard Gran's soft voice singing "All Creatures of Our God and King," and Lily couldn't help but smile. *I'm home,* she thought.

And yet . . .

Was this home? The hallways were so familiar, the sounds and scents like sinking into a warm embrace. But deep within, in a part of herself that seemed as vital as a long-buried root,

Lily already missed the Realm. She missed the magic that Pax imbued into his land.

They gathered around the dinner table as the night deepened and the cricket song intensified. When Dad explained that Mom now knew about the Realm, and then asked Lily to tell them about what she'd endured, Lily's heart felt light. She prattled on about everything she'd experienced, the joys as well as the fears: the Blight, her apprenticeship, Muzzytown and Ash Canyon, the Sea of Oblivion and Pax giving his life for the Realm. The words flew from her mouth like a stream bursting from a hose.

The longer she talked, however, the more her parents' laughter dwindled. She'd expected her parents to lean forward, their forks paused half-wound with pasta, and to ask questions as they'd always done about topics much less important—grades and classes and the games at summer camp. Instead, they avoided her eyes. Worry lines creased her mother's face. Her father stared at his hands. Finally, Lily's monologue petered out, and she studied her parents in confusion. "What is it?" she asked.

Mom drew a breath. "Honestly, Lily, if I never hear another word about that dream world again, it will be too soon."

Lily felt like a deflated balloon. "But it's a wonderful place, Mom! It's such a magical place."

"And deadly," Dad said. "I'll never forgive myself for the pain I put you and Mom through when I was captured. And then, to have you embroiled in the keeper business, too—" He clenched his jaw and stabbed at his food with a fork.

"Dad, didn't you hear anything I just told you?"

"I did. And I'll never forgive myself for putting you through it. The Somnium Realm is no place for a kid."

Lily chewed a mouthful of meatball and tried to sort the emotions twisting inside her. The Somnium Realm was dangerous, but it was also wondrous. Even the meal her mother just cooked, Lily's favorite and the one she requested every birthday, couldn't compare with the sumptuous version Pax had provided on the evening he rose from the tomb. "It's not all awful, Dad," she finally mustered the courage to say. "Don't you remember? You used to love the place. I know you did—just think of all your stories! If you only saw what Pax did—"

"Lily, I used to love the Realm, too, but the stakes are too high. You have a home and a family, and you're just a *kid*. There are plenty of adults in this world who can go into the Realm and be heroes."

"I wasn't trying to be a hero, I was just trying to follow what Pax asked me to do. You should have seen what he did, Dad! He died for the Realm and made everything whole and beautiful again. And then he came back to life! And when I showed others what he'd done, it changed them. Entire kingdoms of lost people, the Icelein and the Forgotten, changed when they learned of what he'd done. It was like they became totally new. This energy came down my arm and shot out of the soothstone, and—"

Dad smacked the table. "Enough, Lily! You should never have gone back."

"But, Dad—"

"You should *never* have gone back, Lily! There's no excuse!"

The sternness in his voice silenced her. She wanted to crawl under the table, or to rush back to the Realm, to the shining waters, mountains, and fields her dad suddenly hated so vehemently. Instead, she gritted her teeth and fought the flush that crept over her cheeks.

"I'm sorry, Scout," Dad said, his demeanor softening. "I just think about what could have happened, and it terrifies me. I could never forgive myself if anything happened to you." His voice cracked. "When Barth brought me your letter, I thought I'd lost you forever."

Lily didn't answer. She pushed the food around on her plate and wondered how she could swing from feeling so overjoyed, to so rotten in an instant. She felt Flint roll over in the front pocket of her pajama top, and in a flight of whimsy she wondered if *he* could convince her parents that the Realm was well worth its dangers. That dreams mattered.

"Excuse me, Mr. McKinley? When did my dad come to see you?"

Dad suddenly looked embarrassed. "Oh, forgive me, Mattie, I'm so sorry. We've been yammering on all this time, and you've been waiting so patiently." He collected his thoughts, and spun his fork between his fingers. "He came about two weeks ago. Apparently, he'd been staying with a friend of yours, Lily?"

"Keisha Reynolds?"

"Right. Her family let him stay with them for a few weeks, and helped him research what happened since he left. He was able to connect with your mother."

Mattie beamed. "My mom! Is she okay? Where is she?"

"She's been through a lot over the years, but she's okay. She's still living in San Francisco."

"And . . . where are we again?"

"Massachusetts."

Her shoulders sagged with disappointment. "Oh, okay. Not nearby. Still, I'm so glad she's all right. When can I see them? Is that where my dad went, to San Francisco to see her?"

"He's not gone to San Francisco yet, Mattie." He paused, weighing his words. "He's looking for you."

"Looking for me?"

"He discovered that you'd disappeared when he last ventured into the Realm. Do you realize exactly how long you've been gone?"

Mattie's smile faded. "A long time. Ages, I guess."

"It's been twenty years, Mattie."

A long pause ensued. A cloud of sorrow descended over Mattie, muting her exuberance.

"You haven't aged at all," Dad said. "It was the Realm, wasn't it? You were in the Realm the whole time?"

Mattie nodded. As she played with strands of her ponytail, she looked wan and frail, a shadow of her usual, vibrant self.

"What exactly happened, Mattie?" Mom pressed gently.

"I followed my dad. I didn't mean to, but he left the house with my sketchbook, and so I ran to grab it from him. Then . . ."

"You transported with him," Dad said.

Mattie nodded.

"Barth suspected as much, but he didn't understand why he didn't come across you during all those years when you were both in the Realm. How did he not know you were there?"

"I was trapped. Deep underground."

"Underground? Where, exactly?"

Mattie didn't answer, but instead stared into her lap and shredded her napkin.

"She was trapped in the lairs of the Forgotten, Dad," Lily said.

Dad's jaw slackened, and sympathy shimmered in his eyes. "I'm so sorry, Mattie. How awful for you."

Mattie shrugged. "I'd rather not talk about it. I'm just glad to be out of there, and I can't wait to finally see him again. Where did he go, after he came to see you?"

Lily's mom shot her father a worried glance. "The news that you'd vanished devastated him," Dad said. "He blames himself, both for your disappearance and for leaving your mom alone for twenty years. He promised your mother that he'd find you."

"But find me how? Not back in the Realm?"

"No, not back in the Realm. He couldn't go back without a soothstone."

"What then? Where did he go?"

Dad twirled the fork more rapidly, a sign of his discomfort. "You have to understand, Mattie, that he felt desperate. He was so determined to find you."

"Mr. McKinley, please, just tell me! Where is my dad? What did he do?"

He drew a breath. "He's trying to go back in time to stop you from entering the Realm."